PENGUIN CLASSICS

FANNY HILL

OR MEMOIRS OF A WOMAN OF PLEASURE

JOHN CLELAND was born in 1710, the eldest son of William Cleland, an officer and friend of Pope. He entered Westminster School in 1721 and remained there until his sudden departure in 1723. Later he joined the East India Company, where he rose from simple soldier to businessman and eventually secretary of the Bombay Council. However, his good fortune did not last and he left Bombay around 1740 and returned to London in 1741. Thereafter Cleland followed a career as literary hack, Grub Street writer and journalist. The life was extremely competitive and though Cleland pursued every promising avenue, both literary writing and factual reporting, he was in constant financial difficulty. He was imprisoned for debt on several occasions and on one of these, between February 1748 and March 1749, he usefully employed his time by revising and rewriting a draft of a novel entitled *Fanny Hill*. Both volumes of *Memoirs of a Woman of Pleasure*, the final title, were published before his release. Cleland enjoyed some success with *Fanny Hill* and he hoped to exploit this with a sequel, *Memoirs of a Coxcomb*; but this and his other attempts at erotic fiction sank into oblivion. Impoverished and virtually unknown, John Cleland died in Westminster in January 1789.

•

PETER WAGNER was born in Germany in 1949 and was educated at the University of the Saarland. He taught at the College of William and Mary in Virginia, USA, and at the University of Bath, England. Since 1981 he has been employed as a tenured lecturer at the Catholic University of Eichstätt in Bavaria. He received doctoral degrees in English from the University of the Saarland in 1978 and from the Sorbonne in 1986. His books in English include a study of Puritanism in colonial New England, a survey of erotica in the age of Enlightenment, and a short history of English and American literature. He is also the editor of Tobias Smollett's *The Life and Adventures of Sir Launcelot Greaves* for Penguin Classics.

JOHN CLELAND

✸

FANNY HILL

OR

MEMOIRS OF A WOMAN OF PLEASURE

EDITED BY PETER WAGNER

PENGUIN BOOKS

PENGUIN BOOKS

Published by the Penguin Group
Penguin Books Ltd, 27 Wrights Lane, London W8 5TZ, England
Penguin Books USA Inc., 375 Hudson Street, New York, New York 10014, USA
Penguin Books Australia Ltd, Ringwood, Victoria, Australia
Penguin Books Canada Ltd, 10 Alcorn Avenue, Toronto, Ontario, Canada M4V 3B2
Penguin Books (NZ) Ltd, 182–190 Wairau Road, Auckland 10, New Zealand

Penguin Books Ltd, Registered Offices: Harmondsworth, Middlesex, England

First published 1748–9
This edition published in Penguin Classics 1985
9 10 8

Introduction and Notes copyright © Peter Wagner, 1985
All rights reserved

Printed in England by Clays Ltd, St Ives plc
Filmset in Monophoto Photina

CONTENTS

Introduction   7

A Note on the Text   31

A Chronological List of French Erotic Fiction
  Published between 1700 and 1748   33

Select Bibliography   35

FANNY HILL *or* MEMOIRS OF A WOMAN OF PLEASURE   37

Notes   225

INTRODUCTION

I

Successful novels often have bizarre publishing histories. The writing and the publication of *Memoirs of a Woman of Pleasure*, commonly known as *Fanny Hill*, are still as much shrouded in mystery as the life of its author, John Cleland, although William H. Epstein's biography has contributed much towards a more satisfactory reconstruction of Cleland's chequered career. Of Scottish parentage, John Cleland was born in 1710, the eldest son of William Cleland, an officer and friend of Pope. John was entered at Westminster School in 1721 and remained there until his sudden departure in 1723. Then, as now, this sort of schooling seemed to have opened the right doors at the right time, for Cleland soon went east, as did many another promising young man, joining the East India Company in 1728. He remained in its services until 1740 and rose from simple soldier to the moderately dizzying heights of businessman and, towards the end of this more fortunate period of his life, secretary of the Bombay Council.

But John Cleland was not born under a lucky star. His career came to an abrupt end in 1740 when he left Bombay and returned to Europe with little financial means left. There is some evidence that he then went on a sort of 'Little Tour' of Europe, not being able to afford the customary 'Grand Tour' of a gentleman. Arriving in London in August 1741, he suffered another blow through the death of Cleland *père*, which to the son meant even more pecuniary difficulties. Cleland joined the poorly paid crowd of Grub Street hacks and on several occasions got to know the inside of a debtor's prison. Between 23 February 1748 and 6 March 1749 he was confined in the Fleet Prison for debt, employing his time by revising and rewriting a draft of a novel entitled *Fanny Hill*. Both volumes of *Memoirs of a Woman of Pleasure*, the final title, were published before Cleland's release, the first in November 1748 and the second in February 1749. It is quite possible that Ralph Griffiths, the publisher of the book, who used his brother's name, Fenton Griffiths, as a cover, secured Cleland's release from prison by paying some of his debts in exchange for the right to publish the novel. Not surprisingly, we find John Cleland three months later as a founding contributor to the *Monthly Review*, a periodical Griffiths published successfully from May/June 1749 and which remained influential beyond the end of the eighteenth century.

Cleland's later career as a literary hack, Grub Street writer, and journalist was not that of a crank, as some critics would have it, but exemplified the life and work of a moderately gifted, if unsuccessful, eighteenth-century man who found himself influenced by the various and sometimes admittedly odd currents of the Enlightenment. Financially, he could hardly have been satisfied with the £20 he was paid by Griffiths for *Memoirs of a Woman of Pleasure* – Griffiths received the lion's share, but with only 750 copies sold of the first edition, John Nichols's claim in the *Gentleman's Magazine* of February 1789 (p. 180) that the novel earned the publisher £10,000 must be dismissed as an exaggerated estimate. Cleland depended on his pen for a living, and he tried every promising avenue, in fiction and literary criticism, and even the sciences. Eighteenth-century authors and publishers were as commercially shrewd as their modern successors in the Hollywood film business. *Memoirs of a Woman of Pleasure* and its cleaned-up version, prepared by Cleland and first sold in 1750, were successful sellers. And success called for at least one sequel. So John Cleland set to work and exploited the newly found mine. In November 1751, he had his *Memoirs of a Coxcomb* published, again anonymously, the title indicating that this was another novel of secret confessions, with Frances Hill replaced by a male hero. In many respects, the plot, the language, and the form of this novel correspond to *Fanny Hill*. However, the amorous adventures of Sir William Delamore, a telling name indeed, did not find many readers, although Smollett gave the novel a laudatory critique in the *Monthly Review*. Smollett was only paying back his due to Cleland who, in March 1751, had favourably reviewed *Peregrine Pickle* in the same periodical. What *Memoirs of a Coxcomb* lacked was the spice of the erotic scenes in *Fanny Hill*. As there was no shortage of erotic novels in the 1750s, with France providing more erotica than English readers could cope with, Cleland's second work of fiction soon sank into oblivion. He tried his hand three more times in the realm of erotic fiction, each time with diminishing success. In May 1752 was published *Memoirs Illustrating the Manners of the Present Age*, a translation of Charles Pineau Duclos's *chronique scandaleuse* of 1751 of which Cleland did volume 11. This second part is concerned with the numerous and entertaining intrigues and gallantries of a young aristocrat, clearly Cleland's literary domain. In the preface, he made some very interesting remarks about the nature of fiction, while defending the moderate use of obscenity for moral purposes – quite a radical opinion for a British writer. He also hinted at his knowledge of French authors, such as Fénelon, Scarron, Lesage, Marivaux, and, most important in view of his influence on Cleland, Crébillon fils. Cleland's translation of Duclos's fictitious memoirs sold badly; his four erotic novellas or 'romances', published after 1760 and collected in *The Surprizes of Love* (Dublin, 1764; reprinted London, 1765) and his last novel, in three volumes, *The Woman of Honour* (London, 1768) were also unsuccessful.

In the eighteenth century life as a literary hack was anything but easy. Competition being as tough as it could be, one had to have one's ear to the ground in almost every area of literature and science to earn sufficient money. Hence it is hardly surprising to find Cleland trying poetry and theatrical writing in the 1750s. But again he was unsuccessful. His tragedy, *Titus Vespasian*, was rejected by Garrick but printed 'for the author' in 1755, quite a normal procedure with plays whether successful or not, and reprinted by Griffiths in 1760. This was followed in 1758 by *Tombo-Chiqui: or, the American Savage*, which, like *The Ladies Subscription*, a light entertainment, was never performed. Cleland's poem, *The Times! An Epistle to Flavian*, a work of 264 lines published in October 1759, merely received a brief notice in the *Monthly Review*. It harped on his favourite themes since 1748 – the balance of reason and erotic passion, the ludicrousness of fashionable life, and the central place of genuine love.

Thereafter, John Cleland launched into non-literary territory, joining such contemporaries as 'Sir' John Hill, who also dabbled in scientific research and wrote fiction. The searching forces of Enlightenment enthusiasm in the sciences produced a welter of para-medical works on sex and sexuality. Whether in botany, where Linnaeus and others applied human sexual terminology to plants and were ridiculed for it, or in medicine, where quacks and 'empiricks' reported on the births of rabbits and monsters to women, there was a great and ever-increasing activity in research and writing, though the writings were not always scientific in the modern sense. Cases of sexual hybrids naturally received ample attention. Even Henry Fielding, a respectable author who was normally above such sexually equivocal matters, published a work in 1746,

9

although protected by anonymity, which is entitled *The Female Husband* and deals in a rather prurient manner with the case of Mary Hamilton, a transvestite arrested and tried at Wells in 1746 for posing and marrying as a man. In 1751, John Cleland tried to jump on the bandwagon of titillating publications on sex with his translation of the Italian Professor Bianchi's account of the transvestite adventures and amours of Catherine Vizzani. The *Monthly Review* announced the elaborate title of the sixty-six page booklet in March 1751:

[An] His[toric]al and Phy[s]ic[al] Dissertation On the Case of Catherine Vizzani, Containing the Adventures of a young Woman, born at Rome, who for eight Years passed in the Habit of a Man, was killed for an Amour with a young Lady; and being found, on Dissection, a true Virgin, narrowly escaped being treated as a Saint by the Populace. With some Curious and Anatomical Remarks on the Nature and Existence of the Hymen. By Giovanni Bianchi, Professor of Anatomy at Sienna, the Surgeon who dissected her. To which are added, certain needful Remarks by the English Editor.

The 'dissertation' catered for the sexual interests of middle-class readers with salacious details published under the veil of medical and scientific respectability. The last quarter of this booklet shows Cleland miles away from the philosophy of erotic pleasure he propagated in *Memoirs of a Woman of Pleasure*. Hard-pressed financially and trying to protect himself and the publisher against prosecution, he succumbed to bourgeois expectations in a moral tone and an unconvincing piety. At any rate, such treatises apparently whetted his appetite for medical research. By 1761 he had finished a work of his own, *The Institutes of Health*, which was marketed by Beckett and Davies. In the style of the notorious, although frequently misunderstood, sexologist James Graham, who caused some stir a decade later, John Cleland explained in this work his loss of 'stamina', due to 'abandoned intemperance of all sorts'. The rescue he prescribed was the Cleland method, a system of personal hygiene and discoveries in 'that capitally interesting branch of physic, the prophylactic'. The title of his last para-medical work indicates the strong speculative element in eighteenth-century scientific writings: *Phisiological Reveries*; it was a pamphlet of not more than twenty-six pages and appeared in the autumn of 1765. The short treatise drew parallels between saliva and semen, expanded on the belief that animals breathe through the pores of their skins and even assessed the danger of fevers. Reacting to this scholarly attempt of an amateur, the *Critical Review* judged Cleland a 'superficial pathologist', while suggesting that he ask 'pardon for the whole performance'. Cleland did not apologize, but he stopped writing on medical subjects and concentrated on linguistics, another hobby-horse of his.

With moderate success, Cleland had already translated in 1753 – again for Ralph Griffiths – Jean-François Dreux du Radier's *Dictionnaire d'amour*, first published at The Hague in 1741. It was reprinted in 1776 and had a considerable number of entries by Cleland, who substituted his own definitions for references to French literature and history in the original. In the late 1760s he tried to prove with the help of etymology that Celtic was the original European language. *The Way to Things by Words and to Words by Things* (1766) was followed only two years later by *Specimen of an Etimological Vocabulary* and complemented in 1769 by *Additional Articles on the Specimen*.

Cleland's unsuccessful attempts as a writer of journalism and as a researcher in medical science and linguistics are by no means singular for the eighteenth century. In the Age of Enlightenment one had to be extraordinary or extraordinarily clever to make one's voice heard in any field. If John Cleland's name has not disappeared and if he has gone down in literary history as a writer, it is because of one book, *Memoirs of a Woman of Pleasure*. Ironically enough, it is not the work he himself cherished most. Defending himself in a letter to Stanhope in November 1749, he pointed out his 'low abject condition' as an excuse for writing a novel he wished 'buried and forgot'. But as he was trying to exonerate himself in this instance, his words ought to be taken with a grain of salt. However, there is every reason to assume that Cleland did not expect his erotic story of a prostitute's rise to respectability to become one of the most successful novels of all time. Impoverished and virtually unknown, John Cleland died in Westminster in January 1789. But *Fanny Hill*, his brain-child, lived on and was at that time just beginning to acquire literary fame.

II

It has often been assumed that it was during his imprisonment that John Cleland wrote *Memoirs of a Woman of Pleasure*. But this was probably not so. He merely revised and enlarged an earlier draft of the novel he had had in his possession since the 1730s. The first volume of the original edition of *Memoirs* was made known to the public in the *General Advertiser* for 21 November 1748:

> This Day is Published, (Price 3s.)
> MEMOIRS of a WOMAN of PLEASURE.
> Written by a PERSON of QUALITY.
> Printed for G. FENTON, in the Strand.

The reference to the 'person of quality' was left out in later ads, and the second volume was announced in the *London Evening-Post* between 14–16 February 1749:

> This Day is publish'd, Price 3s.
> The Second and Last Volume of
> MEMOIRS of a WOMAN of PLEASURE.
> Printed for G. Fenton, at No. 12, in Exeter Exchange in the Strand.

Towards the end of March 1749, the *General Advertiser* carried an ad offering both volumes at six shillings. If this is the publishing history of the novel, its genesis is more complicated. Cleland disclosed some of it in his letter to Lovel Stanhope, the Law Clerk in the Secretary of State's office, when he was asked to give an account of his share in the book. On 13 November 1749, Cleland wrote:

> The plan of the first Part was originally given me by a young gentleman of the greatest hopes that ever I knew, (Brother to a nobleman now Ambassadour at a Foreign Court,) above eighteen years ago, on an occasion immaterial to mention here.
> This I never dreamt of preparing for the Press, till being under confinement in the Fleet, at my leisure hours, I altered, added to, transposed, and in short new-cast: when, on showing it to some whose opinion I unfortunately preferred to my own, and being made to consider it as a ressource, I published the first part. And not till near four months after the Second: which had been promised, and would most surely have never been proceeded to had I been in the least made sensible of the first having given any offence: and indeed I now wonder it could so long, escape the Vigilance of the Guardians of the Public Manners, since, nothing is truer, than that more Clergymen bought it, in proportion, than any other distinction of men.

There is some evidence that would seem to corroborate Cleland's assertion that a manuscript of what was to become *Memoirs of a Woman of Pleasure* was already in existence in the early 1730s. To begin with, it was not at all unusual for licentious books to circulate in manuscript form. In countries such as France, where censorship was stricter than in Britain and thus forced libertine erotica into the underground world of publishing, a great number of novels and such obscene works as *Parapilla* (first published in 1776 and attributed to Charles Borde) and Senac de Meilhan's *La Foutro-Manie* (1780) as well as some of Voltaire's erotica – *La Pucelle d'Orléans*, for instance – were well known as manuscripts before being printed. In Britain, the libertines' clubs aped similar French societies and enjoyed erotic as well as obscene writings which were often provided by their members and were not always in print. Thus John Wilkes's obscene *Essay on Woman* and the ribald poems published with it were probably read to the 'Medmenham monks' forming the Hell-Fire Club before these poems came to prominence and notoriety in the Wilkes scandal. The records of 'The Most Ancient and Puissant Order of the Beggar's Benison and Merryland', a club of would-be libertines flourishing from 1732 to 1836, contain an interesting entry on St Andrew's Day, 1737, when 'two nymphs, eighteen and nineteen, [were] exhibited' and 'Fanny Hill was read'. One of the founding members of this club was Robert Cleland, and if he was related to John Cleland – a possibility Alan Bold, the editor of a recent edition of the records, has failed to explore – it is imaginable that the first draft of the novel was read to the assembled members who 'broke up at 3 o'clock a.m.'. In Boswell's journals there are also two passages where Cleland asserts that a first version of *Memoirs* was written in the 1730s.

John Cleland's arrest on 10 November 1749, in all probability a result of the 'pious indignation of my Lords the Bishops', as Cleland assumed in a letter to the Secretary of State's office cited above, was of course an excellent advertisement for his erotic novel. In his letter, Cleland explained that the bishops could 'take no step towards punishing the Author' that would not 'powerfully contribute to the notoriety of the book'. Just before the government issued a warrant for the arrest of the author, printer, and publisher of *Memoirs of a Woman of Pleasure* on 8 November 1749, Cleland had anonymously published a pamphlet entitled *The Case of the Unfortunate Bosavern Penlez* (7 November 1749), which he reviewed himself in the *Monthly Review* shortly afterwards. In this publication he criticized the government for the recent execution in October of a twenty-year-old peruke-maker, Bosavern Penlez, who had become involved in disturbances in the Strand in which several sailors burned a brothel and incited the local populace to join them.

Although *The Case* had strong political overtones and voiced a good deal of the public sympathy for the young scapegoat, it is highly unlikely that the government would have identified the author of the anonymous pamphlet within a day and then arrested Cleland and Griffiths on a different charge. The persons charged in connection with the publication of *Memoirs of a Woman of Pleasure* were soon released on a recognizance of £100. Within a few months, Cleland had prepared an abridged and bowdlerized version of his novel which the *General Advertiser* announced on 8 March 1750:

> *This Day is Publish'd,*
> *Compleat in One Pocket Volume, Price bound 3s.*
> MEMOIRS of FANNY HILL.
> *If I have painted Vice in its gayest Colours, if I have deck'd*
> *it with Flowers, it has been solely in order to make the worthier,*
> *the solemner Sacrifice of it to* VIRTUE.   *Vide p. 273.*
> Printed for R. Griffiths, at the Dunciad in St. Paul's Church-yard.
> *Of whom may be had, in Two Volumes, Price 6s.*
> Memoirs of the celebrated Mrs. *Lætitia Pilkington.*

After a few days, Thomas Sherlock, the Bishop of London, wrote to Newcastle as Secretary of State. 'I beg of your Grace,' he urged him, 'to give proper orders, to stop the progress of this vile Book, which is an open insult upon Religion and good manners, and a reproach to the Honour of the Government, and the Law of the Country.' Nothing much came of this, despite another warrant for the arrest of the author, printer, and publisher of this version of the novel. Cleland and Griffiths were again arrested on 16 March, but there is no evidence of legal action having been taken. In fact, John Cleland seems to have profited from his subsequent appearance before the Privy Council, for John Earl Granville, the Lord President, apparently arranged for him to receive a pension of £100 per annum, which he seems to have enjoyed until his death, possibly on the tacit agreement that he write journalistic articles in favour of the government.

In view of the literary evaluation of *Memoirs of a Woman of Pleasure* over the centuries, it is of some interest to consider its publishing history after 1749. David Foxon has rightly suggested in his *Libertine Literature* (p. 61) that the action taken against the novel in that year seems to be related to the sodomitical passage in volume II recording Fanny's voyeuristic observation of a homosexual encounter in an inn. Only the first edition includes two paragraphs in Cleland's euphemistic style providing the anatomical details of the episode. All subsequent editions, excepting Drybutter's version of 1757 (he was apparently put in the pillory for this publication), excluded these passages, yet internal evidence and Cleland's reference to sodomy in his letter to the Secretary of State's office on 13 November 1749 suggest that it was indeed Cleland who wrote the episode and that it is not a later addition. The bowdlerized version of the novel Cleland prepared for Griffiths and which appeared in March 1750 as *Memoirs of Fanny Hill* (the first edition of this book is lost) omitted the sexual details, reducing the text by a third and dividing it into eleven letters instead of the original two. Unperturbed by the earlier prosecution, Griffiths tried to 'hype' this abridged version in the *Monthly Review* for March 1750:

> Though this book is said to be taken from a very loose work, printed about two years ago, in two volumes, and on that account a strong prejudice has arisen against it, yet it does not appear to us that this performance, whatever the two volumes might be, (for we have not seen them) has any thing in it more offensive to decency, or delicacy of sentiment and expression, than our novels and books of entertainment in general have: For, in truth, they are most of them (especially our comedies, and not a few of our tragedies) but too faulty in this respect...

> As to the step lately taken to suppress this book, we really are at a loss to account for it; yet, perhaps, all wonder on this head will cease, when we consider how liable great men are to be misinformed, how frequently obliged to see with other men's eyes, and hear with other people's ears.

> *** The news-papers inform us, that the celebrated history of *Tom Jones* has been suppressed in *France*, as an immoral work.

After 1750, *Fanny Hill*, as the book was now often referred to, kept selling slowly but steadily, in several versions and numerous pirate editions, though the text of the first edition was apparently not reprinted after Drybutter's unsuccessful attempt in 1757.

In the 1760s publishers were beginning to turn out illustrated editions of the novel. Rather than enhancing the text, the pictorial material, often badly executed, exaggerated and did much harm to *Memoirs* – a rare exception is the edition of 1766 with engravings attributed to Gravelot. If *Fanny Hill* acquired a bad name and was relegated for more than two centuries to the realm of 'pornography', it was mainly because of the illustrations. James Gillray alluded to *Fanny Hill* as an 'immoral book' in a pictorial satire dated 1786 and entitled 'A Sale of English-

Beauties in the East Indies'. In 1796 Mrs Errington, an alleged nympho-
maniac, was tried for adultery. The published trial report of the case
contains the statement of a witness who deposed that Mrs Errington
had shown her a book on several occasions 'which she said was the
Woman of Pleasure ... that there were a great many indecent pictures
in such book, which she seemed to take pleasure in shewing the deponent'.
By this time, both critical and public opinion had assigned *Memoirs of
a Woman of Pleasure* to the canon of naughty books. In his bibliography
of prohibited books, *Catena Librorum Tacendorum* (London, 1885; reprinted
New York, 1962), Henry Spencer Ashbee listed twenty English editions
of the novel between 1749 and 1845, while the catalogue of the British
Library records eight English registered editions for the eighteenth century.
One may assume that there were many more which are no longer extant.
The major English erotica and the licentious magazines of the late
eighteenth century and the early nineteenth century refer to *Memoirs*
as the classic erotic novel to be read with the works of Ovid, Aretino,
Rochester, and Wilkes.

Given the powerful visual attraction of the pictorial material in many
editions, the text was never discussed objectively in the nineteenth
century. Instead, imitations of the title and form of *Memoirs* tried to
exploit the perennial success of the novel. The bourgeois nineteenth
century could not appreciate the philosophy of sexual pleasure propagated
by Cleland's heroine. *Memoirs* was read mainly because of its erotic appeal,
though its periphrastic style was beginning to disturb readers who were
now demanding more 'realistic' expressions. The twentieth century first
pushed *Memoirs* into the limited-editions bracket while critical voices
still denied the book any claim to literary value. *Fanny Hill* had to stand
trial, first in New York, after the publication of the Putnam edition in
1963, and then in Europe, for the literary discussion of the novel (after
the legal and moral aspects had been debated *ad nauseam*) to be resumed.
Since then, a number of relevant studies, notably Peter Naumann's
formidable and detailed analysis, have proved beyond a doubt that
Memoirs of a Woman of Pleasure is an important, albeit slanted – if not
slandered – work of eighteenth-century fiction that deserves a place beside
the novels of Richardson, Fielding, and Smollett. Until the early 1960s,
scholars of literature found the sexual aspects of *Memoirs* distasteful and
decided that ignoring the history of licentious fiction and eighteenth-
century pornography was preferable to having to deal with the un-

comfortable, if significant, problem of human sexuality as portrayed in literature. Given the importance of literary pornography as a vehicle of revolutionary thought in the Age of Enlightenment, it seems hardly credible that literary historians have sacrificed both historical and literary accuracy for the sake of twentieth-century propriety, ignoring the enormous bulk of aggressive, anti clerical, and anti-aristocratic erotica propagating ideas of moral, philosophical, and political revolution. *Memoirs of a Woman of Pleasure* is revolutionary in its open message to enjoy sex and sexuality, a message that ran counter to what novelists such as Defoe and Richardson had told their readers. Like other eighteenth-century licentious fiction, *Memoirs* is neither worthless nor negligible when seen in relation to the advancement of science, the teaching of the *philosophes*, and the forces behind the French Revolution. John Cleland's novel is unique in that it combines elements of both French and English literature in a secularized parody of the Christian confession; it also combines two literary forms, the whore biography and the whore dialogue, melding them into what became the outstanding novel of English erotic fiction.

III

Cleland's plot in *Memoirs* betrays his borrowing from the whore biography and especially from Hogarth's *A Harlot's Progress*, although Fanny's fate is a prosperous one and thus a mocking parody of the warning moralism as shown in Defoe's novels and Hogarth's engravings. While the lives of the better-known whores in English fiction, poetry, and pictorial series before 1748 ended in misery and death through disease or hanging, Fanny Hill rises from poverty to a middle-class existence as a wife and mother via several stages of prostitution. Like Moll Hackabout in Hogarth's *A Harlot's Progress*, Fanny is initially a naïve and innocent girl. The death of her parents forces her to seek her fortune in London. Left in the lurch by her girlfriend, Fanny is picked up at a registry office by an old bawd, Mrs Brown, who takes her home. Such scenes of innocent country girls being gulled by experienced city dwellers had often been described in both literary and pictorial satire, and Cleland was clearly acquainted with this tradition. It is in Mrs Brown's bawdy-house that Fanny undergoes sexual training, so to speak, advancing from innocence to curiosity and sexual desire while schooled by Phoebe, her bedfellow. As Fanny's tutor, Phoebe is deputized by Mrs Brown to initiate the new disciple into her role as an object of pleasure for men. At this stage, Cleland incorporates into his novel the philosophy of sexual pleasure as exemplified by several decades of libertine French fiction.

Through lesbian sex, Fanny discovers erotic pleasure. However, her first male customer, Mr Crofts, an ugly old lecher who has bought Fanny's maidenhead from Mrs Brown, thoroughly spoils whatever appetite Fanny may have developed. Shocked by his violence, Fanny falls ill. But Phoebe's gentle instruction, and especially scenes of voyeurism, rekindle the heroine's sexual interest and even desire. After secretly watching an encounter between 'the venerable mother abbess herself' and a 'tall, brawny, young horse grenadier', a scene that gains a comical-grotesque dimension by dint of Mrs Brown's physical appearance and Fanny's ironic hindsight report, Fanny loses her moral innocence. And when she has seen her colleague Polly's copulation with an Italian customer, neither Phoebe's lesbian manipulations nor Fanny's auto-eroticism are able to quench the flames of aroused sexuality.

Cleland describes this arousal of sexual desire in minute detail and thus develops both a pornographic dimension and the philosophy of physical and erotic pleasure. Fanny's defloration by Charles, the lover she is to meet again and marry later, may be painful, but she had been longing for it. Her love for the ravisher makes her bear the pain more easily. This episode introduces the sentimental strain. Having found her true love in a brothel, Fanny must leave the world of prostitution for this love to develop in a place that is more acceptable to a middle-class audience. Hence Charles does not deflower Fanny in a bawdy-house but in a public house where both become aware of their love for each other. This discovery of love surpassing mere physical pleasure and attraction is the fourth stage of Fanny's development after the loss of her innocence and the awakening of curiosity and sexual desire. It is interrupted by Charles's sudden disappearance, which is instigated by his father, as Fanny learns much later. Perturbed by the end of her bliss, Fanny, now pregnant, suffers a miscarriage, a realistic and shocking element that would hardly occur if *Memoirs* was merely a 'pornographic' novel.

Fanny's trials, however, have made her much wiser, and she now realizes that money is important to survive. It is for this reason that she does not refuse to become Mr H.'s kept mistress – the next stage of her life and learning – though Mr H. does not compete with Charles in Fanny's affections. She remains faithful to her new keeper until surprising him one day having intercourse with the servant-maid. In a remarkable reversal of the eighteenth-century sexual double standard, Fanny turns the tables on him and seduces his footman, lusty Will. But her happiness with this youth, based only on physical pleasure, doesn't last long. Caught in the act by Mr H., Fanny is rebuked and abandoned by her wealthy keeper. Financially, however, she is now better off than before and advances from kept mistress to woman of pleasure in Mrs Cole's 'academy' in Covent Garden. This step marks the end of letter I and volume I, Fanny mocking the tradition of the epistolary novel in her final remark that 'it is high time to put a period to this'.

In Mrs Cole's establishment Fanny finds happiness and pleasure again in the company of pleasant girls and an understanding and reasonable surrogate mother. Mrs Cole runs a 'bagnio' for well-heeled gentlemen, and the first part of volume II is made up of the tales of Fanny's companions, Emily, Harriet, and Louisa, entertaining themselves with stories of the loss of their maidenheads. Here Cleland has quite obviously quarried the whore dialogue and erotic tales as far back as Boccaccio and Chaucer. The tales are followed by what Fanny terms a 'country-dance' – i.e. an orgy – which demands all Cleland's skill as a writer, for what he describes is a series of copulations whose only difference is the variation of positions. At this point, we are into what Steven Marcus and Mertner/Mainusch have termed 'pornotopia', with several couples in a closed room, the only aim being sexual pleasure from alternately making love and watching others in the act.

With the introduction of Mr Norbert, the novel turns to the description and parody of defloration mania. Mr Norbert pays dearly for what he takes to be Fanny's virginity but which is only a well-hidden sponge filled with blood. As part of her sexual education in the libertine spirit, Fanny samples a wide variety of erotic behaviour. Dissatisfied with Mr Norbert's nocturnal fumbling, she gives herself to a sailor in a public house during a visit in town. What is remarkable about this scene, apart from its overt irony due to style and narrative distance, is Fanny's experience of pure voluptuousness without money being involved. Back at Mrs Cole's house, she has sadomasochistic sex with a flagellant, Mr Barvile, fetishist sex with a 'grave, staid, solemn, elderly gentleman whose peculiar humour was a delight in combing fine tresses of hair', and is a witness to the brutish intercourse between Louisa and an idiot.

While on an outing, Fanny also observes two men having sex at an inn, a scene she describes in detail but immediately afterwards condemns 'in rage and indignation' as criminal. With this explicit description, Cleland broke one of the major sexual taboos of the eighteenth century. Fanny's alleged contempt for homosexuals – pronounced *after* a minute account of the physical details of the sexual act – again caters for the attitudes of the middle-class reader while developing the pornographic potential of the scene.

Fanny's sampling of sex at Mrs Cole's brothel ends with another orgy during a bathing excursion with her colleagues and some gentlemen. When the aged bawd retires to the country, Fanny is ready to enter a new career as a 'young gentlewoman' in a pleasant house at Marylebone. An old bachelor takes her into keeping and, upon his death, she becomes the heiress of a large fortune. Having thus gained financial independence, Fanny remembers Charles, her first and only love. Her distinction between physical-mechanical love and romantic love recalls Prévost's *Manon Lescaut* of 1731 and constitutes Cleland's adaptation of French philosophical ideas of pleasure of aristocratic-libertine origin to an English bourgeois heroine and readership. On a trip to her birthplace, Fanny finally meets her Charles. Fortune has not smiled on her lover, but as Fanny has sufficient money and property for both of them, she can retire to a virtuous middle-class existence of domesticity – to her own satisfaction and that of the readers of the novel. There can be no doubt that the resemblance to the happy ending in *Pamela* is intentional; but Cleland explodes rather than apes Richardson's denouement: for Pamela there could be neither sex nor sexual pleasure before marriage, and she trades her 'virtue' for the marriage licence; Fanny, however, tries to show that vice can also lead to virtue and that there is a difference between sexual and erotic love, her love for Charles being both *eros* and *agape*.

Memoirs of a Woman of Pleasure is a novel dominated by eighteenth-century bourgeois thought, with a sprinkling of French libertinism. Like Pamela, Fanny never aims higher than the status of the 'bourgeoise', and it is this state of mind that controls many aspects of the plot, theme, and style of the book. The need to succeed financially is continually stressed, and like a good pupil Fanny reproduces what she has learned on her social climb, thus perpetuating clichés of middle-class origin. These clichés and prejudices are most obvious in Fanny's comments on, and treatment of, her maid while being a kept mistress of Mr H.

Formally, *Memoirs* is a parody of the Christian confession. When Fanny 'confesses' to the addressee of her letters, an unknown 'Madam', at the very beginning of the novel, 'I shall recall to view those scandalous stages of my life, out of which I emerged at length, to the enjoyment of every blessing in the power of love, health, and fortune to bestow' (at the beginning of her second letter she even uses the word 'confession'), Cleland ironically refers to the tradition of confessions developed by spiritual autobiography and usurped in the eighteenth century by the pornographic and libertine novels. By the time Cleland put pen to paper, the confessional report had become an established form in French licentious fiction, 'Memoirs' promising the titillating disclosure of erotic adventures. Fanny's two 'letters', each comprising a volume, are hardly sufficient reason to call *Memoirs of a Woman of Pleasure* a genuine epistolary novel, though Cleland had his reasons for using a form and a diction that mockingly alluded to Richardson, for *Memoirs* is also one of the numerous anti-*Pamela*s of the mid eighteenth century. Fielding ushered in the wave of parodies on *Pamela* (1740) with his *Shamela* (1741), followed by *Joseph Andrews* in 1742; and Cleland proved a true disciple of Fielding in adopting his spelling in *Shamela* of virtue as 'Vartue', a point all extant modern editions have ignored.

Memoirs has close links with the early history of the English novel. Apart from the influence of Richardson and Fielding in the areas of form and style, which makes itself felt in burlesque rather than in straight, parallel lines, Defoe must be mentioned as another eminent source for Cleland as far as English literature is concerned. Like Richardson, Defoe was a bigot at heart, if not an incipient pornographer, but with *Moll Flanders* (1722) and *Roxana* (1724) he made the whore biography fashionable in English literary circles. Defoe gave pride of place to morality, stating in the preface to *Roxana* that, as 'editor', he had toned down the licentiousness of the 'original' manuscript. 'When Vice is painted in its low-priz'd Colours,' he argued, ''tis not to make People in Love with it, but to expose it; and if the Reader makes a wrong Use of the Figures, the Wickedness is his own.' Edmund Curll, one of the kings of the pornography market in early-eighteenth-century England, defended his wares in much the same words. Significantly, Fanny alludes to Defoe's ostentatious morality in what she concedes is a 'tail-piece of morality' in her confession. Almost repeating Defoe verbatim, she affirms towards the end of volume II: 'if I have painted vice in all its gayest colours, if I have decked it with flowers, it has been solely in order to make the worthier, the solemner, sacrifice of it to virtue'. But unlike Defoe's fictitious editor in *Moll Flanders*, who must 'wrap it up so clean, as not to give room, especially for vicious Readers, to turn it to his Disadvantage', Fanny can be honest and unabashed, as she is addressing a woman who will not 'snuff prudishly, and out of character, at the pictures' Fanny paints. With the covert and false eroticism of Defoe and Richardson in mind, Cleland has Fanny exclaim that, in her description, it is not middle-class decency she adheres to but 'Truth! stark naked truth', and that she 'will not so much as take the pains to bestow the strip of a gauze-wrapper on it, but paint situations such as they rose'. There are many more parallels between *Moll Flanders* and *Memoirs*. Both Moll and Fanny make their way up in society, both attach much importance to money, although Fanny, unlike Moll, can also enjoy sex without the pecuniary aspect in mind.

In addition to the burgeoning English novel of the early eighteenth century, Cleland tapped a few other sources for his bestseller. The currents of sensibility and sentimentality are evident in many places in *Memoirs* and are most obviously expressed in the development of the love between Fanny and Charles. After all, the Abbé Prévost had set the tone in 1731, both for sentimental literature and the theme of the *courtisane vertueuse*, with his *Manon Lescaut*, and Cleland knew French literature very well. But he is even more indebted to materialism, another influential current that was mainly fed by anticlerical and pornographic fiction and was for the most part of French provenance. To find both sentimentality and materialism in one novel may be surprising at first glance; yet Cleland was not the only one who tried such a synthesis; some of Diderot's works and Rousseau's *Confessions* of 1765 (published in 1782) are perhaps the best known in this genre.

It was not so much the philosophical works themselves that had an impact on Cleland. To be sure, he knew one of La Mettrie's major treatises, *L'Homme Machine* of 1747, and may have heard of, or even read, the Frenchman's rehabilitation of the erotic in *L'Art de jouir*, translated into English in 1748. In fact, La Mettrie's mechanism can be traced in Cleland's metaphors – sexual organs in *Memoirs* are compared to pounding 'engines' and thrusting 'machines' – and his implicit view of nature and natural feelings, including the erotic, as a substitute for religion and metaphysics. For Cleland, however, the pervasive influence of French prose fiction was of paramount importance. It was the licentious and often pornographic libertine novels that brought to England the French philosophy of sexual pleasure. It can be argued that if France had not supplied themes, plots, and underlying ideologies in a wave of *romans galants* and salacious novels, England's erotic fiction would have developed quite differently. Indeed, if one views *Memoirs of a Woman of Pleasure* exclusively within the history and tradition of the English novel, Cleland would appear to be the odd man out, a writer whose moral message and libertine ideas on sex were against the literary current, if by this one means the works of Defoe, Richardson, Fielding, and Smollett. However, if one considers the impact of French literature, *Memoirs* appears in a different light.

A brief look at graphic satire corroborates the impression that in the area of erotic fiction French works ruled unchallenged. In the fourth picture of his popular series *Marriage à la Mode*, published in 1746, William Hogarth shows a countess's levee. On the sofa, beside the corrupt and Tartuffe-like Counsellor Silvertongue, lies a book whose title reads *Le Sopha*. This is an extremely successful Oriental tale by Crébillon fils. First published in 1742, it was translated into English in the same year, and by 1801 eighteen registered editions of the translation had appeared. Since the book was so well known, Hogarth's allusion was sufficient evidence for his contemporaries of the moral turpitude of the sycophants assembled at the levee. Diderot's even more explicit *Les Bijoux indiscrets*, translated in 1749 as *The Indiscreet Toys*, did not sell as well as Crébillon's erotica. That the latter was one of the most popular French writers in erotic literature is confirmed by James Gillray. In 1786, Gillray recorded the late-eighteenth-century sexual scene in England in his engraving cited above (pp. 15–16). Among the objects for sale assembled in the picture (aphrodisiacs, pills, condoms, birches) there are also erotic books. Besides *Fanny Hill* and two other English works, Gillray includes Crébillon's *Le Sopha* together with Voltaire's *La Pucelle d'Orléans*.

IV

Critics often forget that in the eighteenth century educated readers of novels, and especially of erotic novels, did not make a distinction between

French and English books. The modern separation of French erotica and 'homespun' English novels is hardly an appropriate way to understand the market of licentious fiction as a reader may have found it in the eighteenth century. A great number of French libertine novels reached England before 1748, and most of them were available in English translation. When in 1748 John Cleland started revising his 'Ur-Fanny' in the Fleet prison, he was able to draw on an impressive series of erotic novels, such as Crébillon's *Lettres de la Marquise de M ... au Comte de R ...* (translated in 1735); *Les Égarements du coeur et de l'esprit* (1736–8); several works by Marivaux and Duclos, and major erotica, including pornography, which literary histories have labelled, somewhat despicably, *'la littérature du deuxième rayon'*, such as Boyer d'Argens's *Les Nones* [sic] *galantes* (1740); the anonymous *Le Canapé couleur de feu* (1714; translated in 1742); Gervaise de Latouche's *Histoire de Dom Bougre* (1741/2; translated in 1743) – one of the most influential pornographic novels of the early part of the eighteenth century – and a few novels from the pen of Godard d'Aucour.

The libertine novel in France can be seen as a reaction against the corruption of manners. The ruling class created a licentious literature dominated by urbane, unpretentious wit. In England, the rise of the novel was accompanied by the growth and influence of a middle-class readership. Realism, in the English novel, came with middle-class authors writing for a bourgeois audience. But in France it was the tradition of vice and worldliness, recorded in fiction from Crébillon fils to Laclos, which contributed to the development of realism. In this process the domain of the erotic had a central function, for it was here that the crucial connection was established between libertine ideas and literature. Philosophical libertinism entered an already existing erotic literature and, with the coming of the ideas of *plaisir* and *volupté*, erotic prose fiction took a decisive turn towards the *libertinage élégant*, where the aims were both philosophical and artistic. La Mettrie asserted the place of sex in man's life with his *L'Art de jouir* (1748) and *La Volupté* (1750), and the new libertine philosophy attacked the bastions of sexual repression – the social contract of the state and, above all, the moral teaching of religion, particularly that of the Catholic Church. This is one of the reasons why libertine pornography is often placed or set in sacred locations. Eighteenth-century pornographic novels set in monasteries break moral, religious, and sexual taboos while demonstrating the corruption of monks and nuns and their mocking of celibacy; but above all these novels show the representatives of the Church advocating, and putting into practice, the *philosophie du plaisir*. This didactic element is often, though not always, present in French libertine fiction, from Boyer d'Argens's *Thérèse philosophe* (1748) in the first half of the century to the philosophy-cum-pornography of Mirabeau, Rétif, and de Sade in the 1790s. Religion, argued the *philosophes*, was to be replaced by an enlightened self-interest, and a number of writers applied this philosophy to their fiction.

The whore dialogue, cast into the form of the novel, absorbed this philosophy, and its modern French branch had a direct influence on Cleland. In fact, *Memoirs of a Woman of Pleasure* is a rather late example of an old literary genre with precedents in Greek literature. By 1748 this genre had been developed to its full pornographic potential. Initially meant as satire and bawdy entertainment, the whore dialogue gradually changed its function until the sexual stimulation of the reader became one of its most obvious features. Pietro Aretino's *Ragionamenti* (Rome, 1534–6; reprinted London, 1584) is the first book of this genre that had a major part in the proliferation of European pornography. It popularized the whore dialogue, and with it the bawdy and obscene satire of religion and clerics as well as the description of the voluptuous pleasures of human sexuality. Aretino found a number of imitators. *La puttana errante*, possibly written by Niccolò Franco, and Ferrante Pallavicino's *La retorica delle puttane* (1642) are worth mentioning. The first book was very popular in France and was still being sold in French translations in the 1790s. Pallavicino's whore dialogues had appeared in an English version, *The Whores Rhetoric*, by 1683. This was an edition rewritten for an English audience, and the subtitle announced it as 'calculated to the meridian of London'.

French authors then continued the line of the whore dialogue, perfecting it towards pornographic fiction. It was with *L'Escole des filles*, translated *c.* 1688 as *The School of Venus* (of which we know only through court records), that a more significant step was taken in the development of the pornographic novel. Attributed to Michel Millot and/or Jean l'Ange, *The School of Venus* shares with the licentious novel a claustrophobic atmosphere, a loss of psychological depth accompanied by an idealization of sex, and an anarchic message undermining the moral teaching of parents and religion. Even more popular was Nicolas Chorier's *Satyra sotadica* (c. 1660), originally published in Latin, which came to be known in French as *L'Académie des dames* (1680) and *Le Meursius francois*; and in English as *The School of Women* (1682) and *A Dialogue Between a Married Lady and a Maid* (1688 and 1744). Numerous versions of this book, with varying titles in Latin, French and English, were sold in the eighteenth century. Lesbian manipulations, orgasm, and sadism are both described in conversations and practised by the characters. This practical part – people engaging in sex – is a novelty in the whore dialogue at this stage of its development. Comic elements have disappeared, and there is much brutality in the description of defloration and flagellation, while the attack on institutions controlling sexual morals – matrimony, the Church – has increased to a degree of striking directness. In the course of the development of the whore dialogue as a literary genre one notices a growing exactness in the description of sexual details. The settings change from brothel to private home and, eventually, to the monastery. Stylistically, the pathetic is substituted for the comic as the audience and literary taste develop and change, and pornographic description displaces obscene satire. The epic mode gradually emerges, replacing the earlier dialogue forms, and leading to autobiographical reports or confessions about sexual experiences including flagellation, homosexuality, and sadism.

The prototype of the anti-monastic novel combining anti-Christian slander and salacity is Jean Barrin's *Venus in the Cloister*, first published in French in 1683 and translated into English in 1692. Edmund Curll published it again in 1724. In many ways this book is still a whore dialogue. In fact, the original edition consisted of three dialogues between two nuns; but later, three epic reports were added that were taken from French collections of tales about amorous monks and nuns. With this novel, pornotopia was finally reached. Voyeurism, masturbation, defloration, and copulation are major themes – sex has become a religion. Consequently, orgasm is described in quasi-religious terms. The new faith, sexual pleasure, is set down in the books Agnès, the major character, receives from her *abbé* – all of them obscene or pornographic. For all its anticlerical attacks – sexy nuns, to English readers, meant anti-Catholic propaganda as well as titillating eroticism – Barrin's book shows a deep interest in sexual deviation, particularly sado-masochism, and it is obvious that the novel is intended to excite the reader sexually. *Venus in the Cloister* remained influential throughout the eighteenth century and paved the way for all the libertine novels set in monasteries and nunneries. Boyer d'Argens's *Thérèse philosophe* (1748), soon afterwards Englished as *The Philosophical Theresa*, and La Morlière's *Les Lauriers ecclésiastiques* (1748) came too late to have been influential for Cleland, but both novels are clearly indebted to Barrin.

If one approaches the French and English pornographic novels of the eighteenth century as one body of literature – a view justified by the translations and the reception in England of French fiction – it is not Cleland's *Memoirs* that marks the height of the development, but Gervaise de Latouche's *Histoire de Dom B.... portier des Chartreux* (*c.* 1741/2). English readers could purchase a translation of this, entitled *History of Don B*, as early as 1743. *Dom Bougre*, to give the novel its full and telling title, appeared in various guises, such as *Portier des Chartreux*; or *Mémoires de Saturnin*; or *Histoire de Gouberdon*, and was frequently reprinted and imitated in sequels that appeared as late as the 1780s. Held as a confessional report, *Dom Bougre* is a parody of the Christian faith and, as a novel, stands in the picaresque tradition. The hero, Saturnin, is of lowly birth. Guided by fortune and misfortune, he records the ups and downs of his life inside and outside the monastery. The novel also has didactic aspects in the conversations between the hero and Suzon, and in the discussion of sexual perversions and corruption in monastic life. There is an anticlerical bias in the detailed description of the fornication of monks and nuns, but it is also obvious that the sexual scenes are pornographic, demonstrating the usual ingredients of the pornographic novel, such as voyeurism and a virtual obsession with sex. The ending of *Dom Bougre*, however, is remarkable in that the hero is castrated. This is quite unusual for pornography, though other features of the book, such as the final remorse and the retiring to a 'decent' life, are typical of pornography written for a non-aristocratic audience. Fanny Hill, too, must finally come to terms with a bourgeois way of life to which she has to adapt her libertine sexual drive. Several years before John Cleland's famous whore made her entrance into the literary world, *Dom Bougre* thus represented the paradigmatic pornographic novel of the Age of Enlightenment, with its propagation of sexual pleasure as a new religion, its seeming rejection of middle-class ideas on sex, and its double morality – quite striking at the end of the book – all couched in a parody of the Christian faith.

What Cleland attempted with *Memoirs of a Woman of Pleasure* is not worthless pornography full of boring repetition, but a unique combination of parody, erotic entertainment, and a philosophical concept of human sexuality borrowed from French sources and adapted to the English bourgeois viewpoint. It is Cleland's fusion of sex and pathetic sentiment that needs some further exploration since it affects the fundamental question of the reception and evaluation of the novel. It has often been stated that *Memoirs* does not contain a single obscene word, a point frequently made in modern editions to appease the law and to justify the publication of the book, the tacit implication being that the absence of obscene language precludes any pornography. To be sure, Cleland has not violated linguistic taboos – which saved him from prison and further prosecution – but he broke those of content, for it is quite possible to describe copulation, for instance, with the help of circumlocutions and euphemisms instead of Anglo-Saxon four-letter words. The message or content thus remain sexually stimulating, but the effect of the description – and this is the crucial point – may run counter to the pornographic intention. In this context it is important to recall that several critics have perceived a comic element in Cleland's description of the sexual scenes. Some scholars even believe that this stylistic comedy was intended by Cleland. This is doubtful. At the beginning of volume II, the author has Fanny remark on the style of her 'memoirs'. Her intention in penning her confession, she tells the lady she writes for, is to write in 'a mean tempered with taste, between the revoltingness of gross, rank, and vulgar expressions, and the ridicule of mincing metaphors and affected circumlocutions'. In other words, *Memoirs* tries to describe sex with the stylistic means employed by contemporary prose fiction. Since Cleland also parodied *Pamela* and the whore biography, what resulted was the stylistic mimicry of the literary sources. While it is true that the autobiographical form, which implies hindsight and hence a certain distance of the narrator from events of the past, allows for a number of comic and ironic aspects in *Memoirs* – as in the first three sex scenes in volume I – the majority of sex scenes, which constitute about one third of the text (thirty-nine episodes) are evidently not intended as comedy and show almost the whole gamut of sexual behaviour known in the eighteenth century. If we find them more amusing than sexually stimulating today we ought to bear in mind that our evaluation of *Memoirs* is fundamentally different from that of an eighteenth-century reader used to the periphrastic style. Cleland obviously had trouble keeping up his 'mean' way in *Memoirs* and often tended to the very 'mincing metaphors' and pathetic clichés which he has Fanny condemn. Especially towards the end of the novel, Fanny finds it extremely difficult to invent still different and more powerful words to convey the feelings of joy and pleasure she experiences in her sexual reunion with Charles.

Since the reader re-creates a novel in the process of reading, a novel's reception and evaluation may vary through the centuries as literary tastes change. This may seem an obvious point, especially in the case of the sentimental novel, which many modern readers find boring if not unpalatable, but it is easily forgotten in the discussion of the pornographic potential and the comic effect of *Memoirs*. On the basis of the predominant literary taste in England around 1750 one can assume that a mid-eighteenth-century reader would not have found Cleland's style comic or odd. In fact, the reading audience probably shared James Boswell's opinion that *Memoirs* was a 'most licentious and inflaming book'. But for the jaded modern reader, Cleland's periphrastic style jars with the pornographic content of the novel. Used to hard-core scenes in books and films (and more often than not repelled by them) presented with a realistically obscene vocabulary, the twentieth-century reader of *Memoirs of a Woman of Pleasure* may feel like George Steiner who sees the book as a 'mock-epic of orgasm ... in which any sane man will take delight' (*Language and Silence*, Harmondsworth, Penguin, 1979, p. 96). And indeed, one cannot help smiling at Cleland's metaphors, such as 'instrument of pleasure', 'machine', and 'abyss of joy', which border on the grotesque. Comic effects, however, whether in style or theme, are detrimental to any sort of pornography, for pornography aims at immediate sexual stimulation whereas laughter defuses erotic tension. Thus time has added another dimension to Cleland's bestseller, and many modern admirers of Fanny Hill may find that, rather than being inflamed like James Boswell, they will be amused at Cleland's entertaining mixture of voluntary and involuntary stylistic comedy.

Whether as a novel, parody, or licentious fiction, *Memoirs of a Woman of Pleasure* is a true product of its time. It has been unjustly denied a place in the history of the English novel; but its rejection of puritanical sexual morals, its assertion of a natural sexuality and sensuality, and its non-repressive message of erotic pleasure controlled by reason characterize it as a voice of the moderate Enlightenment. As such, but also because of its inherent and undeniable literary and historical value, Cleland's *Memoirs* deserves a niche alongside other important novels from the first half of the eighteenth century.

A NOTE ON THE TEXT

This edition is based on the text of the first London edition of the two volumes of *Memoirs of a Woman of Pleasure* (1748/9) as identified by David Foxon in his *Libertine Literature in England 1660–1745* (New Hyde Park, NY, 1965). The novel was printed for Ralph Griffiths, without the author's name, by Thomas Parker. Copies of this original edition are held by the British Library (shelf-mark P.C. 27. a. 44.); Yale; the Bayerische Staatsbibliothek, Munich; and The Bibliothèque Nationale.

Until the appearance of Mr Foxon's authoritative study there had been considerable confusion about the dating and publishing history of *Memoirs*, many modern editions claiming to present 'complete and un-expurgated' texts while excluding the sodomitical passage contained in volume II of the first edition. For additional comments on the publishing of *Memoirs* see William H. Epstein, *John Cleland: Images of a Life* (New York and London, 1974); Patrick J. Kearney, *The Private Case: an Annotated Bibliography of the Private Case Erotica Collection in the British (Museum) Library* (London, Jay Landesman, 1981), pp. 136–41 (nos. 415 and 418); Peter Naumann, *Keyhole und Candle. John Clelands 'Memoirs of a Woman of Pleasure' und die Entstehung des Pornographischen Romans in England* (Heidelberg, Carl Winter Universitätsverlag, 1976), pp. 322–4; and Poul Steen Larsen's unpublished typescript, 'John Cleland's *Memoirs of a Woman of Pleasure*. A Bibliography of the Earliest Editions' (Copenhagen, 1968). Patrick J. Kearney is presently preparing a bibliography of the novel that will no doubt make obsolete the older and less reliable biblio-graphical studies by Henry Spencer Ashbee (alias 'Pisanus Fraxi'), *Catena Librorum Tacendorum. Bio- Biblio- Icono-Graphical and Critical Notes on Curious, Uncommon and Erotic Books* (London, 1885; reprinted London, 1960, and New York, 1962), pp. 60–95; and Paul Englisch, *Memoiren eines Freudenmädchens. Von John Cleland. Ein Bibliographischer Versuch* (Stuttgart, 1929).

In the present text only minor changes have been made for the convenience of the modern reader, the major aim being to preserve as much of the colour and texture of Cleland's prose as possible. I have adjusted the text where punctuation or misspelling might confuse the reader. The eighteenth-century use of italics for proper names and the capitalization of several nouns have been eliminated. Cleland's spelling has been retained when it is consistent, except that elliptical spellings (past participles ending in 'd; thro' etc.) have been expanded; hyphens have been added or eliminated in some cases, and the 'long s' has been replaced by s throughout. In addition, I have corrected several errors. The notes prepared for this edition are at the end of the book.

A CHRONOLOGICAL LIST
OF FRENCH EROTIC FICTION
PUBLISHED BETWEEN 1700 AND 1748

As Cleland has often and exclusively been seen within the context of early eighteenth-century English prose fiction (i.e. as influenced by, or reacting to, Defoe, Richardson, Fielding, and Smollett), the following list provides an idea of the amount and scope of influential erotic prose of French origin, published in the first half of the eighteenth century. In his book reviews, Cleland referred to several French authors he had read, Crébillon and Duclos taking pride of place, and one can assume that he knew the major erotica. Although poetry and drama are excluded here, they ought not to be ignored in an assessment of *Memoirs of a Woman of Pleasure*. The list also excludes such perennial bestsellers as Petronius' *Satyricon*; Apuleius' *The Golden Ass*; Marguerite de Navarre's *L'Heptaméron*, first published in 1559; the anonymous *Les Cent Nouvelles Nouvelles* (1486); Boccaccio's *Decameron*; La Fontaine's *Contes*; and Aretino's *Ragionamenti*, works that appeared in numerous editions, and in several languages, throughout the century and proved important for both French and English literature.

As the list shows, most novels were translated immediately. But the cognoscenti and the educated hardly needed translations, French being the century's international language.

Year of publication	Author and title	Year of English translation
1683, 1702	Barrin, *Vénus dans le cloître*	1692; 1724; 1745
	Chorier, *L'Académie des Dames*	1707; 1740; 1745
1714	*Le Canapé couleur de feu*	1742
1715	Millot/L'Ange, *L'Escole des filles*	1745
1728	Godard de Beauchamps, *Histoire du Prince Apprius*	1728
1731	Prévost, *Manon Lescaut*	
1731–42	Marivaux, *La Vie de Marianne*	1736–42; 1743; 1746; 1747

Year of publication	Author and title	Year of English translation
1734	Crébillon fils, *L'Écumoire*	1735; 1742; 1748
1734–5	Marivaux, *Le Paysan parvenu*	1765
1735	Crébillon fils, *Lettres de la Marquise ...*	1735
1736–8	Crébillon fils, *Les Égarements du coeur*	1751
1740	D'Argens, *Les Nones galantes*	probably translated
1741	Duclos, *Confessions du Comte de ...*	1775
1742	Crébillon fils, *Le Sopha*	1742: 18 editions until 1801
	C. Villaret, *Antipamela*	1742
	Latouche, *Histoire de Dom B.*	1743
1743	Godard d'Aucour, *Mémoires turcs*	
1744	Duclos, *Acajou et Zirphile*	
1745	Meusnier de Querlon, *Histoire de la Tourrière des Carmélites*	
	Godard d'Aucour, *Thémidore*	
1746	La Morlière, *Angola*	
1748	La Morlière, *Les Lauriers ecclésiastiques*	translated after 1750
	D'Argens, *Thérèse philosophe*	1748/9
	Diderot, *Les Bijoux indiscrets*	1749
	Meusnier de Querlon, *Psaphion ou la courtisane de Smyrne*	

SELECT BIBLIOGRAPHY

The standard biography of John Cleland is William H. Epstein, *John Cleland: Images of a Life* (New York and London, Columbia University Press, 1974). For general surveys of erotic literature in seventeenth- and eighteenth-century England and France see Paul Englisch, *Geschichte der erotischen Literatur* (Stuttgart, 1927), parts 4 and 6; David Foxon, *Libertine Literature in England 1660–1745* (New Hyde Park, NY, 1965); and Roger Thompson, *Unfit for Modest Ears. A Study of Pornographic, Obscene and Bawdy Works Written or Published in England in the Second Half of the Seventeenth Century* (London, Macmillan, 1979). In my own *Eros Revived: a Study of Erotica in Eighteenth-Century England and America* (London, Secker & Warburg, 1985) I have tried to discuss eighteenth-century erotica as one body of literature, demonstrating the enormous French influence as well as the literary and political importance of pornography; see especially chapters 2, 3, and 7.

The most detailed and authoritative study of *Memoirs of a Woman of Pleasure*, with a welter of background information, is Peter Naumann's *Keyhole und Candle. John Clelands 'Memoirs of a Woman of Pleasure' und die Entstehung des Pornographischen Romans in England* (Heidelberg, Carl Winter Universitätsverlag, 1976), which has been unjustly ignored in the English-speaking world. The following is a list of relevant studies of *Memoirs* that have appeared in recent years.

Malcolm Bradbury, 'Fanny Hill and the comic novel', *Critical Quarterly*, 13 (1971), 263–75.

Leo Braudy, 'Fanny Hill and materialism', *Eighteenth-Century Studies*, 4 (1970), 21–40.

Edward W. Copeland, 'Clarissa and Fanny Hill: sisters in distress', *Studies in the Novel*, 4 (1972), 343–52.

Hans Giese, *Das obszöne Buch*, Stuttgart, 1965, 56–72.

John Hollander, 'The old last act: some observations on Fanny Hill', *Encounter*, 2 (1963), 69–77.

B. Ivker, 'John Cleland and the Marquis d'Argens: eroticism and natural morality in mid-eighteenth-century English and French fiction', *Mosaic*, 8 (1975), 141–8.

Edgar Mertner/Herbert Mainusch, *Pornotopia. Das Obszöne und die Pornographie in der literarischen Landschaft*, Frankfurt and Bonn, 1970, 265–319.

Roland Mortier, 'Libertinage littéraire et tensions sociales dans la littérature de l'Ancien Régime: de la "picara" à la "fille de joie" ', *Revue de littérature comparée*, 46 (1972), 35–45.

J. H. Plumb, 'Introduction', in John Cleland, *Memoirs of Fanny Hill*, New York, New American Library, 1965, vii–xiv.

Peter Quennell, 'Introduction for Modern Readers', in John Cleland, *Memoirs of a Woman of Pleasure*, New York, Putnam, 1963, v–xiv.

Horst Rüdiger, 'Das Urteil eines Sachverständigen. Winckelmann über Clelands Stil', *Arcadia*, 7 (1972), 272f.

Michael Shinagel, '*Memoirs of a Woman of Pleasure*: pornography and the mid-eighteenth-century novel', in Paul J. Korshin, ed., *Studies in Change and Revolution*, Menston, 1972, 211–36.

B. Slepian and L. J. Morrissey, 'What is *Fanny Hill*?', *Essays in Criticism*, 14 (1964), 65–75.

Stanley J. Solomon, 'Subverting propriety as a pattern of irony in three eighteenth-century novels: *The Castle of Otranto*, *Vathek*, and *Fanny Hill*', *Erasmus Review*, 1 (1971), 107–16.

Stephen Sossaman, 'Sex, love and reason in the novels of John Cleland', *Massachusetts Studies in English*, 6 (1978), 93–106.

M. Taube, '*Moll Flanders* and *Fanny Hill*: a comparison', *Ball State University Forum*, 9 (1968), 76f.

Raymond K. Whitley, 'The libertine hero and heroine in the novels of John Cleland', *Studies in Eighteenth-Century Culture*, 9 (1979), 387–404.

Michael Wilding, '*Paradise Lost* and *Fanny Hill*', *Milton Quarterly*, 5 (1971), 14–15.

MEMOIRS

OF A

WOMAN

OF

PLEASURE.

VOL. I.

LONDON:

Printed for G. FENTON in the *Strand*

M.DCC.XLIX.

*Overleaf is a facsimile of the title-page of the first edition
(reproduced by permission of the British Library)*

MADAM,

I sit down to give you an undeniable proof of my considering your desires as indispensible orders: ungracious then as the task may be, I shall recall to view those scandalous stages of my life, out of which I emerged at length, to the enjoyment of every blessing in the power of love, health, and fortune to bestow, whilst yet in the flower of youth, and not too late to employ the leisure afforded me by great ease and affluence, to cultivate an understanding naturally not a despicable one, and which had, even amidst the whirl of loose pleasures I had been tossed in, exerted more observation on the characters and manners of the world than what is common to those of my unhappy profession, who, looking on all thought or reflexion as their capital enemy, keep it at as great a distance as they can, or destroy it without mercy.[1]

Hating, as I mortally do, all long unnecessary prefaces, I shall give you good quarter in this, and use no farther apology than to prepare you for seeing the loose part of my life, wrote with the same liberty that I led it.

Truth! stark naked truth, is the word, and I will not so much as take the pains to bestow the strip of a gauze-wrapper on it, but paint situations such as they actually rose to me in nature, careless of violating those laws of decency, that were never made for such unreserved intimacies as ours; and you have too much sense, too much knowledge of the *originals* themselves, to snuff prudishly and out of character at the *pictures* of them. The greatest men, those of the first and most leading taste, will not scruple adorning their private closets with nudities, though, in compliance with vulgar prejudices they may not think them decent decorations of the staircase or saloon.[2]

This and enough premised, I go souse into my personal history. My maiden name was Frances Hill. I was born at a small village near Liverpool in Lancashire, of parents extremely poor, and, I piously believe, extremely honest.

My father, who had received a maim on his limbs that disabled him from following the more laborious branches of country-drudgery, got, by making of nets, a scanty subsistence, which was not much enlarged by my mother's keeping a little day-school for the girls in her neighbourhood. They had had several children, but none lived to any age, except myself, who had received from nature a constitution perfectly healthy.

My education, till past fourteen, was no better than very vulgar; reading, or rather spelling, an illegible scrawl, and a little ordinary plainwork, composed the whole system of it: and then all my foundation in virtue was no other than a total ignorance of vice, and the shy timidity general to our sex, in the tender stage of life when objects alarm or frighten more by their novelty than any thing else: but then this is a fear too often cured at the expense of innocence, when Miss, by degrees, begins no longer to look on man as a creature of prey that will eat her.

My poor mother had divided her time so entirely between her scholars and her little domestic cares that she had spared very little of it to my instruction, having, from her own innocence from all ill, no hint or thought of guarding me against any.

I was now entering on my fifteenth year, when the worst of ills befell me in the loss of my tender fond parents, who were both carried off by the smallpox, within a few days of each other; my father dying first, and thereby hastening the death of my mother, so that I was now left an unhappy friendless Orphan: (for my father's coming to settle there was accidental, he being originally a Kentish-man). That cruel distemper which had proved so fatal to them had indeed seized me, but with such mild and favourable symptoms that I was presently out of danger, and, what I then did not know the value of, was entirely unmarked. I skip over here an account of the natural grief and affliction which I felt on this melancholy occasion. A little time, and the giddiness of that age, dissipated too soon my reflections on that irreparable loss; but nothing contributed more to reconcile me to it than the notions that were immediately put into my head of going to London and looking out for a service, in which I was promised all assistance and advice, from one Esther Davis, a young woman that had been down to see her friends and who, after the stay of a few days, was to return to her place.

As I had now nobody left alive in the village who had concern enough about what should become of me to start any objections to this scheme, and the woman who took care of me after my parents' death rather encouraged me to pursue it, I soon came to a resolution of making this

launch into the wide world by repairing to London in order to seek
my fortune, a phrase which, by the bye, has ruined more adventurers
of both sexes, from the country, than ever it made or advanced.

Nor did Esther Davis a little comfort and inspirit me to venture with
her by piquing my childish curiosity with the fine sights that were to
be seen in London: the tombs, the lions, the king, the royal family, the
fine plays and operas, and, in short, all the diversions which fell within
her sphere of life to come at, the detail of all which perfectly turned
the little head of me.

Nor can I remember, without laughing, the innocent admiration, not
without a spice of envy, with which we poor girls, whose church-going
clothes did not rise above dowlass³ shifts and stuff gowns, beheld Esther's
scowered satin-gown, caps bordered with an inch of lace, tawdry ribbons,
and shoes belaced with silver! All which we imagined grew in London
and entered for a great deal into my determination of trying to come
in for my share of them.

The idea, however, of having the company of a townswoman with
her was the trivial and all the motive that engaged Esther to take charge
of me during my journey to town, where she told me, after her manner
and style: as how several maids out of the country had made themselves
and all their kin forever, that by preserving their VARTUE, some had
taken so with their masters that they had married them, and kept them
coaches, and lived vastly grand, and happy, and some, mayhap, came
to be duchesses: Luck was all, and why not I as well as another,⁴ with
other almanacs to this purpose, which set me a tiptoe to begin this
promising journey, and to leave a place which, though my native one,
contained no relations that I had reason to regret and was grown insupportable to me from the change of the tenderest usage into a cold air
of charity, with which I was entertained even at the only friend's house
that I had the least expectations of care and protection from. She was,
however, so just to me as to manage the turning into money the little
matters that remained to me after the debts and burial-charges were
accounted for, and at my departure put my whole fortune into my hands,
which consisted of a very slender wardrobe, packed up in a very portable
box, and eight guineas, with seventeen shillings in silver, stowed in a
spring-pouch, which was a greater treasure than ever I had yet seen
together and which I could not conceive there was a possibility of running
out: and indeed I was so entirely taken up with the joy of seeing myself

mistress of such an immense sum that I gave very little attention to a world of good advice which was given me with it.

Places then being taken for Esther and me in the Chester-Waggon, I pass over a very immaterial scene of leave taking at which I dropt a few tears betwixt grief and joy; and, for the same reasons of insignificance, skip over all that happened to me on the road, such as the Waggoner's looking liquorish[5] on me, the schemes laid for me by some of the passengers, which were defeated by the vigilance of my guardian Esther who, to do her justice, took a motherly care of me, at the same time that she taxed me for her protection by making me bear all travelling charges, which I defrayed with the utmost chearfulness, and thought myself much obliged to her into the bargain. She took indeed great care that we were not over-rated or imposed on, as well as of managing as frugally as possible: expensiveness was not her vice.

It was pretty late in a summer evening when we reached the town, in our slow conveyance, though drawn by six at length. As we passed through the greatest streets that led to our inn, the noise of the coaches, the hurry, the crowds of foot passengers, in short, the new scenery of the shops and houses at once pleased and amazed me.

But guess at my mortification and surprise when we came to the inn, and our things were landed, and delivered to us, when my fellow traveller and protectress, Esther Davis, who had used me with the utmost tenderness during the journey, and prepared me by no preceding signs for the stunning blow I was to receive, when, I say, my only dependance and friend, in this strange place, all of a sudden assumed a strange and cool air towards me, as if she dreaded my becoming a burden to her.

Instead then of proffering me the continuance of her assistance and good offices, which I relied upon and never more wanted, she thought herself, it seems, abundantly acquitted of her engagements to me by having brought me safe to my journey's end; and seeing nothing in her procedure towards me but what was natural and in order, began to embrace me by way of taking leave, whilst I was so confounded, so struck, that I had not spirit or sense enough so much as to mention my hopes or expectations from her experience and knowledge of the place she had brought me to.

Whilst I stood thus stupid and mute, which she doubtless attributed to nothing more than a concern at parting, this idea procured me perhaps a slight alleviation of it in the following harangue: that now we were got safe to London and that she was obliged to go to her place. she advised me by all means to get into one as soon as possible – that I need not fear getting one – there were more places than parish-churches – that she advised me to go to an intelligence office – that if she heard of anything stirring, she would find me out and let me know; that in the mean time I should take a private lodging and acquaint her where to send to me, that she wished me good luck and hoped I should always have the grace to keep myself honest and not bring a disgrace on my parentage. With this she took her leave of me and left me, as it were, on my own hands, full as lightly as I had been put into hers.

Left thus alone, absolutely destitute and friendless, I began then to feel most bitterly the severity of this separation, the scene of which had passed in a little room in the inn; and no sooner was her back turned, but the affliction I felt at my helpless strange circumstances burst out into a flood of tears, which infinitely relieved the oppression of my heart though I still remained stupified and most perfectly perplexed how to dispose of myself.

One of the drawers coming in added yet more to my uncertainty by asking me, in a short way, if I called for anything. To which I replied, innocently, 'no,' but I wished him to tell me where I might get a lodging for that night. He said he would go and speak to his mistress, who accordingly came and told me drily, without entering in the least into the distress she saw me in, that I might have a bed for a shilling and that, as she supposed I had some friends in town (here I fetched a deep sigh in vain!) I might provide for myself in the morning.

It is incredible what trifling consolations the human mind will seize in its greatest afflictions. The assurance of nothing more than a bed to lie on that night calmed my agonies; and being ashamed to acquaint the mistress of the inn that I had no friends to apply to in town, I proposed to myself to proceed, the very next morning, to an intelligence office, to which I was furnished with written directions on the back of a ballad Esther had given me. There I counted on getting information of any place that such a country girl as I might be fit for, and where I could get into any sort of being before my little stock should be consumed. And as to a character, Esther had often repeated to me that I might depend on her managing me one; nor, however affected I was at her leaving me thus, did I entirely cease to rely on her, as I began to think

43

good-naturedly that her procedure was all in course, and that it was only my ignorance of life that had made me take it in the light I at first did.

Accordingly, the next morning I dressed as clean and as neat as my rustic wardrobe would permit me; and having left my box, with special recommendation to the landlady, I ventured out by myself, and without any more difficulty than may be supposed of a young country girl, barely fifteen, and to whom every sign or shop was a gazing trap, I got to the wished-for intelligence office.

It was kept by an elderly woman who sat at the receipt of custom, with a book before her, in great form and order, and several scrolls, ready made out, of directions for places.

I made up then to this important personage, without lifting up my eyes or observing any of the people round me who were attending there on the same errand as myself, and dropping her curtsies nine deep, made just a shift to stammer out my business to her.

Madam having heard me out, with all the gravity and brow of a petty minister of state, and seeing, at one glance over my figure, what I was, made me no answer but to ask me the preliminary shilling, on receipt of which she told me places for women were exceeding scarce, especially as I seemed too slightly built for hard work but that she would look over her book and see what was to be done for me, desiring me to stay a little till she had dispatched some other customers.

On this, I drew back a little, most heartily mortified at a declaration which carried with it a killing uncertainty that my circumstances could not well endure.

Presently, assuming more courage and seeking some diversion from my uneasy thoughts, I ventured to lift up my head a little and sent my eyes on a course round the room where they met full tilt with those of a lady (for such my extreme innocence pronounced her) sitting in a corner of the room, dressed in a velvet manteel[6] (nota bene, in the midst of summer) with her bonnet off; squob-fat,[7] red-faced, and at least fifty.

She looked as if she would devour me with her eyes, staring at me from head to foot, without the least regard to the confusion and blushes her eyeing me so fixedly put me to and which were to her, no doubt, the strongest recommendation and marks of my being fit for her purpose. After a little time, in which my air, person, and whole figure had undergone her strict examination, which I had, on my part, tried to render favourable to me by primming, drawing up my neck, and setting my best looks, she advanced and spoke to me with the greatest demureness:

'Sweat heart, do you want a place?'

'Yes! and please you' (with a curtsy down to the ground).

Upon this she acquainted me that she was actually come to the office herself to look out for a servant, that she believed I might do, with a little of her instructions; that she could take my very looks for a sufficient character, that London was a very wicked, vile place, that she hoped I would be tractable and keep out of bad company. In short, she said all to me that an old experienced practitioner in town could think of and which was much more than was necessary to take in an artless inexperienced country maid, who was even afraid of becoming a wanderer about the streets and therefore gladly jumped at the first offer of a shelter, especially from so grave and matron-like a lady, for such my flattering fancy assured me this now mistress of mine was; I being actually hired under the nose of the good woman that kept the office, whose shrewd smiles and shrugs I could not help observing, and innocently interpreted them as marks of her being pleased at my getting into place so soon: but, as I afterwards came to know, these beldams understood one another very well, and this was a market where Mrs Brown, my mistress, frequently attended on the watch for any fresh goods that might offer there, for the use of her customers and her own profit.

Madam was, however, so well pleased with her bargain, that fearing, I presume, lest better advice or some accident might occasion my slipping through her fingers, she would officiously take me in a coach to my inn where, calling herself for my box, it was, I being present, delivered without the least scruple or explanation as to where I was going.

This being over, she bid the coachman drive to a shop in St Paul's Churchyard, where she bought a pair of gloves, which she gave me and thence renewed her directions to the coachman to drive to her house in — street, who accordingly landed us at her door, after I had been cheered up and entertained by the way with the most plausible flams, without one syllable from which I could conclude anything but that I was by the greatest good luck fallen into the hands of the kindest mistress, not to say friend, that the varsal world could afford; and accordingly I entered her doors with most complete confidence and exultation, promising myself that, as soon as I should be a little settled, I would acquaint Esther Davis with my rare good fortune.

You may be sure the good opinion of my place was not lessened by the appearance of a very handsome back-parlour, into which I was led, and which seemed to me magnificently furnished, who had never seen better rooms than the ordinary ones in inns upon the road. There were two gilt pier-glasses, and a buffet in which a few pieces of plate, set out to the most show, dazzled and altogether persuaded me that I must be got into a very reputable family.

Here my mistress first began her part with telling me that I must have good spirits and learn to be free with her; that she had not taken me to be a common servant, to do domestic drudgery, but to be a kind of companion to her; and that, if I would be a good girl, she would do more than twenty mothers for me; to all which I answered only by the profoundest and the awkwardest curtsies and a few monosyllables, such as 'yes! no! to be sure'.

Presently my mistress touched the bell, and in came a strapping maid-servant who had let us in: 'Here, Martha,' said Mrs Brown, 'I have just hired this young woman to look after my linnen, so step up and show her her chamber; and I charge you to use her with as much respect as you would myself, for I have taken a prodigious liking to her, and I do not know what I shall do for her.'

Martha, who was an arch jade, and being used to this decoy, had her cue perfect, made me a kind of half-curtsy and asked me to walk up with her and accordingly showed me a neat room, two pair of stairs backwards, in which there was a handsome bed where Martha told me I was to lie with a young gentlewoman, a cousin of my mistress's, who she was sure would be vastly good to me. Then she ran out into such affected encomiums on her good mistress! her sweet mistress! and how happy I was to light upon her, that I could not have bespoke a better, with other the like gross stuff, such as would itself have started suspicions in any but such an unpractised simpleton who was perfectly new to life and who took every word she said in the very sense she laid out for me to take it; but she readily saw what a penetration she had to deal with and measured me very rightly in her manner of whistling to me, so as to make me pleased with my cage and blind to its wires.

In the midst of these false explanations of the nature of my future service we were rung for down again, and I was reintroduced into the same parlour where there was a table laid with three covers; and my mistress had now got with her one of her favourite girls, a notable manager of her house, and whose business it was to prepare and break such young fillies as I was to the mounting block: and she was accordingly, in that view, allotted me for a bedfellow; and to give her the more authority, she had the title of cousin conferred on her by the venerable president of this college.

Here I underwent a second survey, which ended in the full approbation of Mrs Phoebe Ayres, the name of my tuteress elect, to whose care and instructions I was affectionately recommended.

Dinner was now set on the table, and in pursuance of treating me as a companion, Mrs Brown, with a tone to cut off all dispute, soon overruled all my most humble and most confused protestations against sitting down with her Ladyship, which my very short breeding just suggested to me could not be right or in the order of things.

At table, the conversation was chiefly kept up by the two madams and carried on in double-meaning expressions, interrupted every now and then by kind assurances to me, all tending to confirm and fix my satisfaction with my present condition; augment it they could not, so very a novice was I then.

It was here agreed that I should keep myself up and out of sight for a few days, till such clothes could be procured for me as were fit for the character I was to appear in, of my mistress's companion, observing withall that on the first impressions of my figure much might depend; and, as they well judged, the prospect of exchanging my country clothes for the London finery made the clause of confinement digest perfectly well with me. But the truth was, Mrs Brown did not care that I should be seen or talked to by any, either of her customers or her does, (as they called the girls provided for them) till she had secured a good market for my maidenhead, which I had at least all the appearances of having brought into her Ladyship's service.

To slip over minuties[8] of no importance to the main of my story, I pass the interval to bedtime in which I was more and more pleased with the views that opened to me of an easy service under these good people; and after supper, being showed up to bed, Miss Phoebe, who observed a kind of modest reluctance in me to strip and go to bed in my shift before her now the maid was withdrawn, came up to me, and beginning with unpinning my handkerchief and gown, soon encouraged me to go on with undressing myself, and, still blushing at now seeing myself naked to my shift, I hurried to get under the bedclothes out of sight. Phoebe laughed and was not long before she placed herself by my side. She was about five and twenty, by her own most suspicious account, in which, according to all appearances, she must have sunk at least ten good years, allowance too being made for the havoc which a long course of hackneyship and hot waters must have made of her constitution and which had already brought on, upon the spur, that stale stage in which those of her profession are reduced to think of *showing* company instead of *seeing* it.

No sooner then was this precious substitute of my mistress's lain down, but she, who was never out of her way when any occasion of lewdness presented itself, turned to me, embraced and kissed me with great eagerness. This was new, this was odd; but imputing it to nothing but pure kindness, which, for aught I knew, it might be the London way to express in that manner, I was determined not to be behind-hand with her and returned her the kiss and embrace with all the fervour that perfect innocence knew.

Encouraged by this, her hands became extremely free and wandered over my whole body, with touches, squeezes, pressures that rather warmed and surprised me with their novelty than they either shocked or alarmed me.

The flattering praises she intermingled with these invasions contributed also not a little to bribe my passiveness and knowing no ill, I feared none especially from one who had prevented all doubt of her womanhood by conducting my hands to a pair of breasts that hung loosely down, in a size and volume that full sufficiently distinguished her sex, to me at least who had never made any other comparison.

I lay then all tame and passive as she could wish, whilst her freedom raised no other emotion but those of a strange, and till then unfelt, pleasure: every part of me was open and exposed to the licentious courses of her hands which, like a lambent fire, ran over my whole body and thawed all coldness as they went.

My breasts, if it is not too bold a figure to call so two hard, firm, rising hillocks that just began to show themselves or signify anything to the touch, employed and amused her hands awhile, till slipping down lower over a smooth track, she could just feel the soft silky down that had but a few months before put forth and garnished the mount-pleasant of those parts and promised to spread a grateful shelter over the sweet seat of the most exquisite sensation, and which had been, till that instant, the seat of the most insensible innocence. Her fingers played and strove to twine in the young tendrils of that moss which nature has contrived at once for use and ornament.

But not contented with these outer posts, she now attempts[9] the main spot, and began to twitch, to insinuate, and at length to force an introduction of a finger into the quick itself, in such a manner that, had she not proceeded by insensible gradations that enflamed me beyond the power of modesty to oppose its resistence to their progress, I should have jumped out of bed and cried out for help against such strange assaults.

Instead of which, her lascivious touches had lighted up a new fire that wantoned through all my veins but fixed with violence in that center appointed them by nature where the first strange hands were now busied in feeling, squeezing, compressing the lips, then opening them again, with a finger between, till an 'Oh!' expressed her hurting me where the narrowness of the unbroken passage refused it entrance to any depth.

In the meantime the extension of my limbs, languid stretchings, sighs, short heavings, all conspired to assure that experienced wanton that I was more pleased than offended at her proceedings, which she seasoned with repeated kisses and exclamations, such as 'Oh! what a charming creature thou art! – What a happy man will he be that first makes a woman of you! – Oh! that I were a man for your sake –!' with the like broken expressions, interrupted by kisses as fierce and salacious as ever I received from the other sex.

For my part, I was transported, confused, and out of myself. Feelings so new were too much for me; my heated and alarmed senses were in a tumult that robbed me of all liberty of thought; tears of pleasure gushed from my eyes and somewhat assuaged the fire that raged all over me.

Phoebe herself, the hackneyed, thoroughbred Phoebe, to whom all modes and devices of pleasure were known and familiar, found, it seems, in this exercise of her art to break young girls the gratification of one of those arbitrary tastes for which there is no accounting. Not that she hated men or did not even prefer them to her own sex; but when she met with such occasions as this was, a satiety of enjoyments in the common road, perhaps to a secret bias, inclined her to make the most of pleasure wherever she could find it, without distinction of sexes. In this view, now well assured that she had, by her touches, sufficiently inflamed me for her purpose, she rolled down the bedclothes gently, and I saw myself stretched naked, my shift being turned up to my neck, whilst I had no power or sense to oppose it; even my glowing blushes expressed more desire than modesty, whilst the candle left, to be sure not undesignedly, burning, threw a full light on my whole body.

'No! (says Phoebe) you must not, my sweet girl, think to hide all these treasures from me, my sight must be feasted as well as my touch – I must devour with my eyes this springing bosom, – Suffer me to kiss it – I have not seen it enough – Let me kiss it once more – What firm, smooth, white flesh is here – How delicately shaped! – Then this delicious down! Oh! let me view the small, dear, tender cleft! – This is too much, I cannot bear it, I must, I must –' Here she took my hand and in a transport carried it where you will easily guess; but what a difference in the state of the same thing! – A spreading thicket of bushy curls marked the full-grown complete woman. Then the cavity to which she guided my hand easily received it; and as soon as she felt it within her, she moved herself to and fro, with so rapid a friction that I presently withdrew it, wet and clammy, when instantly Phoebe grew more composed, after two or three sighs, and heart-fetched Oh's! and giving me a kiss that seemed to exhale her soul through her lips, she replaced the bedclothes over us.

What pleasure she had found I will not say; but this I know, that the first sparks of kindling nature, the first ideas of pollution, were caught by me that night, and that the acquaintance and communication with the bad of our own sex is often as fatal to innocence as all the seductions of the other. But to go on: – when Phoebe was restored to that calm which I was far from the enjoyment of myself, she artfully sounded me on all the points necessary to govern the designs of my virtuous mistress on me, and by my answers, drawn from pure undissembled nature, she had no reason but to promise herself all imaginable success, so far as it depended on my ignorance, easiness, and warmth of constitution.

After a sufficient length of dialogue, my bedfellow left me to my rest, and I fell asleep through pure weariness from the violent emotions I had been led into, when nature (which had been too warmly stirred

and fermented to subside without allaying by some means or other)
relieved me by one of those luscious dreams, the transports of which
are scarce inferior to those of waking, real action.

In the morning I awoke about ten, perfectly gay and refreshed; Phoebe
was up before me and asked me in the kindest manner how I did, how
I had rested, and if I was ready for breakfast, carefully at the same
time avoiding to increase the confusion she saw I was in, at looking
her in the face, by any hint of the night's bed scene. – I told her if
she pleased I would get up and begin any work she would be pleased
to set me about. She smiled; presently the maid brought in the tea equipage, and I just huddled my clothes on, when in waddled my mistress.
I expected no less than to be told off, if not chid for, my late rising,
when I was agreeably disappointed by her compliments on my pure
and fresh looks. I was 'a bud of beauty' (this was her style) and how
vastly all the fine men would admire me! to all which my answers did
not, I can assure you, wrong my breeding: they were as simple and
silly as they could wish, and, no doubt, flattered them infinitely more
than they had proved me enlightened by education and knowledge of
the world.

We breakfasted; and the tea things were scarce removed, when in
were brought two bundles of linen and wearing apparel; in short,
all the necessaries for *rigging me out*, as they termed it, completely.

Imagine to yourself, Madam, how my little coquette-heart fluttered
with joy at the sight of a white lutestring, flowered with silver, scoured
indeed, but passed on me for spick and span new, a Brussels lace cap,
braided shoes, and the rest in proportion, all second-hand finery, and
procured instantly for the occasion by the diligence and industry of the
good Mrs Brown, who had already a chapman for me in the house
before whom my charms were to pass in review; for he had not only
in course insisted on a previous sight of the premises, but also on immediate surrender to him, in case of his agreeing for me; concluding
very wisely that such a place as I was in was of the hottest to trust
the keeping of such a perishable commodity in as a maidenhead.

The care of dressing and tricking me out for the market was then
left to Phoebe, who acquitted herself, if not well, at least perfectly to
the satisfaction of everything but my impatience of seeing myself dressed.
When it was over, and I viewed myself in the glass, I was, no doubt,

too natural, too artless, to hide my childish joy at the change; a change in real truth for much the worse, since I must have much better become the neat easy simplicity of my rustic dress than the awkward, untoward, tawdry finery that I could not conceal my strangeness to.

Phoebe's compliments, however, in which her own share in dressing me was not forgot, did not a little confirm me in now the first notions I had ever entertained concerning my person, which, be it said without vanity, was then tolerable enough to justify a taste for me, and of which it may not be out of place here to sketch you an unflattered picture.

I was tall, yet not too tall for my age, which, as I before remarked, was barely turned of fifteen, my shape perfectly straight, thin waisted, and light and free, without owing anything to stays. My hair was a glossy auburn and as soft as silk, flowing down my neck in natural buckles,[10] and did not a little set off the whiteness of a smooth skin. My face was rather too ruddy, though its features were delicate, and the shape was a roundish oval, except where a pit in my chin had far from a disagreeable effect; my eyes were as black as can be imagined and rather languishing than sparkling, except on certain occasions, when I have been told they struck fire fast enough; my teeth, which I ever carefully preserved, were small, even, and white; my bosom was finely raised, and one might then discern rather the promise than the actual growth of the round, firm breasts that in a little time made that promise good. In short, all the points of beauty that are most universally in request I had, or at least my vanity forbade me to appeal from the decision of our sovereign judges the men, who all that I ever knew at least gave it thus highly in my favour; and I met with, even in my own sex, some that were above denying me that justice, whilst others praised me yet more unsuspectedly by endeavouring to detract from me in points of person and figure that I obviously excelled in. – This is I own, too much, too strong of self-praise; but should I not be ungrateful to nature, and to a form to which I owe such singular blessings of pleasure and fortune, were I to suppress, through an affectation of modesty, the mention of such valuable gifts?

Well then, dressed I was, and little did it then enter into my head that all this gay attire was no more than decking the victim out for sacrifice, whilst I innocently attributed all to sheer friendship and kindness in the sweet good Mrs Brown, who, I was forgetting to mention, had, under pretence of keeping my money safe, got from me, without the least hesitation, the driblet (so I now call it) which remained to me after the expenses of my journey.

After some little time, most agreeably spent before the glass in scarce self-admiration, since my new dress had by much the greatest share in it, I was sent for down to the parlour where the old lady saluted me, and wished me joy of my new clothes, which, she was not ashamed to say, fitted me as if I had worn nothing but the finest all my lifetime; but what was it she could not see me silly enough to swallow? At the same time she presented me to another cousin of her own creation, an elderly gentleman, who got up at my entry into the room, and on my dropping a curtsy to him, saluted me and seemed a little affronted that I had only presented my cheek to him, a mistake which, if one, he immediately corrected by glueing his lips to mine with an ardour which his figure had not at all disposed me to thank him for: his figure, I say, than which nothing could be more shocking or detestable; for ugly and disagreeable were terms too gentle to convey a just idea of it.

Imagine to yourself a man rather past threescore, short and ill made, with a yellow cadaverous hue, great goggling eyes that stared as if he was strangled; an out-mouth from two more properly tushes[11] than teeth, livid lips, and a breath like a jakes.[12] Then he had a peculiar ghastliness in his grin that made him perfectly frightful, if not dangerous to women with child; yet, made as he was thus in mock of man, he was so blind to his own staring deformities as to think himself born for pleasing, and that no woman could see him with impunity; in consequence of which idea he had lavished great sums on such wretches as could gain upon themselves to pretend love to his person, whilst to those who had not art or patience to dissemble the horror it inspired he behaved even brutally. Impotence, more than necessity, made him seek in variety the provocative that was wanting to raise him to the pitch of enjoyment, which too he often saw himself balked of by the failure of his powers: and this always threw him into a fit of rage, which he wreaked, as far as he durst, on the innocent objects of his fit of momentary desire.

This then was the monster to which my conscientious benefactress, who had long been his purveyor in this way, had doomed me, and sent for me down purposely for this examination. Accordingly, she made me stand up before him, turned me round, unpinned my handkerchief, remarked to him the rise and fall, the turn and whiteness of a bosom just beginning to fill; then made me walk, and took even a handle from the rusticity of my gait to inflame the inventory of my charms. In short, she omitted no point of jockeyship;[13] to which he only answered by gracious nods of approbation whilst he looked goats and monkeys at me: for I sometimes stole a corner-glance at him, and, encountering his fiery eager stare, looked another way from pure horror and affright, which he, doubtless in character, attributed to nothing more than maiden modesty, or at least the affectation of it.

However, I was soon dismissed and reconducted to my room by Phoebe, who stuck close to me, by way of not leaving me alone and at leisure, to make such reflections as might naturally rise to anyone not an idiot on such a scene as I had just gone through; but to my shame be it confessed that such was my invincible stupidity, or rather portentous innocence, that I did not yet open my eyes on Mrs Brown's designs, and saw nothing in this titular cousin of her's but a shocking hideous person, which did not at all concern me, unless that my gratitude for my benefactress made me extend my respect to all her cousinhood.

Phoebe, however, began to sift the state and pulses of my heart towards this monster, asking me how I should approve of such a fine gentleman for a husband? (fine gentleman, I suppose she called him, from his being daubed with lace) I answered her very naturally that I had no thoughts of a husband, but that if I was to choose one, it should be among my own degree sure! So much had my aversion to that wretch's hideous figure indisposed me to all *fine gentlemen* and confounded my ideas, as if those of that rank had been necessarily cast in the same mould that he was. But Phoebe was not to be beat off so, but went on with her endeavours to melt and soften me for the purposes of my reception into that hospitable house; and whilst she talked of the sex in general, she had no reason to despair of a compliance, which more than one reason showed her would be easily enough obtained of me. But then she had too much experience not to discover that my particular fixed aversion to that frightful cousin would be a block not so readily to be removed as suited with the consummation of their bargain and sale of me.

Mother Brown had in the meantime agreed the terms with this liquorish old goat, which I afterwards understood were to be fifty guineas peremptory for the liberty of attempting me, and a hundred more at the complete gratification of his desires in the triumph over my virginity; and as for me, I was to be left entirely at the discretion of his liking and generosity. This unrighteous contract being thus settled, he was so eager to be put in possession that he insisted on being introduced to drink tea with me that afternoon, when we were to be left alone; nor would he hearken to the procuress's remonstrances that I was not sufficiently prepared and ripened for such an attack, that I was yet too green and untamed, having been scarce twenty-four hours in her house: it is the character of lust to be impatient, and his vanity arming him against any supposition of other than the common resistance of a maid on those occasions, made him reject all proposals of delay, and my dreadful trial was thus fixed, unknown to me, that very evening.

At dinner, Mrs Brown and Phoebe did nothing but run riot in praises of this wonderful cousin, and how happy that woman would be that he would favour with his addresses. In short, my two gossips exhausted all their rhetoric to persuade me to accept them: that the gentleman was violently smitten with me at first sight ... that he would make my fortune if I would be a good girl and not stand in my own light ... that I should trust his honour ... that I should be made for ever and have a chariot to go abroad in ... with all such stuff as was fit to turn the head of such a silly ignorant girl as I then was. But luckily here my aversion had taken already such deep root in me, my heart was so strongly defended from him by my senses that, wanting the art to mask my sentiments, I gave them no hopes of their employer's succeeding, at least very easily, with me. The glass too marched pretty quick, with a view, I suppose, to make a friend of the warmth of my constitution in the minutes of the imminent attack.

Thus they kept me pretty long at table, and about six in the evening, after I was retired to my own apartment and the tea-board was set, enters my venerable mistress, followed close by that satyr, who came in grinning in a way peculiar to him, and by his odious presence confirmed me in all the sentiments of detestation which his first appearance had given birth to.

He sat down fronting me, and all teatime kept ogling me in a manner that gave me the utmost pain and confusion, all the marks of which he still explained to be my bashfulness and not being used to see company.

Tea over, the commode old lady pleaded urgent business (which indeed was true) to go out, and earnestly desired me to entertain her cousin *kindly* till she came back, both for my own sake and her's; and then, with a 'Pray, sir, be very good, be very tender of the sweet child,' she went out of the room, leaving me staring, with my mouth open and unprepared, by the suddenness of her departure, to oppose it.

We were now alone; and on that idea a sudden fit of trembling seized me: – I was so afraid, without a precise notion of why and what I had to fear, that I sat on the settee by the fireside, motionless and petrified, without life or spirit, not knowing how to look or how to stir.

But long I was not suffered to remain in this state of stupefaction: the monster squatted down by me on the settee, and without farther ceremony, or preamble, flings his arms about my neck, and drawing me pretty forcibly towards him, obliged me to receive, in spite of my struggles to disengage from him, his pestilential kisses, which quite overcame me. Finding me then next to senseless and unresisting, he tears off my neck handkerchief and laid all open there to his eyes and hands; still I endured all without flinching, till emboldened by my sufferance and silence (for I had not the power to speak or cry out), he attempted to lay me down on the settee, and I felt his hand on the lower part of my naked thighs, which were crossed and which he endeavoured to unlock. Oh then! I was roused out of my passive endurance, and springing from him with an activity he was not prepared for, threw myself at his feet and begged him, in the most moving tone, not to be rude, and that he would not hurt me: 'Hurt you, my dear!' says the brute, 'I intend you no harm ... has not the old lady told you that I loved you? ... that I shall do handsomely by you?' 'She has indeed, sir,' said I, 'but I cannot love you, indeed I cannot! – pray, let me alone ... yes! I will love you dearly if you will let me alone, and go away ...' But I was talking to the wind; for whether my tears, my attitude, or the disorder of my dress proved fresh incentives, or whether he was now under the dominion of desires he could not bridle, but snorting and foaming with lust and rage, he renews his attack, seizes me, and again attempts to extend and fix me on the settee; in which he succeeded so far as to lay me along and even to toss my petticoats over my head, and lay my thighs bare, which I obstinately kept close, nor could he, though he attempted with his knee to force them open, effect it so as to stand fair for being master of the main avenue. He was unbuttoned, both waistcoat and breeches, yet I only felt the weight of his body upon me, whilst I lay struggling with indignation, and dying with terrors; but he stopped all of a sudden, and got off, panting, blowing, cursing, and rehearsing upon me *old* and *ugly*! for so I had very naturally called him in the heat of my defence.

The brute had, it seems, as I afterwards understood, brought on, by his eagerness and struggle, the ultimate period of his hot fit of lust, which his power was too short-lived to carry him through the full execution of; of which my thighs and linnen received the effusion.

When it was over he bid me, with a tone of displeasure, get up [saying] that he would not do me the honour to think of me any more ... that the old b—h might look out for another cully ... that he would not be fooled so by ever a country mock modesty in England ... that he supposed I had left my maidenhead with some hobnail in the country, and was come to dispose of my skim-milk in town, with a volley of the like abuse which I listened to with more pleasure than ever fond woman did to protestations of love from her darling minion: for, uncapable as I was of receiving any addition to my perfect hatred and aversion to him, I looked on his railing as my security against his renewing his most odious caresses.

Yet, plain as Mrs Brown's views were now come out, I had not the heart or spirit to open my eyes on them. Still I could not part with my dependence on that beldam; so much did I think myself her's, soul and body; or rather, I sought to deceive myself with the continuation of my good opinion of her, and chose to wait the worst at her hands, sooner than being turned out to starve in the streets, without a penny of money or a friend to apply to: these fears were my folly.

Whilst this confusion of ideas was passing in my head, and I sat pensive by the fire, with my eyes brimming with tears, my neck still bare, and my cap fallen off in the struggle, so that my hair was in the disorder you may guess, the villain's lust began, I suppose, to be again in flow, at the sight of all that bloom of youth which presented itself to his view, a bloom yet unenjoyed and in course not yet indifferent to him.

After some pause, he asked me, with a tone of voice mightily softened, whether I would make it up with him before the old lady returned, and all should be well; he would restore me his affections, at the same time offering to kiss me and feel my breasts. But now my extreme aversion, my fears, my indignation, all acting upon me, gave me a spirit not natural to me, so that breaking loose from him, I ran to the bell and rang it before he was aware, with such violence and effect as brought up the maid to know what was the matter, or whether the gentleman wanted anything? And before he could proceed to greater extremities, she bounced into the room, and seeing me stretched on the floor, my hair all dishevelled, my nose guishing out blood (which did not a little tragedize the scene) and my odious persecutor still intent on pushing his brutal point, unmoved by all my cries and distress, she was herself confounded and did not know what to do.

As much, however, as Martha might be prepared and hardened to transactions of this sort, all womanhood must have been out of her heart, could she have seen this unmoved. Besides that, on the face of things she imagined that matters had gone greater lengths than they really had, and that the courtesy of the house had been actually consummated on me and flung me into the condition I was in: in this notion she instantly took my part and advised the gentleman to go down and leave me to recover myself, and that all would be soon over with me – that when Mrs Brown and Phoebe, who were gone out, were returned, they would take order for everything to his satisfaction – that nothing would be lost by a little patience with the poor tender thing – that for her part, she was frightened – she could not tell what to say to such doings – but that she would stay by me till my mistress came home. As the wench said all this in a resolute tone, and the monster himself began to perceive that things would not mend by his staying, he took his hat and went out of the room murmuring and pleating his brows like an old ape, so that I was delivered from the horrors of his detestable presence.

As soon as he was gone, Martha very tenderly offered me her assistance in anything, and would have got me some hartshorn drops and put me to bed; which last I at first positively refused, in the fear that the monster might return and take me at that advantage. However, with much persuasion and assurances that I should not be molested that night, she prevailed on me to lie down; and indeed I was so weakened by my struggles, so dejected by my fearful apprehensions, so terror-struck, that I had no power to sit up or hardly to give answers to the questions with which the curious Martha plied and perplexed me.

Such, too, and so cruel was my fate that I dreaded the sight of Mrs Brown, as if I had been the criminal and she the person injured, a mistake which you will not think so strange on distinguishing that neither virtue or principles had the least share in the defence I had made but only the particular aversion I had conceived against this first brutal and fright-ful invader of my tender innocence.

I passed then the time till Mrs Brown's return home, under all the agitations of fear and despair that may easily be guessed.

About eleven at night my two ladies came home, and having received rather a favourable account from Martha, who had run down to let them in (for Mr Crofts, that was the name of my brute, was gone out of the house, after waiting till he had tired his patience for Mrs Brown's return), they came thundering upstairs, and seeing me pale, my face bloody, and all the marks of the most thorough dejection, they employed themselves more to comfort and re-inspirit me than in making me the reproaches I was weak enough to fear, I who had so many juster and stronger to retort upon them.

Mrs Brown withdrawn, Phoebe came presently to bed to me, and what with the answers she drew from me, what with her own method of *palpably* satisfying herself, she soon discovered that I had been more frighted than hurt; upon which, I suppose being herself seized with sleep and reserving her lectures and instructions till the next morning, she left me, properly speaking, to my unrest: for after tossing and turning the greatest part of the night, and tormenting myself with the falsest notions and apprehensions of things, I fell, through mere fatigue, into a kind of delirious doze, out of which I waked late in the morning in a violent fever; a circumstance which was extremely critical to reprieve me, at least for a time, from the attacks of a wretch infinitely more terrible to me than death itself.

The interested care that was taken of me during my illness, in order to restore me to a condition of making good the bawd's engagements or of enduring further trials, had, however, such an effect on my grateful disposition that I even thought myself obliged to my undoers for their attentions to promote my recovery, and, above all, for the keeping out of my sight that brutal ravisher, the author of my disorder, on their finding I was too strongly moved at the bare mention of his name.

Youth is soon raised; and a few days were sufficient to conquer the fury of my fever; but what contributed most to my perfect recovery and to my reconciliation with life was the timely news that Mr Crofts, who was a merchant of considerable dealings, was arrested at the king's suit, for near forty thousand pounds, on account of his driving a certain contra-band trade, and that his affairs were so desperate that even were it in his inclination, it would not be in his power to renew his designs upon me: for he was instantly thrown into a prison, which it was not likely that he would get out of in haste.

Mrs Brown, who had touched his fifty guineas, advanced to so little purpose, and lost all hopes of the remaining hundred, began to look upon my treatment of him with a more favourable eye; and as they had observed my temper to be perfectly tractable and conformable to their views, all the girls that composed her flock were suffered to visit me and had their cue to dispose me, by their conversation, to a perfect resignation of myself to Mrs Brown's direction.

Accordingly they were let in upon me, and all that frolic and thought-less gaiety in which those giddy creatures consume their leisure made me envy a condition of which I only saw the fair side; insomuch that the being one of them became even my ambition: a disposition which they all carefully cultivated; and I wanted now nothing but to restore my health, that I might be able to undergo the ceremony of the initiation.

Conversation, example, all, in short, contributed in that house to corrupt my native purity, which had taken no root in education, whilst now the inflammable principle of pleasure, so easily fired at my age, made strange work within me, and all the modesty I was brought up in the habit (not the instruction) of, began to melt away, like dew before the sun's heat; not to mention that I made a vice of necessity, from the constant fears I had of being turned out to starve.

I was soon pretty well recovered, and at certain hours allowed to range all over the house, but cautiously kept from seeing any company, till the arrival of Lord B— from Bath, to whom Mrs Brown, in respect to his experienced generosity on such occasions, proposed to offer the refusal of that trinket of mine, which bears so great an imaginary value; and his lordship being expected in town in less than a fortnight, Mrs Brown judged I should be entirely renewed in beauty and freshness by that time and afford her the chance of a better bargain than she had driven with Mr Crofts.

In the meantime, I was so thoroughly, as they call it, brought over, so tame to their whistle, that, had my cage door been set open, I had no idea that I ought to fly anywhere sooner than stay where I was; nor had I the least sense of regretting my condition, but waited very quietly for whatever Mrs Brown should order concerning me, who on her side, by herself and her agents, took more than the necessary precautions to lull and lay asleep all just reflexions on my destination.

Preachments of morality over the left shoulder,[14] a life of joy painted in the gayest colours, caresses, promises, indulgent treatment; nothing, in short, was wanting to domesticate me entirely and to prevent my going out anywhere to get better advice; alas! I dreamed of no such thing.

Hitherto I had been indebted only to the girls of the house for the corruption of my innocence; their luscious talk, in which modesty was far from respected, their descriptions of their engagements with men, had given me a tolerable insight into the nature and mysteries of their profession, at the same time that they highly provoked an itch of florid warm-spirited blood through every vein; but above all, my bedfellow, Phoebe, whose pupil I more immediately was, exerted her talents in giving me the first tinctures of pleasure: whilst nature now warmed and wantoned with discoveries so interesting, piqued a curiosity which Phoebe artfully whetted, and leading me from question to question of her own suggestion, explained to me all the mysteries of Venus. But I could not long remain in such an house as that, without being an eye-witness of more than I could conceive from her descriptions.

One day about twelve at noon, being thoroughly recovered of my fever, I happened to be in Mrs Brown's dark closet, where I had not been half an hour, resting on the maids settle-bed,[15] before I heard a rustling in the bed-chamber, separated from the closet only by two sash-doors, before the glasses of which were drawn two yellow damask curtains, but not so close as to exclude the full view of the room from any person in the closet.

I instantly crept softly, and posted myself so that, seeing everything minutely, I could not myself be seen; and who should come in but the venerable mother abbess herself! handed in by a tall, brawny, young horse-grenadier, moulded in the Hercules-style; in fine, the choice of the most experienced dame, in those affairs, in all London.

Oh! how still and hush did I keep at my stand, lest any noise should balk my curiosity, or bring madam into the closet!

But I had not much reason to fear either, for she was so entirely taken up with her present great concern that she had no sense of attention to spare to anything else.

Droll was it to see that clumsy fat figure of her's flop down on the foot of the bed, opposite to the closet door, so that I had a full front view of all her charms.

Her paramour sat down by her. He seemed to be a man of very few words, and a great stomach, for proceeding instantly to essentials, he gave her some hearty smacks, and thrusting his hands into her breasts, disengaged them from her stays, in scorn of whose confinement they broke loose and swagged down, navel low at least. A more enormous pair did my eyes never behold, nor of a worse colour, flagging soft, and most lovingly contiguous: yet such as they were, this neck-beef-eater[16] seemed to paw them with a most unenviable gust, seeking in vain to confine or cover one of them with a hand scarce less than a shoulder of mutton. After toying with them thus some time, as if they had been worth it, he laid her down pretty briskly, and canting up her petticoats, made barely a mask of them to her broad red face, that blushed with nothing but brandy.

As he stood on one side for a minute or so, unbuttoning his waistcoat and breeches, her fat brawny thighs hung down; and the whole greasy landscape lay fairly open to my view: a wide open-mouthed gap, overshaded with a grizzly bush seemed held out like a beggar's wallet for its provision.

But I soon had my eyes called off by a more striking object, that entirely engrossed them.

Her sturdy stallion had now unbuttoned, and produced naked, stiff, and erect, that wonderful machine, which I had never seen before, and which, for the interest my own seat of pleasure began to take furiously in it, I stared at with all the eyes I had. However, my senses were too much flurried, too much concentered in that now burning spot of mine, to observe anything more than in general the make and turn of that instrument, from which the instinct of nature, yet more than all I had heard of it, now strongly informed me I was to expect that supreme pleasure which she has placed in the meeting of those parts so admirably fitted for each other.

Long, however, the young spark did not remain, before, giving it two or three shakes, by way of brandishing it, he threw himself upon her, and his back being now towards me, I could only take his being engulfed for granted, by the direction he moved in, and the impossibility of missing so staring a mark; and now the bed shook, the curtains rattled so, that I could scarce hear the sighs and murmurs, the heaves and pantings that accompanied the action, from the beginning to the end; the sound and sight of which thrilled to the very soul of me, and made every vein of my body circulate liquid fires: the emotion grew so violent that it almost intercepted my respiration.

Prepared then, and disposed as I was by the discourse of my companions, and Phoebe's minute detail of everything, no wonder that such a sight gave the last dying blow to my native innocence.

Whilst they were in the heat of the action, guided by nature only, I stole my hand up my petticoat, and with fingers all on fire, seized and yet more inflamed that center of all my senses; my heart palpitated, as if it would force its way through my bosom; I breathed with pain; I twisted my thighs, squeezed and compressed the lips of that virgin slit, and following mechanically the example of Phoebe's manual operation on it, as far as I could find admission, brought on at last the critical ecstasy, the melting flow, into which nature, spent with excess of pleasure, dissolves and dies away.

After which my senses recovered coolness enough to observe the rest of the transaction between this happy pair.

The young fellow had just dismounted, when the old lady immediately sprang up, with all the vigour of youth, derived no doubt from her late refreshment, and making him sit down, began in her turn to kiss him, to pat and pinch his cheeks, and play with his hair, all which he received with an air of indifference and coolness that showed him to me much altered from what he was when he first went on to the breach.

My pious governess, however, not being above calling in auxiliaries, unlocks a little case of cordials that stood near the bed, and made him pledge her in a very plentiful dram; after which and a little amorous parley, madam sat herself down upon the same place at the bed's foot; and the young fellow standing sideways by her, she, with the greatest effrontery imaginable, unbuttons his breeches, and removing his shirt, draws out his affair, so shrunk and diminished that I could not but remember the difference, now crestfallen, or just faintly lifting its head. But our experienced matron very soon, by chafing it with her hands, brought it to swell to that size and erection I had before seen it up to.

I admired then, upon a fresh account, and with a nicer survey, the texture of that capital part of man: the flaming red head as it stood uncapped, the whiteness of the shaft, and the shrub-growth of curling hair that embrowned the roots of it, the roundish bag that dangled down from it, all exacted my eager attention and renewed my flame; but as the main affair was now at the point the industrious dame had laboured to bring it to, she was not in the humour to put off the payment of her pains, but laying herself down, drew him gently upon her, and thus they finished, in the same manner as before, the old last act.

This over, they both went out lovingly together, the old lady having first made him a present, as near as I could observe, of three or four pieces; he being not only her particular favourite on the account of his performances, but a retainer to the house, from whose sight she had taken great care hither to secrete me, lest he might not have had patience to wait for my lord's arrival, but have insisted on being his taster, which the old lady was under too much subjection to him to dare dispute with him; for every girl of the house fell to him in course, and the old lady only now and then got her turn, in consideration of the maintenance he had, and which he could scarce be accused of not earning from her.

As soon as I heard them go downstairs, I stole up softly to my own room, out of which I had been luckily not missed. There I began to breathe a little freer, and to give a loose to those warm emotions which the sight of such an encounter had raised in me. I laid me down on the bed, stretched myself out, joining, and ardently wishing, and requiring any means to divert or allay the rekindled rage and tumult of my desires, which all pointed strongly to their pole, man. I felt about the bed, as if I sought for something that I grasped in my waking dream, and not finding it, could have cried for vexation, every part of me glowing with stimulating fires. At length, I resorted to the only present remedy, that of vain attempts at digitation, where the smallness of the theater did not yet afford room enough for action, and where the pain my fingers gave me in striving for admission, though they procured me a slight satisfaction for the present, started an apprehension, which I could not be easy till I had communicated to Phoebe and received her explanations upon it.

The opportunity, however, did not offer till next morning, for Phoebe did not come to bed till long after I was gone to sleep. As soon then as we were both awake, it was but in course to bring our ly-a-bed chat to land on the subject of my uneasiness, to which a recital of the love-scene I had thus by a chance been spectatress of, served for a preface.

Phoebe could not hear it to the end without more than one interruption by peals of laughter, and my ingenuous way of relating matters did not a little heighten the joke to her.

But on her sounding me how the sight had affected me, without mincing or hiding the pleasurable emotions it had inspired me with, I told her at the same time that one remark had perplexed me, and that very considerably: 'Ay!' says she, 'what was that?' 'Why,' replied I, having very curiously and attentively compared the size of that enormous machine, which did not appear, at least to my fearful imagination, less than my wrist, and at least three of my handfuls long, to that of the tender, small part of me which was framed to receive it, I could not conceive its being possible to afford it entrance there without dying, perhaps in the greatest pain, since she well knew that even a finger thrust in there, hurt me beyond bearing ... 'As to my mistress's and your's ... I can very plainly distinguish the different dimensions of them from mine, palpable to the touch, and visible to the eye, so that in short, great as the promised pleasure may be, I am afraid of the pain of the experiment.'

Phoebe at this redoubled her laugh, and, whilst I expected a very serious solution of my doubts and apprehensions in this matter, only told me that she never heard of a mortal wound being given, in those parts, by that terrible weapon, and that some she knew younger and as delicately made as myself, had outlived the operation, that she believed, at the worst, I would take a great deal of killing ... that true it was, there was a great diversity of sizes in those parts, owing to nature, child-bearing, frequent over-stretching with unmerciful machines; but that at a certain age and habit of body, even the most experienced in those affairs could not well distinguish between the maid and the woman, supposing too an absence of all artifice, and things in their natural situation; but that since chance had thrown in my way one sight of that sort, she would procure me another, that should feast my eyes more delicately, and go a great way in the cure of my fears from that imaginary disproportion.

On this she asked me if I knew Polly Philips. 'Undoubtedly,' says I, 'the fair girl which was so tender of me when I was sick, and has been, as you told me, but two months in the house?' 'The same,' says Phoebe. 'You must know then, she is kept by a young Genoese merchant, whom his uncle, who is immensely rich and whose darling he is, sent over here with an English merchant, his friend, on a pretext of settling some accounts, but in reality to humour his inclinations for travelling and seeing the world. He met casually with this Polly once in company, and taking a liking to her, makes it worth her while to keep entirely to him. He comes to her here twice or thrice a week, and she receives him in the light closet up one pair of stairs, where he enjoys her in a taste I suppose peculiar to the heat, or perhaps the caprices of his own country. I say no more; but tomorrow being his day, you shall see what passes between them, from a place only known to your mistress and myself.'

You may be sure, in the ply I was now taking, I had no objection to the proposal and was rather a-tiptoe for its accomplishment.

At five in the evening then, next day, Phoebe, punctual to her promise, came to me as I sat alone in my own room, and beckoned me to follow her.

We went down the backstairs very softly, and opening the door of a dark closet, where there was some old furniture kept and some cases of liquors, she drew me in after her, and fastening the door upon us, we had no light but what came through a long crevice in the partition between ours and the light closet, where the scene of action lay; so that sitting on those low cases, we could, with the greatest ease as well as clearness, see all objects (ourselves unseen) only by applying our eyes close to the crevice, where the moulding of a panel had warped or started a little on the other side.

The young gentleman was the first person I saw, with his back directly towards me, looking at a print. Polly was not yet come. In less than a minute though, the door opened, and she came in, and at the noise the door made, he turned about, and came to meet her, with an air of the greatest tenderness and satisfaction.

After saluting her, he led her to a couch that fronted us, where they both sat down, and the young Genoese helped her to a glass of wine, with some Naples biscuit on a salver.

Presently, when they had exchanged a few kisses, and questions in broken English on one side, he began to unbutton, and, in fine, stripped into his shirt.

As if this had been the signal agreed on for pulling off all their clothes, a scheme which the heat of the season perfectly favoured, Polly began to draw her pins, and as she had no stays to unlace she was in a trice, with her gallant's officious assistance, undressed to all but her shift.

When he saw this, his breeches were immediately loosened, waist and knee-bands, and slipped over his ankles, clean off; his shirt collar was unbuttoned too. Then first giving Polly an encouraging kiss, he stole as it were the shift off the girl, who, being I suppose broke and familiarized to this humour, blushed indeed, but less than I did, at the apparition of her now standing stark-naked, just as she came out of the hands of pure nature, with her black hair loose, and a-float down her dazzling white neck and shoulders, whilst the deepened carnation of her cheeks went off gradually into the hue of glazed snow; for such were the blended tints and polish of her skin.

This girl could not be above eighteen. Her face regular and sweet-featured, her shape exquisite; nor could I help envying her two ripe enchanting breasts, finely plumped out in flesh, but withal so round, so firm, that they sustained themselves, in scorn of any stay. Then their nipples pointing different ways marked their pleasing separation; beneath them lay the delicious tract of the belly, which terminated in a parting or rift scarce discernible, that modestly seemed to retire downwards, and seek shelter between two plump fleshy thighs: the curling hair that overspread its delightful front, clothed it with the richest sable fur in the universe. In short, she was evidently a subject for the painters to court her sitting to them for a pattern of female beauty, in all the true pride and pomp of nakedness.

The young Italian (still in his shirt) stood gazing and transported at the sight of beauties that might have fired a dying hermit; his eager eyes devoured her, as she shifted attitudes at his discretion; neither were his hands excluded their share of the high feast, but wandered, on the hunt of pleasure, over every part and inch of her body so qualified to afford the most exquisite sense of it.

In the meantime, one could not help observing the swell of his shirt before, that bolstered out, and pointed out the condition of things behind the curtain. But he soon removed it by slipping his shirt over his head; and now, as to nakedness, they had nothing to reproach one another.

The young gentleman, by Phoebe's guess, was about two and twenty: tall and well limbed. His body was finely formed and of a most vigorous make, square-shouldered, and broad-chested. His face was not remarkable in any way, but for a nose inclining to the Roman, eyes large, black, and sparkling, and a ruddiness in his cheeks that was the more a grace for his complexion being of the brownest, not of that dusky dun colour which excludes the idea of freshness, but of that clear, olive gloss, which, glowing with life, dazzles perhaps less than fairness, and yet pleases more, when it pleases at all. His hair, being too short to tie, fell no lower than his neck, in short easy curls; and he had a few sprigs about his paps, that garnished his chest in a style of strength and manliness. Then his grand movement, which seemed to rise out of a thicket of curling hair that spread from the root all round his thighs and belly up to the navel, stood stiff, and upright, but of a size to frighten me, by sympathy, for the small tender part, which was the object of its fury, and which now lay exposed to my fairest view: for he had immediately, on stripping off his shirt, gently pushed her down on the couch, which stood conveniently to break her willing fall. Her thighs were spread out to their utmost extension, and discovered between them the mark of the sex, the red-centred cleft of flesh, whose lips vermillioning inwards, expressed a small rubied line in sweet miniature, such as not Guido's[17] touch or colouring could ever attain to the life or delicacy of.

Phoebe, at this, gave me a gentle jog to prepare me for a whispered question: whether I thought my little maiden-toy was much less? But my attention was too much engrossed, too much enwrapped with all I saw, to be able to give her any answer.

By this time the young gentleman had changed her posture from lying breadth- to length wise on the couch; but her thighs were still spread, and the mark lay fair for him, who, now kneeling between them, displayed to us a side-view of that fierce erect machine of his, which threatened no less than splitting the tender victim, who lay smiling at the uplifted stroke, nor seemed to decline it. He looked upon his weapon himself with some pleasure, and guiding it with his hand to the inviting slit, drew aside the lips and lodged it (after some thrusts, which Polly seemed even to assist) about half way. But there it stuck, I suppose, from its growing thickness. He draws it again, and just wetting it with spittle, re-enters, and with ease sheathed it now up to the hilt, at which Polly gave a deep sigh, which was quite in another tone than one of pain; he thrusts, she heaves, at first gently, and in a regular cadence, but presently the transport began to be too violent to observe any order or measure, their motions were too rapid, their kisses too fierce and fervent for nature to support such fury long; both seemed to me out of themselves, their eyes darted fires; 'Oh! Oh! – I can't bear it – It is too much – I die – I am a going –' were Polly's expressions of ecstasy. His joys were more silent; but soon broken murmurs, sighs heart-fetched, and at length a dispatching thrust, as if he would have forced himself up her body, and then the motionless languor of all his limbs, all showed that the die-away moment was come upon him, which she gave signs of joining with, by the wild throwing of her hands about, closing her eyes, and giving a deep sob, in which she seemed to expire in an agony of bliss.

When he had finished his stroke and got from off her, she lay still without the least motion, breathless, as it should seem, with pleasure. He replaced her again breadthwise on the couch, unable to sit up, with her thighs open, between which I could observe a kind of white liquid, like froth, hanging about the outward lips of that recent opened wound, which now glowed with a deeper red. Presently she gets up, and throwing her arms round him, seemed far from undelighted with the trial he had put her to, to judge at least by the fondness with which she eyed and hung upon him.

For my part, I will not pretend to describe what I felt all over me during this scene; but from that instant, adieu all fears of what man could do unto me; they were now changed into such ardent desires, such ungovernable longings, that I could have pulled the first of that sex that should present himself by the sleeve and offered him the bauble, which I now imagined the loss of would be a gain I could not too soon procure myself.

Phoebe, who had more experience, and to whom such sights were not so new, could not however be unmoved at so warm a scene; and drawing me away softly from the peep-hole, for fear of being overheard, guided me as near the door as possible; all passive and obedient to her least signals.

Here was no room either to sit or lie, but making me stand with my back towards the door, she lifted up my petticoats, and with her busy fingers fell to visit and explore that part of me where now the heat and irritations were so violent that I was perfectly sick and ready to die with desire: that the bare touch of her finger in that critical place had the effect of fire to a train, and her hand instantly made her sensible to what a pitch I was wound up, and melted by the sight she had thus procured me. Satisfied then with her success in allaying a heat that would have made me impatient of seeing the continuation of transactions between our amorous couple, she brought me again to the crevice so favourable to our curiosity.

We had certainly been but a few instants away from it, and yet on our return we saw everything in good forwardness for recommencing the tender hostilities.

The young foreigner was sitting down, fronting us, on the couch; with Polly upon one knee, who had her arms round his neck, whilst the extreme whiteness of her skin was not undelightfully contrasted by the smooth glossy brown of her lover's.

But who could count the fierce unnumbered kisses given and taken in which I could often discover their exchanging the velvet thrust, when both their mouths were double-tongued, and seemed to favour the mutual insertion with the greatest gust and delight.

In the meantime, his red-headed champion, that had so lately fled the pit, quelled and abashed, was now recovered to the top of its condition, perked and crested up between Polly's thighs, who was not wanting on her part to coax and keep it in good humour, stroking it with her head down, and received even its velvet tip between the lips of not its proper mouth; whether she did this out of any particular pleasure, or whether it was to render it more glib and easy of entrance, I could not tell. But it had such an effect that the young gentleman seemed by his eyes, that sparkled with more excited lustre, and his inflamed countenance, to receive increase of pleasure. He got up, and taking Polly in his arms, embraced her and said something too softly for me to hear, leading her withal to the foot of the couch, and taking delight to slap her thighs and posteriors with that stiff sinew of his, which hit them with a spring that he gave it with his hand, and made them resound again, but hurt her about as much as he meant to hurt her, for she seemed to have as frolic a taste as himself.

But guess my surprise, when I saw the lazy young rogue lie down on his back and gently pull down Polly upon him, who giving way to his humour, straddled and with her hands conducted her blind favourite to the right place, and following her impulse, ran directly upon the flaming point of this weapon of pleasure, which she staked herself upon, up-pierced and infixed to the extremest hair-breadth of it: thus she sat on him, a few instants, enjoying and relishing her situation, whilst he toyed with her provoking breasts. – Sometimes she would stoop to meet his kiss; but presently the sting of pleasure spurred them up to fiercer action: then began the storm of heaves, which, from the undermost combatant, were thrusts at the same time, he crossing his hands over her and drawing her home to him with a sweet violence. The inverted strokes of anvil over hammer soon brought on the critical period, in which all the signs of a close conspiring ecstasy informed us of the *point* they were at.

For me, I could bear to see no more: I was so overcome, so inflamed at this second part of the same play that, mad with intolerable desire, I hugged, I clasped Phoebe, as if she had had wherewithal to relieve me. Pleased, however, with, and pitying the taking she could feel me in, she drew me towards the door and opening it as softly as she could, we both got off undiscovered, and she reconducted me to my own room, where unable to keep my legs in the agitation I was in, I instantly threw myself down on the bed, where I lay transported, though ashamed at what I felt.

Phoebe lay down by me and asked me archly if, now that I had seen the enemy and fully considered him, I was still afraid of him? Or did I think I could venture to come to a close engagement with him? To all which not a word on my side. I sighed and could scarce breathe. She takes hold of my hand, and having rolled up her own petticoats, forced it half-strivingly towards those parts, where, now grown more knowing, I missed the main object of my wishes; and finding not even the shadow of what I wanted, where everything was so flat! or so hollow! In the vexation I was in at it, I should have withdrawn my hand, but for fear of disobliging her. Abandoning it then entirely to her management, she made use of it as she thought proper, to procure herself rather the shadow than the substance of any pleasure. For my part, I now pined for more solid food, and promised tacitly to myself that I would not be put off much longer with this foolery from woman to woman, if Mrs Brown did not soon provide me with the essential specific: in short, I had all the air of not being able to wait the arrival of my lord B——, though he was now expected in a very few days: nor did I wait for him, for love itself took charge of the disposal of me, in spite of interest or gross lust.

It was now two days after the closet-scene, that I got up about six in the morning, and leaving my bedfellow fast asleep, stole down, with no other thought than of taking a little fresh air in a small garden, which our back-parlour opened into, and from which my confinement debarred me at the times company came to the house; but now sleep and silence reigned all over it.

I opened the parlour-door, and well surprised was I at seeing, by the side of a fire half out, a young gentleman in the old lady's elbow-chair, with his legs laid upon another, fast asleep, and left there by his thoughtless companions, who had drank him down and then went off with every one his mistress, whilst he stayed behind by the curtesy of the old matron, who would not disturb or turn him out in that condition at one in the morning, and beds, it is more than probable, there were none to spare. On the table still remained the punch-bowl and glasses, strewed about in their usual disorder after a drunken revel.

But when I drew nearer to view the sleeping estray,[18] heavens! what a sight! no! no term of years, no turns of fortune could ever erase the lightening-like impression his form made on me ... Yes! dearest object of my earliest passion, I command for ever the remembrance of thy first appearance to my ravished eyes, – it calls thee up, present; and I see thee now!

Figure to yourself, Madam, a fair stripling, between eighteen and nineteen, with his head reclined on one of the sides of the chair, his hair in disordered curls, irregularly shading a face, on which all the roseate bloom of youth and all the manly graces conspired to fix my eyes and heart. Even the languor and paleness of his face, in which the momentary triumph of the lilly over the rose was owing to the excesses of the night, gave an inexpressible sweetness to the finest features imaginable: his eyes closed in sleep, displayed the meeting edges of their lids beautifully bordered with long eyelashes, over which no pencil could have described two more regular arches than those that graced his forehead, which was high, perfectly white and smooth; then a pair of vermillion lips, pouting and swelling to the touch, as if a bee had freshly stung them, seemed to challenge me to get the gloves of this lovely sleeper, had not the modesty and respect, which in both sexes are inseparable from a true passion, checked my impulses.

But on seeing his shirt collar unbuttoned, and a bosom whiter than a drift of snow, the pleasure of considering it could not bribe me to lengthen it at the hazard of a health that began to be my life's concern. Love, that made me timid, taught me to be tender too: with a trembling hand I took hold of one of his, and waking him as gently as possible, he started, and looking at first a little wildly, said, with a voice that sent its harmonious sound to my heart: 'Pray, child, what a'clock is it?' I told him and added that he might catch cold if he slept longer with his breast open in the cool of the morning air. On this he thanked me, with a sweetness perfectly agreeing with that of his features and eyes; the last now broad open, and eagerly surveying me, carried the sprightly fires they sparkled with directly to my heart.

It seems that having drunk too freely before he came upon the rake with some of his young companions, he had put himself out of a condition to go through all the weapons with them, and crown the night with getting a mistress; so that seeing me in a loose undress, he did not doubt but I was one of the misses of the house, sent in to repair his loss of time; but though he seized that notion, and a very obvious one it was, without hesitation, yet, whether my figure made a more than ordinary impression on him, or whether it was his natural politeness, he addressed me in a manner far from rude, though still on the foot of one of the house-pliers, come to amuse him; and giving me the first kiss that I ever relished from man in my life, asked me if I could favour him with my company, assuring me that he would make it worth my while. But had not even new-born love, that true refiner of lust, opposed so sudden a surrender, the fear of being surprised by the house was a sufficient bar to my compliance.

I told him then, in a tone set me by love itself, that for reasons I had not time to explain to him, I could not stay with him, and might not even ever see him again, with a sigh at these last words which broke from the bottom of my heart. My conqueror, who, as he afterwards told me, had been struck with my appearance, and liked me as much as he could think of liking anyone in my supposed way of life, asked me briskly at once if I would be kept by him, and that he would take a lodging for me directly, and relieve me from any engagements he presumed I might be under to the house. Rash, sudden, undigested, and even dangerous as this offer might be from a perfect stranger, and that stranger a giddy boy, the prodigious love I was struck with for him had put a charm into his voice there was no resisting, and blinded me to every objection: I could, at that instant, have died for him; think if I could resist an invitation to live with him! Thus my heart, beating strong to the proposal, dictated my answer, after scarce a minute's pause, that I would accept of his offer, and make my escape to him, in what way he pleased, and that I would be entirely at his disposal, let it be good or bad. I have often since wondered that so great an easiness did not disgust him, or make me too cheap in his eyes; but my fate had so appointed it that in his fears of the hazard of the town, he had been some time looking out for a girl to take into keeping, and my person happening to hit his fancy, it was by one of those miracles reserved to love that we struck the bargain in the instant, which we sealed by an exchange of kisses, that the hopes of a more uninterrupted enjoyment engaged him to content himself with.

Never, however, did dear youth carry in his person more wherewith to justify the turning of a girl's head, and making her set all consequences at defiance for the sake of following a gallant.

For besides all the perfections of manly beauty which were assembled in his form, he had an air of neatness and gentility, a certain smartness in the carriage and port of his head, that yet more distinguished him: his eyes were sprightly and full of meaning; his looks had in them something at once sweet and commanding. His complexion out-bloomed the lovely coloured rose, whilst its inimitable tender vivid glow clearly saved it from the reproach of wanting life, of raw and dough-like, which is commonly made to those so extremely fair as he was.

Our little plan was that I should get out about seven the next morning (which I could readily promise, as I knew where to get the key of the street-door), and he would wait at the end of the street with a coach to convey me safe off; after which he would send and clear any debt incurred by my stay at Mrs Brown's, who he only judged, in gross, might not care to part with one he thought so fit to draw custom to the house.

I then just hinted to him not to mention in the house his having seen such a person as me, for reasons I would explain to him more at leisure. And then, for fear of miscarrying by being seen together, I tore myself from him with a bleeding heart, and stole up softly to my room, where I found Phoebe still fast asleep, and hurrying off my few clothes, lay down by her, with a mixture of joy and anxiety that may be easier conceived than expressed.

The risks of Mrs Brown's discovering my purpose, of disappointments, misery, ruin, all vanished before this new-kindled flame. The seeing, the touching, the being, if but for a night, with this idol of my fond virgin-heart appeared to me a happiness above the purchase of my liberty or life. He might use me ill! Let him! He was the master! Happy, too happy, even to receive death at so dear a hand.

To this purpose were the reflections of the whole day, of which every minute seemed to me a little eternity. How often did I visit the clock, nay, was tempted to advance the tedious hand, as if that would have advanced the time with it! Had those of the house made the least observations on me, they must have remarked something extraordinary from the discomposure I could not help betraying: especially when at dinner mention was made of the charmingest youth having been there, and stayed breakfast! Oh, he was such a beauty! I should have died for him! They would pull caps for him! and the like fooleries, which, however, was throwing oil on a fire I was sorely put to it to smother the blaze of.

The fluctuations of my mind, the whole day, produced however one good effect; which was that through mere fatigue I slept tolerably well till five in the morning, when I got up, and having dressed myself, waited, under the double tortures of fear and impatience, for the appointed hour. It came at last, the dear, critical, dangerous hour came; and now supported only by the courage love lent me, I ventured a-tip-toe downstairs, leaving my box behind, for fear of being surprised with it in going out.

I got to the street-door, the key whereof was always laid on the chair by our bedside, in trust with Phoebe, who, having not the least suspicion of my entertaining any design to go from them (nor indeed had I but the day before), made no reserve or concealment of it from me. I opened the door then with great ease; love, that emboldened, protected me too: and now, got safe into the street, I saw my new guardian angel waiting at a coach-door ready open. How I got to him I know not: I suppose I flew; but I was in the coach in a trice, and he by the side of me, with his arms clasped round me, and giving me the kiss of welcome. – The coachman had his orders, and drove to them.

My eyes were instantly filled with tears, but tears of the most delicious delight. To find myself in the arms of that beauteous youth was a rapture that my little heart swam in. Past or future were equally out of the question with me. The present was as much as all my powers of life were sufficient to bear the transport of without fainting. Nor were the most tender embraces, the most soothing expressions wanting on his side, to assure me of his love, and of never giving me cause to repent the bold step I had taken in throwing myself thus entirely upon his honour and generosity. But, alas! This was no merit in me, for I was driven to it by a passion too impetuous for me to resist, and I did what I did because I could not help it.

In an instant, for time was now annihilated with me, we were landed at a public house in Chelsea, hospitably commodious for the reception of duet parties of pleasure, where a breakfast of chocolate was prepared for us.

An old jolly stager, who kept it, and understood life perfectly well, breakfasted with us, and leering archly at me, gave us both joy, and said we were well paired, i'faith! that a great many gentlemen and ladies used his house, but he had never seen a handsomer couple, ... he was sure I was a fresh piece ... I looked so country, so innocent! well, my spouse was a lucky man! ... all which common landlord's cant not only pleased and soothed me, but helped to divert my confusion at being with my new sovereign, whom, now the minute approached, I began to fear to be alone with, a timidity which true love had a greater share in than even maiden bashfulness.

I wished, I doted, I could have died for him, and yet I know not how or why I dreaded the point which had been the object of my fiercest wishes; my pulses beat fears, amidst a flush of the warmest desires: this struggle of the passions, however, this conflict betwixt modesty and love-sick longings, made me burst again into tears, which he took, as he had done before, only for the remains of concern and emotion at the suddenness of my change of condition, in committing myself to his care, and in consequence of that idea, did and said all that he thought would most comfort and re-inspirit me.

After breakfast, Charles, the dear familiar name I must take the liberty henceforward to distinguish my Adonis by, with a smile full of meaning, took me gently by the hand and said, 'Come, my dear, and I will show you a room that commands a fine prospect over some gardens.' And without waiting for an answer, in which he relieved me extremely, he led me up into a chamber, airy and lightsome, where all seeing of prospects was out of the question, except that of a bed, which had all the air of having recommended the room to him.

Charles had just slipped the bolt of the door, and running, caught me in his arms, and lifting me from the ground with his lips glued to mine, bore me, trembling, panting, dying with soft fears and tender wishes, to the bed, where his impatience would not suffer him to undress me more than just unpinning my handkerchief and gown, and unlacing my stays.

My bosom was now bare, and rising in the warmest throbs, presented to his sight and feeling the firm hard swell of a pair of young breasts, such as may be imagined of a girl not sixteen, fresh out of the country, and never before handled; but even their pride, whiteness, fashion, pleasing resistance to the touch, could not bribe his restless hands from roving. But giving them the loose, my petticoats and shift were soon taken up, and their stronger center of attraction laid open to their tender invasion. My fears, however, made me mechanically close my thighs; but the very touch of his hand insinuated between them disclosed them and opened a way for the main attack.

In the meantime I lay fairly exposed to the examination of his eyes and hands, quiet and unresisting, which confirmed him in the opinion he proceeded so cavalierly upon, that I was no novice in these matters, since he had taken me out of a common bawdy-house; nor had I said one thing to prepossess him of my virginity; and if I had, he would sooner have believed that I took him for a cully that would swallow such an improbability than that I was still mistress of that darling treasure, that hidden mine, so eagerly sought after by the men, and which they never dig for but to destroy.

Being now too high wound up to bear a delay, he unbuttoned, and drawing out the engine of love-assaults, drove it currently as at a ready-made breach. Then! then! for the first time did I feel that stiff horn-hard gristle battering against the tender part; but imagine to yourself his surprise when he found, after several vigorous pushes, which hurt me extremely, that he made not the least impression.

I complained, but tenderly complained I could not bear it ... indeed! he hurt me. Still he thought no more than that being so young, the largeness of his machine (for few men could dispute size with him) made all the difficulty, and that possibly I had not been enjoyed by any so advantageously made in that part as himself; for still, that my virgin flower was yet uncropped never once entered into his head, and he would have thought it idling with time and words to have questioned me upon it.

He tries again; still no admittance; still no penetration; but he had hurt me yet more, whilst my extreme love made me bear extreme pain almost without a groan: at length, after repeated fruitless trials, he lay down panting by me, kissed my falling tears and asked me tenderly what was the meaning of so much complaining, and if I had not born it better from others than I did from him? I answered, with a simplicity framed to persuade, that he was the first man that ever served me so.

Truth is powerful, and it is not always that we do not believe what we eagerly wish.

Charles, already disposed by the evidence of his senses to think my pretences to virginity not entirely apocryphal, smothers me with kisses, begs me, in the name of love, to have a little patience, and that he will be as tender of hurting me as he would be of himself.

Alas! it was enough I knew his pleasure, to submit joyfully to him, whatever pain I foresaw it would cost me.

He now resumes his attempts in more form: first he put one of the pillows under me, to give the blank of his aim a more favourable elevation, and another under my head, in ease of it; then, spreading my thighs, and placing himself standing between them, made them rest upon his hips; applying then the point of his machine to the slit, into which he sought entrance, it was so small he could scarce assure himself of its being rightly pointed. He looks, he feels, and satisfies himself; then driving forward with fury, its prodigious stiffness thus impacted, wedge-like, breaks the union of those parts and gained him just the insertion of the tip of it, lip-deep which, being sensible of, he improves his advantage, and following well his stroke, in a straight line, forcibly deepens his penetration, but put me to such intolerable pain, from the separation of the sides of that soft passage by a hard thick body, I could have screamed out; but unwilling as I was to alarm the house, I held in my breath and crammed my petticoat (which was turned up over my face) into my mouth, and bit it through in the agony. At length, the tender texture of that tract giving way to such fierce tearing and rending, he pierced something further into me: and now, outrageous, and no longer his own master, but borne headlong away by the fury and over-mettle of that member now exerting itself with a kind of native rage, he breaks in, carries all before him, and one violent merciless lunge sent it, imbrued[19] and reeking with virgin blood, up to the very hilts in me: then! then! all my resolution deserted me; I screamed out and fainted away with the sharpness of the pain; and (as he told me afterwards), on his drawing out, when emission was over with him, my thighs were instantly all in a stream of blood that flowed from the wounded torn passage.

When I recovered my senses, I found myself undressed and abed, in the arms of the sweet relenting murderer of my virginity, who hung mourning tenderly over me, and holding in his hands a cordial, which, coming from the still dear author of so much pain I could not refuse. My eyes, however, moistened with tears and languishingly turned upon him, seemed to reproach him with his cruelty, and ask him if such were the rewards of love. But Charles, to whom I was now infinitely endeared, by his complete triumph over a maidenhead, where he so little expected to find one, in tenderness to that pain which he had put me to in procuring himself the height of pleasure, smothered his exultation and employed himself with so much sweetness, so much warmth, to sooth, to caress, and comfort me in my soft complainings, that breathed indeed more love than resentment, that I presently drowned all sense of pain in the pleasure of seeing him, of thinking that I belonged to him, he who now was the absolute disposer of my happiness, and, in one word, my fate.

The sore was however too tender, the wound too bleeding fresh, for Charles's good nature to put my patience presently to another trial; but as I could not stir or walk across the room, he ordered the dinner to be brought to the bedside, where it could not be otherwise than my getting down the wing of a fowl, and two or three glasses of wine, since it was my adored youth who both served and urged them on me, with that sweet irresistible authority with which love had invested him over me.

After dinner, and every thing but the wine taken away, Charles very impudently asks a leave he might read the grant of in my eyes, to come to bed to me, and accordingly falls to undressing; which I could not see the progress of without strange emotions of fear and pleasure.

He is now in bed with me the first time, and in broad day;[20] but when thrusting up his own shirt and my shift, he laid his naked glowing body to mine – oh! insupportable delight! oh! superhumane rapture! What pain could stand before a pleasure so transporting? I felt no more the smart of my wounds below; but, curling round him like the tendril of a vine, as if I feared any part of him should be untouched or unpressed by me, I returned his strenuous embraces and kisses with a fervour and gust only known to true love, and which mere lust could never rise to.

Yes, even at this time that all the tyranny of the passions is fully over and that my veins roll no longer but a cold tranquil stream, the remembrance of those passages that most affected me in my youth still cheers and refreshes me. Let me proceed then – my beauteous youth was now glued to me in all the folds and twists that we could make our bodies meet in: when no longer able to rein in the fierceness of refreshed desires, he gives his steed the head, and, gently insinuating his thighs between mine, stopping my mouth with kisses of humid fire, makes a fresh irruption, and renewing his thrusts, pierces, tears, and forces his way up the torn tender folds of the sheath that yielded him admission with a smart little less severe than when the breach was first made. I stifled, however, my cries, and bore him with the passive fortitude of an heroine; soon his thrusts, more and more furious, cheeks flushed with a deeper scarlet, his eyes turned up in the fervent fit and rolling nothing but their whites, some dying sighs and an agonizing shudder, announced the approaches of that ecstatic pleasure I was yet in too much pain to come in for my share of.

Nor was it till after a few enjoyments had numbed and blunted the sense of the smart, and giving me to feel the titillating inspersion[21] of balsamic sweets, drew from me the delicious return, and brought down all my passion, that I arrived at excess of pleasure through excess of pain; but when successive engagements had broken and inured me, I began to enter into the true unallayed relish of that pleasure of pleasures, when the warm gush darts through all the ravished inwards. What floods of bliss! what melting transports! what agonies of delight! too fierce, too mighty for nature to sustain: well has she therefore, no doubt, provided the relief of a delicious momentary dissolution, the approaches of which are intimated by a dear delirium, a sweet thrill, on the point of emitting those liquid sweets in which enjoyment itself is drowned, when one gives the languishing stretch-out and dies at the discharge.

How often, when the rage and tumult of my senses has subsided after the melting flow, have I, in a tender meditation, asked myself coolly the question, if it was in nature for any of its creatures to be so happy as I was? Or, what were all the fears of my future fate, put in the scale of one night's enjoyment of anything so transcendently the taste of my eyes and heart, as that delicious, fond, matchless youth?

Thus we spent the whole afternoon, till supper-time, in a continued circle of love-delights, kissing, turtle-billing, toying, and all the rest of the feast. At length, supper was served in, before which Charles had, for I do not know what reason, slipped his clothes on, and sitting down by the bedside, we made table and tablecloth of the bed and sheets, whilst he suffered nobody to attend or serve but himself. He ate with a very good appetite, and seemed charmed to see me eat. For my part,

I was so enchanted with my fortune, so transported with the comparison of the delights I now swarmed in, with all the insipidity of my past scenes of life, that I thought them sufficiently cheap at even the price of my ruin, or the risque of their not lasting. The present possession was all my little head could find room for.

We lay together that night, when after playing repeated prizes of pleasure, nature, overspent and satisfied, gave us up to the arms of sleep; those of my dear youth encircled me, the consciousness of which made even that sleep more delicious.

Late in the morning I waked first; and observing my lover slept profoundly, softly disengaged myself from his arms, scarcely daring to breath, for fear of shortening his repose; my cap, my hair, my shift were all in disorder from the rufflings I had undergone; and I took this opportunity to adjust and set them as well as I could, whilst every now and then, looking at the sleeping youth with inconceivable fondness and delight, and reflecting on all the pain he had put me to, tacitly owned that the pleasure had overpaid me for my sufferings.

It was then broad day. I was sitting up in the bed, the clothes of which were all tossed, or rolled off, by the unquietness of our motions, from the sultry heat of the weather; nor could I refuse myself a pleasure that sollicited me so irresistibly, as this fair occasion of feasting my sight with all those treasures of youthful beauty I had enjoyed, and which lay now almost entirely naked, his shirt being trussed up in a perfect wisp, which the warmth of the room and season made me easy about the consequence of. I hung over him enamoured indeed! and devoured all his naked charms with only two eyes, when I could have wished them at least a hundred, for the fuller enjoyment of the gaze.

Oh! could I paint his figure as I see it now still present to my transported imagination! A whole length of an all-perfect manly beauty in full view. Think of a face without a fault, glowing with all the opening bloom and vernal freshness of an age in which beauty is of either sex, and which the first down over his upper-lip scarce began to distinguish.

The parting of the double ruby pout of his lips seemed to exhale an air sweeter and purer than what it drew in: ah! what violence did it not cost me to refrain the so tempted kiss!

Then a neck exquisitely turned, graced behind and on the sides with his hair playing freely in natural ringlets, connected his head to a body of the most perfect form, and of the most vigorous contexture, in which all the strength of manhood was concealed and softened to appearance by the delicacy of his complexion, the smoothness of his skin, and the plumpness of his flesh.

The platform of his snow-white bosom, that was laid out in a manly proportion, presented, on the vermillion summet of each pap, the idea of a rose about to blow.

Nor did his shirt hinder from observing that symmetry of his limbs, that exactness of shape, in the fall of it towards the loins, where the waist ends and the rounding swell of the hips commences, where the skin, sleek, smooth, and dazzling white, burnishes on the stretch over firm, plump-ripe flesh, that crimped and run into dimples at the least pressure, or that the touch could not rest upon, but slid over as on the surface of the most polished ivory.

His thighs finely fashioned, and with a florid glossy roundness gradually tapering away to the knees, seemed pillars worthy to support that beauteous frame, at the bottom of which I could not, without some remains of terror, some tender emotions too, fix my eyes on that terrible spitfire machine, which had, not so long before, with such fury broke into, torn, and almost ruined those soft tender parts of mine, which had not yet done smarting with the effects of its rage; but behold it now! crest-fallen, reclining its half-capped vermillion head over one of his thighs, quiet, pliant, and to all appearance incapable of the mischiefs and cruelty it had committed. Then the beautiful growth of the hair, in short and soft curls round its root, its whiteness, branched veins, the supple softness of the shaft, as it lay foreshortened, rolled and shrunk up into a squob thickness, languid, and born up from between the thighs by its globular appendage, that wondrous treasure-bag of nature's sweets, which, rivelled round and pursed up in the only wrinkles that are known to please, perfected the prospect, and all together formed the most interesting moving picture in nature, and surely infinitely superior to those nudities furnished by the painters, statuaries, or any art, which are purchased at immense prices, whilst the sight of them in actual life is scarce sovereignly tasted by any but the few whom nature has endowed with a fire of imagination, warmly pointed by a truth of judgment to the spring-head, the originals of beauty of nature's unequalled composition, above all the imitations of art, or the reach of wealth to pay their price.

But everything must have an end. A motion made by this angelic youth, in the listlessness of going-off sleep, replaced his shirt and clothes in a posture that shut up that treasury from longer view.

I lay down then, and carrying my hands to that part of me in which the objects just seen had begun to raise a mutiny that prevailed over the smart of them, my fingers now opened themselves an easy passage; but long I had not the time to consider the wide differences *there*, between the maid and the now finished woman, before Charles waked, and turning towards me, kindly inquired how I had rested, and scarce giving me time to answer, imprinted on my lips one of his burning rapture-kisses, which darted a flame to my heart, that from thence radiated to every part of me: and presently, as if he had proudly meant revenge for the survey I had smuggled of all his naked beauties, he spurns off the bed-clothes, and trussing up my shift as high as it would go, took his turn to feast his eyes with all the gifts nature had bestowed on my person; his busy hands too ranged intemperantly[22] over every part of me. The delicious austerity and hardness of my yet unripe budding breasts, the whiteness and firmness of my flesh, the freshness and regularity of my features, the harmony of my limbs, all seemed to confirm him in his satisfaction with his bargain: but, when curious to explore the havoc he had made in the tender center of his over-fierce attack, he not only directed his hands there, but with a pillow put under, placed me favourably for his wanton purpose of inspection; then, who can express the fire his eyes glistened, his hands glowed with, whilst sighs of pleasure, and tender broken exclamations were all the praises he could utter. By this time his machine, stiffly risen at me, lifted and bore the flap of his shirt out, which, presently fiercely removing, gave me to see it in its highest state and bravery: He feels it himself, seems pleased at its condition, and, smiling loves and graces, seizes one of my hands, and carries it, with a gentle compulsion, to this pride of nature, and its richest masterpiece.

I, struggling faintly, could not help feeling what I could not grasp, a column of the whitest ivory, beautifully streaked with blue veins, and carrying, fully uncapped, a head of the liveliest vermillion: no horn could be harder or stiffer; yet no velvet more smooth or delicious to the touch. Presently he guided my hand lower, to that part in which nature and pleasure keep their stores in concert, so aptly fastened and hung-on to the root of their first instrument and minister, that not improperly he might be styled their purse-bearer too: there he made me feel distinctly, through their soft cover, the contents, a pair of roundish balls, that seemed to play within, and elude all pressure but the tenderest, from without.

But now this visit of my soft warm hand in those so sensible parts had put everything into such ungovernable fury that, disdaining all further preluding, and taking the advantage of my commodious posture, he made the storm fall where I scarce patiently expected, and where he was sure to lay it: presently then, I felt the stiff intersertion between the yielding divided lips of the wound now open for life; where the narrowness no longer put me to intolerable pain, and afforded my lover no more difficulty than what heightened his pleasure, in the strict embrace of that tender warm sheath, round the instrument it was so deliciously adjusted to, and which, now cased home, so gorged me with pleasure that it perfectly suffocated me and took away my breath; then the killing thrusts! the unnumbered kisses! every one of which was a joy inexpressible; and that joy lost in a crowd of yet greater blisses. But this was a disorder too violent in nature to last long: the vessels so stirred and intensely heated soon boiled over, and for that time put out the fire. Meanwhile all this dalliance and disport had so far consumed the morning that it became a kind of necessity to lay breakfast and dinner into one.

In our calmer intervals Charles gave the following account of himself, every tittle of which was true. He was the only son of a father who, having a small post in the revenue, rather overlived his income and had given this young gentleman a very slender education; no profession had he bred him up to, but designed to provide for him in the army by purchasing him an ensign's commission, that is to say, provided he could raise the money, or procure it by interest, either of which clauses was rather to be wished than hoped for by him. On no better a plan, however, than this had this improvident father suffered this youth, and a youth of great promise, to run up to the age of manhood, or near it at least, in next to idleness, and had besides taken no sort of pains to give him even the common premonitions against the vices of the town, and the dangers of all sorts which wait the unexperienced and unwary in it. He lived at home, and at discretion, with his father, who himself kept a mistress, and for the rest, provided Charles did not ask him for money, he was indolently kind to him: he might lie out when he pleased, any excuse would serve, and even his reprimands were so slight that they carried with them rather an air of connivance at the fault than any serious control or constraint. But, to supply his calls for money, Charles, whose mother was dead, had, by her side, a grandmother who doted upon and did not a little help-spoil him. She had a considerable annuity to live upon, and very regularly parted with every shilling she could spare to this darling of her's, to the no little heartburn[23] of his father, who was vexed, not that she by this means fed his son's extravagance, but that she preferred Charles to himself; and we shall too soon see what a fatal turn such a mercenary jealousy could operate on the breast of a father.

Charles was, however, by the means of his grandmother's lavish fondness, very sufficiently enabled to keep a mistress so easily contented as my love made me; and my good fortune, for such I must ever call it, threw me in his way, in the manner above related, just as he was on the look-out for one.

As to his temper, the even sweetness of it made him seem born for domestic happiness: tender, naturally polite, and gentle-mannered, it could never be his fault if ever jars or animosities ruffled a calm he was so qualified every way to maintain or restore. Without those great or shining qualities that constitute a genius, or are fit to make a noise in the world, he had all those humble ones that compose the softer social merit: plain common sense, set off with every grace of modesty and good nature, made him, if not admired, what is much happier, universally beloved and esteemed. But, as nothing but the beauties of his person had at first attracted my regard and fixed my passion, neither was I then a judge of that internal merit, which I had afterwards full occasion to discover, and which perhaps, in that season of giddiness and levity, would have touched my heart very little, had it been lodged in a person less the delight of my eyes and idol of my senses. But to return to our situation.

After dinner, which we ate abed in a most voluptuous disorder, Charles got up, and taking a passionate leave of me for a few hours, he went to town, where, concerting matters with a young sharp lawyer, they went together to my late venerable mistress's, from whence I had but the day before made my elopement, and with whom he was determined to settle accounts in a manner that should cut off all after-reckonings from that quarter.

Accordingly, they went; but by the way, the Templar, his friend, on thinking over Charles's information, saw reason to give their visit another turn, and instead of offering satisfaction, to demand it.

On being let in, the girls of the house flocked round Charles, whom they knew, and from the earliness of my escape, and their perfect ignorance of his ever having so much as seen me, not having the least suspicion of his being accessary to my flight, they were, in their way, *making up* to him; and as to his companion, they took him probably for a fresh cully. But the Templar soon checked their forwardness by inquiring for the old lady, with whom, he said, with a grave judge-like countenance, that he had some business to settle.

Madam was immediately sent for down, and the ladies being desired to clear the room, the lawyer asked her severely if she did not know or had not decoyed, under pretence of hiring as a servant, a young girl just come out of the country, called Frances or Fanny Hill, describing me withall as particularly as he could from Charles's description.

It is peculiar to vice to tremble at the inquiries of justice; and Mrs Brown, whose conscience was not entirely clear upon my account, as knowing as she was of the town, as hackneyed as she was in buffing[24] through all the dangers of her vocation, could not help being alarmed at the question, especially when he went on to talk of a justice of peace, Newgate, the Old Baily, indictments for keeping a disorderly house, pillory, carting, and the whole process of that nature: She, who, it is likely, imagined I had lodged an information against her house, looked extremely blank, and began to make a thousand protestations and excuses. However, to abridge, they brought away triumphantly my box of things, which, had she not been under an awe, she might have disputed with them; and not only that, but a clearance and discharge of any demands on the house, at the expense of no more than a bowl of arrack-punch, the treat of which, together with the choice of the house-conveniences, was offered, and not accepted. Charles all the time acted the chance companion of the lawyer, who had brought him there, as he knew the house, and appeared in no wise interested in the issue, but he had the collateral pleasure of hearing all I had told him verified, so far as the bawd's fears would give her leave to enter into my history, which, if one may guess by the composition she so readily came into, were not small.

Phoebe, my kind tutoress Phoebe, was at that time gone out, perhaps in search of me, or their cooked-up story had not, it is probable, passed so smoothly.

This negotiation had, however, taken up some time, which would have appeared much longer to me, left as I was in a strange house, if the landlady, a motherly sort of woman to whom Charles had liberally recommended me, had not come up and borne me company. We drank tea, and her chat helped to pass away the time very agreeably, since he was our theme; but as the evening deepened, and the hour set for his return was elapsed, I could not dispel the gloom of impatience and tender fears which gathered upon me, and which our timid sex are apt to feel in proportion to their love.

Long, however, I did not suffer, the sight of him overpaid me; and the soft reproach I had prepared for him expired before it reached my lips.

I was still abed, yet unable to use my legs otherwise than awkwardly, and Charles flew to me, catches me in his arms, raised, and, extending mine to meet his dear embrace, gives me an account, interrupted by many a sweet parenthesis of kisses, of the success of his measures.

I could not help laughing at the fright the old woman had been put into, which my ignorance, and indeed my want of innocence, had far from prepared me for bespeaking. She had, it seems, apprehended that I had fled for shelter to some relation I had recollected in town, on my dislike of their ways and proceeding towards me, and that this application came from thence. For, as Charles had rightly judged, not one neighbour had, at that still hour, seen the circumstance of my escape into the coach, or at least noticed him; neither had any in the house the least hint or clue of suspicion of my having spoke to him, much less of my having clapped up such a sudden bargain with a perfect stranger: thus the greatest improbability is not always what we should most mistrust.

We supped with all the gaiety of two young giddy creatures at the top of their desires; and as I had most joyfully given up to Charles the whole charge of my future happiness, I thought of nothing beyond the exquisite pleasure of possessing him.

He came to bed in due time, and this second night, the pain being pretty well over, I tasted, in full draughts, all the transports of perfect enjoyment. I swam, I bathed in bliss, till both fell fast asleep, through the natural consequences of satisfied desires and appeased flames; nor did we wake but to renewed raptures.

Thus, making the most of love and life, did we stay at this lodging in Chelsea about ten days, in which time Charles took care to give his excursions from home a colourable gloss, and to keep his footing with his fond, indulgent grandmother, from whom he drew constant and sufficient supplies for the charge I was to him, and which was very trifling, in comparison with his former less regular course of pleasures.

Charles removed me then to a private ready-furnished lodging in D— street, St James's, where he paid half a guinea a week for two rooms and a closet on the second floor, which he had been some time looking out for, and was more convenient for the frequency of his visits than where he had at first placed me, in a house which I cannot say but I left with regret, as it was infinitely endeared to me by the first possession of my Charles, and the circumstance of losing there that jewel which can never be twice lost. The landlord, however, had no reason to complain of anything but of a procedure in Charles too liberal not to make him regret his loss of us.

Arrived at our new lodgings, I remember I thought them extremely fine, though ordinary enough even at that price; but had it been a dungeon that Charles had brought me to, his presence would have made it a little Versailles.

The landlady, Mrs Jones, waited on us to our apartment, and, with great volubility of tongue, explained to us all its conveniences: that her own maid should wait on us – that the best of quality had lodged at her house – that her first floor was let to a foreign secretary of an embassy and his lady – that I looked like a very good-natured lady. At the word lady, I blushed out of flattered vanity: this was too strong for a girl of my condition; for though Charles had had the precaution of dressing me in a less tawdry flaunting style than were the clothes I escaped to him in, and of passing me for his wife that he had secretly married and kept private (the old story) on account of his friends, I dare swear this appeared extremely apocryphal to a woman who knew the town so well as she did; but that was the least of her concern. It was impossible to be less scruple-ridden than she was; and the advantage of letting her rooms being her sole object, the truth itself would have far from scandalized her, or broken her bargain.

A sketch of her picture and personal history will dispose you to account for the part she is to act in my concerns.

She was about forty-six years old, tall, meager, red-haired, with one of those trivial ordinary faces you meet with everywhere, and go about unheeded and unmentioned. In her youth she had been kept by a gentleman, who, dying, left her forty pounds a year during her life, in consideration of a daughter he had by her; which daughter, at the age of seventeen, she sold, for not a very considerable sum neither, to a gentleman who was going an envoy abroad and took his purchase with him, where he used her with the utmost tenderness, and, it is thought, was secretly married to her; but had constantly made a point of her not keeping up the least correspondence with a mother base enough to make a market of her own flesh and blood. However, as she had no nature, nor indeed any passion but that of money, this gave her no further uneasiness than as she thereby lost a handle of squeezing presents, or other after-advantages, out of the bargain. Indifferent then, by nature or constitution, to every other pleasure but that of increasing the lump by any means whatever, she commenced a kind of private procuress, for which she was not amiss fitted by her grave decent appearance, and sometimes did a job in the matchmaking way; in short, there was nothing that appeared to her under the shape of gain that she would not have undertaken. She knew most of the ways of the town, having not only herself been upon but kept up constant intelligences in it, dealing, besides her practice in promoting a harmony between the two sexes, in private pawn-broking and other profitable secrets. She rented the house she lived in and made the most of it by letting it out in lodgings; and though she was worth, at least, near three or four thousand pounds, she would not allow herself even the necessaries of life, and pinned her subsistence entirely on what she could squeeze out of her lodgers.

When she saw such a young pair come under her roof, her immediate notions doubtless were how she should make the most money of us, by every means that money might be made, and which she rightly judged our situation and inexperience would soon beget her occasions of.

In this hopeful sanctuary, and under the clutches of this harpy,[25] did we pitch our residence. It will not be mighty material to you, or very pleasant to me, to enter into a detail of all the petty cut-throat ways and means with which she used to fleece us; all which Charles indolently chose to bear with, rather than take the trouble of removing, the difference of the expense being scarce attended to by a young gentleman who had no ideas of stint, or even economy, and a raw country girl who knew nothing of the matter.

Here, however, under the wings of my sovereignly beloved, did I flow[26] the most delicious hours of my life; my Charles I had, and in him every thing my fond heart could wish or desire. He carried me to plays, operas, masquerades and every diversion of the town, all which pleased me indeed, but pleased me infinitely the more for his being with me, and explaining everything to me, and enjoying perhaps the natural impressions of surprise and admiration, which such sights at the first never fail to excite in a country girl new to the delights of them. But to me, they sensibly proved the power and full dominion of the sole passion of my heart over me, a passion in which soul and body were concentered and left me no room for any other relish of life but love.

As to the men I saw at those places, or at any other, they suffered so much in the comparison my eyes made of them with my all-perfect Adonis that I had not the infidelity even of one wandering thought to reproach myself with upon his account. He was the universe to me, and all that was not him was nothing to me.

My love, in fine, was so excessive that it arrived at annihilating every suggestion or kindling spark of jealousy, for, one idea only tending that way gave me such exquisite torment that my self-love and dread of worse than death made me for ever renounce and defy it: nor had I indeed occasion, for, were I to enter here on a recital of several instances wherein Charles sacrificed to me women of greater importance than I dare hint (which, considering his form, was no such wonder), I might indeed give you full proof of his unshaken constancy to me, but would not you accuse me of warming up again a feast that my vanity ought long ago to have been satisfied with?

In our cessations from active pleasure, Charles framed himself one, in instructing me, as far as his own lights reached, in a great many points of life that I was, in consequence of my no-education, perfectly ignorant of. Nor did I suffer one word to fall in vain from the mouth of my lovely teacher; I hung on every syllable he uttered, and received as oracles all he said, whilst kisses were all the interruption I could not refuse myself the pleasure of admitting, from lips that breathed more than Arabian sweetness.

I was in a little time enabled, by the progress I had made, to prove the deep regard I had paid to all that he had said to me; repeating it to him almost word for word, and to show that I was not entirely the parrot, but that I reflected upon, that I entered into it, I joined my own comments and asked him questions of explanation.

My country accent and the rusticity of my gait, manners, and deportment began now sensibly to wear off, so quick was my observation, and so efficacious my desire of growing every day worthier of his heart.

As to money, though he brought me constantly all he received, it was with difficulty he even got me to give it room in my bureau, and what clothes I had, he could prevail on me to accept of on no other foot than that of pleasing him by the greater neatness in my dress, beyond which I had no ambition; I could have made a pleasure of the greatest toil, and worked my fingers to the bone, with joy, to have supported him: guess then, if I could harbour any idea of being burdensome to him; and this disinterested turn in me was so unaffected, so much the dictate of my heart, that Charles could not but feel it, and if he did not love me as much as I did him (which was the constant and only matter of sweet contention between us), he managed so at least as to give me the satisfaction of believing it impossible for man to be more tender, more true, more faithful than he was.

Our landlady, Mrs Jones, came frequently up to my apartment, from whence I never stirred on any pretext without Charles; nor was it long before she wormed out, without much art, the secret of our having cheated the church of a ceremony, and, in course, of the terms we lived together upon: a circumstance which far from displeased her, considering the designs she had upon me, and which, alas! she will have too soon room to carry into execution. But in the meantime, her own experience of life let her see that any attempt, however indirect or disguised, to divert or break, at least presently, so strong a cement of hearts as ours was, could only end in losing two lodgers of whom she made very competent advantages, if either of us came to smoke²⁷ her commission, for a commission she had from one of her customers, either to debauch or get me away from my keeper at any rate.

But the barbarity of my fate soon saved her the task of disuniting us. I had now been eleven months with this life of my life, which had passed in one continued rapid stream of delight; but nothing so violent was ever made to last. I was about three months gone with child by him, a circumstance which would have added to his tenderness, had he ever left me room to believe it could receive an addition, when the mortal, the unexpected blow of separation fell upon us. I shall gallop post over the particulars, which I shudder yet to think of, and cannot to this instant reconcile myself to how, or by what means, I could outlive it.

Two live-long days had I lingered through, without hearing from him, I, who breathed, who existed but in him, and had never yet seen twenty-four hours pass without seeing or hearing from him. The third day my impatience was so strong, my alarms had been so severe, that I perfectly sickened with them; and being unable to support the shock longer, I sunk upon the bed, and ringing for Mrs Jones, who had far from comforted me under my anxieties, she came up, and I had scarce breath and spirit enough to find words to beg of her if she would save my life, to fall upon some means of finding out instantly what was become of its only prop and comfort. She pitied me in a way that rather sharpened my affliction than suspended it, and went out upon this commission.

For she had but to go to Charles's house, who lived but at an easy distance, in one of the streets that run into Covent-Garden. There she went into a public-house, and from thence sent for a maid-servant whose name I had given her, as the properest to inform her.

The maid readily came, and as readily, when Mrs Jones inquired of her what was become of Mr Charles, or whether he was gone out of town, acquainted her with the disposal of her master's son, which the very day after was no secret to the servants; such sure measures had he taken for the most cruel punishment of his child for having more interest with his grandmother than he had, though he made use of a pretence, plausible enough to get rid of him in this secret and abrupt manner, for fear her fondness should have interposed a bar to his leaving England, and proceeding on a voyage he had concerted for him, which pretext was that it was indispensably necessary to secure a considerable inheritance that devolved to him by the death of a rich merchant (his own brother) at one of the factories in the South Seas, of which he had lately received advice, together with a copy of the will.

In consequence of which resolution to send away his son, he had, unknown to him, made the necessary preparations for fitting him out, struck a bargain with the captain of a ship, whose punctual execution of his orders he had secured by his interest with his principal owner and patron, and, in short, concerted his measures so secretly and effectually that whilst his son thought he was going down the river, that would take him a few hours, he was stopped on board of a ship, debarred from writing, and more strictly watched than a state criminal.

Thus was the idol of my soul torn from me, and forced on a long voyage, without taking leave of one friend, or receiving one line of comfort, except a dry explanation and instructions from his father how to proceed when he should arrive at his destined port, enclosing withal some letters of recommendation to a factor[28] there: all these particulars I did not learn minutely till some time after.

The maid, at the same time, added that she was sure this usage of her sweet young master would be the death of his grandmama, as indeed it proved true, for the old lady, on hearing it, did not survive the news a whole month; and as her fortune consisted in an annuity, out of which she had laid up no reserves, she left nothing worth mentioning to her so fatally envied darling, but absolutely refused to see his father before she died.

When Mrs Jones returned, and I observed her looks, they seemed so unconcerned and even nearest to pleased that I half flattered myself she was going to set my tortured heart at ease by bringing me good news; but this, indeed, was a cruel delusion of hope: the barbarian, with all the coolness imaginable, stabs me to the heart in telling me succinctly that he was sent away at least on a four years' voyage, (here she stretched maliciously) and that I could not expect in reason ever to see him again; and all this with such pregnant circumstances that I could not escape giving them credit, as in general they were indeed too true!

She had hardly finished her report before I fainted away, and after several successive fits, all the while wild and senseless, I miscarried of the dear pledge of my Charles's love: but the wretched never die when it is fittest that they should die, and women are hard-lived to a proverb.

The cruel and interested care taken to recover me saved an odious life: which, instead of the happiness and joys it had overflowed in, all of a sudden presented no view before me of anything but the depth of misery, horror, and the sharpest affliction.

Thus I lay six weeks, in the struggles of youth and constitution against the friendly efforts of death, which I constantly invoked to my relief and deliverance, but which, proving too weak for my wish, I recovered at length, but into a state of stupefaction and despair that threatened me with a loss of my senses, and a mad-house.

Time, however, that great comforter in ordinary, began to assuage the violence of my suffering, and to numb my feeling of them. My health returned to me, though I still retained an air of grief, dejection, and languor, which, taking off from the ruddiness of my country complexion, rendered it rather more delicate and affecting.

The landlady had all this time officiously provided and seen that I wanted for nothing, and as soon as she saw me retrieved into a condition of answering her purpose, one day after we had dined together, she congratulated me on my recovery, the merit of which she took entirely to herself, and all this by way of introduction to a most terrible and scurvy epilogue: 'You are now,' says she, 'Miss Fanny, tolerably well, and you are very welcome to stay in these lodgings as long as you please, you see I have asked you for nothing this long time, but truly I have a call to make up a sum of money which must be answered,' and, with that, presents me with a bill for arrears of rent, diet, apothecary's charges, nurse, &c. sum total twenty-three pounds, seventeen and six-pence, towards discharging of which I had not in the world (which she well knew) more than seven guineas, left by chance, of my dear Charles's common stock with me. At the same time she desired me to tell her what course I would take for payment. I burst out into a flood of tears, and told her my condition, that I would sell what few clothes I had, and that, for the rest, would pay her as soon as possible; but my distress being favourable to her views, only stiffened her the more. She told me very coolly that she was indeed sorry for my misfortunes, but that she must do herself justice, though it would go to the very heart of her to send such a tender young creature to prison; at the word 'prison' every drop of my blood chilled, and my fright acted so strongly upon me that, turning as pale and faint as a criminal at the first sight of his place of execution, I was on the point of swooning. My landlady, who wanted only to terrify me to a certain point, and not to throw me into a state of body inconsistent with her designs upon it, began to soothe me again, and told me, in a tone composed to more pity and gentleness, that it would be my own fault if she was forced to proceed to such extremities, but she believed there was a friend to be found in the world who would make up matters to both our satisfactions, and that she would bring him to drink tea with us that very afternoon, when she hoped we would come to a right understanding in our affairs. To all this, not a word of answer; I sat mute, confounded, terrified.

Mrs Jones, however, judging rightly that it was her time to strike whilst the impressions were so strong upon me, left me to myself and to all the terrors of an imagination wounded to death by the idea of going to a prison, and, from a principle of self-preservation, snatching at every glimpse of redemption from it.

In this situation I sat near half an hour, swallowed up in grief and despair, when my landlady came in, and, observing a death-like dejection in my countenance, still in pursuance of her plan, put on a false pity, and bidding me be of good heart, things, she said, would not be so bad as I imagined, if I would be but my own friend, and closed with telling me she had brought a very honourable gentleman to drink tea with me, who would give me the best advice how to get rid of all my troubles; upon which, without waiting for a reply, she goes out and returns with this very honourable gentleman, whose very honourable procuress she had been on this as well as other occasions.

The gentleman, on his entering the room, made me a very civil bow, which I had scarce strength, or presence of mind enough to return a curtsey to; when the landlady, taking upon her to do all the honours of this first interview (for I had never, that I remembered, seen the gentleman before), sets a chair for him, and another for herself. All this while not a word on either side: a stupid stare was all the face I could put on this strange visit.

The tea was made, and the landlady, unwilling, I suppose, to lose any time, observing my silence and shyness before this entire stranger: 'Come, Miss Fanny,' says she in a coarse familiar style and tone of authority, 'hold up your head, child, and do not let sorrow spoil that pretty face of yours. What! sorrows are only for a time. Come, be free, here is a worthy gentleman who has heard of your misfortunes and is willing to serve you – you must be better acquainted with him, do not you now stand upon your punctilios, and this and that, but make your market while you may.'

At this so delicate and eloquent harangue, the gentleman, who saw I looked frighted and amazed, and indeed incapable of answering, took her up for breaking things in so abrupt a manner, as rather to shock than incline me to an acceptance of the good he intended me; then, addressing himself to me, told me he was perfectly acquainted with my whole story, and every circumstance of my distress, which he owned was a cruel plunge for one of my youth and beauty to fall into; that he had long taken a liking to my person, for which he appealed to Mrs Jones, there present, but finding me so deeply engaged to another, he had lost all hopes of succeeding, till he heard the sudden reverse of fortune that had happened to me, on which he had given particular orders to my landlady to see that I should want for nothing, and that, had he not been forced abroad to The Hague on affairs he could not refuse himself to, he would himself have attended me during my sickness; that on his return, which was but the day before, he had, on learning my recovery, desired my landlady's good offices to introduce him to me, and was as angry, at least, as I was shocked, at the manner in which she had conducted herself towards obtaining him that happiness, but that to show me how much he disowned her procedure, and how far he was from taking an ungenerous advantage of my situation, and from exacting any security for my gratitude, he would, before my face, that instant, discharge my debt entirely to my landlady and give me her receipt in full, after which I should be at liberty either to reject or grant his suit, as he was much above putting any force upon my inclinations.

Whilst he was exposing his sentiments to me, I ventured just to look up to him and observe his figure, which was that of a very well looking gentleman, well made, of about forty, dressed in a suit of plain clothes, with a large diamond ring on one of his fingers, the lustre of which played in my eyes, as he waved his hand in talking and raised my notions of his importance: in short, he might pass for what is commonly called a comely black[29] man, with an air of distinction natural to his birth and condition.

To all his speeches, however, I answered only in tears that flowed plentifully to my relief, and, choking up my voice, excused me from speaking, very luckily, for I should not have known what to say.

The sight, however, moved him, as he afterwards told me, irresistibly, and by way of giving me some reason to be less powerfully afflicted, he drew out his purse, and calling for pen and ink, which the landlady was prepared for, paid her every farthing of her demand, independant of a liberal gratification, which was to follow unknown to me, and taking a receipt in full, very tenderly forced me to secure it, by guiding my hand, which he had thrust it into, so as to make me passively put it into my pocket.

Still I continued in a state of stupidity, or melancholic despair, as my spirits could not yet recover from the violent shocks they had received, and the commode landlady had actually left the room, and me alone with this strange gentleman, before I observed it, and then observed it without alarm, for I was now lifeless, and indifferent to everything.

The gentleman, however, no novice in affairs of this sort, drew near me, and under the pretence of comforting me, first with his handkerchief dried my tears as they ran down my cheeks; presently, he ventured to kiss me: on my part neither resistance nor compliance. I sat stock-still; and now looking on myself as bought by the payment that had been transacted before me, I did not care what became of my wretched body; and wanting life, spirits, or courage to oppose the least struggle, even that of the modesty of my sex, I suffered tamely whatever the gentleman pleased, who, proceeding insensibly from freedom to freedom, insinuated his hand between my handkerchief and bosom, which he handled at discretion. Finding thus no repulse, and that everything favoured beyond expectation the completion of his desires, he took me in his arms and bore me without life or motion to the bed, on which laying me gently down, and having me at what advantage he pleased, I did not so much as know what he was about, till recovering from a trance of lifeless insensibility, I found him buried in me, whilst I lay passive and innocent of the least sensation of pleasure: a death cold corpse could scarce have had less life or sense in it. As soon as he had thus pacified a passion, which had too little respected the condition I was in, he got off, and after recomposing the disorder of my clothes, employed himself with the utmost tenderness to calm the transports of remorse and madness at myself, with which I was seized, too late, I confess, for having suffered on that bed the embraces of an utter stranger. I tore my hair, wrung my hands, and beat my breast like a madwoman; but when my new master, for in that light I then viewed him, applied himself to appease me, as my whole rage was levelled at myself, no part of which I thought myself permitted to aim at him, I begged him, with more submission than anger, to leave me alone, that I might at least enjoy my affliction in quiet; this he positively refused, for fear, as he pretended, that I should do myself a mischief.

Violent passions seldom last long, and those of women least of any. A dead still calm succeeded this storm, which ended in a profuse shower of tears.

Had anyone, but a few instants before, told me that I should have ever known any man but Charles, I would have spat in his face, or had I been offered infinitely a greater sum of money than that I saw

97

paid for me, I had spurned the proposal in cold blood. But our virtues and our vices depend too much on our circumstances; unexpectedly beset as I was, betrayed by a mind weakened by a long severe affliction, and stunned with the terrors of a goal, my defeat will appear the more excusable, since I certainly was not present at, or a party in any sense, to it. However as the first enjoyment is decisive, and he was now over the bar, I thought I had no longer a right to refuse the caresses of one that had got that advantage over me, no matter how obtained. Conforming myself then to this maxim, I considered myself as so much in his power that I endured his kisses and embraces without affecting struggles or anger; not that they as yet gave me any pleasure, or prevailed over the aversion of my soul to give myself up to any sensation of that sort; what I suffered, I suffered out of a kind of gratitude, and as matter of course after what had passed.

He was, however, so regardful as not to attempt the renewal of those extremities which had thrown me just before into such violent agitations; but, now secure of possession, contented himself with bringing me to temper by degrees, and waiting at the hand of time for those fruits of his generosity and courtship which he since often reproached himself with having gathered much too green, when, yielding to the invitations of my inability to resist him, and overborn by desires, he had wreaked his passion on a mere lifeless spiritless body, dead to all purposes of joy, since, taking none, it ought to have been supposed incapable of giving any. This is, however, certain: my heart never thoroughly forgave him the manner in which I had fallen to him, although, in point of interest, I had reason to be pleased that he found in my person wherewithal to keep him from leaving me as easily as he had had me.

The evening was in the meantime so far advanced that the maid came in to lay the cloth for supper, when I understood with joy that my landlady, whose sight was present poison to me, was not to be with us.

Presently a neat and elegant supper was introduced, and a bottle of Burgundy, with the other necessaries, were set on a dumb-waiter.

The maid quitting the room, the gentleman insisted, with a tender warmth, that I should sit up in the elbow chair by the fire and see him eat, if I could not be prevailed on to eat myself. I obeyed, with a heart full of affliction, at the comparison it made between those delicious tête-à-têtes with my ever dear youth and this forced situation, this new awkward scene, imposed and obtruded on me by cruel necessity.

At supper, after a great many arguments used to comfort and reconcile me to my fate, he told me that his name was H—, brother to the earl of L—, and that, having by the suggestions of my landlady been led to see me, he had found me perfectly to his taste, had given her a commission to procure me at any rate, and that he had at length succeeded as much to his satisfaction as he passionately wished it might be to mine, adding withal some flattering assurances that I should have no cause to repent my knowledge of him.

I had now got down at least half a partridge, and three or four glasses of wine, which he compelled me to drink by way of restoring nature; but whether there was anything extraordinary put into the wine, or whether there wanted no more to revive the natural warmth of my constitution and give fire to the old train, I began no longer to look with that constraint, not to say disgust, on Mr H—, which I had hitherto done; but withal there was not the least grain of love mixed with this softening of my sentiments: any other man would have been just the same to me as Mr H—, that stood in the same circumstances and had done for me, and with me, what he had done.

There are not, on earth at least, eternal griefs; mine were, if not at an end, at least suspended: my heart, which had been so long overloaded with anguish and vexation, began to dilate and open to the least gleam of diversion, or amusement. I wept a little, and my tears relieved me; I sighed, and my sighs seemed to lighten me of a load that oppressed me; my countenance grew, if not cheerful, at least more composed and free.

Mr H—, who had watched, perhaps brought on, this change, knew too well not to seize it. He thrust the table imperceptibly from between us, and bringing his chair to face me, he soon began, after preparing me by all the endearments of assurances and protestations, to lay hold of my hands, to kiss me, and once more to make free with my bosom, which, being at full liberty from the disorder of my loose dishabille, now panted and throbbed, less with indignation than with fear and bashfulness at being used so familiarly by still a stranger; but he soon gave me greater occasion to exclaim, by stooping down and slipping his hand above my garters; thence he strove to regain the pass which he had before found so open and unguarded. But now he could not unlock the twist of my thighs: I gently complained and begged him to let me alone; told him I was not well; however, as he saw there was more form and ceremony in my resistance than good earnest, he made his conditions for desisting from pursuing his point that I should be put instantly to bed, whilst he gave certain orders to the landlady, and that he would return in an hour, when he hoped to find me more reconciled to his passion for me than I seemed at present. I neither assented nor denied, but in my air and manner of receiving this proposal gave him to see that I did not think myself enough my own mistress to refuse it.

Accordingly he went out and left me, when a minute or two after, before I could recover myself into any composure for thinking, the maid came in with her mistress's service, and a small silver porringer of what she called a bridal posset, and desired me to eat it as I went to bed, which consequently I did, and felt immediately a heat, a fire, run like a hue-and-cry through every part of my body; I burnt, I glowed, and wanted even little of wishing for any man.

The maid, as soon as I was lain down, took the candle away, and wishing me a good night, went out of the room and shut the door after her.

She had hardly time to get downstairs before Mr H— opened my room door softly, and came in, now undressed, in his nightgown and cap, with two lighted wax candles, and bolting the door, gave me, though I expected him, some sort of alarm. He came a-tiptoe to the bedside, and saying with a gentle whisper: 'Pray, my dear, do not be startled – I will be very tender and kind to you.' He then hurried off his clothes, and leaped into bed, having given me openings enough, whilst he was stripping, to observe his brawny structure, strong-made limbs, and rough shaggy breast.

The bed shook again when it received this new load. He lay on the outside, where he kept the candles burning, no doubt for the satisfaction of every sense; for as soon as he had kissed me, he rolled down the bedclothes and seemed transported with the view of all my person at full length, which he covered with a profusion of kisses, sparing no part of me. Then, being on his knees between my thighs, he drew up his shirt and bared all his hairy thighs and stiff staring truncheon, red-topped and rooted into a thicket of curls, which covered his belly to his navel and gave it the air of a flesh brush: and soon I felt it joining close to mine, when he had driven the nail up to the head, and left no partition but the intermediate hair on both sides.

I had it now, I felt it now; and beginning to drive, he soon gave nature such a powerful summons down to her favourite quarters that she could no longer refuse repairing thither. All my animal spirits then rushed mechanically[30] to that center of attraction, and presently, inly warmed and stirred as I was beyond bearing, I lost all restraint, and yielding to the force of the emotion, gave down, as mere woman, those effusions of pleasure, which, in the strictness of still faithful love, I could have wished to have held up.

Yet oh! what an immense difference did I feel between this impression of a pleasure merely animal, and struck out of the collision of the sexes by a passive bodily effect, from that sweet fury, that rage of active delight which crowns the enjoyments of a mutual love-passion, where two hearts, tenderly and truly united, club to exalt the joy, and give it a spirit and soul that bids defiance to that end which mere momentary desires generally terminate in, when they die of a surfeit of satisfaction.

Mr H—, whom no distinctions of that sort seemed to distract, scarce gave himself or me breathing time from the last encounter, but as if he had tasked himself to prove that the appearances of his vigour were not signs hung out in vain, in a few minutes he was in a condition for renewing the onset, to which, preluding with a storm of kisses, he drove the same course as before with unbated fervour, and thus, in repeated engagements, kept me constantly in exercise till dawn of morning, in all which time he made me fully sensible of the virtues of his firm texture of limbs, his square shoulders, broad chest, compact hard muscles, in short, a system of manliness that might pass for no bad image of our ancient sturdy barons, when they wielded the battle-ax, whose race is now so thoroughly refined and frittered away into the more delicate modern-built frame of our pap-nerved softlings, who are as pale, as pretty, and almost as masculine as their sisters.

Mr H—, content, however, with having the day break upon his triumphs, resigned me up to the refreshment of a rest we both wanted, and we soon dropped into a profound sleep.

Though he was some time awake before me, yet did he not offer to disturb a repose he had given me so much occasion for; but on my first stirring, which was not till past ten o'clock, I was obliged to endure one more trial of his manhood.

About eleven, in came Mrs Jones, with two basins of the richest soup, which her experience in these matters had moved her to prepare. I pass over the fulsome compliments, the cant of this decent procuress, with which she saluted us both, but though my blood rose at the sight of her, I suppressed my emotions, and gave all my concern to reflections on what would be the consequence of this new engagement.

But Mr H——, who penetrated my uneasiness, did not long suffer me to languish under it and acquainted me that, having taken a solid sincere affection to me, he would begin by giving me one leading mark of it, in removing me out of a house which must for many reasons be irksome and disagreeable to me, into convenient lodgings, where he would take all imaginable care of me; and desiring me not to have any explanations with my landlady, or be impatient till he returned, he dressed and went out, having left me a purse with two and twenty guineas in it, being all he had about him, as he expressed it, to keep my pocket till farther supplies.

As soon as he was gone, I felt the usual consequences of the first launch into vice; (for my love attachment to Charles never appeared to me in that light). I was instantly borne away down the stream, without the power of making back to the shore. My dreadful necessities, my gratitude, and above all, to say the plain truth, the dissipation and diversion I began to find in this new acquaintance, from the black corroding thoughts my heart had been a prey to ever since the absence of my dear Charles, concurred to stun all contrary reflections. If I now thought of my first, my only charmer, it was still with the tenderness and regret of the fondest love, embittered with the consciousness that I was no longer worthy of him. I could have begged my bread with him all over the world, but wretch that I was! I had neither the virtue or courage requisite not to outlive my separation from him.

Yet! had not my heart been thus pre-engaged, Mr H—— might probably have been the sole master of it, but the place was full, and the force of conjunctures alone had made him the possessor of my person, the charms of which had, by the by, been his sole object and passion, and were, of course, no foundation for a love either very delicate or very durable. He did not return till six in the evening to take me away to my new lodgings, and my moveables being soon packed and conveyed into a hackney-coach, it cost me but little regret to take my leave of a landlady whom I thought I had so much reason not to be overpleased with, and as for her part, she made no other difference of my staying or going but what that of the profit created.

We soon got to the house appointed for me, which was that of a plain tradesman, who, on the score of interest, was entirely at Mr H—'s devotion, and who let him the first floor, very genteelly furnished, for two guineas a week, of which I was instated mistress, with a maid to attend me.

He staid with me that evening, and we had a supper from a neighbouring tavern, after which, and a gay glass or two, the maid put me to bed. Mr H— soon followed, and, notwithstanding the fatigues of the preceding night, I found no quarter nor remission from him: he piqued himself, as he told me, on doing the honours of my new apartment.

The morning being pretty well advanced, we got to breakfast: and the ice now broke, my heart, no longer engrossed by love, began to take ease, and to please itself with such trifles as Mr H—'s liberal liking led him to make his court to the usual vanity of our sex. Silks, laces, earrings, pearl-necklace, gold watch, in short, all the trinkets and articles of dress were lavishly heaped upon me, the sense of which, if it did not create returns of love, forced a kind of grateful fondness something like love, a distinction it would be spoiling the pleasure of nine tenths of the keepers in the town to make, and is, I suppose, the very good reason why so few of them ever do make it.

I was now established the kept mistress in form, well lodged, with a very sufficient allowance and lighted up with all the lustre of dress.

Mr H— continued kind and tender to me, yet, with all this I was far from happy; for, besides my regrets for my dear youth, which, though often suspended or diverted, still returned upon me in certain melancholic moments with redoubled violence, I wanted more society, more dissipation.

As to Mr H—, he was so much my superior in every sense that I felt it too much to the disadvantage of the gratitude I owed him; thus he gained my esteem, though he could not raise my taste. I was qualified for no sort of conversation with him, except one sort, and that is a satisfaction which leaves tiresome intervals, if not filled up by love or other amusements.

Mr H—, so experienced, so learned in the ways of women, numbers of whom had passed through his hands, doubtless soon perceived this uneasiness, and without approving or liking me the better for it, had the complaisance to indulge me.

He made suppers at my lodgings, where he brought several companions of his pleasures with their mistresses, and by this means I got into a circle of acquaintance that soon stripped me of all the remains of bashfulness and modesty which might be yet left of my country education, and were, to a just taste, perhaps, the greatest of my charms.

We visited one another in form, and mimicked, as near as we could, all the miseries, the follies, and impertinences of the women of quality, in the round of which they trifle away their time, without its ever entering into their little heads that on earth there cannot subsist anything more silly, more flat, more insipid and worthless than, generally considered, their system of life is: they ought to treat the men as their tyrants indeed! were they to condemn them to it.

But though, amongst the kept mistresses (and I was now acquainted with a good many, besides some useful matrons, who live by their connexions with them) I hardly knew one that did not perfectly detest their keepers, and, of course, made little or no scruple of any infidelity they could safely accomplish, I had still no notion of wronging mine: for, besides that no mark of jealousy on his side started me the hint, or gave me the provocation to play him a trick of that sort, and that his constant generosity, politeness, and tender attentions to please me forced a regard to him, that, without affecting my heart, insured him my fidelity, no object had yet presented that could overcome the habitual liking I had contracted for him. I was on the eve of obtaining from the movements of his own voluntary generosity a modest provision for life, when an accident happened which broke all the measures he had resolved upon in my favour.

I had now lived near seven months with Mr H—, when one day returning to my lodgings from a visit in the neighbourhood, where I used to stay longer, I found the street-door open, and the maid of the house standing at it talking with some of her acquaintance, so that I came in without knocking; and as I passed by, she told me Mr H— was above. I stepped upstairs into my own bedchamber, with no other thought than of pulling off my hat, etc., and then to wait upon him in the dining room, into which my bedchamber had a door, as is common enough. Whilst I was untying my hat-strings, I fancied I heard my maid Hannah's voice, and a sort of tussle, which, raising my curiosity, I stole softly to the door, where a knot in the wood had been slipped out and afforded a very commanding peep-hole to the scene then in agitation, the actors of which had been too earnestly employed to hear my opening my own door, from the landing place of the stairs into my bedchamber.

The first sight that struck me was Mr H— pulling and hauling this coarse country strammel[31] towards a couch that stood in the corner of the dining room; to which the girl made only a sort of an awkward hoydening resistance, crying out so loud that I, who listened at the door, could scarce hear her, 'Pray, Sir, don't – let me alone – I am not for your turn – You cannot, sure, demean yourself with such a poor body as I –. Lord, Sir, my mistress may come home – I must not indeed. I will cry out –' All which did not hinder her from insensibly suffering herself to be brought to the foot of the couch, upon which a push of no mighty violence served to give her a very easy fall, and my gentleman having got up his hands to the stronghold of her *vartue*, she no doubt thought it was time to give up the argument, and that all further defence would be vain: and he, throwing her petticoats over her face, which was now as red as scarlet, discovered a pair of stout, plump, substantial thighs, and tolerably white; he mounted them round his hips, and coming out with his drawn weapon, stuck it in the cloven spot, where he seemed to find a less difficult entrance than perhaps he had flattered himself with (for by the way this blowze[32] had left her place in the country for a bastard), and, indeed, all his motions showed he was lodged pretty much at large. After he had done, his dearee gets up, drops her petticoats down, and smoothes her apron and handkerchief. Mr H— looked a little silly, and taking out some money, gave it her, with an air indifferent enough, bidding her be a good girl and say nothing.

Had I loved this man, it was not in nature for me to have had patience to see the whole scene through: I should have broken in and played the jealous princess with a vengeance; but that was not the case, my pride alone was hurt, my heart not, and I could easier win upon myself to see how far he would go, till I had no uncertainty upon my conscience.

The least delicate of all affairs of this sort being now over, I retired softly into my closet, where I began to consider what I should do: my first scheme naturally was to rush in and upbraid them; this indeed flattered my present emotions and vexations, as it would have given immediate vent to them; but on second thoughts, not being so clear as to the consequence to be apprehended from such a step, I began to doubt whether it was not better to dissemble my discovery till a safer season, when Mr H— should have perfected the settlement he had made overtures to me of, and which I was not to think such a violent explanation, as I was indeed not equal to the management of, could possibly forward, and might destroy. On the other hand, the provocation seemed too gross, too flagrant, not to give me some thoughts of revenge, the very start of which idea restored me to perfect composure, and delighted as I was with the confused plan of it in my head, I was easily mistress enough of myself to support the part of ignorance I had prescribed to myself; and as all this circle of reflections was instantly over, I stole a-tiptoe to the passage-door, and opening it with a noise, passed for having that moment come home; and after a short pause, as if to pull off my things, I opened the door into the dining room, where I found the dowdy blowing the fire, and my faithful shepherd walking about the room and whistling, as cool and unconcerned as if nothing had happened. I think, however, he had not much to brag of having out-dissembled me; for I kept up, nobly, the character of our sex for art, and went up to him with the same open air of frankness as I had ever received him. He staid but a little while, made some excuse for not being able to stay the evening with me, and went out.

As for the wench, she was now spoiled, at least for my servant; and scarce eight and forty hours were gone round, before her insolence, on what had passed between Mr H— and her, gave me so fair an occasion to turn her away at a minute's warning that not to have done it would have been the wonder; so that he could neither disapprove it nor find in it the least reason to suspect my original motive. What became of her afterwards I know not; but generous as Mr H— was, he undoubtedly made her amends: though, I dare answer, that he kept up no farther commerce with her of that sort; as his stooping to such a coarse morsel was only a sudden sally of lust, on seeing a wholesome-looking, buxom country wench, and no more strange than hunger, or even a wimsical appetite's making a flying meal of neck-beef, for a change of diet.

Had I considered this escape of Mr H— in no more than that light and contented myself with turning away the wench, I had thought and acted right; but, flushed as I was with imaginary wrongs, I should have held Mr H— to have been too cheaply off, if I had not pushed my revenge farther, and repaid him, as exactly as I could for the soul of me, in the same coin.

Nor was this worthy act of justice long delayed: I had it too much at heart. Mr H— had, about a fortnight before, taken into his service a tenant's son, just come out of the country, a very handsome young lad, scarce turned of nineteen, fresh as a rose, well shaped and clever-limbed; in short, a very good excuse for any woman's liking, even though revenge had been out of the question; any woman, I say, who was disprejudiced and had wit and spirit enough to prefer a point of pleasure to a point of pride.

Mr H— had clapped a livery upon him; and his chief employ was, after being shown my lodgings, to bring and carry letters or messages between his master and me; and as the situation of all kept ladies is not the fittest to inspire respect even to the meanest of mankind, and perhaps less of it from the most ignorant, I could not help observing that this lad, who was, I suppose, acquainted with my relation to his master by his fellow servants, used to eye me in that bashful confused way, more expressive, more moving, and readier caught at by our sex than any other declarations whatever: my figure had, it seems, struck him, and modest and innocent as he was, he did not himself know that the pleasure he took in looking at me was love, or desire; but his eyes, naturally wanton, and now inflamed by passion, spoke a great deal more than he durst have imagined they did. Hitherto, indeed, I had only taken notice of the comeliness of the youth, but without the least design. My pride alone would have guarded me from a thought that way, had not Mr H—'s condescension with my maid, where there was not half the temptation in point of person, set me a dangerous example; but now I began to look on this stripling as every way a delicious instrument of my designed retaliation upon Mr H—, of an obligation for which I should have made a conscience to die in his debt.

In order then to pave the way for the accomplishment of my scheme, for two or three times that the young fellow came to me with messages, I managed so as without affectation to have him admitted to my bedside, or brought to me at my toilet, where I was dressing; and by carelessly showing or letting him see as if without meaning or design, sometimes my bosom rather more bare than it should be; sometimes my hair, of which I had a very fine head, in the natural flow of it while combing; sometimes a neat leg, that had unfortunately slipped its garter, which I made no scruple of tying before him, easily gave him the impressions favourable to my purpose, which I could perceive to sparkle in his eyes and glow in his cheeks. Then certain slight squeezes by the hand, as I took letters from him, did his business completely.

When I saw him thus moved and fired for my purpose, I inflamed him yet more by asking him several leading questions; such as had he a mistress? – was she prettier than me? – could he love such a one as I was? – and the like; to all which the blushing simpleton answered to my wish, in a strain of perfect nature, perfect undebauched innocence, but with all the awkwardness and simplicity of country breeding.

When I thought I had sufficiently ripened him for the laudable point I had in view, one day that I expected him at a particular hour, I took care to have the coast clear for the reception I designed him. And, as I had laid it, he came to the dining room door, tapped at it, and, on my bidding him come in, he did so and shut the door after him. I desired him then to bolt it on the inside, pretending it would not otherwise keep shut.

I was then lying at length on that very couch, the scene of Mr H—'s polite joys, in an undress which was with all the art of negligence flowing loose, and in a most tempting disorder: no stays, no hoop – no encumbrance whatever; on the other hand, he stood at a little distance that gave me a full view of a fine featured, shapely, healthy, country lad, breathing the sweets of fresh blooming youth: his hair, which was of a perfect shining black, played to his face in natural side-curls and was set out with a smart tuck-up behind; new buckskin breeches that, clipping close, showed the shape of a plump well made thigh, white stockings, garter-laced livery, shoulder-knot, altogether composed a figure in which the beauties of pure flesh and blood appeared under no disgrace from the lowness of a dress, to which a certain spruce neatness seems peculiarly fitted.

I bid him come towards me and give me his letter, at the same time throwing down carelessly a book I had in my hands. He coloured, and came within reach of delivering me the letter, which he held out awkwardly enough for me to take, with his eyes riveted on my bosom, which was, through the designed disorder of my handkerchief, sufficiently bare and rather shaded than hidden.

I, smiling in his face, took the letter, and immediately catching gently hold of his shirt-sleeve, drew him towards me, blushing and almost trembling; for surely his extreme bashfulness and utter inexperience called for at least all these advances to encourage him. His body was now conveniently inclined towards me, and just softly chucking his smooth beardless chin, I asked him, if he was afraid of a lady? – and with that taking and carrying his hand to my breasts, I pressed it tenderly to them. They were now finely furnished and raised in flesh, so that, panting with desire, they rose and fell, in quick heaves, under his touch: at this, the boy's eyes began to lighten with all the fires of inflamed nature, and his cheeks flushed with a deep scarlet; tongue-tied with joy, rapture, and bashfulness, he could not speak, but then his looks, his emotion, sufficiently satisfied me that my train had taken, and that I had no disappointment to fear.

My lips, which I threw in his way, so as that he could not escape kissing them, fixed, fired and emboldened him, and now, glancing my eyes towards that part of his dress which covered the essential object of enjoyment, I plainly discovered the swell and commotion there, and as I was now too far advanced to stop in so fair a way, and was indeed no longer able to contain myself or wait the slower progress of his maiden bashfulness (for such it seemed, and really was), I stole my hand upon his thighs, down one of which I could both see and feel a stiff hard body, confined by his breeches, that my fingers could discover no end to. Curious then, and eager to unfold so alarming a mystery, playing, as it were, with his buttons, which were bursting ripe from the active force within, those of his waistband and foreflap flew open at a touch, when out it started; and now, disengaged from the shirt, I saw with wonder and surprise, what? not the plaything of a boy, not the weapon of a man, but a maypole of so enormous a standard that, had proportions been observed, it must have belonged to a young giant; its prodigious size made me shrink again. Yet I could not, without pleasure, behold and even ventured to feel such a length! such a breadth of animated ivory, perfectly well turned and fashioned, the proud stiffness of which distended its skin, whose smooth polish and velvet softness might vie with that of the most delicate of our sex, and whose exquisite whiteness was not a little set off by a sprout of black curling hair round the root, through the jetty sprigs of which the fair skin showed as, in a fine evening, you may have remarked the clear light ether, through the branchwork of distant trees, overtopping the summet of a hill. Then the broad and bluish-casted incarnate of the head and blue serpentines of its veins altogether composed the most striking assemblage of figure and colours in nature; in short, it stood an object of terror and delight.

But what was yet more surprising, the owner of this natural curiosity (through the want of occasions in the strictness of his home breeding, and the little time he had been in town not having afforded him one) was hitherto an absolute stranger, in practice at least, to the use of all that manhood he was so nobly stocked with; and it now fell to my lot to stand his first trial of it, if I could resolve to run the risks of its disproportion to that tender part of me which such an over-sized machine was very fit to lay in ruins.

But it was now of the latest to deliberate; for by this time, the young fellow, overheated with the present objects, and too high-mettled to be longer curbed in by that modesty and awe which had hitherto restrained him, ventured, under the stronger impulse and instructive promptership of nature alone, to slip his hands, trembling with eager impetuous desires, under my petticoats, and seeing, I suppose, nothing extremely severe in my looks to stop, or dash him, he feels out and seizes gently the center-spot of his ardours. Oh then! the fiery touch of his fingers determines me, and my fears melting away before the growing intolerable heat, my thighs disclose of themselves and yield all liberty to his hand; and now, a favourable movement giving my petticoats a toss, the avenue lay too fair, too open to be missed; he is now upon me. I had placed myself with a jet under him, as commodious and open as possible to his attempts, which were untoward enough, for his machine, meeting with no inlet, bore and battered stiffly against me in random pushes, now above, now below, now beside its point, till, burning with impatience from its irritating touches, I guided gently with my hand this furious fescue[33] to where my young novice was now to be taught his first lesson of pleasure. Thus he nicked at length the warm and insufficient orifice; but he was made to find no breach practicable, and mine, though so often entered, was still far from wide enough to take him easily in.

By my direction, however, the head of his unwieldy machine was so critically pointed that, feeling him foreright against[34] the tender opening, a favourable motion from me met his timely thrust, by which the lips of it, strenuously dilated, gave way to his thus assisted impetuosity, so that we might both feel that he had gained a lodgment; pursuing then his point, he soon, by violent and, to me, most painful piercing thrusts, wedges himself at least so far in as to be now tolerably secure of his entrance: here he stuck; and I now felt such a mixture of pleasure and pain as there is no giving a definition of. I dreaded, alike, his splitting me farther up or his withdrawing: I could not bear either to keep or part with him; the sense of pain, however, prevailing, from his prodigious size and stiffness, acting upon me in those continued rapid thrusts with which he furiously pursued his penetration, made me cry out gently: 'Oh, my dear, you hurt me!' This was enough to check the tender respectful boy, even in his mid-career; and he immediately drew out the sweet cause of my complaint, whilst his eyes eloquently expressed at once his grief for hurting me and his reluctance at dislodging from quarters of which the warmth and closeness had given him a gust of pleasure that he was now desire-mad to satisfy, and yet too much a novice not to be afraid of my withholding his relief, on account of the pain he had put me to.

But I was myself far from being pleased with his having too much regarded my tender exclaims, for now more and more fired with the object before me, as it still stood with the fiercest erection, unbonneted and displaying its broad vermillion head, I first gave the youth a re-encouraging kiss, which he repaid me with a fervour that seemed at once to thank me and bribe my farther compliance, and I soon replaced myself in a posture to receive, at all risks, the renewed invasion, which he did not delay an instant; for, being presently remounted, I once more felt the smooth hard gristle forcing an entrance, which he achieved rather easier than before. Pained, however, as I was, with his efforts of gaining a complete admission, which he was so regardful as to manage by gentle degrees, I took care not to complain. In the meantime, the soft strait passage gradually loosens, yields, and, stretched to its utmost bearing by the stiff, thick, in-driven engine, sensible at once to the ravishing pleasure of the feel and the pain of the distension, let him in about half way, when all the most nervous activity he now exerted to further his penetration gained him not an inch of his purpose; for, whilst he hesitated there, the crisis of pleasure overtook him, and the close com-pressure of the warm surrounding fold drew from him the ecstatic gush, even before mine was ready to meet it, kept up by the pain I had en-dured in the course of the engagement, from the unsufferable size of his weapon, though it was not as yet in above half its length.

I expected then, but without wishing it, that he would draw, but was pleasingly disappointed; for he was not to be let off so. The well-breathed youth, hot-mettled, and flush with genial juices, was now fairly in for making me know my driver. As soon, then, as he had made a short pause, waking, as it were, out of the trance of pleasure (in which every sense seemed lost for a while, whilst, with his eyes shut and short quick breathings, he had yielded down his maiden tribute), he still kept his post, yet unsated with enjoyment, and solacing in these so new delights, till his stiffness, which had scarce perceptibly remitted, being thoroughly recovered to him, who had not once unsheathed, he proceeded afresh to cleave and open to himself an entire entry into me, which was not a little made easy to him by the balsamic injection with which he had just plentifully moistened the whole internals of the passage. Redoubling, then, the active energy of his thrusts, favoured by the fervid appetency[35] of my motions, the soft oiled wards can no longer stand so effectual a picklock, but yield and open him an entrance: and now, with conspiring nature and my industry, strong to aid him, he pierces, penetrates, and at length, winning his way inch by inch, gets entirely in, and finally, a home-made thrust, sheathes it up to the guard; on the information of which, from the close jointure of our bodies (insomuch that the hair on both sides perfectly interweaved and encurled[36] together), the eyes of the transported youth sparkled with more joyous fires, and all his looks and motions acknowledged excess of pleasure, which I now began to share, for I felt him in my very vitals! I was quite sick with delight! stirred beyond bearing with its furious agitations within me, and gorged and crammed even to a surfeit: thus I lay gasping, panting, under him, till his broken breathings, faultering accents, eyes twinkling with humid fires, lunges more furious, and an increased stiffness gave me to hail the approaches of the second period: – it came – and the sweet youth, overpowered with ecstasy, died away in my arms, melting in a flood that shot in genial warmth into the innermost recesses of my body, every conduit of which, dedicated to that pleasure, was on flow to mix with it. Thus we continued for some instants, lost, breathless, senseless of everything and in every part but those favourite ones of nature, in which all that we enjoyed of life and sensation was now totally concentered.

When our mutual trance was a little over, and the young fellow had withdrawn that delicious stretcher with which he had most plentifully drowned all thoughts of revenge in the sense of actual pleasure, the widened wounded passage refunded a stream of pearly liquids, which flowed down my thighs, mixed with streaks of blood, the marks of the ravage of that monstrous machine of his, which had now triumphed over a kind of second maidenhead. I stole, however, my handkerchief to those parts and wiped them as dry as I could, whilst he was readjusting, and buttoning up.

I made him now sit down by me, and as he had gathered courage from such extreme intimacy, he gave me an aftercourse of pleasure, in a natural burst of tender gratitude and joy, at the new scenes of bliss I had opened to him; scenes positively so new that he had never before had the least acquaintance with that mysterious mark, the cloven stamp of female distinction, though nobody better qualified than he to penetrate into its deepest recesses or do it nobler justice. But when, by certain motions, certain unquietnesses of his hands, that wandered not without design, I found he languished for satisfying a curiosity natural enough, to view and handle those parts which attract and concenter the warmest force of imagination, charmed as I was to have any occasion of obliging and humouring his young desires, I suffered him to proceed as he pleased, without check or control, to the satisfaction of them.

Easily, then, reading in my eyes the full permission of myself to all his wishes, he scarce pleased himself more than me, when, having insinuated his hands under my petticoat and shift, he presently removed those bars to the sight by slily lifting them upwards, under favour of a thousand kisses, which he thought, perhaps, necessary to divert my attention to what he was about. All my drapery being now rolled up to my waist, I threw myself into such a posture upon the couch as gave up to him, in full view, the whole region of delight, and all the luxurious landscape round it. The transported youth devoured everything with his eyes and tried with his fingers to lay more open to his sight the secrets of that dark and delicious deep: he opens the folding lips, the softness of which, yielding entry to anything of a hard body, close round it, and oppose the sight; and feeling further, meets with, and wonders at, a soft fleshy excrescence, which, limber and relaxed after the late enjoyment, now grew, under the touch and examination of his fiery fingers, more and more stiff and considerable, till the titillating ardours of that so sensible part made me sigh as if he had hurt me. On which he withdrew his curious probing fingers, asking me pardon, as it were, in a kiss that rather increased the flame *there*.

Novelty ever makes the strongest impressions, and in pleasures especially: no wonder then that he was swallowed up in raptures of admiration of things so interesting by their nature, and now seen and handled for the first time. On my part, I was richly overpaid for the pleasure I gave him, in that of examining the power of those objects thus abandoned to him, naked and free to his loosest wish, over the artless, natural stripling: his eyes streaming fire, his cheeks glowing with a florid red, his fervid frequent sighs, whilst his hands convulsively squeezed, opened, pressed together again the lips and sides of that deep flesh-wound or gently twitched the over-growing moss; and all proclaimed the excess, the riot of joys, in having his wantonness thus humoured. But he did not long abuse my patience, for the objects before him had now put him by all his, and coming out with that formidable machine of his, he lets the fury loose, and pointing it directly to the pouting-lipped mouth that bid him sweet defiance in dumb-show, squeezes in the head, and driving with refreshed rage, breaks in and plugs up the whole passage of that soft pleasure-conduit, where he makes all shake again, and put once more all within me into such an uproar as nothing could still but a fresh inundation from the very engine of those flames, as well as from all the springs with which nature floats that reservoir of joy, when risen to its floodmark.

I was now so bruised, so battered, so spent with this over-match that I could hardly stir or raise myself, but lay palpitating, till the ferment of my senses subsiding by degrees, and the hour striking at which I was obliged to dispatch my young man, I tenderly advised him of the necessity there was for parting, which I felt as much displeasure at as he could do, who seemed eagerly disposed to keep the field, and to enter on a fresh action; but the danger was too great, and after some hearty kisses of leave and recommendations of secrecy and discretion, I forced myself to force him away, not without assurances of seeing him again, to the same purpose, as soon as possible, and thrust a guinea into his hands: not more, lest, being too flush of money, a suspicion or discovery might arise from thence, having everything to fear from the dangerous indiscretion of that age in which young fellows would be too irresistible, too charming, if we had not that terrible fault to guard against.

Giddy and intoxicated as I was with such satiating draughts of pleasure, I still lay on the couch, supinely stretched out, in a delicious languor diffused over all my limbs, hugging myself for being thus revenged to my heart's content, and that in a manner so precisely alike, and on the identical spot, in which I had received the supposed injury. No reflections on the consequences ever once perplexed me, nor did I make myself one single reproach for having, by this step, completely entered myself of a profession more decried than disused. I should have held it ingratitude to the pleasure I had received to have repented of it; and since I was now over the bar, I thought by plunging over head and ears into the stream I was hurried away by, to drown all sense of shame or reflection.

Whilst I was thus making these laudable dispositions, and whispering to myself a kind of tacit vow of incontinency, enters Mr H—. The consciousness of what I had been doing deepened yet the glowing of my cheeks, flushed with the warmth of the late action, which, joined to the piquant air of my dishabille, drew from Mr H— a compliment on my looks, which he was proceeding to back the sincerity of with proofs, and that with so brisk an action as made me tremble for fear of a discovery from the condition those parts were left in from their late severe handling: the orifice dilated and inflamed, the lips swollen with their uncommon distension, the ringlets pressed down, crushed and uncurled with the overflowing moisture that had wet everything round it, the different feel and state of things, in short, would hardly have passed, upon one of Mr H—'s nicety and experience, unaccounted for but by the real cause. But here the woman saved me: I pretended a violent disorder of my head, and feverish heat that indisposed me too much to receive his embraces. He gave in to this, and good-naturedly desisted. Soon after, an old lady coming in, made a third, very *à propos* for the confusion I was in, and Mr H—, after bidding me take care of myself and recommending me to my repose, left me much at ease and relieved by his absence.

In the close of the evening, I took care to have prepared for me a warm bath of aromatic and sweet herbs; in which, having fully laved and solaced myself, I came out voluptuously refreshed in body and spirit.

The next morning, waking pretty early after a night's perfect rest and composure, it was not without some dread and uneasiness, that I thought of what innovation that tender soft system of mine might have sustained from the shock of a machine so sized for its destruction.

Struck with this apprehension, I scarce dared to carry my hand thither, to inform myself of the state and posture of things.

But I was soon agreeably cured of my fears.

The silky hair that covered round the borders, now smoothed and repruned, had resumed its wonted curl and trimness; the fleshy pouting lips, that had stood the brunt of the engagement, were no longer swollen or moisture-drenched: and neither they nor the passage into which they opened, that had suffered so great a dilatation, betrayed any the least

alteration, outward or inwardly, to the most curious research, notwithstanding also the laxity that naturally follows the warm bath.

This continuation of that grateful stricture which is in us, to the men,
the very jet of their pleasure, I owed, it seems, to a happy habit of body,
juicy, plump, and furnished towards the texture of those parts, with
a fullness of soft springy flesh that, yielding sufficiently as it does to
almost any distension, soon recovers itself so as to retighten that strict
compression of its mantlings and folds, which form the sides of the passage
wherewith it so tenderly embraces and closely clips any foreign body
introduced into it, such as my exploring finger then was.

Finding then everything in due tone and order, I remembered my
fears, only to make a jest of them to myself. And now, palpably mistress
of any size of man, and triumphing in my double achievement of pleasure
and revenge, I abandoned myself entirely to the ideas of all the delight
I had swum in. I lay stretching out, glowingly alive all over, and tossing
with burning impatience for the renewal of joys that had sinned but
in a sweet excess; nor did I lose my longing, for about ten in the morning,
according to expectation, Will, my new humble sweetheart, came with
a message from his master, Mr H—, to know how I did. I had taken
care to send my maid on an errand into the city, that I was sure would
take up time enough; and from the people of the house I had nothing
to fear, as they were plain good sort of folks, and wise enough to mind
no more of other people's business than they could well help.

All dispositions then made, not forgetting that of lying in bed to receive
him; when he was entered the door of my bedchamber, a latch, that
I governed by a wire, descended and secured it.

I could not but observe that my young minion was as much spruced
out as could be expected from one in his condition; a desire of pleasing
that could not be indifferent to me, since it proved that I pleased him,
which I assure you was now a point I was not above having in view.

His hair trimly dressed, clean linnen, and, above all, a hale, ruddy,
wholesome country look, made him out as pretty a piece of woman's
meat as you should see, and I should have thought anyone much out
of taste that could not have made a hearty meal of such a morsel as
nature seemed to have designed for the highest diet of pleasure.

And why should I here suppress the delight I received from this
amiable creature in remarking each artless look, each motion of pure
undissembled nature, betrayed by his wanton eyes, or showing trans-

parently, the glow and suffusion of blood through his fresh, clear skin, whilst even his sturdy, rustic pressures wanted not their peculiar charm? Oh! but, say you, this was a young fellow in too low a rank of life to deserve so great a display. May be so: but was my condition, strictly considered, one jot more exalted? Or had I really been much above him, did not his capacity of giving such exquisite pleasure sufficiently raise and ennoble him to me at least? Let who would, for me, cherish, respect, and reward the painter's, the statuary's, [37] the musician's arts, in proportion to the delight taken in them; but at my age, and with my taste for pleasure, a taste strongly constitutional to me, the talent of pleasing, with which nature has endowed a handsome person, formed to me the greatest of all merits, compared to which the vulgar prejudices in favour of titles, dignities, honours, and the like, held a very low rank indeed! Nor, perhaps, would the beauties of the body be so much affected to be held cheap, were they in their nature to be bought and delivered; but for me, whose natural philosophy all resided in the favourite center of sense, [38] and who was ruled by its powerful instinct in taking pleasure by its right handle, I could scarce have made a choice more to my purpose.

Mr H—'s loftier qualifications of birth, fortune, and sense laid me under a sort of subjection and constraint that were far from making harmony in the concert of love; nor had he, perhaps, thought me worth softening that superiority to; but with this lad I was more on that level which love delights in.

We may say what we please, but those we can be the easiest and freest with are ever those we like, not to say love, the best.

With this stripling, all whose art of love was the action of it, I could without check of awe or restraint, give a loose to joy and execute every scheme of dalliance my fond fancy might put me on, in which he was, in every sense, a most exquisite companion. And now my great pleasure lay in humouring all the petulances, all the wanton frolic of a raw novice just fleshed, and keen on the burning scent of his game, but unbroken to the sport: and, to carry on the figure, who could better thread the wood than he, or stand fairer for the heart of the hunt?

He advanced then to my bedside, and whilst he faltered out his message, I could observe his colour rise, and his eyes lighten with joy, in seeing me in a situation as favourable to his loosest wishes as if he had bespoke the play.

I smiled, and put out my hand towards him, which he kneeled down to (a politeness taught him by love alone, that great master of it) and greedily kissed. After exchanging a few confused questions and answers, I asked him if he would come to bed to me for the little time I could venture to detain him. This was just asking a person dying with hunger to feast upon the dish on earth the most to his palate. Accordingly, without farther reflection, all his clothes were off in an instant; when, blushing still more at this new liberty, he got under the bedclothes I held up to receive him, and was now in bed with a woman for the first time in his life.

Here began the usual tender preliminaries, as delicious perhaps as the crowning act of enjoyment itself; which they often beget an impatience of that makes pleasure destructive of itself by hurrying on the final period, and closing that scene of bliss, in which the actors are generally too well pleased with their parts not to wish them an eternity of duration.

When we had sufficiently graduated our advances towards the main point, by toying, kissing, clipping, feeling my breasts, now round and plump, feeling that part of me I might call a furnace-mouth, from the prodigious intense heat his fiery touches had rekindled there, my young sportsman, emboldened by every freedom he could wish, wantonly takes my hand and carries it to that enormous machine of his that stood with a stiffness! a hardness! an upward bent of erection! and which, together with its bottom dependence, the inestimable bulse[39] of lady's jewels, formed a grand show out of goods indeed! Then its dimensions, mocking either grasp or span, almost renewed my terrors. I could not conceive how, or by what means, I could take or put such a bulk out of sight. I stroked it gently, on which the mutinous rogue seemed to swell and gather a new degree of fierceness and insolence; so that finding it grew not to be trifled with any longer, I prepared for rubbers in good earnest.

Slipping then a pillow under me, that I might give him the fairest play, I guided officiously with my hand this furious battering-ram whose ruby head, presenting nearest the resemblance of a heart, I applied to its proper mark, which lay as finely elevated as we could wish, my hips being born up and my thighs at their utmost extension; the gleamy warmth that shot from it made him feel that he was at the mouth of the indraught, and driving foreright, the powerfully divided lips of that pleasure-thirsty channel received him. He hesitated a little; then, settled well in the passage, he makes his way up the straights of it, with a difficulty nothing more than pleasing, widening as he went, so as to distend and smooth each soft furrow: our pleasure increasing deliciously, in proportion as our points of mutual touch increased in that so vital part of me in which I had now taken him, all indriven and completely sheathed, and which, crammed as it was, stretched splitting ripe, gave it so gratefully straight an accommodation! so strict a fold! a suction so fierce, that gave and took unutterable delight! We had now reached the closest point of union; but when he backened to come on the fiercer, as if I had been actuated by a fear of losing him, in the height of my fury, I twisted my legs round his naked loins, the flesh of which, so firm, so springy to the touch, quivered again under the pressure; and now I had him every way encircled and begirt; and having drawn him home to me, I kept him fast there, as if I had sought to unite bodies with him at that point. This bred a pause of action, a pleasure stop; whilst that delicate glutton, my nethermouth, as full as it could hold, kept palating, with exquisite relish, the morsel that so deliciously engorged it. But nature could not long endure a pleasure that so highly provoked without satisfying it; pursuing then its darling end, the battery recommenced with redoubled exertion; nor lay I inactive on my side, but encountering him with all the impetuosity of motion I was mistress of, the downy clothing of our meeting mounts was now of real use to break the violence of the tilt; and soon, too soon indeed! the high-wrought agitation, the sweet urgency of this to-and-fro friction, raised the titillation on me to its height, so that, finding myself on the point of going, and loath to leave the tender partner of my joys behind me, I employed all the forwarding motions and arts my experience suggested to me to promote his keeping me company to our journey's end. I not only then tightened the pleasure-girth round my restless inmate, by a secret spring of suction and compression that obeys the will in those parts, but stole my hand softly to that store-bag of nature's prime sweets which is so pleasingly attached to its conduit-pipe, from which we receive them; there feeling, and most gently indeed, squeezing those tender globular reservoirs, the magic touch took instant effect, quickened, and brought on upon the spur the symptoms of that sweet agony, the melting moment of dissolution, when pleasure dies by pleasure, and the mysterious engine of it overcomes the titillation it has raised in those parts by plying them with the stream of a warm liquid, that is itself the highest of all titillations, and which they thirstily express and draw in like the hot-natured leech, which, to cool itself, tenaciously attracts all the moisture within its sphere of exsuction: chiming then to me, with exquisite consent, as I melted away, his oily balsamic injection mixing deliciously with the sluices in flow from me, sheathed and blunted all the stings of pleasure, whilst it flung us into an ecstasy that extended us fainting, breathless, entranced. Thus we lay, whilst a voluptuous languor possessed and still maintained us motionless, and fast locked in one another's arms. Alas! that these delights should be no longer-lived! for now the point of pleasure, unedged by enjoyment, and all the brisk sensations flattened upon us, resigned us up to the cool cares of insipid life. Disengaging myself then from his embrace, I made him sensible of the reasons there were for his present leaving me; on which, though reluctantly, he put on his clothes with as little expedition, however, as he could help, wantonly interrupting himself between whiles with kisses, touches, and embraces, I could not refuse myself to; yet he happily returned to his master before he was missed; but at taking leave, I forced him (for he had sentiments enough to refuse it) to receive money enough to buy a silver watch, that great article of subaltern finery, which he at length accepted as a remembrance he was carefully to preserve of my affections.

And here, Madam, I ought perhaps to make you an apology for this minute detail of things that dwelt so strongly upon my memory after so deep an impression. But, besides that this intrigue bred one great revolution in my life, which historical truth requires I should not sink upon[40] you; may I not presume that so exalted a pleasure ought not to be ungratefully forgotten or suppressed by me, because I found it in a character in low life where, by the by, it is oftener met with, purer and more unsophisticated, than amongst the false ridiculous refinements with which the great suffer themselves to be so grossly cheated by their pride: the great! than whom there exist few amongst those they call the vulgar who are more ignorant of, or who cultivate less, the art of living than they do; they, I say, who forever mistake things the most foreign to the nature of pleasure itself, whose capital favourite object is enjoyment of beauty, wherever that rare invaluable gift is found, without distinction of birth or station.

As love never had, so now revenge had no longer any share in my commerce with this handsome youth. The sole pleasures of enjoyment were now the link I held to him by: for though nature had done such great matters for him in his outward form, and especially in that superb piece of furniture she had so liberally enriched him with; though he was thus qualified to give the senses their richest feast, still there was something more wanting to create in me and constitute the passion of love. Yet Will had very good qualities, too; gentle, tractable, and, above all, grateful: silentious,[41] even to a fault, he spoke at any time very little but made it up emphatically with action; and to do him justice, he never gave me the least reason to complain either of any tendency to encroach upon me for the liberties I allowed him or of his indiscretion in blabbing them. There is, then, a fatality in love, or have loved him I must; for he was really a treasure, a bit for the *bonne bouche* of a duchess; and, to say the truth, my liking for him was so extreme that it was distinguishing very nicely to deny that I loved him.

My happiness, however, with him did not last long, but found an end from my own imprudent neglect. After having taken even superfluous precautions against a discovery, our success in repeated meetings emboldened me to omit the barely necessary ones. About a month after our first intercourse, one fatal morning (the season Mr H— rarely or never visited me in) I was in my closet, where my toilet stood, in nothing but my shift, a bed-gown, and under-petticoat. Will was with me, and both ever too well disposed to balk an opportunity: for my part, a warm whim, a wanton toy had just taken me, and I had challenged my man to execute it on the spot, who hesitated not to comply with my humour. I was sat in the armchair, my shift and petticoat up, my thighs wide spread and mounted over the arms of the chair, presenting the fairest mark to Will's drawn weapon, which he stood in act to plunge into me, when, having neglected to secure the chamber door, and that of the closet standing ajar, Mr H— stole in upon us, before either of us was aware, and saw us precisely in these convicting attitudes.

I gave a great scream, and dropped my petticoat: the thunderstruck lad stood trembling and pale, waiting his sentence of death. Mr H— looked sometimes at one, sometimes at the other, with a mixture of indignation and scorn, and, without saying a word, spun upon his heel and went out.

As confused as I was, I heard him very distinctly turn the key and lock the chamber door upon us, so that there was no escape but through the dining room, where he himself was walking about with distempered strides, stamping in a great chase, and doubtless debating what he should do with us.

In the meantime, poor William was frightened out of his senses, and as much need as I had of spirits to support myself, I was obliged to employ them all to keep his a little up. The misfortune I had now brought upon him endeared him the more to me, and I could have joyfully suffered any punishment he had not shared in. I watered plentifully with my tears the face of the frightened youth, who sat, not having strength to stand, as cold and as lifeless as a statue.

Presently Mr H— comes in to us again, and made us go before him into the dining room, trembling and dreading the issue. Mr H— sat down on a chair, whilst we stood like criminals under examination, and, beginning with me, asked me with an even firm tone of voice, neither soft nor severe, but cruelly indifferent, what I could say for myself for having abused him in so unworthy a manner with his own servant, too, and how he had deserved this of me?

Without adding to the guilt of my infidelity that of an audacious defence of it, in the old style of a common kept Miss, my answer was modest and, often interrupted by my tears, in substance as follows: that I had never had a single thought of wronging him (which was true) till I had seen him taking the last liberties with my servant-wench, (here he coloured prodigiously) and that my resentment at that which I was over-awed from giving a vent to by complaints, or explanations with him, had driven me to a course that I did not pretend to justify; but that, as to the young man, he was entirely faultless, for that in the view of making him the instrument of my revenge, I had downright seduced him to what he had done, and therefore hoped, whatever he determined about me, he would distinguish between the guilty and the innocent; and, that, for the rest, I was entirely at his mercy.

Mr H—, on hearing what I said, hung his head a little; but instantly recovering himself, he said to me, as near as I can retain, to the following purpose:

'Madam, I take shame to myself and confess you have fairly turned the tables upon me. – It is not with one of your cast of breeding and sentiments that I should enter into a discussion of the very great difference of the provocations: be it sufficient that I allow you so much reason on your side as to have changed my resolutions, in consideration of what you reproach me with; and I own, too, that your clearing that rascal there is fair and honest in you; renew with you I cannot; the affront is too gross. I give you a week's warning to go out of these lodgings: whatever I have given you remains to you; and as I never intend to see you more, the landlord will pay you fifty pieces on my account, with which, and every debt paid, I hope you will own I do not leave you in a worse condition than what I took you up in, or than you deserve of me. – Blame yourself only that it is no better.'

Then, without giving me time to reply, he addressed himself to the young fellow.

'For you, spark, I shall for your father's sake take care of you: the town is no place for such an easy fool as thou art; and tomorrow you shall set out under the charge of one of my men, well recommended, in my name, to your father, not to let you return and be spoiled here.'

At these words he went out, after my vainly attempting to stop him by throwing myself at his feet: he took me off, though he seemed greatly moved, too, and took Will away with him, who, I dare swear, thought himself very cheaply off.

I was now once more adrift, and left upon my own hands by a gentleman whom I certainly did not deserve. And all the letters, arts, friends' entreaties that I employed within the week of grace in my lodging could never win on him so much as to see me again. He had irrevocably pronounced my doom, and submission to it was my only part. Soon after, he married a lady of birth and fortune, to whom I have heard he proved an irreproachable husband.

As for poor Will, he was immediately sent down to the country, to his father, who was an easy⁴² farmer, where he was not four months before an inn-keeper's buxom young widow, with a very good stock both in money and trade, fancied and, perhaps pre-acquainted with his secret excellencies, married him; and I am sure there was at least one good foundation for their living happily together.

Though I should have been charmed to see him before he went, such measures were taken by Mr H—'s orders that it was impossible; otherwise I should certainly have endeavoured to detain him in town, and would have spared neither offers nor expense to have procured myself the satisfaction of keeping him with me: he had such powerful holds upon my inclinations as were not easily to be shaken off or replaced; as to my heart, it was quite out of the question; glad, however, I was from my soul that nothing worse, and, as things turned out, probably nothing better, could have happened to him.

As to Mr H—, though views of conveniency made me at first exert myself to regain his affection, I was giddy and thoughtless enough to be much easier reconciled to my failure than I ought to have been; but as I never had loved him, and his leaving me gave me a sort of liberty that I had often longed for, I was soon comforted; and flattering myself that the stock of youth and beauty I was going into trade with could hardly fail of procuring me a maintenance, I saw myself under a necessity of trying my fortune with them, rather with pleasure and gaiety than with the least idea of despondence.

In the meantime, several of my acquaintance amongst the sisterhood, who had soon got wind of my misfortune, flocked to insult me with their malicious consolations: most of them had long envied me the affluence and splendour I had been maintained in; and though there was scarce one of them that did not at least deserve to be in my case, and would probably sooner or later come to it, it was equally easy to remark, even in their affected pity, their secret pleasure at seeing me thus disgraced and discarded, and their secret grief that it was still no worse with me. Unaccountable malice of the human heart! and which is not confined to the class of life they were of.

But as the time approached for me to come to some resolution how to dispose of myself, and I was considering round where to shift my quarters to, Mrs Cole,⁴³ a middle-aged discreet sort of woman, who had been brought into my acquaintance by one of the misses that visited me, upon learning my situation, came to offer her cordial advice and service to me; and as I had always taken to her more than to any of my female acquaintance, I listened the easier to her proposals; and as it happened, I could not have put myself into worse or into better hands in all London: into worse, because keeping a house of conveniency, there were no lengths in lewdness she would not advise me to go, in compliance with her customers, no schemes of pleasure, or even unbounded debauchery, she did not take even a delight in promoting; into better, because nobody having had more experience of the wicked part of the town than she had, was fitter to advise and guard one against the worst dangers of our profession; and what was rare to be met with in those of hers, she contented herself with a moderate living profit upon her industry and good offices and had nothing of their greedy rapacious turn. She was really too a gentlewoman born and bred, but through a train of accidents reduced to this course, which she pursued: partly through necessity, partly through choice, as never woman delighted more in encouraging a brisk circulation of the trade, for the sake of the trade itself, or better understood all the mysteries and refinements of it than she did; so that she was consummately at the top of her profession, and dealt only with customers of distinction; to answer the demands of whom she kept a competent number of her daughters in constant recruit: So she called those whom their youth and personal charms recommended to her adoption and management, several of whom, by her means and through her tuition and instructions, succeeded very well in the world.

This useful gentlewoman, upon whose protection I now threw myself, having her reasons of state, respecting Mr H——, for not appearing too much in the thing herself, sent a friend of hers, on the day appointed for my removal, to conduct me to my new lodgings at a brush-makers in R—— street, Covent-Garden, the very next door to her own house, where she had no conveniences to lodge me herself; lodgings that, by having been for several successions tenanted by ladies of pleasure, the landlord of them was familiarized to their ways; and provided the rent was duly paid, everything else was as easy and as commodious as one could desire.

The fifty guineas promised me by Mr H——, at his parting with me, having been duly paid me, all my clothes and movables chested up, which were at least of two hundred pounds' value, I had them conveyed into the coach, where I soon followed them, after taking a civil leave of the landlord and his family, with whom I had never lived in a degree of familiarity enough to regret the removal; but still, the very circumstance of its being a removal drew tears from me. I left, too, a letter of thanks for Mr H——, from whom I concluded myself, as I really was, irretrievably separated.

My maid I had discharged the day before, not only because I had her of Mr H——, but that I suspected her of having somehow or other been the occasion of his discovering me, in revenge, perhaps, for my not having trusted her in it.

We were soon got to my lodgings, which, though not so handsomely furnished nor so showy as those I left, were to the full as convenient, and at half price, though on the first floor. My trunks were safely landed and stowed in my apartments, where my neighbour and now gouvernante, Mrs Cole, was ready with my landlord to receive me, to whom she took care to set me out in the most favourable light, that of one from whom there was the clearest reason to expect the regular payment of his rent: all the cardinal virtues attributed to me would not have had half the weight of that recommendation alone.

I was now settled in lodgings of my own, abandoned to my own conduct, and turned loose upon the town, to sink or swim, as I could manage with the current of it: and what were the consequences, together with the number of adventures which befell me in the exercise of my new profession, will compose the matter of another letter; for, surely, it is high time to put a period to this.

I am,
MADAM,
    Yours, &c. &c. &c.
        * * * * * * *

MEMOIRS

OF A

WOMAN

OF

PLEASURE.

VOL. II.

LONDON:

Printed for G. Fenton in the *Strand*.
M.DCC.XLIX

*Overleaf is a facsimile of the title-page of the first edition
(reproduced by permission of the British Library)*

MADAM,

If I have delayed the sequel of my history, it has been purely to afford myself a little breathing time, not without some hopes that, instead of pressing me to a continuation, you would have acquitted me of the task of pursuing a confession, in the course of which my self-esteem has so many wounds to sustain.

I imagined, indeed, that you would have been cloyed and tired with the uniformity of adventures and expressions, inseparable from a subject of this sort, whose bottom or groundwork being, in the nature of things, eternally one and the same, whatever variety of forms and modes the situations are susceptible of, there is no escaping a repetition of near the same images, the same figures, the same expressions, with this further inconvenience added to the disgust it creates that the words *joys, ardours, transports, ecstasies,* and the rest of those pathetic terms so congenial to, so received in the *practice of pleasure,* flatten and lose much of their due spirit and energy by the frequency they indispensibly recur with, in a narrative of which that *practice* professedly composes the whole basis. I must therefore trust to the candour of your judgment for your allowing for the disadvantage I am necessarily under in that respect, and to your imagination and sensibility the pleasing task of repairing it by their supplements, where my descriptions flag or fail: the one will readily place the pictures I present before your eyes; the other give life to the colours where they are dull, or worn with too frequent handling.

What you say besides, by way of encouragement, concerning the extreme difficulty of continuing so long in one strain, in a mean tempered with taste, between the revoltingness of gross, rank, and vulgar expressions, and the ridicule of mincing metaphors and affected circumlocutions, is so sensible as well as good-natured that you greatly justify me to myself for my compliance with a curiosity that is to be satisfied so extremely at my expense.

*

Resuming now where I broke off in my last I am in my way to remark to you that it was late in the evening before I arrived at my new lodgings, and Mrs Cole, after helping me to range and secure my things, spent the whole evening with me in my apartment, where we supped together, in giving me the best advice and instruction with regard to this new stage of my profession I was now to enter upon, and passing thus from a private devotee to pleasure into a public one, to become a more general good, with all the advantages requisite to put my person out to use, either for interest or pleasure, or both. But then she observed, as I was a kind of new face upon the town, that it was an established rule, and mystery of trade, for me to pass for a maid and dispose of myself as such on the first good occasion, without prejudice, however, to such diversions as I might have a mind to the interim; for that nobody could be a greater enemy than she was to the losing of time. That she would, in the meantime, do her best to find out a proper person, and would undertake to manage this nice point for me, if I would accept of her aid and advice to such good purpose that, in the loss of a fictitious maiden-head, I should reap all the advantages of a native one.

As a great delicacy of sentiments did not extremely belong to my character at that time, I confess against myself that I perhaps too readily closed with a proposal which my candour and ingenuity gave me some repugnance to; but not enough to contradict the intention of one to whom I had now thoroughly abandoned the direction of all my steps. For Mrs Cole had, I do not know how, unless by one of those unaccountable invincible sympathies that nevertheless form the strongest links, especially of female friendship, won and got entire possession of me. On her side, she pretended that a strict resemblance she fancied she saw in me to an only daughter, whom she had lost at my age, was the first motive of her taking to me so affectionately as she did; it might be so: there exist as slender motives of attachments that gathering force from habit and liking, have proved often more solid and durable than those founded on much stronger reasons; but this I know, that, though I had had no other acquaintance with her than seeing her at my lodgings when I lived with Mr H——, where she had made errands to sell me some millinary ware, she had by degrees insinuated herself so far into my confidence that I threw myself blindly into her hands and came, at length, to regard, love, and obey her implicitly; and, to do her justice, I never experienced at her hands other than a sincerity of tenderness and care for my interest hardly heard of in those of her profession. We parted that night, after having settled a perfect unreserved agreement; and the next morning Mrs Cole came and took me with her to her house for the first time.

Here, at the first sight of things, I found everything breathe an air of decency, modesty, and order.

In the outer parlour, or rather shop, sat three young women, very demurely employed on millinary work, which was the cover of a traffic in more precious commodities: but three beautifuller creatures could hardly be seen. Two of them were extremely fair, the eldest not above nineteen, and the third, much about that age, was a piquant brunette whose black sparkling eyes and perfect harmony of features and shapes left her nothing to envy in her fairer companions. Their dress, too, had the more design in it, the less it appeared to have, being in a taste of uniform correct neatness and elegant simplicity. These were the girls that composed the small and domestic flock which my governess trained up with surprising order and management, considering the giddy wildness of young girls once got upon the loose. But then she never continued any in her house whom, after a due noviciate, she found untractable or unwilling to comply with the rules of it. Thus had she insensibly formed a little family of love, in which the members found so sensibly their account in a rare alliance of pleasure with interest, and of a necessary outward decency with unbounded secret liberty, that Mrs Cole, who had picked them as much for their temper as their beauty, governed them with ease to herself and them too.

To these pupils then of hers, whom she had prepared, she presented me as a new boarder, and one that was to be immediately admitted to all the intimacies of the house; upon which these charming girls gave me all the marks of a welcome reception, and indeed of being perfectly pleased with my figure, that I could possibly expect from any of my own sex; but they had been effectually brought to sacrifice all jealousy or competition of charms to a common interest and considered me as a partner that was bringing no despicable stock of goods into the trade of the house: they gathered round me, viewed me on all sides; and, as my admission into this joyous troop made a little holiday, the show of work was laid aside, and Mrs Cole, giving me up, with special recommendation, to their caresses and entertainment, went about her ordinary business of the house.

The sameness of our sex, age, profession, and views soon created as unreserved a freedom and intimacy as if we had been for years acquainted. They took and showed me the house, their respective apartments, which were furnished with every article of conveniency and luxury, and, above all, a spacious drawing room, where a select revelling band usually met in general parties of pleasure; the girls supping with their sparks, and acting their wanton pranks with unbounded licentiousness, whilst a defiance of awe, modesty, or jealousy were their standing rules, by which, according to the principles of their society, whatever pleasure was lost on the side of sentiment was abundantly made up to the senses in the poignancy of variety and the charms of ease and luxury. The authors and supporters of this secret institution would, in the height of their humour, style themselves the restorers of the liberty of the golden age and its simplicity of pleasures, before their innocence became so unjustly branded with the names of guilt and shame.

As soon then as the evening began, and the shew[44] of a shop was shut, the academy opened, the mask of mock-modesty was completely taken off, and all the girls delivered over to their respective calls of pleasure or interest with their men; and none of that sex were promiscuously admitted, but only such as Mrs Cole was previously satisfied of their character and discretion. In short, this was the safest, politest, and, at the same time, the most thorough house of accommodation in town, everything being conducted so that decency made no intrenchment[45] upon the most libertine pleasures, in the practice of which, too, the choice familiars of the house had found the secret so rare and difficult of reconciling even all the refinements of taste and delicacy with the most gross and determinate gratifications of sensuality.

After having consumed the morning in the endearments and instructions of my new acquaintance, we went to dinner, when Mrs Cole, presiding at the head of her cluck,[46] gave me the first idea of her management and address, in inspiring these lively amiable girls with so sensible a love and respect for her. There was no stiffness, no reserve, no airs of pique, or little jealousies, but all was unaffectedly gay, cheerful, and easy.

After dinner, Mrs Cole, seconded by the young ladies, acquainted me that there was a chapter[47] to be held that night in form, for the ceremony of my reception into the sisterhood, and in which, with all due reserve to my maidenhead that was to be occasionally cooked up for the first proper chapman, I was to undergo a ceremonial of initiation they were sure I should not be displeased with.[48]

Embarked as I was, and moreover captivated with the charms of my new companions, I was too much prejudiced in favour of any proposal they could make, to so much as hesitate an assent, which, therefore, readily giving, in the style of a *carte blanche*, I received fresh kisses of compliment from them all, in approval of my docility and good nature. Now I was a 'sweet girl –' I came into things 'with a good grace –' I was 'not affectedly coy –' I should be the 'pride of the house –' and the like.

This point thus adjusted, the young women left Mrs Cole to talk and concert matters with me, when she explained to me that I should be introduced that very evening to four of her best friends, one of whom she had, according to the custom of the house, favoured with the preference of engaging me in the first party of pleasure, assuring me at the same time that they were all young gentlemen agreeable in their persons, and unexceptionable in every respect; that, united and holding together by the band of common pleasures, they composed the chief support of her house, and made very liberal presents to the girls that pleased and humoured them, so that they were, properly speaking, the founders and patrons of this little seraglio. Not but that she had, at proper seasons, other customers to deal with, whom she stood less upon punctilio with than with these: for instance, it was not on one of them she could attempt to pass me for a maid; they were not only too knowing, too much town-bred to bite at such a bait, but they were such generous benefactors to her that it would be unpardonable to think of it.

Amidst all the flutter and emotion which this promise of pleasure, for such I conceived it, stirred up in me, I preserved so much of the woman as to feign just reluctance enough to make some merit of sacrificing it to the influence of my patroness, whom I likewise, still in character, reminded of it perhaps being right for me to go home and dress in favour of my first impressions.

But Mrs Cole, in opposition to this, assured me that the gentlemen I should be presented to were, by their rank and taste of things, infinitely superior to the being touched with any glare of dress or ornaments, such as silly women rather confound, and overlay, than set off their beauty with; that these veteran voluptuaries knew better than not to hold them in the highest contempt; they with whom the pure native

133

charms alone could pass current, and who would at any time leave a sallow, washy, painted duchess on her own hands, for a ruddy, healthy, firm-fleshed country maid; and as for my part, that nature had done enough for me to set me above owing the least favour to art; concluding withal, that for the instant occasion there was no dress like an undress.

I thought my governess too good a judge of these matters not to be easily overruled by her; after which she went on preaching very pathetically the doctrine of passive obedience and nonresistance to all those arbitrary tastes of pleasure which are by some styled the refinements, and by others the deprivations of it; between whom it was not the business of a simple girl, who was to profit by pleasing, to decide, but to conform.

Whilst I was edifying by these wholesome lessons, tea was brought in, and the young ladies, returning, joined company with us.

After a great deal of mixed chat, frolic, and humour, one of them, observing that there would be a good deal of time on hand before the assembly hour, proposed that each girl should entertain the company with that critical period of her personal history in which she first exchanged the maiden state for womanhood. The proposal was approved, with only one restriction of Mrs Cole, that she, on the account of her age, and I, on the account of my titular maidenhood, should be excused, at least till I had undergone the forms[49] of the house. This obtained me a dispensation, and the promotress of this amusement was desired to begin.[50]

Her name was Emily —, a girl fair to excess, and whose limbs were, if possible, too well made, since their plump fullness was rather to the prejudice of that delicate slimness of shape required by the nicer judges of beauty: her eyes were blue and streamed inexpressible sweetness, and nothing could be prettier than her mouth and lips, which closed over a range of the evenest, whitest teeth. Thus she began:

'Neither my extraction, nor the most critical adventure of my life, are sublime enough to impeach me of any vanity in the advancement of the proposal you have approved of. My father and mother were, and for aught I know, are still, farmers in the country, not above forty miles from town. Their barbarity to me, in favour of a son, on whom only they vouchsafed to bestow their tenderness, had a thousand times determined me to fly their house and throw myself on the wide world; but at length an accident forced me on this desperate step, at the age of fifteen. I had broken a china-bowl, the pride and idol of both their hearts, and as an unmerciful beating was the least I had to depend on at their hands, in the silliness and timidity of those tender years, I left the house, and, at all adventures, took the road to London. How my loss was resented I do not know, for till this instant I have not heard a syllable about them. My whole stock was two broadpieces[51] of my godmother's, a few shillings, silver shoe-buckles, and a thimble. Thus equipped, with no more clothes than the ordinary ones I had on my back, and frightened at every foot or noise I heard behind me, I hurried on and, I dare swear, walked a dozen miles before I stopped through mere weariness and fatigue. I sat down on a stile,[52] where I wept bitterly, and yet was still rather under increased impressions of fear on the account of my escape; which made me dread, worse than death, the going back to face my unnatural parents. Refreshed by this little repose, and relieved by my tears, I was proceeding onward, when I was overtaken by a sturdy country lad who was going to London to see what he could do for himself there, and, like me, had given his friends the slip. He could not be above seventeen, was ruddy, well featured enough, with uncombed flaxen hair, a little flapped hat, a kersey frock,[53] yarn stockings; in short, a perfect ploughboy. I saw him come whistling behind me, with a bundle tied to the end of a stick: his travelling equipage. We walked by one another for some time without speaking, at length we joined company and agreed to keep together till we got to our journey's end. What his designs or ideas were, I know not; the innocence of mine I can solemnly protest. As night drew on, it became us to look out for some inn, or shelter; to which perplexity another was added, and that was, what we should say for ourselves, if we were questioned. After some puzzle, the young fellow started a proposal, which I thought the finest that could be; and what was that? Why, that we should pass for husband and wife; I never once dreamed of consequences. We came presently, after having agreed on this notable expedient, to one of those hedge-accommodations[54] for foot-passengers, at the door of which stood an old crazy beldam, who, seeing us trudge by, invited us to lodge there. Glad of any cover, we went in, and my fellow-traveller taking all upon him, called for what the house afforded, and we supped together as man and wife, which, considering our figures and ages, could not have passed on anyone, but such as anything could pass on. But when bedtime came on, we had neither of us the courage to contradict our first account of ourselves;

and what was extremely pleasant, the young lad seemed as perplexed as I was, how to evade the lying together, which was so natural for the state we had pretended to. Whilst we were in this quandary, the landlady takes the candle and lights us to our apartment, through a long yard, at the end of which it stood, separate from the body of the house. Thus we suffered ourselves to be conducted without saying a word in opposition to it, and there, in a wretched room, with a bed answerable,[55] we were left to pass the night together, as a thing quite in course. For my part, I was so incredibly innocent, as not even then to think much more harm of going into bed with the young man than with one of our dairy-wenches; nor had he perhaps any other notions than those of innocence, till such a fair occasion put them into his head. Before either of us undressed, however, he put out the candle; and the bitterness of the weather made it a kind of necessity for me to get into bed. Slipping then my clothes off, I crept under the bedclothes, where I found the young stripling already nestled, and the touch of his warm flesh rather pleased than alarmed me. I was indeed too much disturbed with the novelty of my condition to be able to sleep; but then I had not the least thought of harm. But oh! how powerful are the instincts of nature, and how little is there wanting to set them in action! The young man, sliding his arm under my body, drew me gently towards him, as if to keep himself and me warmer; and the heat I felt from joining our breasts kindled another that I had hitherto never felt and was even then a stranger to the nature of. Emboldened, I suppose, by my easiness, he ventured to kiss me, and I insensibly returned it, without knowing the consequence of returning it: for on this encouragement, he slipped his hand all down from my breast to that part of me where the sense of feeling is so exquisitely critical, as I then experienced by its instant taking fire upon the touch and glowing with a strange tickling heat. There he pleased himself and me by feeling, till, growing a little too bold, he hurt me and made me complain; then he took my hand, which he guided, not unwillingly on my side, between the twist of his closed thighs, which were extremely warm; there he lodged and pressed it, till raising it by degrees, he made me feel the proud distinction of his sex from mine. I was frightened at the novelty, and drew back my hand; yet pressed and spurred on by sensations of a strange pleasure, I could not help asking him what that was for. He told me he would show me if I would let him; and without waiting for my answer, which he prevented by stopping my mouth with kisses I was far from disrelishing, he got atop of me, and inserting one of his thighs between mine, opened them so as to make way for himself and fixed me to his purpose; whilst I was so much out of my usual sense, so subdued by the present power of a new one that, between fear and desire, I lay utterly passive, till the piercing pain roused and made me cry out: but it was too late; he was too firm fixed in the saddle for me to compass[56] flinging him, with all the struggles I could use, some of which only served to further his point, and at length an omnipotent thrust murdered at once my maidenhead and almost me: I now lay a bleeding witness of the necessity imposed on our sex, to gather the first honey off the thorns.

But the pleasure rising, as the pain subsided, I was soon reconciled to fresh trials, and before morning, nothing on earth could be dearer to me than this rifler of my virgin sweets. He was everything to me now. How we agreed to join fortunes, how we came up to town together, where we lived some time, till necessity parted us and drove me into this course of life, in which I had been long ago battered and torn to pieces before I came to this age, as much through my easiness as through my inclination, had it not been for my finding refuge in this house; these are all circumstances which pass the mark I proposed, so that here my narrative ends.'

In the order of our sitting, it was Harriet's turn to go on. Amongst all the beauties of our sex that I had before or have since seen, few indeed were the forms that could dispute excellence with hers; it was not delicate, but delicacy itself incarnate. Such was the symmetry of her small but exactly fashioned limbs. Her complexion, fair as it was, appeared yet more fair from the effect of two black eyes, the brilliancy of which gave her face more vivacity than belonged to the colour of it, which was only defended from paleness by a sweetly pleasing blush in her cheeks, that grew fainter and fainter, till at length it died away insensibly into the overbearing white. Then her miniature features joined to finish the extreme sweetness of it, which was not belied by that of a temper turned to indolence, languor, and the pleasures of love. Pressed to subscribe her contingent,[57] she smiled, blushed a little, and thus complied with our desires:

'My father was neither better nor worse than a miller, near the city of York; but both he and my mother dying whilst I was an infant, I fell under the care of a widow and childless aunt, housekeeper to my lord N—, at his seat in the county of —, where she brought me up with all imaginable tenderness. I was not seventeen, as I am not now eighteen, before I had, on the account of my person purely (for fortune I had notoriously none), several advantageous proposals; but whether nature was slow in making me sensible of her favourite passion, or that I had not seen any of the other sex who had stirred up the least emotion or curiosity to be better acquainted with it, I had till that age preserved a perfect innocence even of thought, whilst my fears of I did not well know what made me no more desirous of marrying than of dying. My aunt, good woman, favoured my timorousness, which she looked on as a childish affection that her own experience might probably assure her would wear off in time, and gave my suiters proper answers for me.

The family had not been down at this seat for years, so that it was neglected and committed entirely to my aunt and two more old domestics to take care of it.

Thus I had the full range of a spacious lonely house, and gardens, situated at above half a mile's distance from any other habitation, except perhaps a straggling cottage or so.

Here, in tranquility and innocence, I grew up, without any memorable accident, till, one fatal day, I had, as I had often done before, left my aunt fast asleep and secure for some hours, after dinner; and resorting to a kind of ancient summer-house at some distance from the house, I carried my work with me and sat over a rivulet, which its door and window faced upon. Here I fell into a gentle breathing slumber, which stole upon my senses as they fainted under the excessive heat of the season at that hour. A cane couch, with my work-basket for a pillow, were all the conveniences of my short repose, for I was soon waked and alarmed by a flounce and noise of splashing in the water. I got up to see what was the matter; and what indeed should it be but the son of a neighbouring gentleman, as I afterwards found (for I had never seen him before), who had strayed that way with his gun, and heated by his sport and the sultriness of the day, had been tempted by the freshness of the clear stream, so that presently stripping, he jumped into it on the other side which bordered on a wood, some trees whereof, inclined down to the water, formed a pleasing, shady recess, commodious to undress and leave his clothes under.

My first emotions, at the sight of this youth naked in the water, were, with all imaginable respect to truth, those of surprise and fear; and in course I should immediately have run out, had not my modesty, fatally for itself, interposed the objection of the door and window being so situated that it was scarce possible to get out and make my way along the bank to the house without his seeing me: which I could not bear the thought of, so much ashamed and confounded was I at having seen him. Condemned then to stay till his departure should release me, I was greatly embarrassed how to dispose of myself. I kept some time, betwixt terror and modesty, even from looking through the window, which being an old-fashioned casement, without any light behind me, could hardly betray anyone's being there to him from within; then the door was so secure that without violence, or my own consent, there was no opening it from without.

But now, by my own experience, I found it too true that objects which afright us, when we cannot get from them, draw our eyes as forcibly as those that please us. I could not long withstand that nameless impulse which, without any desire of this novel sight, compelled me towards it: emboldened, too, by my certainty of being at once unseen and safe, I ventured by degrees to cast my eyes on an object so terrible and alarming to my virgin modesty as a naked man. But as I snatched a look, the first gleam that struck me, was, in general, the dewy lustre of the whitest skin imaginable, which the sun playing upon, made the reflection of it perfectly beamy. His face, in the confusion I was in, I could not well distinguish the lineaments of any farther than that there was a great deal of youth and freshness in it. The frolic and various play of all his fine polished limbs, as they appeared above the surface in the course of his swimming or wantoning with the water, amused and insensibly delighted me: sometimes he lay motionless on his back, water-borne, and dragging after him a fine head of hair, that, floating, swept the stream in a bush of black curls. Then the overflowing water would make a separation between his breast and glossy white belly, at the bottom of which I could not escape observing so remarkable a distinction as a black mossy tuft, out of which appeared to emerge a round, softish, limber, white something, that played every way, with every the least motion or whirling eddy. I cannot say but that part chiefly, by a kind of natural instinct, attracted, detained, captivated my attention: it was out of the power of all my modesty to command my eye away from it, and seeing nothing so very dreadful in its appearance, I sensibly looked away all my fears; but as fast as they gave way, new desires and strange wishes took place, and I melted as I gazed. The fire of nature, that had so long lain dormant or concealed, began to break out and make me feel for my sex for the first time. He had now changed his posture and swam prone on his belly, striking out with his legs and arms, finer modelled than which could not have been cast, whilst his floating locks played over a neck and shoulders whose whiteness they delightfully set off. Then the luxuriant swell of flesh that rose from the small of his back, and terminated its double cope at where the thighs are sent off, perfectly dazzled one with its watery glistening gloss.

By this time I was so affected by this inward revolution of sentiments, so softened by this sight, that now, betrayed into a sudden transition from extreme fears to extreme desires, I found these last so strong upon me, the heat of the weather, too, perhaps conspiring to exalt their rage, that nature almost fainted under them. Not that I so much as knew precisely what was wanting to me; my only thought was that so sweet a creature as this youth seemed to me could only make me happy; but then the little likelihood there was of compassing an acquaintance with him, or perhaps of ever seeing him again, dashed my desires and turned them into torments. I was still gazing with all the powers of my sight on this bewitching object, when, in an instant, down he went. I had heard of such things as a cramp seizing on even the best swimmers and occasioning their being drowned; and imagining this so sudden eclipse to be owing to it, the inconceivable fondness this unknown had given birth to distracted me with the most killing terrors, insomuch that, my concern giving me wings, I flew to the door, opened it, ran down to the banks of the canal, guided thither by the madness of my fears for him and the intense desire of being an instrument to save him, though I was ignorant how or by what means to effect it; but was it for fear, and a passion so sudden as mine, to reason? All this took up scarce the space of a few moments. I had then just life enough to reach the green borders of the water-piece, where wildly looking round for the young man and missing him still, my fright and concern sunk me down in a deep swoon, which must have lasted me some time; for I did not come to myself till I was roused out of it by a sense of pain that pierced me to the vitals, and waked me to the most surprising circumstance of finding myself not only in the arms of this very same young gentleman I had been so solicitous to save, but taken at such an advantage in my unresisting condition that he had actually completed his entrance into my body so far that, weakened as I was by all the preceding conflicts of mind I had suffered, and struck dumb by the violence of my surprise, I had neither the power to cry out, nor the strength to disengage myself from his strenuous embraces, before, urging his point, he had forced his way into me and completely triumphed over my virginity, as he might now as well see by the streams of blood that followed his drawing out, as he had felt by the difficulties he had met with in consummating his penetration. But the sight of the blood, and the sense of my condition had (as he told me afterwards), since the ungovernable rage of his passion was somewhat appeased, now wrought so far on him that at all risks, even of the worst consequences, he could not find in his heart to leave me and make off, which he might easily have done. I still lay all discomposed in bleeding ruin, palpitating, speechless, unable to get off, and frightened and fluttering like a poor wounded partridge, and ready to faint away again at the sense of what had befallen me. The young gentleman was by me, kneeling, kissing my hand, and with tears in his eyes, beseeching me to forgive him and offering all the reparation in his power. It is certain that could I, at the instant of regaining my senses, have called out, or taken the bloodiest revenge, I would not have stuck at it: the violation was attended too with such aggravating circumstances! though he was ignorant of them, since it was to my concern for the preservation of his life that I owed my ruin.

But how quick is the shift of passions from one extreme to another! And how little are they acquainted with the human heart who dispute it! I could not see this amiable criminal, so suddenly the first object of my love and as suddenly of my just hate, on his knees, bedewing my hand with his tears, without relenting. He was still stark naked, but my modesty had been already too much wounded in essentials to be so much shocked as I should have otherwise been with appearances only; in short, my anger ebbed so fast, and the tide of love returned so strong upon me that I felt it a point of my own happiness to forgive him: the reproaches I made him were murmured in so soft a tone, my eyes met his with such glances, expressing more languor than resentment, that he could not but presume his forgiveness was at no desperate distance: but still he would not quit his posture of submission, till I had pronounced his pardon in form; which, after the most fervent entreaties, protestations, and promises, I had not the power to withhold.

On which, with the utmost marks of a fear of again offending, he ventured to kiss my lips, which I neither declined or resented: but on my mild expostulations with him upon the barbarity of his treatment, he explained the mystery of my ruin, if not entirely to the clearance, at least much to the alleviation of his guilt, in the eyes of a judge so partial in his favour as I was grown. It seems that the circumstance of his going down or sinking, which in my extreme ignorance I had mistaken for something very fatal, was no other than a trick of diving, which I had not ever heard or at least attended to the mention of; and he was so long-breathed at it that in the few moments in which I ran out to save him he had not yet emerged before I fell into the swoon, in which, as he rose, seeing me extended on the bank, his first idea was that some young woman was upon some design of frolic or diversion with him, for he knew I could not have fallen asleep there without his having seen me before; agreeable to which notion he had ventured to approach, and finding me without sign of life, and still perplexed as he was what to think of the adventure, he took me in his arms at all hazards and carried me into the summer-house, of which he observed the door open: there he laid me down on the couch and tried, as he protested in good faith, by several means to bring me to myself again, till fired, as he said beyond all bearing, by the sight and touch of several parts of me which were unguardedly exposed to him, he could no longer govern his passion; and the less, as he was not quite sure that his first idea of this swoon being a feint, was not the very truth of the case: seduced then by this flattering notion, and overcome by the present, as he styled them, super-humane temptations, combined with the solitude and seeming security of the attempt, he was not enough his own master not to make it. Leaving me then just only whilst he fastened the door, he returned with redoubled eagerness to his prey, when, finding me still entranced, he ventured to place me as he pleased, whilst I felt, no more than the dead, what he was about, till the pain he put me to, roused me just time enough to be witness of a triumph I was not able to defeat and now scarce regretted: for, as he talked, the tone of his voice sounded, methought, so sweetly in my ears, the sensible nearness of so new and interesting an object to me wrought so powerfully upon me that, in the rising perception of things in a new and pleasing light, I lost all sense of the past injury. The young gentleman soon discerned the symptoms of a reconciliation in my softened looks, and hastening to receive the seal of it from my lips, pressed them tenderly to pass his pardon in the return of a kiss so melting fiery that the impression of it being carried to my heart, and thence to my new-discovered sphere of Venus, I was melted into a softness that could refuse him nothing. When now he managed his caresses and endearments so artfully as to insinuate the most soothing consolations for the past pain and the most pleasing expectations of future pleasure, but whilst mere modesty kept my eyes from seeking his and rather declined them, I had a glimpse of that instrument of the mischief which was now, obviously even to me who had scarce had snatches of a comparative observation of it, resuming its capacity to renew it and grew greatly alarming with its increase of size, as he bore it no doubt designedly, hard and stiff, against one of my hands carelessly dropped; but then he employed such tender prefacing, such winning progressions, that my returning passion of desire being now so strongly prompted by the engaging circumstances of the sight and incendiary touch of his naked glowing beauties I yielded at length to the force of the present impressions, and he obtained of my tacit blushing consent all the gratifications of pleasure left in the power of my poor person to bestow, after he had cropped its richest flower, during my suspension of life and abilities to guard it.

Here, according to the rule laid down, I should stop; but I am so much in motion that I could not if I would. I shall only add, however, that I got home without the least discovery or suspicion of what had happened. I met my young ravisher several times after, whom I now passionately loved and who, though not of age to claim a small but independent fortune, would have married me; but as the accidents that prevented it, and their consequences which threw me on the public, contain matter too moving and serious to introduce at present, I cut short here.'

Louisa, the brunette whom I mentioned at first, now took her turn to treat the company with her history. I have already hinted to you the graces of her person, than which nothing could be more exquisitely touching; I repeat touching, as a just distinction from striking, which is ever a less lasting effect and more generally belongs to the fair complexions; but leaving that decision to everyone's taste, I proceed to give you Louisa's narrative, as follows.

'According to my practical maxims of life, I ought to boast of my birth, since I owe it to pure love, without marriage; but this I know, it was scarce possible to inherit a stronger propensity to that cause of my being than I did: I was the rare production of the first essay of a journey-man cabinet-maker on his master's maid: the consequence of which was a big belly, and the loss of her place. He was not in circumstances to do much for her; and yet, after all this blemish, she found means, after she had dropped her burden and disposed of me at a poor relation's in the country, to repair it by marrying a pastry cook here in London, in thriving business, on whom she soon, under favour of the complete ascendant he had given her over him, passed me for a child she had by her first husband. I had, on that footing, been taken home and was not six years old when this stepfather died and left my mother in tolerable circumstances and without any children by him. As to my natural father, he had betaken himself to the sea, where, when the truth of things came out, I was told that he died, not immensely rich you may think, since he was no more than a common sailor. As I grew up, under the eye of my mother who kept on the business, I could not but see in her severe watchfulness the marks of a slip which she did not care should be hereditary; but we no more choose our passions than our features or complexion, and the bent of mine was so strong to the forbidden pleasure that it got the better, at length, of all her care and precaution. I was scarce twelve years old before that part of me which she wanted so much to keep out of harm's way made me feel its impatience to be taken notice of and come into play: already had it put forth the signs of forwardness in the sprout of a soft down over it, which had often flattered, and I might also say, grown under my constant touch and visitation; so pleased was I with what I took to be a kind of title to womanhood, that state I pined to be entered of, for the pleasures I conceived were annexed to it; and now the growing importance of that part of me, and the new sensations in it, demolished at once all my girlish playthings and amusements: nature now pointed me strongly to more solid diversions, while all the stings of desire settled so fiercely in that little centre of them that I could not mistake the spot I wanted a playfellow in.

I now shunned all company in which there was no hopes of coming at the object of my longings, and used to shut myself up to indulge in solitude some tender meditation on the pleasures I strongly perceived the overture of, in feeling and examining what nature assured me must be the chosen avenue, the gates for the unknown bliss to enter at, that I panted after.

But these meditations only increased my disorder and blew the fire that consumed me. It was yet worse when yielding at length to the insupportable irritations of the little fairy charm that tormented me; I searched it with my fingers, teasing it to no end. Sometimes, in the furious excitations of desire, I threw myself on my bed, spread my thighs abroad, and lay, as it were, expecting the longed-for relief, till finding my illusion, I shut and squeezed them together again, burning and fretting. In short, this devilish thing, with its impetuous girds[58] and itching fires, led me such a life that I could neither, night or day, be at peace with it or myself. In time, however, I thought I had gained a prodigious prize, when figuring to myself that my fingers were something of the shape of what I pined for, I worked my way in for one of them with great agitation and delight; yet not without pain, too, did I deflower myself as far as it could reach; proceeding with such a fury of passion, in this solitary and last shift of pleasure, as extended me at length breathless on the bed in an amorous melting trance.

But frequency of use dulling the sensation, I soon began to perceive that this finger-work was but a paltry shallow expedient that went but a little way to relieve me, and rather raised more flame than its dry insignificant titillation could rightly appease.

Man alone, I almost instinctively knew, as well as by what I had industriously picked up at weddings and christenings, was possessed of the only very remedy that could reduce this rebellious disorder; but watched, and overlooked as I was, how to come at it was the point, and that, to all appearance, an invincible one: not that I did not rack my brains and invention how at once to elude my mother's vigilance and procure myself the satisfaction of my impetuous curiosity and longings for this mighty and untasted pleasure. At length, however, a singular chance did at once the work of a long course of alertness. One day that we had dined at an acquaintance's over the way, together with a gentlewoman-lodger that occupied the first floor of our house, there started an indispensible necessity for my mother's going down to Greenwich to accompany her: the party was settled, when I do not know what genius whispered me to plead a headache, that I certainly had not, against my being included in a jaunt that I had not the least relish for; the pretext however passed, and my mother, with much reluctance, prevailed with herself to go without me, but took particular care to see me safe home, where she consigned me into the hands of an old trusty maid-servant who served in the shop, for we had not a male creature in the house.

As soon as she was gone, I told the maid I would go up and lie down on our lodger's bed, mine not being made, with a charge to her at the same time not to disturb me, as it was only rest I wanted. This injunction probably proved of eminent service to me. As soon as I got into the bed-chamber I unlaced my stays and threw myself on the outside of the bedclothes in all the loosest undress. Here I gave myself up to the old insipid privy shifts of self-viewing, self-touching, self-enjoying, in fine, to all the means of self-knowledge I could devise, in search of the pleasure that fled before me and tantalized me with that unknown something that was out of my reach; thus all only served to inflame myself, and to provoke violently my desires, whilst the one thing needful to their satisfaction was not at hand, and I could have bitten my fingers for representing it so ill. After then wearying and fatiguing myself with grasping of shadows, whilst that more sensible part of me disdained to content itself with less than realities, the strong yearnings, the urgent struggles of nature towards the melting relief, and the extreme self-agitations I had used to come at it had wearied and thrown me into a kind of unquiet sleep, for if I tossed and threw about my limbs in proportion to the distraction of my dreams, as I had reason to believe I did, a bystander could not have helped seeing all for love.⁵⁹ And one there was, it seems; for waking out of my very short slumber, I found my hand locked in that of a young man, who was kneeling at my bedside and begging my pardon for his boldness, but that, being son to the lady to whom this bed-chamber, he knew, belonged, he had slipped by the servant of the shop, as he supposed, unperceived, when, finding me asleep, his first ideas were to withdraw; but that he had been fixed and detained there by a power he could better account for than resist. What shall I say? My emotions of fear and surprise were instantly subdued by those of the pleasure I bespoke in great presence of mind from the turn this adventure might take: he seemed to me no other than a pitying angel, dropped out of the clouds; for he was young and perfectly handsome, which was more than even I had asked for, *Man*, in general, being all that my utmost desires had pointed at. I thought then I could not put too much encouragement into my eyes and voice; I regretted no leading advances, no matter for his after-opinion of my forwardness, so it might bring him to the point of answering my pressing demands of present ease. It was not now with his thoughts, but his actions, that my business immediately lay. I raised then my head and told him in a soft tone that tended to prescribe the same key to him that his mama was gone out and would not return till late at night; which I thought no bad hint. But, as it proved, I had nothing of a novice to deal with: the impressions I had made on him, from the discoveries I had betrayed of my person in the disordered motions of it during his view of me asleep had, as he afterwards told me, so fixed and charmingly prepared him that, had I known his dispositions, I had more to hope for from his violence than to fear from his respect. And even less than the extreme tenderness which I threw into my voice and eyes would have served to encourage him to make the most of the opportunity. Finding then that his kisses imprinted on my hand were taken as tamely as he could wish, he rose to my lips, and glueing his to them, made me so faint with over-coming joy and pleasure that I fell back, and he with me, in course, on the bed, upon which I had, by insensibly shifting from the side to near the middle, invitingly made room for him. He is now lain down by me, and the minutes being too precious to consume in untimely ceremony or dalliance, my youth proceeds immediately to those extremities which all my looks, flushings, and palpitations had assured him he might attempt without the fear of repulse. Those rogues, the men, read us admirably on these occasions! I lay then, at length, panting for the imminent attack, with wishes far beyond my fears, and for which it was scarce possible for a girl barely thirteen, but tall and well grown, to have better dispositions. He threw up my petticoat and shift, whilst my thighs were by an instinct of nature unfolded to their best; and my desires had so thoroughly destroyed all modesty in me that even their being now naked and all laid open to him was part of the prelude that pleasure deepened my blushes at, more than shame. But when his hand and touches, naturally attracted to their center, made me feel all their wantonness and warmth in and round it, oh! how immensely different a sense of things did I perceive there than when under my own insipid handling. And now his waistcoat was unbuttoned, and the confinement of the breeches burst through, when out started to view the amazing, pleasing object of all my wishes, all my dreams, all my

147

love, the king-member indeed! I gazed at, I devoured it, length and breadth with my eyes intently directed to it, till his getting upon me and placing it between my thighs took from me the enjoyment of its sight to give me a far more grateful one in its touch, in that part, where its touch is so exquisitely affecting: applying it then to the minute opening, for such at that age it certainly was, I met with too much good will, I felt with too great a rapture of pleasure the first insertion of it to heed much the pain that followed. I thought nothing too dear to pay for this the richest treat of the senses, so that, split up, torn, bleeding, mangled, I was still superiorly pleased and hugged the author of all this delicious ruin; but when soon after he made his second attack, sore and red-raw as everything was, the smart was soon put away by the sovereign cordial; all my soft complainings were silenced, and the pain melting fast away into pleasure, I abandoned myself over to all its transports, and gave it the full possession of my whole body and soul. For now all thought was at an end with me; I lived but in what I felt only: and who could describe those feelings, those agitations, yet exalted by the charm of their novelty and surprise? When that part of me which had so long hungered and thirsted for the dear morsel that now so delightfully crammed it, forced all my vital sensations to fix their home there, during the stay of my new and beloved guest, who too soon paid me for his hearty welcome in a dissolvent, far richer than that I have heard of some queen treating her paramour with, in liquefied pearl, and ravishingly poured into me where, now myself too much melted to give it a dry reception, I hailed it with the warmest confluence of sweets on my side, amidst all those ecstatic raptures not unfamiliar, I presume, to this good company. Thus, however, I arrived at the very top of all my wishes by an accident unexpected indeed, but not so wonderful; for this young gentleman was just arrived in town from college, and came familiarly to his mother at her apartment, where he had once before been, though, by mere chance, I had not seen him, so that we knew one another by hearsay only. And finding me stretched on his mother's bed, he readily concluded, from her description, who it was. The rest you know. This affair had however no ruinous consequences, the young gentleman escaping then, and many more times, undiscovered. But the warmth of my constitution, that made the pleasures of love a kind of necessary of life to me, having betrayed me into indiscretions fatal to my private fortune, I fell at length to the public, from which, it is probable, I might have met with the worst of ruin, if my better fate had not thrown me into this safe and agreeable refuge.'

Here Louisa ended; and these little histories having brought the time for the girls to retire and to prepare for the revels of the evening, I staid with Mrs Cole till Emily came and told us the company was met, and waited for us.

Mrs Cole on this, taking me by the hand, with a smile of encouragement, led me upstairs, preceded by Louisa, who was come to hasten us, and lighted us with two candles, one in each hand.

On the landing place of the first pair of stairs we were met by a young gentleman, extremely well dressed, and a very pretty figure, to whom I was to be indebted for the first essay of the pleasures of the house. He saluted me with great gallantry and handed me into the drawing room, the floor of which was over-spread with a Turkey-carpet, and all its furniture voluptuously adapted to every demand of the most studied luxury. Now too it was, by means of a profuse illumination, enlivened by a light scarce inferior to, and perhaps more favourable to joy, more tenderly pleasing than that of broad sunshine.

On my entrance into the room, I had the satisfaction to hear a buzz of approbation run through the whole company, which now consisted of four gentlemen, including my particular (this was the cant term of the house for one's gallant for the time), the three young women, in a neat flowing dishabille, the mistress of the academy, and myself. I was welcomed and saluted by a kiss all round, in which, however, it was easy to discover, in the superior warmth of that of the men, the distinction of the sexes.

Awed and confounded as I was at seeing myself surrounded, caressed, and made court to by so many strangers, I could not immediately familiarize myself to all that air of gaiety and joy, which dictated their compliments and animated their caresses. They assured me that I was so perfectly their taste as to have but one fault against me, which I might easily be cured of; and that was my modesty: this, they observed, might pass for a beauty the more with those who wanted it for a heightener; but their maxim was that it was an impertinent mixture, and dashed the cup so as to spoil the sincere draught of pleasure. They considered it accordingly as their mortal enemy, and gave it no quarter wherever they met with it; this was a prologue not unworthy of the revels that ensued.

In the midst of all the frolic and wantonnesses, which this joyous band had presently and all naturally run into, an elegant supper was served in, and we sat down to it, my spark elect placing himself next to me, and the other couples without order or ceremony. The delicate cheer and good wine soon banished all reserve; the conversation grew as lively as could be wished, without taking too loose a turn. These professors of pleasure knew too well to stale the impressions of it, or evaporate the imagination in words, before the time of action. Kisses, however, were snatched at times, or where a handkerchief round the neck interposed its feeble barrier, it was not extremely respected: the hands of the men went to work with their usual petulance, till the provocations on both sides rose to such a pitch that my particular's proposal for beginning the country dances was received with instant assent: for, as he laughingly added, he fancied the instruments were in tune. This was a signal for preparation that the complaisant Mrs Cole, who understood life, took for her cue of disappearing; no longer so fit for personal service herself, and content with having settled the order of battle, she left us the field to fight it out at discretion.

As soon as she was gone, the table was removed from the middle and became a sideboard; a couch was brought into its place, of which when I whisperingly inquired the reason, of my particular, he told me that as it was chiefly on my account that this convention was met, the parties intended at once to humour their taste of variety in pleasures, and by an open public enjoyment, to see me broken of any taint of reserve or modesty, which they looked on as the poison of joy; that though they occasionally preached pleasure, and lived up to the text, they did not enthusiastically set up for its missionaries, and only indulged themselves in the delights of a practical instruction of all the pretty women they liked well enough to bestow it upon, and fell properly in the way of it; but that as such a proposal might be too violent, too shocking for a young beginner, the older standers were to set an example, which he hoped I would not be averse to follow, since it was to him I was devolved in favour of the first experiment; but that still I was perfectly at my liberty to refuse the party, which being in its nature one of pleasure, supposed an exclusion of all force or constraint.

My countenance expressed, no doubt, my surprise, as my silence did my acquiescence. I was now embarked and thoroughly determined on any voyage the company would take me on.

The first that stood up to open the ball were a cornet of horse[60] and that sweetest of olive-beauties, the soft and amorous Louisa. He led her to the couch, 'nothing loth', on which he gave her the fall and extended her at her length with an air of roughness and vigour, relishing high of amourous eagerness and impatience. The girl, spreading herself to the best advantage, with her head upon the pillow, was so concentered in what she was about that our presence seemed the least of her care or concern. Her petticoats, thrown up with her shift, discovered to the company the finest turned legs and thighs that could be imagined, and in a broad display that gave us a full view of that delicious cleft of flesh into which the pleasingly hair-grown mount over it parted and presented a most inviting entrance, between two close ledges, delicately soft and pouting. Her gallant was now ready, having disencumbered himself from his clothes, overloaded with lace, and presently, his shirt removed, shewed us his forces in high plight,[61] bandied[62] and ready for action. But giving us no time to consider dimensions, and proving the stiffness of his weapon by his impatience of delay, he threw himself instantly over his charming antagonist, who received him as he pushed at once dead at mark, like a heroine, without flinching, for surely never was girl constitutionally truer to the taste of joy, or sincerer in the expressions of its sensations, than she was: we could observe the pleasure lighten in her eyes as he introduced his plenipotentiary instrument into her, till at length, having indulged her its utmost reach, its irritations grew so violent, and gave her the spurs so furiously that, collected within herself, and lost to everything but the enjoyment of her favourite feelings, she retorted his thrusts with a just concert of springy heaves, keeping time so exactly with the most pathetic sighs that one might have numbered the strokes in agitation by their distinct murmurs, whilst her active limbs kept wreathing and intertwisting with his in convulsive folds. Then the turtle-billing kisses, and the poignant painless love-bites, which they both exchanged in a rage of delight, all conspiring towards the melting period, it soon came on, when Louisa, in the ravings of her pleasure-frenzy, impotent of all restraint, cried out: 'Oh Sir! – Good Sir! – pray do not spare me! ah! ah! – I can no more.' And all her accents now faultering into heart-fetched sighs, she closed her eyes in the sweet death, in the instant of which she was deliciously embalmed by an injection, of which we could easily see the signs in the quiet, dying, languid posture of her late so furious driver, who was stopped of a sudden, breathing short, panting, and, for that time, giving up the spirit of pleasure.

As soon as he was dismounted, Louisa sprang up, shook her petticoats, and running up to me, gave me a kiss and drew me to the sideboard, to which she was herself handed by her gallant, where they made me pledge them in a glass of wine, and toast a droll health of Louisa's proposal in high frolic: that of 'the miraculous thing which wets where it tickles, and tickles where it wets'.

By this time the second couple was ready to enter the lists, which were a young baronet and that delicatest of charmers, the winning tender Harriet. My gentle esquire came to acquaint me with it, and brought me back to the scene of action.

And surely, never did one of her profession accompany her dispositions for the bare-faced part she was engaged to play with such a peculiar grace of sweetness, modesty, and yielding coyness, as she did. All her air and motions breathed only unreserved, unlimited complaisance, without the least mixture of impudence or prostitution. But, what was yet more surprising, her spark elect, in the midst of the dissolution of a public open enjoyment, doted on her to distraction, and had, by dint of love and sentiments, touched her heart, though for a while the restraint of their engagement to the house laid him under a kind of necessity of complying with an institution which he himself had had the greatest share in establishing.

Harriet then was led to the vacant couch by her gallant, blushing as she looked at me, and with eyes made to justify anything, tenderly bespeaking of me the most favourable construction of the step she was thus irresistibly drawn into.

Her lover, for such he was, sat her down at the foot of the couch, and passing his arms round her neck, preluded with a kiss fervently applied to her lips, that visibly gave her life and spirit to go through with the scene. And as he kissed, he gently inclined his head, till it fell back on a pillow disposed to receive it, and leaning himself down all the way with her, at once countenanced and endeared her fall to her. There as if he had guessed our wishes, or meant to gratify at once his pleasure and his pride in being the master, by title of present possession, of beauties delicate beyond imagination, he discovered her breasts to his own touch and our common view. But oh! what delicious manuals of love-devotion! How inimitably fine-moulded! small, round, firm, and excellently white; then the grain of their skin, so soothing, so flattering to the touch! and their nipples, that crowned them the sweetest buds of beauty! When he had feasted his eyes with the touch and perusal, feasted his lips with kisses of the highest relish, imprinted in those all-delicious twin orbs, he proceeded downwards.

Her legs still kept the ground; and now, with the tenderest attention not to shock or alarm her too suddenly, he, by degrees, rather stole than rolled up her petticoats, at which, as if a signal had been given, Louisa and Emily took hold of her legs, in pure wantoness and yet in ease, too, to her, kept them stretched wide abroad. Then lay exposed, or, to speak more properly, displayed, the greatest parade in nature of female charms. The whole company, who, except myself, had often seen them, seemed as much dazzled, surprised, and delighted as anyone could be who had now beheld them for the first time. Beauties so excessive could not but enjoy the privileges of eternal novelty. Her thighs were so exquisitely fashioned that, either more in or more out of flesh than they were, they would have declined from that point of perfection they presented. But what infinitely enriched and adorned them was the sweet intersection formed, where they met, at the bottom of the smoothest, roundest, whitest belly, by that central furrow which nature had sunk there, between the soft relievo[63] of two pouting ridges, and which in this girl was in perfect symmetry of delicacy and miniature with the rest of her frame. No! nothing in nature could be of a beautifuller cut. Then the dark umbrage of the downy sprig-moss that over-arched it, bestowed, on the luxury of the landscape, a touching warmth, a tender finishing, beyond the expression of words or even the paint of thought.

Her truly enamoured gallant, who had stood absorbed and engrossed by the pleasure of the sight long enough to afford us time to feast ours (no fear of glutting!), addressed himself at length to the materials of enjoyment; and lifting the linen veil that hung between us and his master-member of the revels, exhibited one whose eminent size proclaimed the owner a true woman's hero. He was, besides, in every other respect an accomplished gentleman and in the bloom and vigour of youth. Standing then between Harriet's legs, which were supported by her two companions at their widest extension, with one hand he gently disclosed the lips of that luscious mouth of nature, whilst with the other, he stooped his mighty machine to its lure, from the height of its stiff stand-up towards his belly; the lips, kept open by his fingers, received its broad shelving head of coral hue; and when he had nestled it in, he hovered there a little, and the girls then delivered over to his hips the agreeable office of supporting her thighs. And now, as if he meant to spin out his pleasure and give it the more play for its life, he passed up his instrument so slow that we lost sight of it inch by inch, till at length it was wholly taken into the soft labaratory of love, and the mossy mounts of each fairly met together. In the meantime, we could plainly mark the prodigious effect the progressions of this delightful energy wrought in this delicious girl, gradually heightening her beauty as they heightened her pleasure. Her countenance, and whole frame grew more animated; the faint blush of her cheeks, gaining ground on the white, deepened into a florid vivid vermillion glow; her naturally brilliant eyes now sparkled with ten-fold lustre; her languor was vanished, and she appeared quick-spirited and alive all over. He had now fixed, nailed, this tender creature with his home-driven wedge, so that she lay passive per force, and unable to stir, till beginning to play a strain of arms[64] against this vein of delicacy, as he urged the to-and-fro constriction, he awakened, roused, and touched her so to the heart that, unable to contain herself, she could not but reply to his motions as briskly as her nicety of frame would admit of, till the raging stings of the pleasure, rising towards the point, made her wild with the intolerable sensations of it, and she now threw her legs and arms about at random, as she lay lost in the sweet transport; which on his side again declared itself by quicker, eagerer thrusts, convulsive grasps, burning sighs, swift laborious breathings, eyes darting humid fires: all faithful tokens of the imminent approaches of the last gasp of joy. It came on at length: the baronet led the ecstasy, which she critically joined in, as she felt the melting symptoms from him, in the nick of which, glueing more ardently than ever his lips to hers, with eyes lifted up in a trance, he showed all the signs of that agony of bliss being strong upon him, in which he sent his soul, distilled in liquid sweets, up the body of that charming creature and gave her the finishing titillation; inly thrilled with which, we saw plainly that she answered it down with all the effusion of spirit and matter she was mistress of, whilst a general soft shudder ran through all her limbs, which she gave a stretch-out of, and lay motionless, breathless, dying with dear delight; and in the heighth of its expression showing, through the nearly closed lids of her eyes, just the edges of their black, the rest being rolled strongly upwards in her ecstasy. Then her sweet mouth

appeared languishingly open, with the tip of her tongue leaning negli-
gently towards the lower range of her white teeth, whilst the natural
ruby colour of her lips glowed with heightened life. Was this a subject
not to dwell upon? And accordingly her lover still kept on her with
an abiding delectation, till compressed, squeezed, and distilled to the last
drop, he slipped out at last and took leave with one fervent kiss, expressing
satisfied desires but unextinguished love.

As soon as he was off, I ran to her, and sitting down on the couch
by her, raised her head, which she declined gently and hung in my
bosom, to hide her blushes and confusion at what had passed, till by
degrees she recomposed herself and accepted of a restorative glass of
wine from my spark, who had left me to fetch it her, whilst her own
was re-adjusting his affairs and buttoning up, after which he led her,
leaning languishingly upon him, to our stand of view round the couch.

And now Emily's partner had taken her out for her share in the
dance, when this transcendently fair and sweet-tempered creature readily
stood up: and if a complexion to put the rose and lily out of countenance,
extreme pretty features, and that florid health and bloom for which the
country girls are so lovely might pass her for a beauty, she certainly
was one, and one of the most striking of the fair ones.

Her gallant began first, as she stood, to disengage her breasts and
restore them to the liberty of nature, from the easy confinement of no
more than a pair of jumps;[65] but on their coming out to view, we thought
a new light was added to the room, so superiorly shining was their
whiteness; then they rose in so happy a swell as to compose her a well-
formed fullness of bosom, that had such an effect on the eye as to seem
flesh hardening into marble, of which it emulated the polished gloss,
and far surpassed even the whitest in the life and lustre of its colours,
white veined with blue. Who could refrain from such provoking entice-
ments to it in reach? He touched her breasts first lightly when the glossy
smoothness of the skin eluded his hand, and made it slip along the surface;
he pressed them, and the springy flesh that filled them, thus pitted by
force, rose again reboundingly with his hand and on the instant effaced
the dint of the pressure: and alike indeed was the consistence of all
those parts of her body throughout, where the fullness of flesh compacts
and constitutes all that fine firmness which the touch is so highly attached
to. When he had thus largely pleased himself with this branch of dalliance
and delight, he trussed up her petticoat and shift in a wisp to her waist,

where being tucked in, she stood fairly naked on every side. A blush at this overspread her lovely face, and her eyes, downcast to the ground, seemed to beg for quarter, when she had so great a right to triumph in all the treasures of youth and beauty that she now so victoriously displayed. Her legs were perfectly well shaped, and her thighs, which she kept pretty close, showed so white, so round, so substantial, and abounding in firm flesh, that nothing could offer a stronger recommendation to the luxury[66] of the touch, which he accordingly did not fail to indulge himself in. Then gently removing her hand, which in the first emotion of natural modesty she had carried thither, he gave us rather a glimpse than a view of that soft narrow chink, running its little length downwards and hiding the remains of it between her thighs: but plain was to be seen the fringe of light-brown curls, in beauteous growth over it, that, with their silky gloss, created a pleasing variety from the surrounding white, whose lustre, too, their gentle embrowning shade considerably raised. Her spark then endeavoured, as she stood, by disclosing her thighs, to gain us a completer sight of that central charm of attraction, but not obtaining it so conveniently in that attitude, he led her to the foot of the couch, and bringing to it one of the pillows, gently inclined her head down, so that as she leaned with it over her crossed hands, straddling with her thighs wide spread and jutting her body out, she presented a full back-view of her person, naked to her waist. Her posteriors, plump, smooth, and prominent, formed luxuriant tracts of animated snow that splendidly filled the eye, till it was commanded down the parting or separation of those exquisitely white cliffs, by their narrow vale, and was there stopped, and attracted by the embowered bottom-cavity, that terminated this delightful vista and stood moderately gaping from the influence of her bended posture, so that the agreeable interior red of the sides of the orifice came into view, and with respect to the white that dazzled round it, gave somewhat the idea of a pink flash in the glossiest white satin. Her gallant, who was a gentleman about thirty, of an immense fortune, somewhat inclined to a fatness that was in no sort displeasing, improving the hint thus tendered him of this mode of enjoyment, after settling her well in this posture and encouraging her with kisses and caresses to stand him through, drew out his affair ready erected, and whose extreme length, rather disproportioned to its breadth, was the more surprising as that excess is not often the case of those of his corpulent habit. Making then the right and direct application, he drove it up to the guard, whilst the round bulge of those Turkish beauties of hers tallying with the hollow made by the bent of his belly and thighs, as they curved inwards, brought all those parts, surely not undelightfully, into warm touch and close conjunction; his hands he kept passed round her body and employed in toying with her enchanting breasts. As soon too as she felt him as home as he could reach, she lifted her head a little from the pillow, and turning her neck without much straining, but her cheeks glowing with the deepest scarlet and a smile of the tenderest satisfaction, met the kiss he pressed forward to give her, as they were thus close joined together. When leaving him to pursue his delights, she hid again her face and blushes with her hands and pillow, and thus stood passively and as favourably too as she could, whilst he kept laying at her with repeated thrusts and making the meeting flesh on both sides resound again with the violence of them. Then ever as he backened from her, we could see between them part of his long white staff foamingly in motion, till, as he went on again and closed with her, the interposing hillocks took it out of sight. Sometimes he took his hands from the semi-globes of her bosom and transferred the pressure of them to those larger ones, the present subjects of his soft blockade, which he squeezed, grasped, and played with, till at length a pursuit of driving, so hotly urged, brought on the height of the fit with such symptoms of over-powering pleasure that his fair partner became now necessary to support him, panting, fainting, and dying as he discharged, which she no sooner felt the killing sweetness of than, unable to keep her legs and yielding to the mighty intoxication, she reeled, and falling forward on the couch, made it a necessity for him, if he would preserve the warm pleasure-hold, to fall upon her, where they perfected, in a continued conjunction of body and ecstatic flow, their scheme of joys for that time.

As soon as he had disengaged, the charming Emily got up, and we crowded round her with congratulations and other officious little services; for it is to be noted that, though all modesty and reserve were banished the transaction of these pleasures, good manners and politeness were inviolably observed: here was no gross ribaldry, no offensive or rude behaviour, or ungenerous reproaches to the girls for their compliance with the humours and desires of the men. On the contrary, nothing was wanting to soothe, encourage, and soften the sense of their condition to them. Men know not in general how much they destroy of their own pleasure, when they break through the respect and tenderness due to our sex, and even to those of it who live only by pleasing them. And this was a maxim perfectly well understood by these polite voluptuaries, these profound adepts in the great art and science of pleasure, who never showed these votaries of theirs a more tender respect than at the time of those exercises of their complaisance, when they unlocked their treasures of concealed beauty, and showed out in the pride of their native charms, ever more touching surely than when they parade it in the artificial ones of dress and ornament.

The frolic was now come round to me, and it being my turn of subscription to the will and pleasure of my particular elect, as well as that of the company, he came to me, and saluting me very tenderly, with a flattering eagerness, put me in mind of the compliances my presence there authorized the hopes of, and at the same time repeated to me that if all this force of example had not surmounted any repugnance I might have to concur with the humours and desires of the company, that though the play was bespoke for my benefit, and great as his own private disappointment might be, he would suffer anything sooner than be the instrument of imposing a disagreeable task on me.

To this I answered, without the least hesitation or mincing grimace, that, had I not even contracted a kind of engagement to be at his disposal without the least reserve, the example of such agreeable companions would alone determine me, and that I was in no pain about anything but my appearing to so great a disadvantage after such superior beauties: and take notice that I thought as I spoke. The frankness of the answer pleased them all; my particular was complimented on his acquisition and, by way of indirect flattery to me, openly envied.

Mrs Cole, by the way, could not have given me a greater mark of her regard than in managing for me the choice of this young gentleman for my master of the ceremonies; for, independent of his noble birth and the great fortune he was heir to, his person was even uncommonly pleasing, well shaped and tall; his face, marked with the smallpox, but no more than what added a grace of more manliness to features rather turned to softness and delicacy, was marvellously enlivened by eyes which were of the clearest sparkling black; in short, he was one whom any woman would, in the familiar style, readily call a very pretty fellow.

I was now handed by him to the cockpit of our match, where, as I was dressed in nothing but a white morning gown, he vouchsafed to play the male Abigail[67] on the occasion, and spared me the contusion that would have attended the forwardness of undressing myself. My gown then was loosened in a trice, and I divested of it; my stays next offered an obstacle which quickly gave way, Louisa very readily furnishing a pair of scissors to cut the lace: off went that shell; and dropping my upper coat, I was now reduced to my under one and my shift, the open bosom of which gave the hands and eyes all the liberty they could wish. Here I imagined the stripping was to stop; but I reckoned short: my spark, at the desire of the rest, tenderly begged that I would not suffer the small remains of a covering to rob them of a full view of my whole person; and for me, who was too flexibly obsequious to dispute any point with them, and who considered the little more that remained as very immaterial, I readily assented to whatever he pleased. In an instant, then, my under petticoat was untied and at my feet, and my shift drawn over my head, so that my cap, slightly fastened, came off with it and brought all my hair down (of which, be it again remembered without vanity, I had a very fine head) in loose disorderly ringlets, over my neck and shoulders, to no unfavourable set-off of my skin.

I now stood before my judges in all the truth of nature, to whom I could not appear a very disagreeable figure, if you please to recollect what I have before said of my person, which time, that at certain periods of life robs us every instant of our charms, had, at that of mine then greatly improved into full and open bloom, for I wanted some months of eighteen. My breasts, which in the state of nudity are ever capital points, now in no more than grateful plenitude, maintained a firmness and steady independence on any stay or support that dared and invited the test of the touch. Then I was as tall, as slim-shaped as could be consistent with all that juicy plumpness of flesh ever the most grateful to the senses of sight and touch, which I owed to the health and youth of my constitution. I had not, however, so thoroughly renounced all innate shame as not to suffer great confusion at the state I saw myself in. But the whole troop round me, men and women, relieved me with every mark of applause and satisfaction, every flattering attention to raise and inspire me with even sentiments of pride on the figure I made, which, my friend gallantly protested, infinitely out-shone all other birthday finery whatever; so that, had I leave to set down, for sincere, all the compliments these connoisseurs overwhelmed me with upon this occasion, I might flatter myself with having passed my examination with approbation of the learned.

My friend however, who for this time had alone the disposal of me, humoured their curiosity, and perhaps his own, so far that he placed me in all the variety of postures and lights imaginable, pointing out every beauty under every aspect of it, not without such parentheses of kisses, such inflammatory liberties of his roving hands, as made all shame fly before them and a blushing glow give place to a warmer one of desire, which led me even to find some relish in the present scene.

But in this general survey, you may be sure, the most material spot of me was not excused the strictest visitation; nor was it but agreed that I had not the least reason to be diffident of passing even for a maid, on occasion. So inconsiderable a flaw had my preceding adventures created there, and so soon had the blemish of an over-stretch been repaired and worn out, at my age and in my naturally small make in that part.

Now, whether my partner had exhausted all the modes of regaling the touch or sight, or whether he was now ungovernably wound up to strike, I know not; but briskly throwing off his clothes, the prodigious heat bred by a close room, a great fire, numerous candles, and even the inflammatory warmth of these scenes induced him to lay aside his shirt too, when his breeches, before loosened, now gave up their contents to view, and showed in front the enemy I had to engage with, stiffly bearing up the port of its head unhooded and glowing red; then I plainly saw what I had to trust to: it was one of those just true-sized instruments of which the masters have a better command than the more unwieldy, inordinate sized ones are generally under. Straining me then close to his bosom, as he stood up foreright against me, and applying to the obvious niche its peculiar idol, he aimed at inserting it, which, as I forwardly favoured, he effected at once by canting up my thighs over his naked hips, and made me receive every inch, and close home; so that stuck upon the pleasure-pivot, and clinging round his neck, in which and his hair I hid my face burningly flushing with my present feelings as much as with shame, my bosom glued to his, he carried me once round the couch, on which he then, without quitting the middle-fastness or dischannelling, laid me down and began the pleasure-grist. But so provokingly predisposed and primed[68] as we were, by all the moving sights of the night, our imagination was too much heated not to melt us of the soonest; and accordingly, I no sooner felt the warm spray darted up my inwards from him, but I was punctually on flow to share the momentary ecstasy. But I had yet greater reason to boast of our harmony: for finding that all the flames of desire were not yet quenched within me but that rather, like wetted coals, I glowed the fiercer for this sprinkling, my hot-mettled spark, sympathyzing with me, and loaded for a double-fire, recontinued the sweet battery with undying vigour, greatly pleased at which, I gratefully endeavoured to accommodate all my motions to his best advantage and delight. Kisses, squeezes, tender murmurs, all came into play, till our joys, growing more turbulent and riotous, threw us into a fond disorder, and, as they raged to a point, bore us far from ourselves into an ocean of boundless pleasures, into which we both plunged together in a transport of taste. Now all the impressions of burning desire, from the lively scenes I had been spectatress of, ripened by the heat of this exercise, and, collecting to a head, throbbed and agitated me with insupportable irritations: I perfectly fevered and maddened with their excess. I did not now enjoy a calm of reason enough to perceive, but I, ecstatically indeed! *felt* the policy and power of such rare and exquisite provocatives as the examples of the night had proved towards thus exalting our pleasures, which, with great joy, I sensibly found my gallant shared in, by his nervous and home[69] expressions of it: his eyes flashing eloquent flames, his action infuriated with the stings of it, all conspiring to raise my delight by assuring me of his. Lifted then to the utmost pitch of joy that human life can bear, undestroyed by excess, I touched that sweetly critical point, when, scarce prevented by the spermatic injection from my partner spurting liquid fire up to my vitals, I dissolved, and breaking out into a deep drawn sigh, sent my whole sensitive soul down to that passage where escape was denied it, by its being so deliciously plugged and choked up. Thus we lay a few blissful instants, overpowered, still, and languid; till, as the sense of pleasure stagnated, we recovered from our trance, and he slipped out of me, not, however, before he had protested his extreme satisfaction by the tenderest kiss and embrace, as well as by the most cordial expressions.

The company, who had stood round us in a profound silence, when all was over, helped me to hurry on my clothes in an instant and complimented me on the sincere homage they could not escape observing had been done (as they termed it) to the sovereignty of my charms, in my receiving a double payment of tribute at one juncture. But my partner, now dressed again, signalized, above all, a fondness unbated by the circumstance of recent enjoyment. The girls, too, kissed and embraced me, assuring me that for that time, or indeed any other, unless I pleased, I was to go through no further public trials, and that I was now consummately initiated, and one of them.

As it was an inviolable law for every gallant to keep to his partner, for the night especially, and even till he relinquished possession over to the community, in order to preserve a pleasing property and to avoid the disgusts and indelicacy of another arrangement, the company, after a short refection[70] of biscuits and wine, tea and chocolate, served in at now about one in the morning, broke up and went off in pairs. Mrs Cole had prepared my spark and me an occasional field-bed, to which we retired, and there ended the night in one continued strain of pleasure, sprightly and uncloyed enough for us not to have formed one wish for its ever knowing an end. In the morning, after a restorative breakfast in bed, he got up, and with very tender assurances of a particular regard for me, left me to the composure and refreshment of a sweet slumber; waking out of which, and getting up to dress before Mrs Cole should come in, I found in one of my pockets a purse of guineas, which he had slipped there; and just as I was musing on a liberality I had certainly not expected, Mrs Cole came in, to whom I immediately communicated the present, and naturally offered her whatever share she pleased. But assuring me that the gentleman had very nobly rewarded her, she would on no terms, no entreaties, no shape I could put it in, receive any part of it. Her denial, she observed, was not affectation or grimace, and proceeded to read me such admirable lessons on the economy of my person and my purse as I became amply paid for my *general* attention and conformity to in the course of my acquaintance with the town. After which, changing the discourse, she fell on the pleasures of the preceding night, where I learned, without much surprise, as I began to enter her character, that she had seen everything that had passed from a convenient place, managed solely for that purpose, and of which she readily made me the confidante.

She had scarce finished with this, when the little troop of love, the girls my companions, broke in and renewed their compliments and caresses. I observed with pleasure that the fatigues and exercises of the night had not usurped in the least on the life of the complexion or the freshness of their bloom: this, I found by their confession, was owing to the management and advice of our rare directress. They went down then to figure[71] it, as usual, in the shop; whilst I repaired to my lodgings, where I employed myself till I returned to dinner at Mrs Cole's.

Here I staid, in constant amusement, with one or other of these charming girls, till about five in the evening: when, seized with a sudden drowsy fit, I was prevailed on to go up and doze it off on Harriet's bed, who left me on it to my repose. There then I lay down in my clothes and fell fast asleep, and had now enjoyed, by guess, about an hour's rest, when I was pleasingly disturbed by my new and favourite gallant, who, inquiring for me, was readily directed where to find me. Coming then into my chamber and seeing me lie alone, with my face turned from the light towards the inside of the bed, he, without more ado, just slipped off his breeches, for the greater ease and enjoyment of the naked touch; and softly turning up my petticoat and shift behind, opened himself the prospect of the back avenue to the genial seat of pleasure; where, as I lay at my side-length, inclining rather face downward, I appeared full fair and liable to be entered. Laying himself then gently down by me, he invested me behind, and giving me to feel the warmth of his body as he applied his thighs and belly close to me, and the endeavours of that machine, whose touch has something so exquisitely singular in it, to make its way good into me, I waked, pretty much startled at first; but seeing who it was, disposed myself to turn to him, when he gave me a kiss; and desiring me to keep my posture, just lifted up my upper thigh, and ascertaining the right opening, soon drove it up to the farthest. Satisfied with which and solacing himself with lying so close in full touch of flesh in those parts, he suspended all motion, and thus steeped in pleasure, kept me lying on my side, in, to him, spoon-fashion, as he termed it, from the snug indent of the back part of my thighs, and all upwards, into the space of the bending between his thighs and belly; till, after some time, that restless and turbulent inmate, impatient by nature of longer quiet, urged him to action, which now prosecuting with all the usual train of toying, kissing, and the like, ended at length in the liquid proof on both sides that we had not been exhausted, or at least were quickly recruited[72] of last night's draughts of pleasure on us.

With this noble and agreeable youth I lived in perfect joy and constancy. He was full bent on keeping me to himself, for the honey-month at least; but his stay in London was not even so long. His father, who had a great post in Ireland, taking him abruptly with him on his repairing thither. Yet even then I was near keeping hold of his affection and person, for he had proposed, and I had consented to follow his order to go to Ireland after him, as soon as he should be settled there; but meeting with an agreeable and advantageous match in that kingdom he chose the wiser part and forbore sending for me, but at the same time took care that I should receive a magnificent present, which did not, however, compensate for all my deep regret on my loss of him.

This event also created a chasm in our little society, which Mrs Cole, on the foot of her usual caution, was in no haste to fill up. But then it redoubled her attention to procure me in the advantages of the traffic for a counterfeit maidenhead, some consolation for the sort of widowhood I had been left in; and this was a scheme she had never lost prospect of, and only waited for a proper person to bring it to bear with.

But I was, it seems, fated to be my own caterer in this, as I had been in my first trial of the market.

I had now passed near a month in the enjoyment of all the pleasures of familiarity and society with my companions, whose particular favourites (the baronet excepted, who soon after took Harriet home) had all, on the terms of community established in the house, solicited the gratification of their taste for variety in my embraces. But I had with the utmost art and address, on various pretexts, eluded their pursuit without giving them cause to complain: and this reserve I used neither out of dislike to them or disgust of the thing, but my true reason was my attachment to my own, and my tenderness of invading the choice of my companions who, outwardly exempt, as they seemed, from jealousy, could not but in secret like me the better for the regard I had for, without making a merit of it to, them. Thus easy, and beloved by the whole family, did I go on, when one day that, about five in the afternoon, I stepped over to a fruiterer's shop in Covent-Garden to pick some table fruit for myself and the young women, I met with the following adventure.

Whilst I was chaffering[73] for the fruit I wanted, I observed myself followed by a young gentleman, whose rich dress first attracted my notice; for the rest, he had nothing remarkable in his person, except that he was pale, thin-made, and ventured himself upon legs rather of the slenderest. Easy was it to perceive, without seeming to perceive it, that it was me he wanted to be at, by his making a full set at and keeping his eyes fixed on me, till he came to the same basket that I stood at, and cheapening, or rather giving the first price asked for the fruit, began his approaches. Now most certainly I was not at all out of figure to pass for a modest girl. I had neither the feathers nor *fumet* [74] of a tawdry town-miss;[75] a straw hat, a white gown, clean linen, and above all, a certain natural and easy air of modesty (which the appearances of never forsook me, even on those occasions that I most broke in upon it in practice) were all signs that gave him no opening to conjecture my condition. He spoke to me, and this address from a stranger, throwing a blush into my cheeks that still set him wider off the truth, I answered him with an awkwardness and confusion the more apt to impose as there was really a mixture of the genuine in them. But when proceeding, on the foot of having broken the ice, to join discourse, he went into other leading questions, I put so much innocence, simplicity, and even childishness into my answers that on no better foundation, liking my person as he did, I will answer for it that he would have been sworn for my modesty. There is, in short, in the men, when once they are caught by the eye especially, a fund of cullibility[76] that their lordly wisdom little dreams of, and in virtue of which the most sagacious of them are seen so often our dupes. Amongst other queries he put to me, one was whether I was married. I replied that I was too young to think of that this many a year. To that of my age, I answered, and sunk a year upon him, passing myself for not seventeen. As to my way of life, I told him I had served an apprenticeship to a milliner in Preston and was come to town after a relation that I found, on my arrival, was dead, and I now lived journey-woman to a milliner in town. That last article indeed was not much on the side of what I pretended to pass for; but it did pass, under favour of the growing passion I had inspired him with. After he had next got out of me, very dextrously as he thought, what I had no sort of design to make a reserve of, my own, my mistress's name, and place of abode, he loaded me with fruit, all the rarest and dearest he could pick out, and sent me home, pondering on what might be the consequence of this adventure.

As soon then as I came to Mrs Cole's I related to her all that had passed, on which she very judiciously concluded that, if he did not come after me there was no harm done and that, if he did, as her presage suggested to her he would, his character and his views should be well sifted, so as to know whether the game was worth the springs;[77] that in the meantime nothing was easier than my part in it, since no more rested on me than to follow her cue and promptership throughout, to the last act.

The next morning, after an evening spent on his side, as we afterwards learnt, in perquisitions into Mrs Cole's character in the neighbourhood (than which nothing could be more favourable to her designs upon him), my gentleman came in his chariot to the shop, where Mrs Cole alone had an inkling of his errand. Asking then for her, he easily made a beginning of acquaintance by bespeaking some millinary ware, when, as I sat without lifting up my eyes, and pursuing the hem of a ruffle with the utmost composure and simplicity of industry, Mrs Cole took notice that the first impressions I made on him ran no risk of being destroyed by those of Louisa and Emily, who were then sitting at work with me. After vainly endeavouring to catch my eyes in rencounter[78] with his, as I held my head down, affecting a kind of consciousness of guilt for having, by speaking to him, given him encouragement and means of following me home, and after giving Mrs Cole direction when to bring herself the things home, and the time he should expect them, he went out, taking with him some goods that he paid for liberally, for the better grace of his introduction.

The girls all this time did not in the least smoke the mystery of this new customer; but Mrs Cole, as soon as we were conveniently alone, insured me, in virtue of her long experience in these matters, that for this bout my charms had not missed fire; for that by his eagerness, his manner and looks, she was sure he had it. The only point now in doubt was his character and circumstances, which her knowledge of the town would soon gain her sufficient acquaintance with, to take her measures upon.

And effectively, in a few hours, her intelligence served her so well that she learned that this conquest of mine was no other than Mr Norbert, a gentleman originally of a great fortune, which, with a constitution naturally not the best, he had greatly impaired by his over-violent pursuit of the vices of the town, in the course of which, having worn out and staled all the more common modes of debauchery, he had fallen into a taste of maiden-hunting, in which chase he had ruined a number of girls, sparing no expense to compass his ends, and generally using them well till tired, or cooled by enjoyment, or springing a new face, he could with more ease disembarrass himself of the old ones, and resign them up to their fate, as his sphere of achievements of that sort lay only amongst such as he could proceed with by way of bargain and sale.

Concluding from these premises, Mrs Cole observed that a character of this sort was ever lawful prize; that the sin would be not to make the best of our market of him; and that she thought such a girl as me only too good for him at any rate, and on any terms.

She went then, at the hour appointed, to his lodgings in one of our Inns of Court,[79] which were furnished in a taste of grandeur that had a special eye to all the conveniences of luxury and pleasure. Here she found him in ready waiting, and after finishing her business of pretence, and a long circuit of discussions concerning her trade, which she said was very bad, the qualities of her servants, 'prentices, journey-women, the discourse naturally landed at length on me, when Mrs Cole, acting admirably the good old prating gossip, who lets everything escape her when her tongue is set in motion, cooked him up a story so plausible of me, throwing in every now and then such strokes of art, with all the simplest air of nature, in praise of my person and temper as finished him finely for her purpose; whilst nothing could be better counterfeited than her innocence of his. But when now fired and on edge, he proceeded to drop hints of his design and views upon me, after he had with much confusion and pains brought her to the point (she kept as long aloof from as she thought proper) of understanding him, without now affecting to pass for a dragoness of virtue by flying out into those violent and ever suspicious passions, she stuck with a better grace and effect to the character of a plain, honest, good sort of a woman, that knew no harm, and that, getting her bread in an honest way, was made of easy and flexible stuff enough to be wrought upon to his ends by his superior skill and address. But, however, she managed so artfully that three or four meetings took place before he could obtain the least favourable hope of her assistance, without which, he had, by a number of fruitless messages, letters, and other direct trials of my disposition, convinced himself there was no coming at me, all which too raised at once my character and price with him.

Regardful, however, of not carrying these difficulties to such a length as might afford time for starting discoveries or incidents unfavourable to her plan, she at last pretended to be won over by mere dint of entreaties, promises and, above all, by the dazzling sum she took care to wind him up to the specification of, when it was now even a piece of art to feign, at once, a yielding to the allurements of a great interest, as a pretext for her yielding at all, and the manner of it such as might persuade him she had never before dipped her virtuous fingers in an affair of that sort.

Thus she led him through all the gradations of difficulty and obstacles necessary to enhance the value of the prize he aimed at; and in conclusion, he was so struck with the little beauty I was mistress of, and so eagerly bent on gaining his ends of me, that he left her even no room to boast of her management in bringing him up to her mark, he drove so plum[80] of himself into everything tending to make him swallow the bait. Not that in other respects Mr Norbert was not clear-sighted enough, not that he did not perfectly know the town, and even by experience, the very branch of imposition now in practice upon him; but we had his passion to friend so much, he was so blinded and hurried on by it that he would have thought any undeception a very ill office done to his pleasure. Thus concurring, even precipitantly, to the point she wanted him at, Mrs Cole brought him at last to hug himself on the cheap bargain he considered the purchase of my imaginary jewel was to him, at no more than three hundred guineas to myself, and a hundred to the broker-ess; being a slender recompense for all her pains, and all the scruples of conscience she had now sacrificed to him for this the first time of her life; which sums were to be paid down on the nail, upon livery of my person, exclusive of some not inconsiderable presents that had been made in the course of the negotiation: during which I had occasionally, but sparingly, been introduced into his company, at proper times and hours, in which it is incredible how little it seemed necessary to strain my natural disposition to modesty higher, in order to pass it upon him for that of a very maid. All my looks and gestures ever breathing nothing but that innocence which the men so ardently require in us, for no other end than to feast themselves with the pleasure of destroying it, and which they are so grievously, with all their skill, subject to mistakes in.

When the articles of the treaty had been fully agreed on, the stipulated payments duly secured, and nothing now remained but the execution of the main point, which centered in the surrender of my person up to his free disposal and use, Mrs Cole managed her objections, especially to his lodgings, and insinuations so nicely, that it became his own mere motion and urgent request that this copy of a wedding should be finished at her house. At first, indeed, she did not care, not she, to have such doings in it – she would not for a thousand pounds have any of the servants or 'prentices know it – her precious good name would be gone for ever – with the like excuses: however, on superior objections to all other expedients, whilst she took care to start none but those that were most liable to them, it came round at last to the necessity of her obliging him in that conveniency, and of doing a little more where she had already done so much.

The night then was fixed, with all possible respect to the eagerness of his impatience, and in the meantime Mrs Cole had omitted no instructions, nor even neglected any preparation that might enable me to come off with honour, in regard to the appearance of virginity, except that, favoured as I was by nature, with all the narrowness of stricture in that part requisite to conduct my designs, I had no occasion to borrow those auxiliaries of art that create a momentary one, easily discovered by the test of a warm bath; and as to the usual bloody symptoms of defloration, which, if not always, are generally attendants on it, Mrs Cole had made me the mistress of an invention of her own, which could hardly miss its effect, and of which more in its place.

Everything then being disposed and fixed for Mr Norbert's reception, he was at the hour of eleven at night, with all the mysteries of silence and secrecy, let in by Mrs Cole herself, and introduced into her bedchamber, where, in an old-fashioned bed of hers, I lay fully undressed and panting, if not with the fears of a real maid, at least with those perhaps greater of a dissembled one, which gave me an air of confusion and bashfulness that maiden-modesty had all the honour of, and was indeed scarce distinguishable from it, even by less partial eyes than those of my lover, so let me call him, for I ever thought the term *cully*[81] too cruel a reproach to the men for their abused weakness for us.

As soon as Mrs Cole, after the old gossipery, on those occasions, used to young women abandoned for the first time to the will of man, had left us alone in her room, which, by the by, was well lighted up, at his previous desire, that seemed to bode a stricter examination than he afterwards made. Mr Norbert, still dressed, sprung towards the bed, where I had got my head under the clothes, and defended them a good while before he could even get at my lips, to kiss them: so true it is, that a false virtue, on this occasion, ever makes a greater rout and resistance than a true one! From thence he descended to my breasts, the feel of which I disputed tooth and nail with him, till tired with my resistance, and thinking probably to give a better account of me when got into bed to me; he hurried his clothes off in an instant, and came into bed.

Meanwhile, by the glimpse I stole of him, I could easily discover a person far from promising any such doughty performances as the storming of maidenheads generally requires, and whose flimsy consumptive texture gave him more the air of an invalid that was pressed than of a volunteer on such hot service.

At scarce thirty, he had already reduced his strength of appetite down to a wretched dependance on forced provocatives, very little seconded by the natural powers of a body jaded and wracked off[82] to the lees by constant repeated overdraughts of pleasure, which had done the work of sixty winters on his springs of life, leaving him at the same time all the fire and heat of youth in his imagination, which served at once to torment and to spur him down the precipice.

As soon as he was in bed, he threw off the bedclothes, which I suffered him to force from my hold, and I now lay as exposed as he could wish, not only to his attacks, but his visitation[83] of the sheets, where, in the various agitations of my body, through my endeavours to defend myself, he could easily assure himself there was no preparation or stain of blood, though, to do him justice, he seemed less strict an examinant than I had apprehended from so experienced a practitioner. My shift then he fairly tore open, finding I made too much use of it to barricade my breasts as well as the more important avenue. Yet in everything else he proceeded with all the marks of tenderness and regard to me, whilst the art of my play was to show none for him. I acted then all the niceties, apprehensions, and terrors supposable for a girl perfectly innocent to feel at so great a novelty as a naked man in bed with her for the first time. He scarce even obtained a kiss but what he ravished; I put his hand away twenty times from my breasts, where he had satisfied himself of their hardness and consistence with passing for hitherto unhandled goods. But when grown impatient for the main point, he now threw himself upon me, and first trying to examine me with his finger, sought to make himself further way, I complained of his usage bitterly: I thought he would not have served a body so. I was ruined – I did not know what I had done – I would get up, so I would, and at the same time kept my thighs so fast locked that it was not for a strength like his to force them open or do any good. Finding thus my advantages, and that I had both my own and his motions at command, the deceiving him became so easy that it was perfect playing upon velvet. In the meantime, his machine, which was one of those sizes that slip in and out without being minded, kept pretty stiffly bearing against that part which the shutting my thighs barred access to; but finding, at length, he could do no good by mere dint of bodily strength, he resorted to entreaties and arguments; to which I only answered, with a tone of shame and timidity, that I was afraid it would kill me – Lord! – I would not be served so – I was never so used in all my born days – I wondered he was not ashamed of himself, so I did – With such silly infantile moods of repulse and complaint as I judged best adapted to express the characters of innocence, and fright. Pretending, however, to yield at length to the vehemence of his insistence, in action and words, I sparingly disclosed my thighs, so that he could just touch the cloven inlet with the tip of his instrument, but as he fatigued and toiled to get it in, a twist of my body, so as to receive it obliquely, not only thwarted his admission, but, giving a scream as if he had pierced me to the heart, I shook him off me, with such violence that he could not with all his might to it keep the saddle. Vexed indeed at this he seemed, but not in the style of any displeasure with me for my skittishness; on the contrary, I dare swear he held me the dearer and hugged himself for the difficulties that even hurt his instant pleasure. Fired, however, now, beyond all bearance of delay, he remounts and begged of me to have patience, stroking and soothing me to it by all the tenderest endearments and protestations of what he would moreover do for me, at which, feigning to be something softened, and abating of the anger that I had shown at his hurting me so prodigiously, I suffered him to lay my thighs aside, and make way for a new trial; but I watched the directions and management of his point so well that no sooner was the orifice in the least open to it, but I gave such a timely jerk as seemed to proceed, not from the evasion of his entry, but from the pain his efforts at it put me to: a circumstance too that I did not fail to accompany with proper gestures, sighs, and cries of complaint, of which, that he had hurt me – he killed me – I should die – were the most frequent interjections. But now, after repeated attempts, in which he had not made the least impression towards gaining his point, at least for that time, the pleasure rose so fast upon him that he could not check or delay it, and in the vigour and fury, which the approaches of the height of it inspired him, he made one fierce thrust that had almost put me by my guard, and lodged it so far that I could feel the warm inspersion just within the exterior orifice, which I had the cruelty not to let him finish there, but threw him out again, not without a most piercing loud exclamation, as if the pain had put me beyond all regard of being overheard. It was easy then to observe that he was more satisfied, more highly pleased, with the supposed motives of his balk of consummation than he would have been at the full attainment of it. It was on this foot that I salved[84] to myself all the falsity I employed to procure him that blissful pleasure in it, which most certainly he would not have tasted in the truth of things. Eased, however, and relieved by one discharge, he now applied himself to soothe, encourage, and put me into humour and patience to bear his next attempt, which he began to prepare and gather force for, from all the incentives of the touch and sight which he could think of, by examining every individual part of my whole body, which he declared his satisfaction with in raptures of applause, kisses universally imprinted, and sparing no part of me, in all the eagerest wantonnesses of feeling, seeing and toying. His vigour, however, did not return so soon, and I felt him more than once pushing at the door, but so little in a condition to break in that I question whether he had the power to enter, had I held it ever so open. But this he then thought me too little acquainted with the nature of things to have any regret or confusion about, and he kept fatiguing himself and me for a long time before he was in any state of stiffness to resume his attempts with any prospect of success. And then I breathed him so warmly, and kept him so at bay, that before he had made any sensible progress in point of penetration he was deliciously sweated and wearied out indeed, so that it was deep in the morning before he had achieved his second let-go, about half way of entrance, I all the time crying and complaining of his prodigious vigour, and the immensity of what I appeared to suffer splitting up with. Tired, however, at length, with such athletic drudgery, my champion began now to give out and to gladly embrace the refreshment of some rest. Kissing me then with much affection, and recommending me to my repose, he presently fell fast asleep; which, as soon as I had well satisfied myself of, I, with much composure of body, so as not to wake him by any motion, with much ease and safety, too, played off Mrs Cole's device for perfecting the signs of my virginity.

In each of the head bedposts, just above where the bedsteads are inserted into them, there was a small drawer so artfully adapted to the mouldings of the timber-work that it might have escaped even the most curious search; which drawers were easily opened or shut by the touch of a spring, and were fitted each with a shallow glass tumbler full of a prepared fluid blood; in which lay soaked, for ready use, a sponge that required no more than gently reaching the hand to it, taking it out, and properly squeezing between the thighs, when it yielded a great deal more of the red liquid than would save a girl's honour; after which, replacing it, and touching the spring, all possibility of discovery or even of suspicion, was taken away; and all this was not the work of the fourth part of a minute, and on whichever side one lay, the thing was equally easy and practicable by the double care taken to have each bedpost provided alike. True it is that, had he waked and caught me in the fact, it would at least have covered me with shame and confusion; but then, that he did not, was, with the precautions I took, a risk of a thousand to one in my favour.

At ease now, and out of all fear of any doubt or suspicion on his side, I addressed myself in good earnest to my repose, but could obtain none. And in about half an hour's time, my gentleman waked again, and turning towards me, I feigned a sound sleep, which he did not long respect; but girding himself again to renew the onset, he began to kiss and caress me, when now making as if I just waked, I complained of the disturbance and of the cruel pain that this little rest had stolen my senses from. Eager, however, for the pleasure as well as honour of con- summating an entire triumph over my virginity, he said and did every- thing that could overcome my resistance, and bribe my patience to the end, which now I was ready to listen to, from being secure of the bloody proofs I had prepared of his victorious violence, though I still thought it good policy not to let him in yet a while. I answered then only to his importunities in sighs and moans that I was so hurt, I could not bear it – I was sure he had done me a mischief; that he had, – he was such a sad[85] man! Turning, at this, down the clothes, and viewing the field of battle by the glimmer of a dying taper, he saw plainly my thighs, shift, and sheets, all yet wet and stained with what he readily took for virgin gore,[86] proceeding from his last half-penetration: convinced and transported at which, nothing could equal his joy and exultation. The illusion was complete; no other conception entered his head but that of his having been at work upon an unopened mine, which idea, upon so strong an evidence, redoubled at once his tenderness for me and his ardour for breaking it wholly up. Kissing me then with the utmost rapture, he comforted me, and begged my pardon for the pain he had put me to, observing, withal, that it was only a thing in course, but the worst was certainly past, and that with a little courage and constancy I should get it once well over, and never after experience anything but the greatest pleasure. By little and little I suffered myself to be prevailed on, and giving, as it were, up the point to him, I made my thighs, insensibly spreading them, yield him liberty of access, which, improving, he got a little within me, when, by a well managed reception, I worked the female screw so nicely that I kept him from the easy mid-channel direction, and, by dexterous wreathings and contortions, creating an artificial difficulty of entrance, made him win it inch by inch, with the most laborious struggles, I all the time sorely complaining, till at length, with might and main, winding his way in, he got it completely home, and giving my virginity, as he thought, the *coup de grâce*, furnished me the cue of setting up a terrible outcry, whilst he, triumphant and like a cock clapping his wings over his down-trod mistress, pursued his pleasure, which presently rose, in virtue of this idea of a complete victory, to a pitch that made me soon sensible of his melting period, whilst I now lay acting the deep wounded, breathless, frightened, undone, no longer maid.

You will ask me, perhaps, whether all this time I enjoyed any perception of pleasure? I assure you, little or none; till just towards the latter end, a faintish sense of it came on mechanically, from so long a struggle and frequent fret in that ever sensible part. But, in the first place, I had no taste for the person I was suffering the embraces of, on a purely mercenary account, and then I was not entirely delighted with myself for the jade's part I was playing, whatever excuses I might have to plead for being brought into it; but then this insensibility kept me so much the mistress of my mind and motions that I could the better manage so close a counterfeit, through the whole scene of deception.

Recovered at length to more show of life, by his tender condolences, kisses, and embraces, I upbraided him and reproached him for my ruin, in such natural terms as added to his satisfaction with himself for having accomplished it; and guessing, by certain observations of mine, that it would be rather favourable to him to spare him, when he sometime

after, feebly enough, came on again to the assault, I resolutely with-
stood any further endeavours, on a pretext that flattered his prowess,
of my being so violently hurt and sore that I could not possibly endure
a fresh trial. He then graciously granted me a respite, and the morning
soon after advancing, I got rid of further importunity, till Mrs Cole, being
rung for by him, came in, and was made acquainted, in terms of the
utmost joy and rapture, with his triumphant certainty of my virtue,
and the finishing stroke he had given it, in the course of the night;
of which, he added, she would see proof enough, in bloody characters,
on the sheets.

You may guess how a woman of her turn of address and experience
humoured the jest and played him off with mixed exclamations of shame,
anger, compassion for me, and of her being pleased that all was so well
over; in which last, I believe, she was perfectly sincere. And now, as
the objection (which she had represented as an invincible one) to my
lying the first night at his lodgings (which were studiously calculated
for a freedom of intrigues), on the account of my maiden fears and terrors
at the thoughts of going to a gentleman's chambers, and being alone
with him in bed, was surmounted, she pretended to persuade me, in
favour to him, that I should go there to him, whenever he pleased,
and still keep up all the necessary appearances of working with her,
that I might not lose, with my character, the prospect of getting a good
husband, and at the same time her house would be kept the safer from
scandal. All this seemed so reasonable, so considerate, to Mr Norbert
that he never once perceived that she did not want him to resort to
her house, lest he might in time discover certain inconsistencies with
the character she had set out with to him; besides that this plan greatly
flattered his own ease and views of liberty.

Leaving me then to my much wanted rest, he got up, and Mrs Cole,
after settling with him all points relating to me, got him undiscovered
out of the house. After which, and I was awake, she came in and gave
me due praises on my success. Behaving, too, with her usual moderation
and disinterestness, she refused any share of the sum I had thus earned
and put me into such a secure and easy way of disposing of my affairs,
which now amounted to a kind of little fortune that a child of ten years
old might have kept the account and property of them safe in its hands.

I was now restored again to my former state of a kept mistress, and
used punctually to wait on Mr Norbert at his chambers whenever he

sent a messenger for me, which I constantly took care to be in the way of, and managed with so much caution that he never once penetrated the nature of my connexions with Mrs Cole; but indolently given up to ease and the town dissipations, the perpetual hurry to them hindered him from looking into his own affairs, much less into mine.

In the meantime, if I may judge from my own experience, none are better paid or better treated during their reign than the mistresses of those who, enervated by nature, debaucheries, or age, have the least employment for the sex: sensible that a woman must be satisfied some way, they ply her with a thousand little tender attentions, presents, caresses, confidences, and exhaust their invention in means and devices to make up for the capital deficiency; and even towards lessening that, what arts, what modes, what refinements of pleasure have they not recourse to to raise their languid powers and press nature into the service of their sensuality! But here is their misfortune, that, when by a course of teasing, worrying, handling, wanton postures, lacivious motions, they have at length accomplished a flashy enervated enjoyment, they have at the same time lighted up a flame in the object of their passion that, not having the means themselves to quench, drives her for relief into the next person's arms, who can finish their work: and thus they become bawds to some secret favourite, tried and approved of for a more vigorous and satisfactory execution; for with women, of our turn especially, however well our hearts may be disposed, there is a controlling part, or queen-seat[87] in us, that governs itself by its own maxims of state, amongst which not one is stronger in practice with it than, in matter of its dues, never to accept the will for the deed.

Mr Norbert, who was much in this ungracious case, though he professed and showed to like me extremely, could but seldom consummate the main joy itself with me, without such a length and variety of preparations as were at once wearisome and inflammatory.

Sometimes he would strip me stark naked on a carpet, by a good fire; when he would contemplate me almost by the hour, disposing me in all the figures and attitudes of body that it was susceptible of being viewed in; kissing me in every part, the most secret and critical one so far from excepted that it received most of that branch of homage. Then his touches were so exquisitely wanton and luxuriously diffused, and penetrative at times, that he made me perfectly rage with titillating fires, when, after all, and with much ado, he had gained a short-lived erection, he would perhaps melt it away in a washy sweat, or a premature abortive effusion, that provokingly mocked my eager desires; or, if carried home, how faltered and unnervous[88] the execution! how insufficient the sprinkle of a few heat-drops to extinguish all the flames he had kindled.

One evening I cannot help remembering, that, returning home from him with a spirit he had raised in a circle his wand had proved too weak to lay, as I turned the corner of a street, I was overtaken by a young sailor. I was then in that spruce, neat, and plain dress, which I ever affected, and perhaps might have in my trip a certain air of restlessness unknown to the composure of cooler thoughts. However, he seized me as a prize, and, without ceremony, threw his hands round my neck, and kissed me boisterously and sweetly. I looked at him with a beginning of anger and indignation at his rudeness, that softened away into other sentiments as fast I viewed him: for he was tall, manly-carriaged, handsome of body and face, so that I ended my stare with asking him, in a tone turned to tenderness, what he meant. At which, with the same frankness and vivacity as he had begun with me, he proposed treating me with a glass of wine. Now, certain it is that, had I been in a calmer state of blood than I was; had I been less under the dominion of unappeased irritations and desires, I should have refused him without hesitation. But I do not know how it was, my pressing calls, his figure, the occasion, and, if you will, the powerful combination of all these, with a start of curiosity to see the end of an adventure so novel to me as being thus treated like a common street-plyer,[89] made me give a silent consent: in short, it was not my head that I now obeyed. I suffered myself then to be towed along, as it were, by this man-of-war, who took me under his arm as familiarly as if he had known me all his lifetime, and led me into the next convenient tavern, where we were shown into a little room on one side of the passage. Here, scarce allowing himself patience till the drawer brought in the wine called for, he fell directly on board[90] me: when, untucking my handkerchief and giving me a smacking buss, he laid my breasts bare at once, which he handled with that keenness of gust that abridges a ceremonial ever more tiresome than pleasing on such pressing occasions; and now hurrying towards the main point, we found no conveniency for our purpose, two or three disabled chairs, and a rickety table composing the whole furniture of the room.

Without more ado, he plants me with my back standing against the wall, and my petticoats up; and coming out with a splitter indeed, made it shine, as he brandished it, in my eyes, and going to work with an impetuosity and eagerness, bred very likely by a long fast at sea, went to give me the taste of it. I straddled, I humoured my posture, and did my best in short to buckle to it; I took part in it too. But still things did not jee[91] to his thorough liking: changing then in a trice his system of battery, he leads me to the table, and with a master-hand lays my head down on the edge of it, and with the other canting up my petticoat and shift, bared my naked posteriors to his blind and furious guide. It forces its way between them, and I feeling pretty sensibly that it was not going by the right door and knocking desperately at the wrong one, I told him of it: 'Pooh,' says he, 'my dear, any port in a storm.' Altering, however, directly his course, and lowering his point, he fixed it right, and driving it up with a delicious stiffness, made all foam again and gave me the *tout* with such fire and spirit that in the fine disposition I was in when I submitted to him, and stirred up so fiercely as I was, I got the start of him, and went away into the melting swoon; and squeezing him, whilst in the convulsive grasp of it, drew from him such a plenteous bedewal of balmy sweets as joined to my own effusion, perfectly floated those parts, and drowned in a deluge all my raging conflagration of desire.

When this was over, how to make my retreat was my concern; for, though I had been so extremely pleased with the difference between this warm broadside, poured so briskly into me, and the tiresome pawing and toying to which I had owed the unappeased flames that had driven me into this step, now I was grown cooler, I began to apprehend the danger of contracting an acquaintance with this however agreeable stranger; who, on his side, spoke of passing the evening with me and continuing our intimacy, with an air of determination that made me afraid of its being not so easy to get away from him as I could wish. In the meantime I carefully concealed my uneasiness, and readily pretended to consent to stay with him, telling him I should only step to my lodgings to leave a necessary direction, and then instantly return. This he very glibly swallowed, on the notion of my being one of those unhappy street-errants who devote themselves to the pleasure of the first ruffian that will stoop to pick them up, and, of course, that I would scarce bilk myself of my hire, by not returning to make the most of the job. Thus he parted with me, not before, however, he had ordered, in my hearing, a supper which I had the barbarity to disappoint him of my company to.

But when I got home, and told Mrs Cole my adventure, she represented so strongly to me the nature and dangerous consequences of my folly, the risks to my health in being so open-legged and free of my flesh, that I not only took resolutions never to venture so rashly again, which I inviolably preserved, but passed a good many days in continual uneasiness lest I should have met with other reasons, besides the pleasure of that rencounter, to remember it. But these fears wronged my pretty sailor, for which I gladly make him this reparation.

I had now lived with Mr Norbert near a quarter of a year, in which space I circulated my time very pleasantly between my amusements at Mrs Cole's and a proper attendance on that gentleman, who paid me profusely for the unlimited complaisance with which I passively humoured every caprice of pleasure, and which had won upon him so greatly that, finding, as he said, all that variety in me alone which he had sought for in a number of women, I had made him lose his taste for inconstancy and new faces. But what was yet at least as agreeable to me as his fondness and attachment, as well as much more flattering: the love I had inspired him with bred a deference to me that was of great service to his health. For having by degrees, and with most pathetic representations, brought him to some husbandry⁹² of it, and to ensure the duration of his pleasures by moderating their use and correcting those excesses in them he was so addicted to, and which had shattered his constitution and destroyed his powers of life in the very point for which he seemed chiefly desirous to live, he was grown more delicate, more temperate, and all in course more healthy; his gratitude for which was taking a turn very favourable for my fortune, when once more the caprice of it dashed the cup from my lips.

His sister, Lady L—, for whom he had a great affection, desiring him to accompany her down to Bath for her health, he could not refuse her such a favour, and accordingly, though he counted on staying away from me no more than a week at farthest, he took his leave of me with an ominous heaviness of heart, and left with me a sum far above the state of his fortune and very inconsistent with the intended shortness of his journey; but it ended in the longest that can be, and is never but once taken: for, arrived at Bath, he was not there two days before he fell into a debauch of drinking with some gentlemen that threw him into a high fever which carried him off in four days' time, never once out of a delirium. Had he been in his senses to make a will,[93] perhaps he might have made favourable mention of me in it. Thus, however, I lost him; and as no condition of life is more subject to revolutions than that of a woman of pleasure, I soon recovered my cheerfulness, and now beheld myself once more struck off the list of kept mistresses and returned into the bosom of the community, from which I had been in some manner taken.

Mrs Cole, still continuing her friendship, offered me her assistances and advice towards another choice; but I was now in a state of ease and affluence enough to look about me at leisure; and as to any constitutional calls of pleasure, their pressure or sensibility was greatly lessened by a consciousness of the ease with which they were to be satisfied at Mrs Cole's house, where Louisa and Emily still continued in the old way; and my great favourite, Harriet, used often to come and see me, and entertain me, with her head and heart full of the happiness she enjoyed with her dear baronet, whom she loved with tenderness and constancy, even though he was her keeper and, what is yet more, had made her independent by a handsome provision for her and hers.

I was then in this vacancy from any regular employ of my person, in my way of business, when one day Mrs Cole, in the course of the constant confidence we lived in, acquainted me that there was one Mr Barvile,[94] a gentleman who used her house, just come to town, whom she was not a little perplexed about providing a suitable companion for; which was indeed a point of difficulty, as he was under the tyranny of a cruel taste: that of an ardent desire, not only of being unmercifully whipped himself, but of whipping others, in such sort that, though he paid extravagantly those who had the courage and complaisance to submit to his humour, there were few, delicate as he was in the choice of his subjects, who would exchange turns with him so terribly at the expense of their skin. But what yet increased the oddity of this strange fancy was the gentleman's being young; whereas it generally attacks, it seems, such as are, through age, obliged to have recourse to this experiment for quickening the circulation of their sluggish juices, and determining a conflux of the spirits of pleasure towards those flagging, shrivelly parts that rise to life only by virtue of those titillating ardours created by the discipline of their opposites, with which they have so surprising a consent.

This Mrs Cole could not well acquaint me with, in any expectation of my offering my service; for sufficiently easy as I was in my circumstances, it must have been the temptation of an immense interest indeed that could have induced me to embrace such a job; neither had I ever expressed, or indeed felt, the least impulse or curiosity to know more of a taste that promised so much more pain than pleasure, to those that stood in no need of such violent goads: what then should move me to subscribe myself voluntarily to a party of pain, foreknowing it such? Why, to tell the plain truth, it was a sudden caprice, a gust of fancy for trying a new experiment, mixed with the vanity of approving my personal courage to Mrs Cole, that determined me, at all risks, to propose myself to her and relieve her from any farther look-out. Accordingly, I at once pleased and surprised her with a frank and unreserved tender[95] of my person to her, and her friend's absolute disposal on this occasion.

My good temporal mother was, however, so kind as to use all the arguments she could imagine to dissuade me. But as I found they only turned on a motive of tenderness to me, I persisted in my resolution, and thereby acquitted my offer of any suspicion of its not having been sincerely made, or out of compliment only. Acquiescing then thankfully in it, Mrs Cole assured me that, bating[96] the pain I should be put to, she had no scruple to engage me in this party, which, she assured me, I should be liberally paid for, and which the secrecy of the transaction preserved safe from the ridicule that otherwise vulgarly attended it; that for her part, she considered pleasure of one sort or other as the universal port of destination, and every wind that blew thither a good one, provided it blew nobody any harm; that she rather compassionated than blamed those unhappy persons who are under a subjection they cannot shake off to those arbitrary tastes that rule their appetites of pleasure with an unaccountable control: tastes, too, as infinitely diversified, as superior to and independent of all reasoning as the different relishes or palates of mankind in their viands;[97] some delicate stomachs nauseating plain meats,[98] and finding no favour but in high-seasoned, luxurious dishes; whilst others again pique themselves upon detesting them.

I stood now in no need of this preamble of encouragement or justification: my word was given, and I was determined to fulfil my engagements. Accordingly the night was set, and I had all the necessary previous instructions how to act and conduct myself. The dining room was duly prepared and lighted up, and the young gentleman posted there in waiting for my introduction to him.

I was then, by Mrs Cole, handed in and presented to him in a loose dishabille, fitted, by her direction, to the exercise I was to go through, all in the finest linen and a thorough white uniform: gown, petticoat, stockings, and satin slippers, like a victim led to the sacrifice; whilst my dark auburn hair, falling in drop-curls over my neck, created a pleasing distinction of colour from the rest of my dress.

As soon as Mr Barvile saw me, he got up with a very visible air of pleasure and surprise, and after saluting me, asked Mrs Cole if it was possible that so fine and delicate a creature would voluntary submit to such sufferings and rigours as were the subject of this assignation. She answered him properly, and now reading in his eyes that she could not too soon leave us together, she went out, after recommending him to use moderation with so tender a novice.

But whilst she was employing his attention, mine had been taken up with examining the figure and person of this unhappy young gentleman, who was thus unaccountably condemned to have his pleasure lashed into him, as boys have their learning.

He was exceedingly fair, and smooth-complexioned; and appeared to me no more than twenty at most, though he was three years older than what my conjectures gave him; but then he owed this favourable mistake to a habit of fatness, which spread through a short, squab stature; and a round, plump, fresh-coloured face gave him greatly the look of a Bacchus, had not an air of austerity, not to say sternness, very unsuitable even to his shape of face, dashed that character of joy necessary to complete the resemblance. His light-brown hair was pretty thick, uncurled, and looked as if it had been trimmed with a bowl-dish, as we are told the Roundheads were in Oliver's times. His dress was extremely neat, but plain, and far inferior to the ample fortune he was in full possession of: this too was a taste in him, and not avarice.

As soon as Mrs Cole was gone, he seated me near him, when now his face changed upon me into an expression of the most pleasing sweetness and good humour, the more remarkable for its sudden shift from the other extreme, which, I found afterwards, when I knew more of his character, was owing to an habitual state of conflict with and dislike of himself for being enslaved to so peculiar a gust,[99] by the fatality of a constitutional ascendant that rendered him incapable of receiving any pleasure till he submitted to these extraordinary means of procuring it at the hands of pain, whilst the constancy of this repining consciousness, stamped at length that cast of sourness and severity on his features which was, in fact, very foreign to the natural sweetness of his temper.

After then a competent preparation by apologies and encouragement to go through my part with spirit and constancy, he stood up near the fire, whilst I went to fetch the instruments of discipline out of a closet hard by: these were several rods, made each of two or three strong twigs of birch tied together, which he took, handled, and viewed with as much pleasure as I did with a kind of shuddering presage.

Next we took from the side of the room a long broad bench, made easy to lie at length on by a soft cushion in a calico-cover: and everything being now ready, he took his coat and waistcoat off and, at his motion and desire, I unbuttoned his breeches and, rolling his shirt up rather above his waist, tucked it in securely there. When directing naturally my eyes to that humoursome master-movement, in whose favour all these dispositions were making, it seemed almost shrunk into his belly, scarce showing its tip above the sprout of hairy curls that clothed those parts, as you may have seen a wren peep its head out of the grass.

Stooping then to untie his garters, he gave them me for the use of tying him down to the legs of the bench, a circumstance no farther necessary than, as I suppose, it made part of the humour of the thing, since he prescribed it to himself, amongst the rest of the ceremonial.

I led him then to the bench, and according to my cue, played at forcing him to lie down: which, after some little show of reluctance, for form's sake, he submitting to, was straightway extended flat upon his belly on the bench, with a pillow under his face; and as he thus tamely lay, I tied him slightly hand and foot, to the legs of it; which done, his shirt remaining trussed up over the small of his back, I drew his breeches quite down to his knees; and now he lay, in all the fairest, broadest display of that part of the back-view in which a pair of chubby, smooth-cheeked and passing[100] white posteriors rose cushioning upwards from two stout, fleshful thighs, and, ending their cleft, or separation, by a union at the small of the back, presented a bold mark that swelled, as it were, to meet the scourge.

Seizing now one of the rods, I stood over him, and, according to his direction, gave him, in one breath, ten lashes with much good will and the utmost nerve and vigour of arm that I could put to them, so as to make those fleshy orbs quiver again under them, whilst himself seemed no more concerned, or to mind them, than a lobster would a flea-bite. In the meantime, I viewed intently the effects of them, which to me at least appeared surprisingly cruel: every lash had skimmed the surface of those white cliffs, which they deeply reddened, and lapping round the side of the furthermost from me, cut, especially into the dimple of it, such livid weals as the blood either spun out from or stood in large drops on; and from some of the cuts I picked out even the splinters of the rod, that had stuck in the skin; nor was this raw work to be wondered at, considering the greenness of the twigs, and the severity of the infliction, whilst the whole surface of his skin was so smooth-stretched over the hard and firm pulp of flesh that filled it as to yield no play or elusive swagging under the stroke, which thereby took place the more plum, and cut into the quick.[101]

I was, however, already so moved at the piteous sight that I from my heart repented the undertaking, and would willingly have given over, thinking he had full enough; but he, encouraging and beseeching me earnestly to proceed, I gave him ten more lashes, and then resting, surveyed the increase of bloody appearances, and at length, steeled to the sight by his stoutness in suffering, I continued the discipline, by intervals, till I observed him wreathing and twisting his body in a way that I could plainly perceive was not the effect of pain, but of some new and powerful sensation; curious to dive into the meaning of which, in one of my pauses of intermission, I approached, as he still kept working and grinding his belly against the cushion under him; and first, stroking the untouched and unhurt side of the flesh-mount next me, then softly insinuating my hand under his thigh, felt the posture things were in forwards, which was indeed surprising; for that machine of his, which I had, by its appearance, taken for an impalpable or at best a very diminutive subject, was now, in virtue of all that smart and havock of his skin behind, grown not only to a prodigious stiffness of erection, but to a size that frighted even me: a non-pareil thickness indeed! The head of it alone filled the utmost capacity of my grasp; and when, as he heaved and wriggled to and fro in the agitation of his strange pleasure, it came into view, it had something of the air of a round fillet of the whitest veal – like its owner, squob and short in proportion to its breadth; but when he felt my hand there, he begged I would go on briskly with my jerking, or he should never arrive at the last stage of pleasure.

Resuming then the rod and the exercise of it, I had fairly worn out three bundles, when, after an increase of struggles and motion, and a deep sigh or two, I saw him lie still and motionless. And now he desired me to desist, which I instantly did, and proceeding to untie him, I could not but be amazed at his passive fortitude, on viewing the skin of his butchered, mangled posteriors, late so white, smooth, and polished, now all one side of them, a confused cut-work of weals, livid flesh, gashes and gore, insomuch that when he stood up, he could scarce walk; in short, he was in sweet briars.[102]

Then I plainly perceived on the cushion the marks of a plenteous effusion of white liquid, and already had his sluggard member run up to its old nestling-place, and ensconced itself again, as if ashamed to show its head, which nothing, it seems, could raise but stripes inflicted on its opposite neighbours, who were thus constantly obliged to suffer for his caprice.

My gentleman had now put on his clothes and recomposed himself, when giving me a kiss and placing me by him, he sat down himself as gingerly as possible, with the one side off the cushion, which was too sore for him to bear resting any part of his weight on.

Here he thanked me extremely for the pleasure I had procured him, and seeing perhaps some marks in my countenance of terror and apprehension of retaliation on my own skin for what I had been the instrument of his suffering in his, he assured me he was ready to give up to me any engagement I might deem myself under to stand him, as he had done me; but that if I proceeded in my consent to it, he would consider the difference of my sex, its greater delicacy, and incapacity to undergo pain. Reheartened at which, and piqued in honour, as I thought not to flinch so near the trial, especially as I well knew Mrs Cole was an eye-witness, from her stand of espial,[103] to the whole of our transactions, I was now less afraid of my skin than of his not furnishing me an opportunity of signalizing my resolution.

Consonant to this disposition was my answer, but my courage was still more in my head than in my heart, and as cowards rush into the danger they fear, in order to be the sooner rid of the pain of that sensation, I was entirely pleased with his hastening matters into execution.

He had then little to do, but to unloose the strings of my petticoat, and lift them, together with my shift, naval-high, where he just tucked them up loosely girt, and might be slipped up higher at pleasure. Then viewing me round with great seeming delight, he laid me at my length on my face upon the bench, and when I expected he would tie me, as I had done him, and held out my hands, not without fear and a little trembling, he told me he would by no means terrify me unnecessarily with such a confinement; for that though he meant to put my constancy to some trial, the standing it was to be completely voluntary on my side, and therefore I was to be at full liberty to get up whenever I found the pain too much for me. You cannot imagine how much I thought myself bound by being thus allowed to remain loose, and how much spirit this confidence in me gave me, so that I was, even from my heart, careless how much my flesh might suffer in honour of it.

All my back parts, naked halfway up, were now fully at his mercy: and first he stood at a convenient distance, delighting himself with a gloating survey of the attitude I lay in, and of all the secret stores I thus exposed to him in fair display; then springing eagerly towards me, he covered all those naked parts with a fond confusion of kisses. And now taking hold of the rod, rather wantoned with me, in gentle inflictions on those tender trembling masses of my flesh behind, than any way hurt them, till, by degrees, he began to tingle them with smarter lashes, so as to provoke a red colour into them, which I knew, as well by the flagrant glow I felt there as by his telling me, they now emulated the native roses of my other cheeks. When he had then amused himself with admiring and toying with them, he went on to strike harder, and more hard, so that I needed all my patience not to cry out, or complain at least; at last he twigged me so smartly as to fetch blood in more than one lash, at sight of which he flung down the rod, flew to me, kissed away the starting drops, and, sucking the wounds, eased a good deal of my pain. But now raising me on my knees, and making me kneel with them straddling wide, that tender part of me, naturally the province of pleasure, not of pain, came in for its share of suffering, for now, eying it wistfully, he directed the rod so that the sharp ends of the twigs lighted there so sensibly that I could not help winching[104] and writhing my limbs with smart; so that my contortions of body must necessarily throw it into an infinite variety of postures and points of view, fit to feast the luxury of the eye. But still I bore everything without crying out: when presently, giving me another pause, he rushed, as it were, on that part whose lips and round-about had felt his cruelty, and by way of reparation, glues his own to them. Then he opened, shut and squeezed them, plucked softly the overgrowing moss, and all this in a style of wild passionate rapture and enthusiasm that expressed excess of pleasure; till betaking himself to the rod again, encouraged by my passiveness, and infuriated with this strange taste of delight, he made my poor posteriors pay for the ungovernableness of it; for now, showing them no quarter,[105] the traitor cut me so that I wanted but very little of fainting away, when he gave over. And yet I did not utter one groan or angry expostulation; but in my heart I resolved nothing so seriously as never to expose myself again to the like severities.

You may guess then in what a curious pickle those flesh-cushions of mine were, all sore, raw, and, in fine, terribly clawed off; but so far from feeling any pleasure in it that the recent smart made me pout a little; and not with the greatest air of satisfaction receive the compliments and after-caresses of the author of my pain.

As soon as my clothes were huddled on in a little decency, a supper was brought in by the discreet Mrs Cole herself, which might have piqued the sensuality of a cardinal, accompanied with a choice of the richest wines; all which she set before us, and went out again without having by a word, or even by a smile, given us the least interruption or confusion in those instants of secrecy that we were not yet ripe for the admission of a third to.

I sat down then, still scarce in charity with my butcher, for such I could not help considering him, and was moreover not a little piqued at the gay, satisfied air of his countenance, which I thought myself insulted by. But when the now necessary refreshment to me of a glass of wine and a little eating (all the time observing a profound silence) had somewhat cheered and restored me to spirits; and as the smart began to go off, my good humour returned accordingly, which alteration not escaping him, he said and did everything that could confirm me in and indeed exalt it.

But scarce was supper well over, before a change so incredible was wrought in me, such violent yet pleasingly irksome sensations took possession of me that I scarce knew how to contain myself: smart of the lashes was now converted into such a prickly heat, such fiery tinglings, as made me sigh, squeeze my thighs together, shift and wriggle about my seat with a furious restlessness; whilst these itching ardours, thus excited in those parts on which the storm of discipline had principally fallen, detached legions of burning, subtile,[106] stimulating spirits to their opposite spot and center of assemblage, where their titillation raged so furiously that I was even stinging-mad with them. No wonder then, that in such a taking, and devoured by flames that licked up all modesty and reserve, my eyes now charged brimful of the most intense desire, fired on my companion very intelligible signals of distress: my companion, I say, who grew in them every instant more amiable and more necessary to my urgent wishes and hopes of immediate ease.

Mr Barvile, no stranger by experience to these situations, soon knew the pass I was brought to, soon perceived my extreme disorder; in favour of which, removing the table out of the way, he began a prelude that flattered me with instant relief, which I was not, however, so near as I imagined: for as he was unbuttoned to me, and tried to provoke and rouse to action his inactive, torpid machine, he blushingly owned that no good was to be expected from it, unless I took in hand to re-excite its languid, loitering powers by just refreshing the smart of the yet recent, blood-raw cuts, seeing it could, no more than a boy's top, keep up without lashing. Sensible then that I should work as much for my own profit as his, I hurried my compliance with his desire, and abridging the ceremonial, whilst he leaned his head against the back of a chair, I had scarce gently made him feel the lash before I saw the object of my wishes give signs of life, and presently, as it were with a magic touch, it started up into a noble size and distinction indeed! Hastening then to give me the benefit of it, he threw me down on the bench; but such was the refreshed soreness of those parts behind, on my leaning so hard on them, as became me to compass the admission of that stupendous head of his machine, that I could not possibly bear it. I got up then and tried, by leaning forwards and turning the crupper[107] on my assailant, to let him in at the back avenue; but here it was likewise impossible to stand his bearing so fiercely against me in his agitations and endeavours to enter that way, whilst his belly battered directly against the recent sore: what should we do now, both intolerably heated, both all in one fury? But pleasure is ever inventive for its own ends: he strips me in a trice, stark naked, and placing a broad settee cushion on the carpet before the fire, oversets me gently topsy-turvy on it; and handling me only at the waist, whilst you may be sure I savoured all his dispositions, brought my legs round his neck; so that my head was kept from the floor only by my hands and the velvet cushion, which was now bespread with my flowing hair. Thus I stood on my head and hands, supported by him in such manner that, whilst my thighs clung round him, so as to expose to his sight all my back figure, including the theatre of his bloody pleasure, the center of my forepart fairly bearded the now worthy object of its rage that now stood in fine condition to give me satisfaction for the injuries of its neighbours. But as this posture was certainly not the easiest, and our imagination, wound up to the height, could suffer no delay, he first, with the utmost eagerness and effort, just lip-lodged that broad, acorn-fashioned head of his instrument; and still friended[108] by the fury with which he had made that impression, he soon stuffed in the rest; when now, with a pursuit of thrusts fiercely urged, he absolutely overpowered and absorbed all sense of pain and uneasiness, whether from my wounds behind, my most untoward posture, or the oversize of his stretcher, in an infinitely predominant delight. When now, all my whole spirits of life and sensation, rushing impetuously to the cock-pit, where the prize of pleasure was hotly in dispute, and clustering to a point there, I soon received the dear relief of nature from these over-violent strains and provocations of it, harmonizing with which, my gallant spouted into me such a potent overflow of the oily balsamic injection as softened and unedged all those irritating stings of a new species of titillation, which I had been so intolerably maddened with, and restored the ferment of my senses to some degree of composure.

I had now achieved this rare adventure, ultimately much more to my satisfaction than I had bespoke the nature of it to turn out; nor was it much lessened, you may think, by my spark's lavish praises of my constancy and complaisance, which he gave weight to by a present that greatly passed my utmost expectation, besides his gratification to Mrs Cole.

I was not, however, at any time re-enticed to renew with him, or resort again to the violent expedient of lashing nature into more haste than good speed, which by the way, I conceive acts somewhat in the manner of a dose of Spanish flies,[109] with more pain perhaps but less danger, and might be necessary to him; but was nothing less so than to me, whose appetites wanted the bridle more than the spur.

Mrs Cole, to whom this adventurous exploit had more and more endeared me, looked on me now as a girl after her own heart, afraid of nothing, and, on a good account, hardy enough to fight all the weapons of pleasure through. Attentive then, in consequence of these favourable conceptions, to promote either my profit or pleasure, she had special regard for the first, in a new gallant of a very singular turn that she procured for and introduced to me.

This was a grave, staid, solemn, elderly gentleman whose peculiar humour was a delight in combing fine tresses of hair, and as I was perfectly headed to his taste, he used to come constantly at my toilette hours, when I let down my hair as loose as nature, and abandoned it to him to do what he pleased with it. And accordingly he would keep me an hour or more in play with it, drawing the comb through it, winding the curls round his fingers, even kissing it as he smoothed it, and all this led to no other use of my person, or any other liberties whatever, any more than if a distinction of sexes had not existed.

Another peculiarity of taste he had, which was to present me at once with a dozen pair of the whitest kid-gloves at a time: these he would divert himself with drawing on me, and then biting off their fingers' ends; all which fooleries of a sickly appetite the old gentleman paid more liberally for than most others did for more essential favours. This lasted till a violent cough, seizing and laying him up, delivered me from this most innocent and most insipid trifler; for I never heard more of him after his first retreat.

You may be sure a by-job of this sort interfered with no other pursuit or plan of life, which I led in truth with a modesty and reserve that was less the work of virtue than of exhausted novelty, a glut of pleasure, and easy circumstances, that made me indifferent to any engagements in which pleasure and profit were not eminently united. And such I could, with the less impatience, wait for at the hands of time and fortune, as I was satisfied I could never mend my pennyworths,[110] having evidently been served at the top of the market and even been pampered with dainties; besides that, in the sacrifice of a few momentary impulses, I found a secret satisfaction in respecting myself as well as preserving the life and freshness of my complexion. Louisa and Emily did not carry indeed their reserve as high as I did, but still they were far from cheap or abandoned, though two of their adventures seemed to contradict this general character, which for their singularity I shall give you in course, beginning first with Emily's.

Louisa and she went one night to a ball, the first in the habit of a shepherdess, Emily in that of a shepherd: I saw them in their dresses before they went, and nothing in nature could represent a prettier boy than this last did, being so extremely fair and well limbed. They had kept together for some time, when Louisa, meeting with an old acquaintance of hers, very cordially gives her companion the drop, and leaves her under the protection of her boy's habit, which was not much, and of her discretion, which was, it seems, yet less. Emily, finding herself deserted, sauntered thoughtlesly about a while, and as much for coolness and air, as anything else, pulled off her mask at length and went to the side-board, where, eyed and marked out by a gentleman in a very handsome domino, she was accosted by and fell into chat with him. The domino, after a little discourse, in which Emily doubtless distinguished her good nature and easiness more than her wit, began to make violent love to her, and drawing her insensibly to some benches at the lower end of the masquerade-room, got her to sit by him, where he squeezed her hands, pinched her cheeks, praised and played with her fair hair, admired her complexion, and all in a style of courtship dashed with a certain oddity that, not comprehending the mystery of, poor Emily attributed to his falling in with the humour of her disguise, and being naturally not the cruellest of her profession, began to incline to a parley on essentials; but here was the stress of the joke: he took her really for what she appeared to be, a smock-faced[111] boy, and she, forgetting her dress, and of course ranging quite wide of his ideas, took all those addresses to be paid to herself as a woman, which she precisely owed to his not thinking her one. However, this double error was pushed to such a height on both sides that Emily, who saw nothing in him but a gentleman of distinction by those points of dress to which his disguise did not extend, warmed too by the wine he had plied her with, and the caresses he had lavished upon her, suffered herself to be persuaded to go to a bagnio[112] with him. And thus, losing sight of Mrs Cole's cautions, with a blind confidence put herself into his hands to be carried wherever he pleased. For his part, equally blinded by his wishes, whilst her egregious simplicity favoured his deception more than the most exquisite art could have done, he supposed, no doubt, that he had lighted on some soft simpleton fit for his purpose, or some kept minion broken to his hand, who understood him perfectly well and entered into his designs. But be that as it would, he led her to a coach, went into it with her, and brought her into a very handsome apartment, with a bed in it; but whether it was a bagnio or not, she could not tell, having spoken to nobody but himself. But when they were alone together, and her *inamorato*[113] began to proceed to those extremities which instantly discover the sex, she remarked that no description could paint up to the life, the mixture of pique, confusion, and disappointment that appeared in his countenance, which joined to the mournful exclamation: 'By heavens, a woman!' This at once opened her eyes, which had hitherto been shut in downright stupidity. However, as if he had meant to retrieve that escape, he still continued to toy with and fondle her, but with so staring an alteration from extreme warmth into a chill and forced civility that even Emily herself could not but take notice of it, and now began to wish she had paid more regard to Mrs Cole's premonitions against ever engaging with a stranger. And now an excess of timidity succeeded to an excess of confidence, and she thought herself so much at his mercy and discretion that she stood passive throughout the whole progress of his prelude. For now, whether the impressions of so great a beauty had even made him forgive her her sex, or whether her appearance or figure in that dress still humoured his first illusion, he recovered by degrees a good part of his first warmth, and keeping Emily with her breeches still unbuttoned, stripped them down to her knees, and gently impelling her to lean down, with her face against the bedside, placed her so that the double-way between the double rising behind presented the choice fair to him, and he was so fiercely set on a mis-direction as to give the girl no small alarms for fear of losing a maidenhead she had not dreamt of. However, her complaints, and a resistance, gentle but firm, checked and brought him to himself again; so that turning his steed's head, he drove him at length in the right road, in which, his imagination having probably made the most of those resemblances that flattered his taste, he got with much ado whip and spur to his journey's end. After which he led her out himself, and walking with her two or three streets length, got her a chair,[114] when making her a present not anything inferior to what she could have expected, he left her, well recommended to the chairmen, who, on her directions, brought her home.

This she related to Mrs Cole and me the same morning, not without the visible remains of the fear and confusion she had been in, still stamped on her countenance. Mrs Cole's remark was that her indiscretion, proceeding from a constitutional facility, there were little hopes of anything curing her of it but repeated severe experience. Mine was that I could not conceive how it was possible for mankind to run into a taste, not only universally odious but absurd,[115] and impossible to gratify, since, according to the notions and experience I had of things, it was not in nature to force such immense disproportions. Mrs Cole only smiled at my ignorance and said nothing towards my undeception, which was not effected but by ocular demonstration, some months after, which a most singular accident furnished me and I will here set down that I may not return again to so disagreeable a subject.

I had, on a visit intended to Harriet, who had lodgings at Hampton-Court, hired a chariot to go out thither, Mrs Cole having promised to accompany me. But some indispensible business intervening to detain her, I was obliged to set out alone; and scarce had I got a third of my way before the axle-tree broke down, and I was well off to get out safe and unhurt into a public-house of a tolerably handsome appearance, on the road. Here the people told me that the stage[116] would come by in a couple of hours at farthest, upon which, determining to wait for it, sooner than lose the jaunt I had got so far forward on, I was carried into a very clean decent room up one pair of stairs, which I took possession of for the time I had to stay, in right of calling for sufficient to do the house justice.

Here, whilst I was amusing myself with looking out of the window, a single horse-chaise stopped at the door, out of which lightly leaped two young gentlemen, for so they seemed, who came in, as it were, only to bait[117] and refresh a little, for they gave their horse to be held in a readiness against[118] they came out. And presently I heard the door of the next room to me open, where they were let in and called about them briskly; and as soon as they were served, I could just hear that they shut and fastened the door on the inside.

A spirit of curiosity, far from sudden, since I do not know when I was without it, prompted me, without any particular suspicion, or other drift or view, to see who they were, and examine their persons and behaviour. The partition of our rooms was one of those moveable ones that, when taken down, served occasionally to lay them into one, for the convenience of a large company; and now my nicest search could not show me the shadow of a peep-hole, a circumstance which probably had not escaped the review of the parties on the other side, whom much it stood upon not to be deceived in it; but at length I observed a paper patch of the same colour as the wainscot, which I took to conceal some flaw. But then it was so high that I was obliged to stand on a chair to reach it, which I did as softly as possible, and with the point of a bodkin soon pierced it and opened myself espial-room sufficient: and now applying my eye close, I commanded the room perfectly, and could see my two young sparks romping and pulling one another about, entirely to my imagination, in frolic and innocent play.

The eldest might be, on my nearest guess, towards nineteen, a tall comely young man, in a white fustian frock, with a green velvet cape, and a cut bob-wig.

The youngest could not be above seventeen, fair, ruddy, completely well made, and, to say the truth, a sweet pretty stripling. He was, I fancy too, a country lad, by his dress, which was a green plush frock, and breeches of the same, white waistcoat and stockings, a jockey cap, with his yellowish hair long and loose in natural curls.

But after a look of circumspection, which I saw the eldest cast every way round the room, probably in too much hurry and heat not to overlook the very small opening I was posted at, especially at the height it was, whilst my eye too close to it, kept the light from shining through and betraying it, he said something to his companion that presently changed the face of things.

For now the elder began to embrace, to press, to kiss the younger, to put his hands in his bosom, and give such manifest signs of an amorous intention as made me conclude the other to be a girl in disguise, a mistake that nature kept me in countenance[119] in, for she had certainly made one, when she gave him the male stamp.

In the rashness then of their age, and bent as they were to accomplish their project of preposterous pleasure, at the risk of the very worst of consequences,[120] where a discovery was nothing less than improbable, they now proceeded to such lengths as soon satisfied me what they were.[121]

For presently the eldest unbuttoned the other's breeches, and removing the linen barrier, brought out to view a white shaft, middle-sized and scarce fledged, when, after handling and playing with it a little, with other dalliance, all received by the boy without other opposition than certain wayward coynesses, ten times more alluring than repulsive, he got him to turn round, with his face from him, to a chair that stood hard by; when knowing, I suppose, his office, the Ganymede now obsequiously leaned his head against the back of it, and projecting his body, made a fair mark, still covered with his shirt, as he thus stood in a side-view to me but fronting his companion, who, presently un-masking his battery, produced an engine that certainly deserved to be put to a better use, and very fit to confirm me in my disbelief of the possibility of things being pushed to odious extremities, which I had built on the disproportion of parts. But this disbelief I was now to be cured of, as by my consent all young men should likewise be, that their innocence may not be betrayed into such snares, for want of knowing the extent of their danger; for nothing is more certain than that ignorance of a vice is by no means a guard against it.

Slipping then aside the young lad's shirt, and tucking it up under his clothes behind, he showed to the open air those globular, fleshy eminences that compose the mount-pleasants of Rome, and which now, with all the narrow vale that intersects them, stood displayed and exposed to his attack: nor could I, without a shudder, behold the dispositions he made for it. First then, moistening well with spittle his instrument, obviously to render it glib, he pointed, he introduced it, as I could plainly discern, not only from its direction and my losing sight of it, but by the writhing, twisting, and soft murmured complaints of the young sufferer. But, at length, the first straights of entrance being pretty well got through, everything seemed to move and go pretty currently on, as in a carpet-road, without much rub or resistance. And now, passing one hand round his minion's hips, he got hold of his red-topped ivory toy, that stood perfectly stiff, and showed that if he was like his mother behind he was like his father before; this he diverted himself with, whilst with the other he wantoned with his hair, and leaning forward over his back, drew his face, from which the boy shook the loose curls that fell over it in the posture he stood him in, and brought it towards his, so as to receive a long-breathed kiss, after which, renewing his driving, and thus continuing to harrass his rear, the height of the fit came on with its usual symptoms, and dismissed the action.

All this, so criminal a scene, I had the patience to see to an end, purely that I might gather more facts, and certainty against them in my full design to do their deserts instant justice, and accordingly, when they had readjusted themselves and were preparing to go out, burning as I was with rage and indignation, I jumped down from my chair, in order to raise the house upon them, with such an unlucky impetuosity that some nail or ruggedness in the floor caught my foot, and flung me on my face with such violence that I fell senseless on the ground, and must have lain there some time before anyone came to my relief, so that they, alarmed, I suppose, by the noise of my fall, had more than the necessary time to make a safe retreat, which they effected, as I learnt, with a precipitation nobody could account for, till, when come to myself and composed enough to speak, I acquainted those of the house with the transaction I had been evidence to.

When I came home again and told Mrs Cole this adventure, she very sensibly observed to me that there was no doubt of due vengeance one time or other overtaking these miscreants, however they might escape for the present; and that, had I been the temporal instrument of it, I should have been, at least, put to a great deal more trouble and confusion than I imagine: that as to the thing itself, the less said of it was the better; but that though she might be suspected of partiality, from its being the common cause of womankind, out of whose mouths this practice tended to take something more precious than bread, yet she protested against any mixture of passion, with a declaration extorted from her by pure regard to truth, which was that whatever effect this infamous passion had in other ages and other countries, it seemed a peculiar blessing on our air and climate that there was a plague-spot visibly imprinted on all that are tainted with it, in this nation at least; for that among numbers of that stamp whom she had known, or at least were universally under the scandalous suspicion of it, she could not name an exception hardly of one of them whose character was not in all other respects the most worthless and despicable that could be, stripped of all the manly virtues of their own sex and filled up with only the very worst vices and follies of ours; that, in fine, they were scarce less execrable than ridiculous in their monstrous inconsistency of loathing and condemning women, and all at the same time aping their manners, airs, lisp, skuttle, and, in general, all their little modes of affectation, which become them at least better than they do these unsexed male misses.[122]

But here, washing my hands of them, I replunge into the stream of my history, into which I may very properly ingraft a terrible sally[123] of Louisa's, since I had some share in it myself and have besides engaged myself to relate it, in point of countenance to poor Emily. It will add, too, one more example to thousands in confirmation of the maxim that

when women get once out of compass, there are no lengths of licentiousness they are not capable of running.

One morning then, that both Mrs Cole and Emily were gone out for
the day, and only Louisa and I (not to mention the house-maid) were
left in charge of the house, whilst we were loitering away the time in
looking through the shop windows, the son of a poor woman who earned
very hard bread indeed by mending of stockings, in a stall in the neighbourhood, offers us some nosegays ranged round a small basket; by selling
of which the poor boy eked out his mother's maintenance of them both;
nor was he fit for any other way of livelihood, since he was not only
a perfect changeling, or idiot, but stammered so that there was no understanding even those sounds that his half-a-dozen, at most, animal ideas
prompted him to utter.

The boys and servants in the neighbourhood had given him the nick-
name of Good-natured Dick, from the soft simpleton's doing everything
he was bid to do at the first word, and from his naturally having no
turn to mischief. Then, by the way, he was perfectly well made, stout,
and clean-limbed, tall of his age, as strong as a horse, and, withal, pretty
featured; so that he was not absolutely such a figure to be snuffed at
neither, if your nicety could, in favour of such essentials, have dispensed
with a face unwashed, hair tangled for want of combing, and so ragged
a plight that he might have disputed points of show with any heathen
philosopher of them all.

This boy we had often seen, and bought his flowers, out of pure compassion, and nothing more: but just at this time, as he stood presenting
us his basket, a sudden whim, a start of wayward fancy seized Louisa,
and without consulting me, she calls him in, and, beginning to examine
his nosegays, culls out two, one for herself, another for me, and pulling
out half a crown, very currently gives it him to change, as if she had
really expected he could have changed it: but the boy, scratching his
head, made his signs explain his inability, in place of words, that he
could not, with all his struggling, articulate.

Louisa at this, says: 'Well, my lad, come upstairs with me, and I will
give you your due.' Winking at the same time to me, and beckoning
me to accompany her, which I did, securing first the street-door, that
by this means, together with the shop, became wholly the care of the
faithful house-maid.

As we went up, Louisa whispered me that she had conceived a strange longing to be satisfied, whether the general rule held good with regard to this changeling, and how far nature had made him amends in her best bodily gifts for her denial of the sublimer intellectual ones; begging at the same time my assistance in procuring her this satisfaction.[124] A want of complaisance was never my vice, and I was so far from opposing this extravagant frolic that now, bit with the same maggot, and my curiosity conspiring with hers, I entered plum into it, on my own account.

Consequently, as soon as we came into Louisa's bed-chamber, whilst she was amusing him with picking out his nosegays, I undertook the lead and began the attack. As it was not then very material to keep much measures with a mere natural,[125] I made presently very free with him, though at my first motion of meddling, his surprise and confusion made him receive my advances but awkwardly; nay, insomuch that he bashfully shied, and shied back a little, till encouraging him with my eyes, plucking him playfully by the hair, sleeking his cheeks, and forwarding my point by a number of little wantonnesses, I soon turned him familiar, and gave nature her sweetest alarm; so that aroused and beginning to feel himself, we could, amidst all the innocent laugh and grin I had provoked him into, perceive the fire lighting in his eyes, and, diffusing over his cheeks, blend its glow with that of his blushes; the emotion, in short, of animal pleasure glared distinctly in the simpleton's countenance. Yet struck with the novelty of the scene, he did not know which way to look or move; but tame, passive, simpering, with his mouth half open, in stupid rapture, stood and tractably suffered me to do what I pleased with him: his basket was dropped out of his hands, which Louisa took care of.

I had now, through more than one rent, discovered and felt his thighs, the skin of which seemed the smoother and fairer for the coarseness and even dirt of his dress; as the teeth of negroes seem the whiter for the surrounding black. And poor indeed of habit, poor of understanding, he was, however, abundantly rich in personal treasures, such as flesh, firm, plump, and replete with the sweet juices of youth, and robust well-knit limbs. My fingers too had now got within reach of the true, the genuine sensitive plant,[126] which, instead of shrinking from the touch, joys to meet it, and swells and vegetates under it: mine pleasingly informing me that matters were so ripe for the discovery we meditated that they were too mighty for the confinement they were ready to break.

A waistband that I unskewered,[127] and a rag of shirt that I removed, and which could not have covered a quarter of it, revealed the whole of the idiot's standard of distinction, erect, in full pride and display: but such a one! it was positively of so tremendous a size that, prepared as we were to see something extraordinary, it still, out of measure, surpassed our expectation, and astonished even me, who had not been used to trade in trifles. In fine, it might have answered very well the making a show of: its enormous head seemed, in hue and size, not unlike a common sheep's heart; then you might have trolled[128] dice securely along the broad back of the body of it; the length of it, too, was prodigious; then the rich appendage of the treasure-bag beneath, large in proportion, gathered, and crisped up, round, in shallow furrows, helped to fill the eye, and complete the proof of his being a natural, not quite in vain, since it was full manifest that he inherited, and largely too, the prerogative of majesty, which distinguishes that otherwise most unfortunate condition, and gives rise to the vulgar saying that 'a fool's bauble is a lady's play-fellow'.[129] Nor wholly without reason; for, generally speaking, it is in love as it is in war, where the longest weapon carries it. Nature, in short, had done so much to him in those parts, that she perhaps held herself acquitted for doing so little for his head.

For my part, who had sincerely no intention to push the joke further than simply satisfying my curiosity with the sight of it alone, I was content, in spite of the temptation that stared me in the face, with having raised a maypole for another to hang a garland; for by this time, easily reading Louisa's desires in her wishful eyes, I acted the commodious part, and made her, who sought no better sport, significant signs of encouragement to go through-stitch[130] with the adventure; intimating too that I would stay and see fair play; in which, indeed, I had in view to humour a new-born curiosity to observe what appearances active nature would put on in a natural, in the course of this her darling operation.

Louisa, whose appetite was up, and who, like the industrious bee, was, it seems, not above gathering the sweets of so rare a flower, though she found it planted on a dung-hill, was but too readily disposed to take the benefit of my cession: urged then strongly by her own desires, and emboldened by me, she presently determined to risk a trial of parts with the idiot, who was by this time nobly inflamed for her purpose by all the irritations we had used to put the principles of pleasure effectually into motion, and to wind up the springs of its organ to their supreme pitch; and it stood accordingly stiff and straining, ready to burst with the blood and spirits that swelled it to a bulk! No! I shall never forget it.

Louisa then, taking and holding the fine handle that so invitingly offered itself, led the ductile youth by that master-tool of his, as she stepped backward towards the bed, which he joyfully gave way to, under the incitations of instinct, and palpably delivered up to the goad of desire.

Stopped then by the bed, she took the fall she loved, and leaned to the most, gently backward upon it, still holding fast what she held and taking care to give her clothes a convenient toss up, so that her thighs, duly disclosed and elevated, laid open all the outward prospect of the treasure of love: the rose-lipped ouverture[131] presenting the cock-pit so fair that it was not in nature even for a natural to miss it. Nor did he; for Louisa, fully bent on grappling with it, and impatient of dalliance or delay, directed faithfully the point of the battering piece, and bounded up with a rage of so voracious appetite to meet and favour the thrust of insertion that the fierce activity on both sides effected it, but effected it with such a pain of distention that Louisa cried out violently that she was hurt beyond all bearing, that she was killed. But it was too late; the storm was up, and force was on her to give way to it. For now the man-machine,[132] strongly worked upon by the sensual passion, felt so manfully his advantages and superiority, felt withal the sting of pleasure so intolerable that, maddening with it, his joys began to assume a character of furiousness, which made me tremble for the too tender Louisa. He seemed at this juncture greater than himself; his countenance, before so void of meaning or expression, now grew big with the importance of the act he was upon. In short, it was not now that he was to be played the fool with; but what is pleasant enough, I myself was awed into a sort of respect for him by the comely terrors his emotions dressed him in, his eyes shooting sparks of fire, his face glowing with ardours that gave all another life to it; his teeth churning; his whole frame agitated with a raging ungovernable impetuosity, all sensibly betraying the formidable fierceness with which the genial instinct acted upon him. Butting then and goring all before him, and mad and wild like an overdriven[133] steer, he ploughs up the tender furrow, all insensible of Louisa's complaints; nothing can stop, nothing can keep out a fury like this; which, having once got its head in, its blind rage soon made way for the rest, piercing, rending, and breaking open all obstruction. The torn, split, wounded girl cries, struggles, invokes me to her rescue, and endeavours to get from under the young savage, or shake him off, but alas, in vain! Her breath might as soon have stilled or stemmed a storm in winter as all her strength have quelled his rough assault, or put him out of his course. And indeed all her efforts and struggles were managed in such disorder that they served rather to entangle and fold her the faster in the twine of his boisterous arms; so that she was tied to the stake and obliged to fight the match out, if she died for it. For his part, instinct-ridden as he was, the expressions of his animal passion, partaking something of ferocity, were rather worryings[134] than kisses, intermixed with eager ravenous love-bites on her cheeks and neck, the prints of which did not wear out for some days after.

Poor Louisa, however, bore up at length better than could have been expected; and though she suffered, and greatly too, yet ever true to the good old cause, she suffered with pleasure and enjoyed her pain. And soon now, by dint of an enraged enforcement, the brute-machine, driven like a whirlwind, made all smoke again, and wedging his way up to the utmost extremity, left her, in point of penetration, nothing either to fear or to desire; and now,

> Gorged with the dearest morsel of the earth,
>
> (Shakespeare)

Louisa lay, pleased to the heart, pleased to her utmost capacity of being so, with every fibre in those parts stretched almost to breaking, on a rack of joy, whilst the instrument of all this overfulness searched her senses with its sweet excess, till the pleasure gained upon her so, its point stung her so home that, catching at length the rage from her furious driver, and sharing the riot of his wild rapture, she went wholly out of her mind into that favourite part of her body, the whole intenseness of which was so fervorously[135] filled and employed: there alone she existed, all lost in those delirious transports, those ecstasies of the senses, which her winking eyes, the brightened vermillion of her lips and cheeks, and sighs of pleasure, deeply fetched, so pathetically expressed. In short, she was now as mere a machine as much wrought on, and had her motions as little at her own command as the natural himself, who thus broke in upon her, made her feel with a vengeance his tempestuous tenderness and the force of mettle he battered with.

Their active loins quivered again with the violence of their conflict, till
the surge of pleasure, foaming and raging to a height, drew down the
pearly shower that was to allay this hurricane. The purely sensitive
idiot then first shed those tears of joy that attend its last moments,
not without an agony of delight, and even almost a roar of rapture,
as the gush escaped him, so sensibly too for Louisa that she kept him
faithful company, going off in consent with the old symptoms: a delicious
delirium, a tremulous convulsive shudder, and the critical dying 'oh!'
And now, on his getting off, she lay pleasure-drenched and regorging[136]
its essential sweets: but quite spent, gasping for breath, without other
sensation of life than in those exquisite vibrations that trembled yet on
the strings of delight, which had been so ravishingly touched, and which
nature had been too intensely stirred with, for the senses to be quickly
at peace from.

As for the changeling, whose curious engine had been thus successfully played off, his shift of countenance and gesture had even something
droll or rather tragi-comic in it: there was now an air of sad, repining
foolishness superadded to his natural one of no meaning and idiotism,
as he stood with his label of manhood, now lank, unstiffened, becalmed,
and flapping against his thighs, down which it reached halfway, terrible
even in its fall; whilst, under the dejection of spirit and flesh, which
naturally followed, his eyes, by turns cast down towards his stricken
standard, or piteously lifted to Louisa, seemed to require at her hands
what he had so sensibly parted from to her and now ruefully missed.
But the vigour of nature, soon returning, dissipated this blast of faintness
which the common-law of enjoyment had subjected him to; and now
his basket re-became his main concern, which I looked for and brought
him, whilst Louisa restored his dress to its usual condition, and afterwards
pleased him perhaps more by taking all his flowers off his hands, and
paying him at his rate for them, than if she had embarrassed him by
a present that he would have been puzzled to account for, and might
have put others on tracing the motives of it.

Whether she ever returned to the attack, I know not, and, to say
the truth, I believe not; she had had her freak-out[137] and had pretty
plentifully drowned her curiosity in a glut of pleasure, which, as it happened, had no other consequence than that the lad, who retained only
a confused memory of the transaction, would, when he saw her, for
some little time after, express a grin of joy and familiarity, after his idiot

manner, and soon forgot her, probably in favour of the next woman tempted, on the report of his parts, to take him in.

Louisa, too, herself did not long outstay this adventure at Mrs Cole's (to whom, by the by, we took care not to boast of our exploit, till all fear of consequences was clearly over), for, an occasion presenting itself of proving her passion for a young fellow, at the expense of her discretion, proceeding all in character, she packed up her toilet, at half a day's warning, and went with him abroad, since which I lost entirely sight of her; and it never fell in my way to hear what became of her.

But a few days after she had left us, two very pretty young gentlemen, who were Mrs Cole's especial favourites, and free of her academy, easily obtained her consent for Emily's and my acceptance of a party of pleasure, at a little but agreeable house belonging to one of them, situated not far up the river Thames, on the Surrey side.

Everything being settled, and it being a fine summer day, but rather of the warmest, we set out after dinner, and got to our rendezvous about four in the afternoon, where, landing at the foot of a neat, joyous pavilion, Emily and I were handed into it by our Squires, and there drank tea with a cheerfulness and gaiety that the beauty of the prospect, the serenity of the weather, and tender politeness of our sprightly gallants naturally led us into.

After tea, and taking a turn in the garden, my particular, who was the master of the house, and had in no sense schemed this party of pleasure for a dry one, proposed to us, with that frankness which his familiarity at Mrs Cole's entitled him to, as the weather was excessively hot, to bathe together, under a commodious shelter that he had prepared expressly for that purpose, in a creek of the river, with which a side-door of the pavilion immediately communicated, and where we might be sure of having our diversion out, safe from interruption, and with the utmost privacy.

Emily, who never refused anything, and I, who ever delighted in bathing, and had no exception to the person who proposed it, or to those pleasures it was easy to guess it implied, took care, on this occasion, not to wrong our training at Mrs Cole's, and agreed to it with as good a grace as we could. Upon which, without loss of time, we returned instantly to the pavilion, one door of which opened into a tent, pitched before it, that with its marquise[138] formed a pleasing defence against the sun, or the weather, and was besides as private as we could wish.

The lining of it, embossed cloth, represented a wild forest-foliage, from the top down to the sides, which, in the same stuff, were figured with fluted pilasters, with their spaces between filled with flower vases, the whole having a gay effect upon the eye, wherever you turned it.

Then it reached sufficiently into the water, yet contained convenient benches round it, on the dry ground, either to keep our clothes, or, – or, – in short, for more uses than resting upon. There was a side-table, too, loaded with sweatmeats, jellies, and other eatables, and bottles of wine and cordials, by way of occasional relief from any rawness, or chill of the water, or from any faintness from whatever cause; and, in fact, my gallant, who understood *chere entière*[139] perfectly, and who, for taste (even if you would not approve this specimen of it) might have been comptroller of pleasures to a Roman emperor, had left no requisite towards convenience or luxury unprovided.

As soon as we had looked round this inviting spot, and every preliminary of privacy was duly settled, strip was the word: when the young gentlemen soon dispatched the undressing each his partner, and reduced us to the naked confession of all those secrets of person which dress generally hides, and which the discovery of was, naturally speaking, not to our disadvantage. Our hands, indeed, machinally carried towards the most interesting part of us, screened at first all from the tufted cliff downwards, till we took them away at their desire and employed them, in doing them the same office, of helping them off with their clothes, in the process of which there passed all the little wantonnesses and frolic that you may easily imagine.

As for my spark, he was presently undressed, all to his shirt, the fore-lappet[140] of which, as he leaned languishingly on me, he smilingly pointed to me to observe as it bellied out, or rose, and fell, according to the unruly starts of the motion behind it; but it was soon fixed, for now, taking off his shirt, and naked as a Cupid, he showed it me at so upright a stand as prepared me indeed for his application to me for instant ease. But though the sight of its fine size was fit enough to fire me, the cooling air, as I stood in this state of nature, joined to the desire I had of bathing first, enabled me to put him off, and tranquillize him, with the remark that a little suspense would only set a keener edge on the pleasure. Leading then the way, and showing our friends an example of continency, which they were giving signs of losing respect to, we went hand in hand into the stream, till it took us up to our neck, where the no more than grateful coolness of the water gave my senses a delicious refreshment from the sultriness of the season, and made me more alive, more happy in myself, and, in course, more alert and open to voluptuous impressions.

Here I laved and wantoned with the water, or sportively[141] played with my companion, leaving Emily to deal with hers at discretion. Mine, at length, not content with making me take the plunge over head and ears, kept splashing me, and provoking me by all the little playful tricks he could devise, and which I strove not to remain in his debt for. We gave, in short, a loose to mirth. And now, nothing would serve him but giving his hands the regale of going over every part of me, neck, breast, belly, thighs, and all the sweet *et cetera*, so dear to the imagination, under the pretext of washing and rubbing them; as we both stood in the water, no higher now than the pit of our stomachs, and which did not hinder him from feeling and toying with that leak that distinguishes our sex and is so wonderfully water-tight: for his fingers, in vain dilating and opening it, only let more flame than water into it, be it said without a figure; at the same time he made me feel his own engine, which was so well wound up as to stand even the working in water, and he accordingly threw one arm round my neck, and was endeavouring to get the better of that harsher constriction bred by the surrounding fluid, and had in effect won his way so far as to make me sensible of the pleasuring stretch of those nether lips, from the in-driving machine; when, independent of my not liking that awkward mode of enjoyment, I could not help interrupting him, in order to become joint spectators of a plan of joy in hot operation between Emily and her partner, who, impatient of the fooleries and dalliance of the bath, had led his nymph to one of the benches on the green bank, where he was very cordially proceeding to teach her the difference betwixt jest and earnest.

There, setting her on his knee, and gliding one hand over the surface of that smooth polished, snow-white skin of hers, which now doubly shone with a dew-bright lustre, and presented to the touch something like what one would imagine of animated ivory, especially in those ruby-nippled globes which the touch is so fond of and delights to make love to; with the other, he was lusciously exploring the sweet secret of nature, in order to make room for a stately piece of machinery that stood up-reared between her thighs, as she continued sitting on his lap, and pressed hard for instant admission, which the tender Emily, in a fit of humour deliciously protracted, affecting to decline and elude the very pleasure she sighed for, but in a style of waywardness so prettily put on and managed as to render it only ten times more poignant. Then her eyes, amidst all the softest, dying languishment, expressed at once a mock-denial and extreme desire, whilst her sweetness was zested with a coyness so pleasingly provoking, her moods of keeping him off were so attractive that they redoubled the impetuous rage with which he covered her with kisses and kisses that, whilst she seemed to shy from or scuffle for, the cunning wanton contrived such sly returns of as were doubtless the sweeter for the gust she gave them of being stolen or ravished.

Thus Emily, who knew no art but that which nature itself, in favour of her principal end, pleasure, had inspired her with, the art of yielding, coyed it indeed, but coyed it to the purpose; for with all her straining, her wrestling, and striving to break from the clasp of his arms, she was so far wiser yet than to mean it, that in her struggles it was visible that she aimed at nothing more than multiplying points of touch with him, and drawing yet closer the folds that held them everywhere entwined, like two tendrils of a vine intercurling together, so that the same effect, as when Louisa strove in good earnest to disengage from the idiot, was now produced by different motives.

Meanwhile, their emersion out of the cold water had caused a general glow, a tender suffusion of heightened carnation[142] over their bodies, both equally white and smooth-skinned; so that, as their limbs were thus amorously interwoven in sweet confusion, it was scarce possible to distinguish who they respectively belonged to, but for the brawnier, bolder muscles of the stronger sex.

In a little time, however, the champion was fairly in with her, and had tied at all points the true lover's knot, when now, adieu all the little refinements of a finessed[143] reluctance! adieu the tender friendly feint! she was presently driven forcibly out of the power of using any art: and indeed, what art but must give way when nature, corresponding with her sweet assailant, invaded in the heart of her capital and, carried by storm, lay at the mercy of the proud conqueror, who had his entry triumphantly and completely; soon however to become a tributary! For the engagement, growing hotter and hotter at close quarters, she presently brought him to the pass of paying down the dear debt to nature, which she had no sooner collected in but, like a duellist who has laid his antagonist at his feet, when he has himself received a mortal wound, Emily had scarce time to plume herself upon her victory, but, shot with the same discharge, she, in a loud expiring sigh, in the closure of her eyes, the stretch-out of her limbs, and a remission of her whole frame, gave manifest signs that all was as it should be, and happily well over with her.

For my part, who had not with the calmest patience stood in the water all this time, to view this warm action, I leaned tenderly on my gallant, and, at the close of it, seemed to ask him with my eyes, what he thought of it. But he, more eager to satisfy me by his actions than by words or looks, as we shoaled[144] the water together towards the shore, showed me the staff of love so intensely set up that, had not even charity, beginning at home in this case, urged me to our mutual relief, it would have been cruel indeed to have suffered the youth to burst with straining, when the remedy was so obvious and so near at hand.

Accordingly, we took to a bench, whilst Emily and her spark, who belonged, it seems, to the sea, stood at the side-board, drinking to our good voyage, for, as the last observed, we were well under way with a fair wind up channel, and full-freighted: nor indeed were we long before we finished our trip to *Cythera* and unloaded in the old haven; but as the circumstances did not admit of much variation, I shall spare you the description.

At the same time, allow me to place you here an excuse I am conscious of owing you for having perhaps too much affected the figurative style; though, surely, it can pass nowhere more allowably than in a subject which is so properly the province of poetry, nay! is poetry itself, pregnant with every flower of imagination and loving metaphors, even where not the natural expressions, for respects of fashion and sound necessarily forbid it.

Resuming now my history, you may please to know that, what with a competent number of repetitions, all in the same strain, (and, by the by, we have a certain natural sense that those repetitions are very much to the taste of), what with a circle of pleasures delicately varied, there was not a moment lost to joy all the time we stayed there; till, late in the night, we were re-escorted home by our 'squires, who delivered us safe to Mrs Cole, with generous thanks for our company.

This, too, was Emily's last adventure in our way. For scarce a week after, she was, by an accident too trivial to detail to you the particulars, found out by her parents, who were in very good circumstances, and who had been punished for their partiality to their son in the loss of him, occasioned by a circumstance of their overindulgence to his appetite; upon which, the so long engrossed stream of fondness, running violently in favour of this lost and inhumanly abandoned child, whom, if they had not neglected all inquiry about, they might long before have recovered, they were now so overjoyed at their retrieval of her that, I presume, it made them much the less strict in examining to the bottom of things. For they seemed very glad to take for granted, in the lump, everything that the grave and decent Mrs Cole was pleased to pass upon them, and soon afterwards sent her, from the country, a handsome acknowledgment.

But it was not so easy to replace to our community the loss of so sweet a member of it; for, not to mention her beauty, she was one of those mild, pliant characters that, if one does not entirely esteem, one can scarce help loving, which is not such a bad compensation neither. Owing all her weaknesses to a good nature and an indolent facility that kept her too much at the mercy of first impressions, she had just sense enough to know that she wanted leading strings, and thought herself so much obliged to any who would take the pains to think for her, and guide her, that with a very little management, she was capable of being made a most agreeable, nay, a most virtuous wife. For vice, it is probable, had never been her choice, or her fate, if it had not been for occasion or example, or had she not depended less upon herself than upon her circumstances: this presumption her conduct afterwards verified. For presently meeting with a match, that was ready cut and dry for her, with a neighbour's son of her own rank, and a young man of sense and order, who took her as the widow of one lost at sea (for so it seems one of her gallants, whose name she had made free with, really was), she naturally struck into all the duties of her domestic[145] with as much simplicity of affection, with as much constancy and regularity, as if she had never swerved from a state of undebauched innocence from her youth.

These desertions had, however, now so far thinned Mrs Cole's cluck that she was left with only me, like a hen with one chicken. But though she was earnestly entreated and encouraged to recruit her *corps*, her growing infirmities, and above all the tortures of a stubborn hip-gout, which she found would yield to no remedy, determined her to break up her business, and retire with a decent pittance into the country, where I promised myself nothing so sure as my going down to live with her, as soon as I had seen a little more of life and improved my small matters into a competency that would create me an independence on the world; for I was now, thanks to Mrs Cole, wise enough to keep that essential in view.

Thus I was then to lose my preceptress, as did the philosophers of the town the white crow of their profession;[146] for, besides that she never ransomed[147] her customers, whose taste too she ever studiously consulted; besides that she never racked her pupils with unconscionable extortions, nor ever put their hand earnings, as she called them, under the contribution of poundage, she was a severe enemy to the seduction of innocence, and confined her acquisitions solely to those unfortunate young women who, having lost it, were but the juster objects of compassion. Amongst these, indeed, she picked out such as suited her views, and taking them under her protection, rescued them from the danger of the public sinks of ruin and misery, to place or form them, well or ill, in the manner you have seen. Having then settled her affairs, she set out on her journey, after taking the most tender leave of me and, at the end of some excellent instructions, recommending me to myself, with an anxiety, perfectly maternal: in short, she affected me so much that I was not presently reconciled to myself for suffering her, at any rate, to go without me; but fate had, it seems, otherwise disposed of me.

I had, on my separation from Mrs Cole, taken a pleasant convenient house near Marylebone, but easy to rent and manage, from its smallness; which I furnished neatly and modestly. There, with a reserve of eight hundred pounds, the fruit of my deference to Mrs Cole's counsels, exclusive of clothes, some jewels, some plate, I saw myself in purse for a long time, to wait without impatience for what the chapter of accidents might produce in my favour.[148]

Here, under the new character of a young gentlewoman whose husband was gone to sea, I had marked me out such lines of life and conduct as, leaving me at a competent liberty to pursue my views, either of pleasure or fortune, bounded me nevertheless strictly within the rules of decency and discretion: a disposition in which you cannot escape observing a true pupil of Mrs Cole's.

I was scarce, however, well warm in my new abode when, going out one morning pretty early to enjoy the freshness of it, in the pleasing outlet of the fields, accompanied only by a maid whom I had hired; as we were carelessly walking among the trees, we were alarmed with the noise of a violent coughing: turning our heads towards which, we distinguished a plain well-dressed elderly gentleman, who, attacked with a sudden fit, was so much overcome as to be forced to give way to it and sit down at the foot of a tree, where he seemed suffocating with the severity of it, being perfectly black in the face. Not less moved than frightened with which, I flew on the instant to his relief, and using the rote[149] of practice I had observed on the like occasion, I loosened his cravat, and clapped him on the back; but whether to any purpose, or whether the cough had had its course, I know not; but the fit went immediately off; and now recovered to his speech, and legs, he returned me thanks, with as much emphasis as if I had saved his life. This naturally engaging a conversation, he acquainted me where he lived, which was a considerable distance from where I met with him, and where he had strayed insensibly on the same intention of a morning walk.

He was, as I afterwards learned in the course of the intimacy which this little accident gave birth to, an old bachelor turned of sixty, but of a fresh, vigorous complexion, insomuch that he scarce marked five and forty, having never racked or forced his constitution, by permitting his desires to overtax his ability.

As to his birth and condition, his parents, honest and failed mechanics, had, by the best traces he could get of them, left him an infant orphan on the parish; so that it was from a charity school that, by honesty and industry, he made his way into a merchant's compting-house;[150] from whence, being sent to a house in Cadiz, he there, by his talents and activity, acquired a fortune, but an immense one; with which he returned to his native country, where he could not, however, so much as fish one single relation out of the obscurity he was born in. Taking then a taste for retirement, and pleased to enjoy life, like a mistress in the dark, he flowed[151] his days in all the ease of opulence, without the least parade of it, and rather studying the concealment than the show of a fortune, looking down on a world he perfectly knew; himself, to his wish unknown and unmarked by it.

But as I propose to devote a letter entirely to the pleasure of retracing to you all the particulars of my acquaintance with this ever, to me, memorable friend, I shall, in this, transiently touch on no more than may serve as mortar to cement, or form the connexion of my history, and to obviate your surprise that one of my high blood and relish of life should count a gallant of threescore such a catch.

Referring then to a more explicit narrative, to explain by what progressions our acquaintance, certainly innocent at first, insensibly changed nature, and ran into unplatonic lengths, as might well be expected from one of my condition of life, and above all from that principle of electricity which scarce ever fails of producing fire, when the sexes meet, I shall only here acquaint you that, as age had not subdued his tenderness for our sex, neither had it robbed him of the power of pleasing, since whatever he wanted in the bewitching charms of youth, he atoned for or supplemented with the advantages of experience, the sweetness of his manners, and, above all, his flattering address in touching the heart by an application to the understanding. From him it was that I first learned to any purpose, and not without infinite pleasure, that I had such a portion of me worth bestowing some regard on; from him I received my first essential encouragement, and instructions, how to put it into that train of cultivation which I have since pushed to the little degree of improvement you see it at; he it was who first taught me to be sensible that the pleasures of the mind were superior to those of the body, at the same time that they were so far from obnoxious to, or incompatible with each other that, besides the sweetness in the variety and transition, the one served to exalt and perfect the taste of the other to a degree that the senses alone can never arrive at.

Himself a rational pleasurist, as being much too wise to be ashamed of the pleasures of humanity, loved me indeed, but loved me with dignity, in a mean[152] equally removed from that sourness or forwardness which age is unpleasingly characterised by, and from that childish silly dotage that so often disgraces it, and which he himself used to turn into ridicule and compare to an old goat affecting the frisk of a young kid.

In short, everything that is generally unamiable in his season of life was, in him, repaired by so many advantages that he existed a proof manifest, at least to me, that it is not out of the power of age to please, if it lays out to please, and if, making just allowances, those in that class do not forget that it must cost them more pains and attention than what youth, the natural springtime of joy, stands in need of: as fruits out of season require proportionably more skill and cultivation to force them.

With this gentleman then, who took me home soon after our acquaintance commenced, I lived near eight months, in which time, my constant complaisance, my docility, my attention to deserve his confidence and love, and a conduct, in general, devoid of the least art and founded on my sincere esteem and regard for him, won and attached him so firmly to me that, after having generously trusted me with a genteel,[153] independent settlement, proceeding to heap marks of affection on me, he appointed me, by an authentic will, his sole heiress and executrix; a disposition which he did not outlive two months, being taken from me by a violent cold that he contracted as he unadvisedly ran to the window, on an alarm of fire, at some streets' distance, and stood there naked-breasted and exposed to the fatal impressions of a damp night-air.

After acquitting myself of my duty towards my deceased benefactor, and paying him a tribute of unfeigned sorrow, which a little time changed into the most tender, grateful memory of him that I shall ever retain, I grew somewhat comforted by the prospect that now opened to me, if not of happiness, at least of affluence and independence.

I saw myself then, in the full bloom and pride of youth (for I was not yet nineteen), actually at the head of so large a fortune as it would have been even the height of impudence in me to have raised my wishes, much more my hopes, to; and that this unexpected elevation did not turn my head, I owed to the pains my benefactor had taken to form and prepare me for it, as I owed his opinion of my management of the vast possessions he left me to what he had observed of the prudential economy I had learned under Mrs Cole, of which the reserve he saw I had made was a proof and encouragement to him.

But alas! how easily is the enjoyment of the greatest sweets in life, in present possession, poisoned by the regret of an absent one! But my regret was a mighty and a just one, since it had my only truly beloved Charles for its object.

Given him up I had, indeed, completely, having never once heard from him since our separation; which, as I found afterwards, had been my misfortune, and not his neglect, for he wrote me several letters which had all miscarried; but forgotten him I never had: and amidst all my personal infidelities, not one had made a pin's point impression on a heart impenetrable to the true love-passion, but for him.

As soon, however, as I was mistress of this unexpected fortune, I felt more than ever how dear he was to me, from its insufficiency to make me happy, whilst he was not to share it with me. My earliest care, consequently, was to endeavour at getting some account of him. But all my researches produced me no more light than that his father had been dead some time, not so well as even with the world, and that Charles had reached his port of destination in the South Seas, where, finding the estate he was sent to recover dwindled to a trifle, by the loss of two ships, in which the bulk of his uncle's fortune lay, he was come away with the small remainder, and might perhaps, according to the best advice, in a few months return to England, from whence he had, at the time of this my inquiry, been absent two years and seven months: a little eternity in love!

You cannot conceive with what joy I embraced the hopes thus given me of seeing the delight of my heart again; but as the term of months was assigned it, in order to divert and amuse my impatience for his return, after settling my affairs with much ease and security, I set out on a journey for Lancashire, with an equipage suitable to my fortune, and with a design purely to revisit my place of nativity, for which I could not help retaining a great tenderness, and might naturally not be sorry to show myself there, to the advantage I was now in pass to do, after the report Esther Davis had spread of my being spirited away to the Plantations, for on no other supposition could she account for the suppression of myself to her, since her leaving me so abruptly at the inn. Another favourite intention I had, to look out for my relations, though I had none besides distant ones, and to prove a benefactress to them. Then Mrs Cole's place of retirement, lying in my way, was not amongst the least of the pleasures I had proposed to myself in this expedition.

I had taken nobody with me but a discreet decent woman, to figure it as my companion, besides my servants, and was scarce got into an inn, about twenty miles from London, where I was to sup and pass the night, when such a storm of wind and rain sprang up as made me congratulate myself on having got under shelter before it began.

This had continued a good half hour when, bethinking me of some directions to be given to the coachman, I sent for him, and not caring that his shoes should soil the very clean parlour in which the cloth was laid, I stepped into the hall-kitchen, where he was, and where, whilst I was talking to him, I slantingly observed two horsemen driven in by the weather, and both wringing wet; one of whom was asking if they could be assisted with a change, till their clothes could be dried. But heavens! who can express what I felt at the sound of a voice, ever present to my heart, and that it now rebounded at! or when pointing my eyes towards the person it came from, they confirmed its information, in spite of so long an absence, and of a dress one would have imagined studied for a disguise: a horseman's great coat with a stand-up cape, and his hat flapped; but what could escape the piercing alertness of a sense surely guided by love? A transport then, like mine, was above all consideration or schemes of surprise, and I, that instant, with the rapidity of the emotions that I felt the spur of, shot into his arms, crying out as I threw mine round his neck: 'My life! – my soul! – my *Charles!*' and, without further power of speech, swooned away under the oppressing agitations of joy and surprise.

Recovered out of my entrancement, I found myself in my charmer's arms, but in the parlour, surrounded by a crowd which this event had gathered round us, and which immediately, on a signal from the discreet landlady, who currently took him for my husband, cleared the room, and desirably left us alone to the raptures of this reunion, my joy at which had like to have proved, at the expense of my life, its power superior to that of grief at our fatal separation.

The first object then that my eyes opened on was their supreme idol, and my supreme wish, Charles, on one knee, holding me fast by the hand and gazing at me in a transport of fondness. Observing my recovery, he attempted to speak, and give vent to his impatience of hearing my voice again, to satisfy him once more that it was me; but the mightiness and suddenness of the surprise continuing to stun him, choked his utterance. He could only stammer out a few broken, half-formed, faultering accents,[154] which my ears greedily drinking in, spelt, and put together so as to make out their sense: 'After so long! – so cruel! – an absence, – my dearest *Fanny!* – Can it? Can it be you? –' stifling me at the same time with kisses that, stopping my mouth, at once prevented the answer that he panted for, and increased the delicious disorder in which all my senses were rapturously lost. Amidst, however, this crowd of ideas, and all blissful ones, there obtruded only one cruel doubt, that poisoned nearly all this transcendent happiness: and what was it but my dread of its being too excessive to be real! I trembled now with the fear of its being no more than a dream, and of my waking out of it into the horrors of finding it one: under this fond apprehension, imagining I could not make too much of the present prodigious joy before it should vanish and leave me in the desert again, nor verify its reality too strongly, I clung to him, I clasped him, as if to hinder him from escaping me again. 'Where have you been? – how could you, could you leave me? – Say you are still mine – that you still love me, – and thus! thus!' (kissing him as if I would consolidate lips with him) 'I forgive you – forgive my hard fortune in favour of this restoration.' All these interjections breaking from me, in that wildness of expression that justly passes for eloquence in love, drew from him all the returns my fond heart could wish or require. Our caresses, our questions, our answers, for some time, observed no order; all crossing or interrupting one another in sweet confusion, whilst we exchanged hearts at our eyes, and renewed the ratifications of a love unabated by time or absence: not a breath, not a motion, not a gesture on either side but what was strongly impressed with it. Our hands, locked in each other, repeated the most passionate squeezes, so that their fiery thrill went to the heart again.

Thus absorbed, and concentered in this unutterable delight, I had not attended to the sweet author of it, being thoroughly wet and in danger of catching cold; when, in good time, the landlady, whom the appearance of my equipage (which, by the by, Charles knew nothing of) had gained me an interest in, for me and mine, interrupted us by bringing in a decent shift of linen and clothes, which now, somewhat recovered into a calmer composure by the coming in of a third person, I pressed him to take the benefit of, with a tender concern and anxiety that made me tremble for his health.

The landlady leaving us again, he proceeded to shift, in the act of which, though he proceeded with all that modesty which became these first solemner instants of our re-meeting, after so long an absence, I could not contain certain snatches of my eyes, lured by the dazzling discoveries of his naked skin, that escaped him as he changed his linen, and which I could not observe the unfaded life and complexion of without emotions of tenderness and joy, that had himself too purely for their object to partake of a loose or mis-timed desire.

He was soon dressed in these tempory clothes, which neither fitted him nor became the light my passion placed him in, to me at least. Yet as they were on him, they looked extremely well, in virtue of that magic charm which love put into everything that he touched or had relation to him; and where indeed was that dress that a figure like his would not give grace to? For now, as I eyed him more in detail, I could not but observe the even favourable alteration which the time of his absence had produced in his person.

There were still the same exquisite lineaments, still the same vivid vermillion and bloom reigning in his face, but now the roses were more fully blown: the tant[155] of his travels and a beard somewhat more distinguishable, had, at the expense of no more delicacy than what he could better spare than not, given it an air of becoming manliness and maturity that symmetrized nobly with that air of distinction and empire[156] with which nature had stamped it, in a rare mixture with the sweetness of it. Still nothing had he lost of that smooth plumpness of flesh which, glowing with freshness, blooms florid to the eye and delicious to the touch; then, his shoulders were grown more square, his shape more formed, more portly, but still free and airy. In short, his figure showed riper, greater, and perfecter to the experienced eye than in his tender youth; and now, he was not much more than two and twenty.

In this interval, however, I picked out of the broken, often pleasingly interrupted account of himself that he was, at that instant, actually on his road to London, in not a very paramount plight or condition, having been wrecked on the Irish coast, for which he had prematurely embarked, and lost the little all he had brought with him from the South Seas, so that he had not, till after great shifts and hardships, in the company of his fellow traveller, the captain, got so far on his journey; that so it was (having heard of his father's death and circumstances), he had now the world to begin again, on a new account; a situation, which, he assured me, in a vein of sincerity that, flowing from his heart, penetrated mine, gave him no farther pain than that he had it not in his power to make me as happy as he could wish. My fortune, you will please to observe, I had not entered upon any overture of, reserving to feast myself with the surprise of it to him in calmer instants. And as to my dress, it could give him no idea of the truth, not only as it was mourning but likewise in a style of plainness and simplicity that I have ever kept to with studied art. He pressed me indeed tenderly to satisfy his ardent curiosity, both with regard to my past and present state of life since his being torn away from me. But I had the address[157] to elude his questions by answers that, showing his satisfaction at no great distance, won upon him to waive his impatience in favour of the thorough confidence he had in my not delaying it; but for respects I should in good time acquaint him with.

Charles, however, thus returned to my longing arms, tender, faithful, and in health, was already a blessing too mighty for my conception! But, Charles in distress! – Charles reduced and broken down to his naked personal merit, was such a circumstance, in favour of the sentiments I had for him, as exceeded my utmost desires. And, accordingly, I seemed so visibly charmed, so out of time and measure pleased at his mention of his ruined fortune that he could account for it no way but that the joy of seeing him again had swallowed up every other sense or concern.

In the meantime, my woman had taken all imaginable care of Charles's travelling companion; and, as supper was coming in, he was introduced to me, when I received him as became my regard for all of Charles's acquaintance or friends.

We four then supped together in the style of joy, congratulation, and pleasing disorder that you may guess. For my part, though all these agitations had left me not the least stomach but for that uncloying feast, the sight of my adored youth, I endeavoured to force it, by way of example for him, who, I conjectured, must want such a recruit after riding, and, indeed, he ate like a traveller, but gazed at and addressed me all the time like a lover.

After the cloth was taken away, and the hour of repose came on, Charles and I were, without further ceremony, in quality of man and wife, shown up together to a very handsome apartment, and, all in course, the bed, they said, to be the best in the inn.

And here, decency forgive me! if, once more I violate thy laws and, keeping the curtains undrawn,[158] sacrifice thee for the last time to that confidence, without reserve, with which I engaged to recount to you the most striking circumstances of my youthful disorders.

As soon then as we were in the room together, left to ourselves, the sight of the bed starting the remembrance of our first joys, and the thought of my being instantly to share it with the dear possessor of my virgin heart, moved me so strongly that it was well I leaned upon him, or I must have fainted again, under the overpowering sweet alarm. Charles saw into my confusion, and forgot his own, that was scarce less, to apply himself to the removal of mine.

But now the true refining passion had regained thorough possession of me, with all its train of symptoms; a sweet sensibility, a tender timidity, love-sick yearnings, tempered with diffidence and modesty, all held me in a subjection of soul incomparably dearer to me than the liberty of heart which I had been long, too long! the mistress of, in the course of those grosser gallantries, the consciousness of which now made me sigh with a virtuous confusion and regret. No real virgin, in short, in view of the nuptial bed, could give more bashful blushes to unblemished innocence than I did to a sense of guilt; and indeed I loved Charles too truly not to feel severely that I did not deserve him.

As I kept hesitating and disconcerted under this soft distraction, Charles, with a fond impatience, took the pains to undress me, and all I can remember amidst the flutter and discomposure of my senses was some fluttering exclamations of joy and admiration, more especially at the feel of my breasts, now set at liberty from my stays, and which, panting and rising in tumultuous throbs, swelled upon his dear touch, and gave it the welcome pleasure of finding them well formed and unfailed in firmness.

I was soon laid in bed, and scarce languished an instant for the darling partner of it, before he was undressed and got between the sheets, with his arms clasped round me, giving and taking, with a gust inexpressible, a kiss of welcome that my heart, rising to my lips, stamped with its warmest impression, concurring to my bliss with that delicate and voluptuous emotion which Charles alone had the secret to excite, and which constitutes the very life, the essence of pleasure.

Meanwhile, two candles lighted on a side-table near us, and a joyous wood-fire, threw a light into the bed that took from one sense, of great importance to our joys, all pretext of complaining of its being shut out of its share of them; and indeed, the sight of my idolized youth was alone, from the ardour with which I had wished for it, without other circumstance, a pleasure to die of.

But as action was now a necessity to desires so much on edge as ours, Charles, after a very short prelusive dalliance, lifting up my linen and his own, laid the broad treasures of his manly chest close to my bosom, both beating with the tenderest alarms; when now, the sense of his glowing body in naked touch with mine, took all power over my thoughts out of my own disposal, and delivered up every faculty of my soul to the sensiblest of joys that, affecting me infinitely more with my distinction of the person than of the sex, now brought my conscious heart deliciously into play; my heart, which, eternally constant to Charles, had never taken any part in my occasional sacrifices to the calls of constitution, complaisance, or interest. But, ah! what became of me, when, as the powers of solid pleasure thickened upon me, I could not help feeling the stiff stake that had been adorned with the trophies of my despoiled virginity bearing hard and inflexible against one of my thighs, which I had not yet opened, from a true principle of modesty revived by a passion too sincere to suffer any aiming at the false merit of difficulty, or my putting on an impertinent mock-coyness.

I have, I believe, somewhere before remarked that the feel of that favourite piece of manhood has, in the very nature of it, something inimitably pathetic.[159] Nothing can be dearer to the touch, or can affect it with a more delicious sensation. Think then! as a lover thinks, what must be the consummate transport of that quickest of our senses, in their central seat too! when, after so long a deprival, it felt itself re-inflamed under the pressure of that peculiar scepter-member which commands us all, but especially my darling elect from the face of the whole earth. And now, at its mightiest point of stiffness, it felt to me something so subduing, so active, so solid, and agreeable that I know not what name to give its singular impression; but the sentiment of consciousness of its belonging to my supremely beloved youth gave me so pleasing an agitation and worked so strongly on my soul that it sent all its sensitive spirits to that organ of bliss in me dedicated to its reception. There concentering to a point, like rays in a burning glass, they glowed, they burnt with the intensest heat; the springs of pleasure were, in short, wound up to such a pitch, I panted now with so exquisitely keen an appetite for the imminent enjoyment, that I was even sick with desire, and unequal[160] to support the combination of two distinct ideas that delightfully distracted me! For all the thought I was capable of was that I was now in touch at once with the instrument of pleasure and the great-seal of love; ideas that, mingling streams, poured such an ocean of intoxicating bliss on a weak vessel, all too narrow to contain it, that I lay overwhelmed, absorbed, lost in an abyss of joy, and dying of nothing but immoderate delight.

Charles then roused me somewhat out of this ecstatic distraction with a complaint softly murmured, amidst a crowd of kisses, at the position, not so favourable to his desires, in which I received his urgent insistence for admission, where that insistence was alone so engrossing a pleasure that it made me inconsistently suffer a much dearer one to be kept out. But how sweet to correct such a mistake! My thighs, now obedient to the intimations of love and nature, gladly disclose, and with a ready submission resign up the lost gateway to entrance at pleasure: I see! I feel! the delicious velvet tip! – he enters might and main with – oh! – my pen drops from me here in the ecstasy now present to my faithful memory! Description, too, deserts me and delivers over a task, above its strength of wing, to the imagination; but it must be an imagination exalted by such a flame as mine, that can do justice to that sweetest, noblest of all sensations that hailed and accompanied the stiff insinuation all the way up, till it was at the end of its penetration, sending up, through my eyes, the sparks of the love-fire that ran all over me, and blazed in every vein and every pore of me: a system incarnate of joy all over.

I had now totally taken in love's true arrow, from the point up to the feather, in that part where, making no new wound, the lips of the original one of nature, which had owed its first breathing to this dear instrument, clung, as if sensible of gratitude, in eager suction round it, whilst all its inwards embraced it tenderly with a warmth of gust, a compressive energy, that gave it, in its way, the heartfelt welcome in nature; every fibre there gathering tight round it, and straining ambitiously to come in for its share of the blissful touch.

As we were giving then a few moments of pause to the delectation of the senses, in dwelling with the highest relish on this intimatest point of reunion, and chewing the cud of enjoyment, the impatience natural to the pleasure soon drove us into action. Then began the driving tumult on his side, and the responsive heaves on mine, which kept me up to him; whilst, as our joys grew too mighty for utterance, the organs of our voice, voluptuously intermixing, became organs of the touch. And, oh, that touch, how delicious! how poignantly luscious! – And now! now! I felt to the heart of me, I felt the prodigious keen edge with which love, presiding over this act, points the pleasure. Love! that may be styled the Attic salt[161] of enjoyment: and indeed, without it, the joy, great as it is, is still a vulgar one, whether in a king or a beggar: for it is undoubtedly love alone that refines, ennobles, and exalts it.

Thus happy then, by the heart, happy by the senses, it was beyond all power, even of thought, to form the conception of a greater delight than what I was now consummating the fruition of.

Charles, whose whole frame all convulsed with the agitation of his rapture, whilst the tenderest fires trembled in his eyes, all assured me of a perfect concord of joy, penetrated me so profoundly, touched me so vitally, took me so much out of my own possession, whilst he seemed himself so much in mine that in a delicious enthusiasm I imagined such a transfusion of heart and spirit as that, coaliting[162] and making one body and soul with him, I was him, and he, me.

But all this pleasure, tending, like life from its first instants, towards its own dissolution, lived too fast not to bring on upon the spur its delicious moment of mortality; for presently the approach of the tender agony discovered itself by its usual signals, that were quickly followed by my dear love's liquid emanation of himself, that spun out and shot feelingly indeed up the ravished indraught, where the sweetly soothing balmy titillation opened at the warm jerk all the sluices of joy on my side, which, ecstatically in flow, helped to allay the prurient glow, and drowned our pleasure for a while, soon, however, to be on float again! For Charles, true to nature's laws, in one breath expiring and ejaculating, languished not long in the dissolving trance, but, recovering spirit again, soon gave me to feel that the true mettle springs of his instrument of pleasure were by love, and perhaps by a long vacation, wound up too high to be let down by a single explosion: his stiffness still stood my friend. Resuming then the action afresh, without dislodging or giving me the trouble of parting from my sweet tenant, we played over again the same opera, with the same delightful harmony and concert; our ardours, like our love, knew no remission. And, all as the tide served, my lover, lavish of his stores and pleasure-milked, overflowed me once more from the fulness of those his oval reservoirs of the genial emulsion; whilst, on my side, a convulsive grasp, in the instant of my giving down my liquid contribution, rendered me sweetly subservient at once to the increase of his joy and of its effusions, moving me so as to make me exert all those springs of the compressive exsuction, with which the sensitive mechanism of that part thirstily draws and drains the nipple of love, with much such an instinctive eagerness and attachment as, to compare great with less, kind nature engages infants at the breast, by the pleasure they find in the motion of their little mouths and cheeks to extract the milky stream prepared for their nourishment.

But still there was no end of his vigour; this double discharge had so far from extinguished his desires, for that time, that it had not even calmed them. And, at his age, desires are power: he was proceeding then, amazingly, to push it to a third triumph, still without uncasing. If a tenderness, natural to true love, had not inspired me with self-denial enough to spare, and not overstrain him, and, accordingly, entreating him to give himself and me quarter,[163] I obtained at length a short suspension of arms, but not before he had exultingly satisfied me that he gave out standing.

The remainder of the night, with what we borrowed upon the day, we employed with unwearied fervour in celebrating thus the festival of our re-meeting, and got up pretty late in the morning, gay, brisk, and alert, though rest had been a stranger to us; but the pleasures of love had been to us what the joy at victory is to an army: repose, refreshment, everything.

The journey into the country being now entirely out of the question, and orders having been given overnight for turning the horses' heads towards London, we left the inn as soon as we had breakfasted, not without a liberal distribution of the tokens of my grateful sense of the happiness I had met with in it.

Charles and I were in my coach, the captain and my companion in a chaise[164] hired purposely for them, to leave us the conveniency of a tête-à-tête.

Here, on the road, as the tumult of my senses was tolerably composed, I had command enough of head to break properly to him the course of life that the consequences of my separation from him had driven me into, which, at the same time that he tenderly deplored with me, he was the less shocked at as, on reflecting how he had left me circumstanced, he could not be entirely unprepared for it.

But when I opened the state of my fortune to him, and with that sincerity which, from me to him, was so much a nature in me, I begged of him his acceptance of it, on his own terms, I should appear to you perhaps too partial to my passion, were I to attempt the doing his delicacy justice. I shall content myself then with assuring you that, after his flatly refusing the unreserved, unconditional donation that I long persecuted him in vain to accept, it was at length, in obedience to his serious commands (for I stood out unaffectedly, till he exerted the sovereign authority which love had given him over me), that I yielded my consent to wave the remonstrance I did not fail of making strongly to him, against his degrading himself and incurring the reflection, however unjust, of

having, for respects of fortune, bartered his honour for infamy and prostitution, in making one his wife who thought herself too much honoured
in being but his mistress.

The plea of love then overruling all objections, Charles, entirely won
with the merit of my sentiments for him, which he could not but read
the sincerity of in a heart ever open to him, obliged me to receive his
hand, by which means I was in pass, amongst other innumerable blessings, to bestow a legal parentage on those fine children you have seen
by this happiest of matches.[165]

Thus, at length, I got snug into port, where, in the bosom of virtue,
I gathered the only uncorrupt sweets: where, looking back on the course
of vice I had run, and comparing its infamous blandishments with the
infinitely superior joys of innocence, I could not help pitying, even in
point of taste, those who, immersed in a gross sensuality, are insensible
to the so delicate charms of VIRTUE, than which even PLEASURE has
not a greater friend, nor than VICE a greater enemy. Thus temperance
makes men lords over those pleasures that intemperance enslaves them
to: the one, parent of health, vigour, fertility, cheerfulness, and every
other desirable good in life; the other, of diseases, debility, barrenness,
self-loathing, with only every evil incident to human nature.

You laugh perhaps at this tail-piece of morality,[166] expressed from[167]
me by the force of truth resulting from compared experiences: you think
it, no doubt, out of place; out of character; possibly, too, you may look
on it as the paltry finesse of one who seeks to mask a devotee to vice
under a rag of a veil, impudently smuggled from the shrine of virtue;
just as if one was to fancy oneself completely disguised at a masquerade,
with no other change of dress than turning one's shoes into slippers;
or as if a writer should think to shield a treasonable libel by concluding
it with a formal prayer for the king. But, independent of my flattering
myself that you have a juster opinion of my sense and sincerity, give
me leave to represent to you that such a supposition is even more injurious
to virtue than to me, since, consistently with candour and good nature,[168]
it can have no foundation but in the falsest of fears, that its pleasures
cannot stand in comparison with those of vice, but let truth dare to
hold it up in its most alluring light: then mark! how spurious, how
low of taste, how comparatively inferior its joys are to those which virtue
gives sanction to, and whose sentiments are not above making even
a sauce for the senses, but a sauce of the highest relish; whilst vices

are the harpies[169] that infect, and foul the feast. The paths of vice are sometimes strewed with roses, but then they are for ever infamous for many a thorn, for many a cankerworm;[170] those of virtue are strewed with roses purely, and those eternally unfading ones.

If you do me then justice, you will esteem me perfectly consistent in the incense I burn to virtue: if I have painted vice all in its gayest colours, if I have decked it with flowers, it has been solely in order to make the worthier, the solemner, sacrifice of it to virtue.

You know Mr C— O—, you know his estate, his worth, and good sense: can you, will you pronounce it ill meant, at least of him, when, anxious for his son's morals, with a view to form him to virtue, and inspire him with a fixed, a rational contempt for vice, he condescended to be his master of the ceremonies, and led him by the hand through the most noted bawdy-houses in town, where he took care that he should be familiarized with all those scenes of debauchery so fit to nauseate a good taste? The experiment, you will cry, is dangerous. True – on a fool; but are fools worth the least attention to?

I shall see you soon, and in the meantime think candidly of me, and believe me ever,

    Madam,
      Yours, &c. &c. &c.

       * * * * * *

NOTES

1 (p. 39). The opening puts Fanny's 'memoirs' clearly in the tradition of both the epistolary novel and the autobiographical confession, though Cleland explodes these forms through satire; at the end of volume I and letter I, Fanny remarks, rather tongue-in-cheek, that it is 'high time to put a period to this'. The literary confession, again referred to at the beginning of volume II, is a mimicry of the religious sacrament while providing the conditions for the development of libertine themes and voyeurism.

2 (p. 39). This is an allusion to the collections of pictorial erotica that could be found in the homes of eighteenth-century aristocrats. Casanova, in his autobiography, and the English caricaturists Rowlandson and Gillray frequently commented on such collections and the mania for erotic pictures. Rowlandson produced a series of licentious illustrations for his temporary friend, the Prince Regent.

3 (p. 41). A kind of strong calico or linen.

4 (p. 41). Cleland's spelling of virtue as VARTUE is a first and deliberate ironic allusion to Richardson's *Pamela* (1740). Fielding had used this spelling in *Shamela* (1741), and Cleland, by adopting it, indicated both his admiration for Fielding's burlesque satire and his own intention to write another anti-*Pamela*. See also the ribald use of the word on p. 105.

Esther, however, also refers to the rags-to-riches stories of some eighteenth-century courtesans; a few of them indeed became duchesses. On the interesting biographies of the more important courtesans like Kitty Fisher and Nancy Parsons, and the vast body of literature written on their minor and major scandals, see Horace William Bleackley, *Ladies Fair and Frail. Sketches of the Demi-Monde during the Eighteenth Century* (London & New York, 1909).

5 (p. 42). Lecherously; lustfully.

6 (p. 44). Some kind of cape or mantle worn by ladies.

7 (p. 44). Squob; short and fat.

8 (p. 47). The correct plural form is minutiae; but this must not necessarily be a misspelling. On several occasions, Fanny tries to impress the lady she writes to with Latin and French expressions. If this is not a mistake, Cleland may have tried to characterize his heroine as the country girl come to town and trying to catch what was then called the *bon ton*.

9 (p. 49). Such switches from the past to the present tense, and vice versa, are typical verbal inconsistencies of eighteenth-century prose fiction: cf. also pp. 56, 63, 68, 78, 79, 83 and 110, and volume II, pp. 147 and 220. The sudden change to the present tense was meant to express the immediacy of action

and feeling and can also be found in French fiction of the same period, the French term being the *présent historique*.

10 (p. 52). Ringlets, curls.

11 (p. 53). Tusks; long pointed teeth.

12 (p. 53). Toilet; water-closet.

13 (p. 54). Abilities, advantages, assets.

14 (p. 61). Ambiguous; what is said is to be interpreted by contraries.

15 (p. 61). A bench adapted for alternative use as a seat or bed.

16 (p. 62). A well-fed menial, beef from the necks of cattle being of inferior quality and beef-eater being used in a derogatory sense.

17 (p. 68). The reference is probably to Guido Reni (1575–1642), a master of the Bolognese school of painting and one of the most admired artists of the period of incipient decadence in Italy. Guido was acquainted and studied with Annibale, Agostino, and Lodovico Carraci at their academy.

Fanny's reference to the painter is to show her knowledge of art and again proves the popularity of continental erotic pictures among eighteenth-century English connoisseurs.

18 (p. 72). Normally used for a stray animal; here it means an abandoned person.

19 (p. 78). Stained or dyed.

20 (p. 79). The phrasing of this sentence is reminiscent of Pamela's reports to her parents about Mr B.'s seductive attempts. A satirical allusion is possibly intended, since Fanny's attitude towards her lover is quite different from Pamela's view of Mr B.

21 (p. 80). Sprinkling.

22 (p. 83). Wanting moderation.

23 (p. 85). Jealousy, discontent, enmity.

24 (p. 86). To stand firm, to resist; or to bluff, if it is a misspelling.

25 (p. 89). In Greek and Latin mythology: a fabulous monster, rapacious and filthy, having a woman's face and body and a bird's wings and claws, and supposed to act as a minister of divine vengeance; hence a cruel, greedy, hard-hearted woman; cf. also volume II, p. 224.

26 (p. 90). To pass.

27 (p. 91). To get an inkling of; to suspect (a design).

28 (p. 93). Agent; manager or merchant buying and selling on commission.

29 (p. 96). Having 'dark' purposes.

30 (p. 101). This term and Cleland's description of the penis as a machine (cf. pp. 77, 78, 83, 110) bespeak his adoption of a French mechanistic materialism, and in particular the philosophy of La Mettrie explaining man as a 'pleasure animal'.

31 (p. 105). An ill-favoured person.

32 (p. 105). A beggar's trull; a fat, red-faced wench.

33 (p. 110). A small stick or pin; a pointer.

34 (p. 110). Directly opposite.

35 (p. 112). Desire; instinctive inclination; passion.

36 (p. 112). Twisted, interlaced.

37 (p. 117). Sculptor.

38 (p. 117). Fanny's philosophizing, in this instance, expresses once again Cleland's belief in the French philosophy of pleasure as based on the senses and including the sexual. Influenced by the erotic–philosophical novels of Crébillon *fils* and Duclos, and by La Mettrie's justification of a natural sexuality, Cleland attempted to find a middle way in *Memoirs* between libertinism and romantic love, a compromise advocating pleasure controlled by reason.

39 (p. 118). A package of diamonds or gold-dust.

40 (p. 120). To avoid mentioning to; to pass over; to leave out of consideration.

41 (p. 121). Given to silence.

42 (p. 123). Lenient; gentle.

43 (p. 124). As a benevolent, kind, and generous bawd, Mrs Cole is an exception when compared to the rapacious beldams who had figured as bawds in English literary and pictorial history before the publication of *Memoirs*. Mrs Cole may be modelled on Mrs Douglas, a historical figure who appears in several of Hogarth's engravings, such as no. 10 of the series 'Industry and Idleness' and 'Enthusiasm Delineated'. But 'Mother' Douglas, more often than not, was shown as a shady and negative character, especially in literary satires dealing with the world of prostitution. On notorious eighteenth-century bawds, such as 'Mother Goadby', see *Nocturnal Revels: or, the History of King's-Place, and Other Modern Nunneries, Containing their Mysteries, Devotions, and Sacrifices. Comprising also, the Ancient and Present State of Promiscuous Gallantry: with the Portraits of the Most Celebrated Demireps and Courtezans of This Period: as well as Sketches of their Professional and Occasional Admirers. By a Monk of the Order of St. Francis* (London, 1779). The author of this satirical guide through London's brothels and night haunts was probably Sir Francis Dashwood, one of the members of the Hellfire Club.

In addition to such satires, catalogues of prostitutes circulated in the larger cities, London's most popular publication being *Harris's List of Covent Garden Ladies, or the Man of Pleasure's Kalender*, which is known to have existed from 1760 onwards. Similar catalogues probably circulated before. For a discussion of the vast literature, often satirical, on bawds, prostitutes, and their customers, see my *Eros Revived. A Study of Erotica in Eighteenth-Century England and America* (London, Secker & Warburg, 1985), chapter 5.

VOLUME II

44 (p. 132). Sham.

45 (p. 132). Encroachment, intrusion.

46 (p. 132). The *Oxford English Dictionary* gives no meaning for this noun,

except as 'cluck' for a hen and the sound made by hens. However, it gives 'cleck', to hatch, and 'cletch', a hatching of chickens. This would accord with the use of the word on p. 208.

47 (p. 132). The general meeting of all the canons of a cathedral church, or the members of a monastery or convent.

48 (p. 133). The religious jargon of this paragraph (chapter, ceremony, sisterhood, initiation) is typical of eighteenth-century libertine prose fiction, especially if the aim was satire or burlesque. For reasons of mimicry and parody, writers of libertine and ribald works frequently expressed sensual pleasure in the language of devotional writing; see, for instance, the title cited in note 43 and the obscene parodies of prayers appended to John Wilkes's *Essay on Woman*. For a detailed discussion, see my *Eros Revived*, chapter 2.

The *double entendre* borrowed from the religious sphere has a long history in the English language. In Shakespeare's time, nunnery was already used in the sense of brothel, and Fanny's ironic description of Mrs Brown in vol. I, p. 61 as the 'venerable mother abbess' indicates the ironic use of 'abbess' signifying bawd and prostitute. See also volume II, p. 150.

The satirical use of religious terms and language developed gradually with erotic literature. Amorous monks and nuns had figured as stock characters in erotic prose fiction for several centuries when *Memoirs* appeared, the most influential sources being the frequently bawdy fabliaux, the *Cent nouvelles nouvelles*; the *Heptaméron*; Boccaccio's *Decameron*; and La Fontaine's *Contes*. Many of the French pornographic novels preceding *Memoirs* thrived on this tradition; they were often set in monasteries, thus allowing the authors to slander the Catholic Church and propagate their libertine philosophy couched in pornographic description.

49 (p. 134). Etiquette; particular way of behaving.

50 (p. 134). The following tales by Emily, Harriet, and Louisa, all concerned with the 'exchange of the maiden state for womanhood', owe much to erotic collections of stories and 'contes' of earlier centuries, both in form and content.

51 (p. 135). A twenty-shilling piece: the name was introduced after 1663.

52 (p. 135). An arrangement of steps, rungs, or the like, contrived to allow passage over or through a fence to one person at a time, while forming a barrier to the passage of sheep or cattle.

53 (p. 135). A kind of coarse, narrow cloth, woven from long wool and usually ribbed; hence plain, homely.

54 (p. 135). Of mean, inferior, common quality.

55 (p. 136). Adequate; fitting; commensurate.

56 (p. 137). To plan, to devise, to consider.

57 (p. 137). An accident; something arriving by chance.

58 (p. 145). A sudden movement or jerk.

59 (p. 146). Because of love.

60 (p. 151). The fifth commissioned officer in a troop of cavalry, who carried the colours.

61 (p. 151). Condition, state.

62 (p. 151). Curved.

63 (p. 153). Relief.

64 (p. 154). A piece of music played by soldiers.

65 (p. 155). A kind of under (or undress) bodice worn by women, especially during the eighteenth century; from c. 1740 usually used in the plural form, 'jumps', or 'a pair of jumps'.

66 (p. 156). Lasciviousness.

67 (p. 159). A waiting-woman; a lady's maid: from the name of the 'waiting gentlewoman' in Beaumont and Fletcher's popular play, *The Scornful Lady*, published in the early seventeenth century.

68 (p. 160). Stimulated.

69 (p. 161). Familiar.

70 (p. 162). A light meal.

71 (p. 163). To play a role; to make an appearance (as a character).

72 (p. 163). Refreshed, recovered.

73 (p. 164). To trade, to bargain, to haggle.

74 (p. 165). Scent or smell.

75 (p. 165). A derogatory term implying that the person has a questionable reputation.

76 (p. 165). Gullibility.

77 (p. 165). Snare, noose.

78 (p. 166). A meeting of two things or bodies.

79 (p. 167). A building of one of the (now four) law societies in London.

80 (p. 168). Softly, easily.

81 (p. 169). One who is cheated or imposed upon; a simpleton.

82 (p. 170). Completely ruined; destroyed. One meaning of 'rack' is 'to draw off from the lees'.

83 (p. 170). Inspection.

84 (p. 172). To excuse, vindicate or overcome.

85 (p. 173). Causing sorrow; calamitous; deplorably bad.

86 (p. 173). Blood.

87 (p. 176). A special place.

88 (p. 177). Weak.

89 (p. 177). A common prostitute.

90 (p. 177). The seaman's jargon and the sailor's bawdy remark in the following passage contribute to the humour of the scene, toning down the pornographic element; cf. such expressions as 'battery' 'any port in a storm', 'course'; and 'broadside' on pp. 177–8.

91 (p. 178). To move, to stir.

92 (p. 179). Thrift; careful management.

93 (p. 180). Fanny's bourgeois materialism emerges at this point. Unconcerned by Mr Norbert's death, she speculates on the chances of getting some of his money.

94 (p. 180). Most modern editions of *Memoirs* have rendered this name as Barville. However, Cleland may have intended a pun on barvel or barvell, a kind of leather apron, especially since the man is a flagellant and fetishist in matters concerning sex.

95 (p. 181). Offering.

96 (p. 181). Except; excepting.

97 (p. 181). Articles of food; victuals.

98 (p. 181). Food in general; dishes.

99 (p. 183). Liking; inclination.

100 (p. 183). Excellent.

101 (p. 184). Tender or sensitive flesh.

102 (p. 185). A species of wild rose with fragrant leaves and shoots.

103 (p. 185). The action of spying or keeping watch.

104 (p. 186). To recoil in fear; to wince.

105 (p. 187). Mercy.

106 (p. 188). Acute; keen.

107 (p. 188). Posteriors; back.

108 (p. 189). To assist or help.

109 (p. 189). Cantharides: the pharmacopoeia name of the dried beetle *Cantharis vesicatoria*, used externally as a rubefacient and vesicant; internally as a diuretic and sexual stimulant. It was formerly considered an aphrodisiac.

110 (p. 190). Improve my value.

111 (p. 191). Effeminate-looking.

112 (p. 191). A brothel.

113 (p. 192). Lover.

114 (p. 192). A sedan-chair.

115 (p. 193). The words 'odious' and 'absurd' express Fanny's first reaction to homosexuality as practised by men. Lesbianism was tolerated in the eighteenth century, or at least not condemned, and the lesbian scenes in volume I of *Memoirs* evince an acceptance of this form of sexual intercourse, even though it was considered not 'natural'. Male homosexuality, however, 'the unnatural vice' as it was termed, was constantly attacked and rejected by writers and novelists. Hence Fanny merely voices the bourgeois view of homosexuality.

116 (p. 193). Stage-coach.

117 (p. 193). To have a snack.

118 (p. 193). When; in time for; by the time that.

119 (p. 194). Belief; conviction.

120 (p. 194). Until the early nineteenth century, sodomy was punishable by death if penetration could be proved.

121 (p. 194). The following passage, pp. 194–5, appeared only in the first edition and in a pirated version published by Drybutter later in the century. Cleland suppressed it in his bowdlerized edition of the novel, published in 1750, and it has not been published in modern versions of *Fanny Hill*.

122 (p. 196). Mrs Cole, in this passage, voices the predominant eighteenth-century

attitude towards male homosexuals. The 'mollies', as they were referred to, were considered perverts, as sodomy was generally seen as non-procreative, and since it was condemned in the Bible and by the Church Fathers. In addition, the idea of the homosexual as a passive, effeminate man threatened a culture founded on male aggression. Nevertheless, London and other large cities had homosexual sub-cultures throughout the century. See Randolph Trumbach, 'London's sodomites: homosexual behaviour and Western culture in the eighteenth century', *Journal of Social History*, 2 (1977), 1–33.

From the very beginning of the century homosexuals served as the butt of satirical attacks, the underlying ideas being that the 'vice' was of foreign origin ('bugger' is derived from Bulgaria), a notion Mrs Cole alludes to on p. 196 ('our air and climate'), and that sodomites were freaks and criminals. See, for instance, John Dunton's *The He-Strumpets* (1707); Edward Ward's *History of the London Clubs* (1709–11); and the anonymous *Hell upon Earth* (1729) and *Satan's Harvest Home: or the Present State of Whorecraft, Adultery, Fornication, Procuring, Pimping, Sodomy, and the Game of Flatts . . .* (1749). As the cliché of the homosexual as an effeminate, misogynist pervert was also propagated in prose fiction, it is understandable that the crowds reacted violently to convicted sodomites standing in the pillory. In 1761, a young homosexual of Cornhill, London, who had been sentenced for an attempt of buggery, was almost lynched by the furious mob, and two years later, two men, similarly sentenced, were killed by the crowd. For a more detailed discussion of the literary and semi-literary treatment of sodomy in eighteenth-century England see my *Eros Revived*, chapter 1.

123 (p. 196). Adventure: experience.

124 (p. 198). Louisa refers to the widely held belief that idiots have special sexual powers, which was just one of the many prevailing sexual myths of the eighteenth century. They were disseminated by such popular sex guides as *Aristotle's Masterpiece*; Nicolas Venette's *Tableau de l'amour conjugal*; and the numerous treatises on midwifery, venereal diseases, and masturbation. For a more detailed discussion see Paul Gabriel Boucé, 'Livres de médecine populaire et mythes sexuels en Grande-Bretagne au XVIIIe siècle', *Cahiers de l'Université de Pau et des Pays de l'Adour*, 10 (1980); ibid., 'Aspects of sexual tolerance and intolerance in eighteenth-century England', *The British Journal for Eighteenth-Century Studies*, 3 (1980), 173–93; and my *Eros Revived*, chapter 1.

125. (p. 198). A half-witted person; one naturally deficient in intellect.

126 (p. 198). This is an allusion to the welter of early eighteenth-century ribald, and mainly poetic, satires comparing genitalia to plants. There is, of course, in poetic erotica a history of geographical or topographical allegory. Charles Cotton's *Erotopolis. The Present State of Betty-land* (1684) – often 'revisited' in the eighteenth century – being the best-known example. In 1740 Thomas Stretser continued this tradition with his bawdy *A New Description of Merryland*.

But there is also a close relation between scientific research in botany and its satirical reflection in humorous bawdy writings. By 1, hundreds of scholars and would-be-scholars were engaged in botanic research in several European countries and even in America. Botanists wrote about the sex life of plants, and in the early decades of the eighteenth century authorities like Philip Miller and Linnaeus put much emphasis on this aspect. Linnaeus writing of 'weddings', 'nuptial beds', and 'husbands and wives' among plants.

As can be expected, this tickled the fancy of the satirists, who, by 1730, began to make fun of botanists and gardeners. See, for instance, the following satires comparing the penis to plants: Thomas Stretser, *Arbor Vitae: or, the Tree of Life* (1732); the anonymous *The Lady's Delight* (1732), which included Stretser's earlier poem and a lampoon on John Tyers and Heidegger; and *Mimosa or the Sensitive Plant* (1779), attributed to James Perry. Ribald satires on the vagina are *The Natural History of the Frutex Vulvaria or the Flowering Shrub* (1741); and *Teague-Root Displayed* (1746). See my *Eros Revived*, chapter 6, for an assessment of these poetic satires.

127 (p. 199). Unfastened.

128 (p. 199). To roll or spin.

129 (p. 199). Bauble is defined by the *Oxford English Dictionary* as (1) an instrument consisting of a stick with a mass of lead fixed or appended at one end, used for weighing (now obsolete); (2) a baton or stick, surmounted by a fantastically carved head with asses' ears, formerly carried by the court fool; (3) a child's toy (obsolete).

Here, it is used as a *double entendre*, alluding to the penis: see, for instance, the ribald verse tale, *The Bauble. A Tale* (1721).

130 (p. 199). To carry on and finish.

131 (p. 200). Opening.

132 (p. 200). See note 30 on mechanism and materialism.

133 (p. 200). Driven too hard.

134 (p. 201). The action of strangling or of biting and tearing by the throat.

135 (p. 201). Ardently; warmly.

136 (p. 202). To cast up or back again.

137 (p. 202). A caper; a whim or prank.

138 (p. 203). Marquee.

139 (p. 204). Good or excellent cheer; entertainment.

140 (p. 204). A loose or overlapping part of a garment, forming a flap or fold.

141 (p. 205). Amorously and playfully.

142 (p. 206). Flesh-colour; a light rosy pink.

143 (p. 206). Playful; pretending.

144 (p. 207). To swim.

145 (p. 208). Household; home; family.

146 (p. 209). A reference and allusion to the way oracles were read and given in Greece, and later, Rome ('town' probably meaning Athens). The augurs interpreted signs from birds, with reference to the direction of their flight, and also

NOTES

to their singing, or uttering other sounds. To the first class of augurs, called
alites in ancient Rome, belonged the eagle and the vulture; to the second, called
oscines, the owl, the crow and the raven.

147 (p. 209). To blackmail.

148 (p. 209). Fanny's materialism, and concern about money, again come to
the fore, indicating her bourgeois ideas and the shadow of Defoe's *Moll Flanders*.

149 (p. 210). Practice or custom.

150 (p. 210). A counting-house; a commercial agency or factory.

151 (p. 210). To pass; cf. also note 26.

152 (p. 211). That which is in the middle; moderation; measure.

153 (p. 212). Liberal, handsome (sum of money).

154 (p. 214). Words; sounds.

155 (p. 216). Tint; colour or hue.

156 (p. 216). Dignity.

157 (p. 216). Adroitness; skill; dexterity.

158 (p. 217). An allusion to Fielding in particular, but also to other early-
eighteenth-century novelists, who 'drew the curtains' when it came to the description of sex scenes.

159 (p. 219). Moving; stirring; passionate.

160 (p. 219). Unable.

161 (p. 220). Refined, delicate, poignant wit.

162 (p. 221). Coalescing.

163 (p. 222). Pause; relief or mercy. See also note 105.

164 (p. 222). A term applied to various pleasure or travelling carriages, the
exact application having varied from time to time.

165 (p. 223). Fanny's reference to her motherhood and her children is another
indication of the non-pornographic elements of *Memoirs*; children do not normally
occur in pornographic fiction (excluding the perverse), and it would, indeed, be
misleading to classify Cleland's novel as mere pornography. While there is no
doubt that it was written to provide erotic entertainment, it is also a *Bildungsroman*
delineating Fanny's career and education, and has, in addition, philosophical
and satirical elements.

166 (p. 223). This is Fanny's final attempt to justify her career as a moral one,
which has taught her the value of true love and the pleasure of the senses. Recent
research stresses, paradoxically at first glance, that John Cleland is not a salacious
but a moral writer, as he tones down erotic events through distancing and imposes
reason and common sense on French hedonism. See especially Stephen Sossaman,
'Sex, love and reason in the novels of John Cleland', *Massachusetts Studies in
English*, 6 (1978), 93–106; and Raymond K. Whitley, 'The libertine hero and
heroine in the novels of John Cleland', *Studies in Eighteenth-Century Culture*, 9
(1979), 387–404.

167 (p. 223). Extracted or forced from.

168 (p. 223). Natural goodness of character.
169 (p. 224). See note 25.
170 (p. 224). A caterpillar that destroys buds and leaves; also used figuratively.

READ MORE IN PENGUIN

In every corner of the world, on every subject under the sun, Penguin represents quality and variety – the very best in publishing today.

For complete information about books available from Penguin – including Puffins, Penguin Classics and Arkana – and how to order them, write to us at the appropriate address below. Please note that for copyright reasons the selection of books varies from country to country.

In the United Kingdom: Please write to *Dept. JC, Penguin Books Ltd, FREEPOST, West Drayton, Middlesex UB7 OBR*

If you have any difficulty in obtaining a title, please send your order with the correct money, plus ten per cent for postage and packaging, to *PO Box No. 11, West Drayton, Middlesex UB7 OBR*

In the United States: Please write to *Penguin USA Inc., 375 Hudson Street, New York, NY 10014*

In Canada: Please write to *Penguin Books Canada Ltd, 10 Alcorn Avenue, Suite 300, Toronto, Ontario M4V 3B2*

In Australia: Please write to *Penguin Books Australia Ltd, 487 Maroondah Highway, Ringwood, Victoria 3134*

In New Zealand: Please write to *Penguin Books (NZ) Ltd,182–190 Wairau Road, Private Bag, Takapuna, Auckland 9*

In India: Please write to *Penguin Books India Pvt Ltd, 706 Eros Apartments, 56 Nehru Place, New Delhi 110 019*

In the Netherlands: Please write to *Penguin Books Netherlands B.V., Keizersgracht 231 NL–1016 DV Amsterdam*

In Germany: Please write to *Penguin Books Deutschland GmbH, Friedrichstrasse 10–12, W–6000 Frankfurt/Main 1*

In Spain: Please write to *Penguin Books S. A., C. San Bernardo 117–6° E–28015 Madrid*

In Italy: Please write to *Penguin Italia s.r.l., Via Felice Casati 20. I–20124 Milano*

In France: Please write to *Penguin France S. A., 17 rue Lejeune, F–31000 Toulouse*

In Japan: Please write to *Penguin Books Japan, Ishikiribashi Building, 2–5–4, Suido, Tokyo 112*

In Greece: Please write to *Penguin Hellas Ltd, Dimocritou 3, GR–106 71 Athens*

In South Africa: Please write to *Longman Penguin Southern Africa (Pty) Ltd, Private Bag X08, Bertsham 2013*

READ MORE IN PENGUIN

PENGUIN CLASSICS

Netochka Nezvanova   Fyodor Dostoyevsky

Dostoyevsky's first book tells the story of 'Nameless Nobody' and introduces many of the themes and issues which dominate his great masterpieces.

Selections from the Carmina Burana   A verse translation by David Parlett

The famous songs from the *Carmina Burana* (made into an oratorio by Carl Orff) tell of lecherous monks and corrupt clerics, drinkers and gamblers, and the fleeting pleasures of youth.

Fear and Trembling   Søren Kierkegaard

A profound meditation on the nature of faith and submission to God's will which examines with startling originality the story of Abraham and Isaac.

Selected Prose   Charles Lamb

Lamb's famous essays (under the strange pseudonym of Elia) on anything and everything have long been celebrated for their apparently innocent charm; this major new edition allows readers to discover the darker and more interesting aspects of Lamb.

The Picture of Dorian Gray   Oscar Wilde

Wilde's superb and macabre novella, one of his supreme works, is reprinted here with a masterly Introduction and valuable notes by Peter Ackroyd.

A Treatise of Human Nature   David Hume

A universally acknowledged masterpiece by 'the greatest of all British Philosophers' – A. J. Ayer

READ MORE IN PENGUIN

PENGUIN CLASSICS

A Passage to India E. M. Forster

Centred on the unresolved mystery in the Marabar Caves, Forster's great work provides the definitive evocation of the British Raj.

The Republic Plato

The best-known of Plato's dialogues, *The Republic* is also one of the supreme masterpieces of Western philosophy whose influence cannot be overestimated.

The Life of Johnson James Boswell

Perhaps the finest 'life' ever written, Boswell's *Johnson* captures for all time one of the most colourful and talented figures in English literary history.

Metamorphoses Ovid

A golden treasury of myths and legends which has proved a major influence on Western literature.

A Nietzsche Reader Friedrich Nietzsche

A superb selection from all the major works of one of the greatest thinkers and writers in world literature, translated into clear, modern English.

Madame Bovary Gustave Flaubert

With *Madame Bovary* Flaubert established the realistic novel in France; while his central character of Emma Bovary, the bored wife of a provincial doctor, remains one of the great creations of modern literature.

READ MORE IN PENGUIN

PENGUIN CLASSICS

John Aubrey	Brief Lives
Francis Bacon	The Essays
George Berkeley	Principles of Human Knowledge and Three Dialogues between Hylas and Philonous
James Boswell	The Life of Johnson
Sir Thomas Browne	The Major Works
John Bunyan	The Pilgrim's Progress
Edmund Burke	Reflections on the Revolution in France
Thomas de Quincey	Confessions of an English Opium Eater
	Recollections of the Lakes and the Lake Poets
Daniel Defoe	A Journal of the Plague Year
	Moll Flanders
	Robinson Crusoe
	Roxana
	A Tour Through the Whole Island of Great Britain
Henry Fielding	Jonathan Wild
	Joseph Andrews
	The History of Tom Jones
Oliver Goldsmith	The Vicar of Wakefield
Richard Gough	The History of Myddle

READ MORE IN PENGUIN

PENGUIN CLASSICS

Matthew Arnold	Selected Prose
Jane Austen	Emma
	Lady Susan, The Watsons, Sanditon
	Mansfield Park
	Northanger Abbey
	Persuasion
	Pride and Prejudice
	Sense and Sensibility
Anne Brontë	Agnes Grey
	The Tenant of Wildfell Hall
Charlotte Brontë	Jane Eyre
	Shirley
	Villette
Emily Brontë	Wuthering Heights
Samuel Butler	Erewhon
	The Way of All Flesh
Thomas Carlyle	Selected Writings
Wilkie Collins	The Moonstone
	The Woman in White
Charles Darwin	The Origin of Species
	The Voyage of the Beagle
Benjamin Disraeli	Sybil
George Eliot	Adam Bede
	Daniel Deronda
	Felix Holt
	Middlemarch
	The Mill on the Floss
	Romola
	Scenes of Clerical Life
	Silas Marner
Elizabeth Gaskell	Cranford and Cousin Phillis
	The Life of Charlotte Brontë
	Mary Barton
	North and South
	Wives and Daughters

READ MORE IN PENGUIN

PENGUIN CLASSICS

Charles Dickens	American Notes for General Circulation
	Barnaby Rudge
	Bleak House
	The Christmas Books
	David Copperfield
	Dombey and Son
	Great Expectations
	Hard Times
	Little Dorrit
	Martin Chuzzlewit
	The Mystery of Edwin Drood
	Nicholas Nickleby
	The Old Curiosity Shop
	Oliver Twist
	Our Mutual Friend
	The Pickwick Papers
	Selected Short Fiction
	A Tale of Two Cities
Edward Gibbon	The Decline and Fall of the Roman Empire
George Gissing	New Grub Street
William Godwin	Caleb Williams
Edmund Gosse	Father and Son
Thomas Hardy	The Distracted Preacher and Other Tales
	Far From the Madding Crowd
	Jude the Obscure
	The Mayor of Casterbridge
	The Return of the Native
	Tess of the d'Urbervilles
	The Trumpet Major
	Under the Greenwood Tree
	The Woodlanders